'I love you.' He could not hide his despair; the thought of losing her was a physical agony as though a knife had been driven between his ribs. 'I didn't mean those things, it's just... Jessie, I'll make it up to you. I swear on my life. Sweetheart don't leave me.'

'Only for a week or two,' she said. 'Perhaps all we need is a little time apart. When I come back, we'll both know better how we feel.' She took his hands. 'I'll write every day. And if I'm not back in a fortnight . . . well, you must come and fetch me, that's all.'

She kissed him on the cheek, drawing away when he would have held her close. As she reached the door he cried out, 'You said once – you said that together, we'd be a match for the best and worst.'

'Tell me that in two weeks' time,' she said, 'and I'll never doubt you again.'

About the author

Jill Salkeld was born in Eastleigh, Hampshire, the eldest of five children. She was educated at Barton Peveril Grammar School and at Southampton College of Art, gaining a diploma in Graphic Design.

Having been employed as a mother's help in Surrey, Athens and Corinth, she moved back to Hampshire and now lives in the village of Botley, where she works for the Drugs Research Trust.

When not involved in writing and research, her hobbies are sailing, portrait-painting, and navigation.

Race Before The Wind

Jill Salkeld

CORONET BOOKS
Hodder and Stoughton

First published in Great Britain in 1988 by Kindredson Publishing Ltd

Coronet edition 1990

British Library C.I.P.

Salkeld, Jill
  Race before the wind.
  I. Title
  823'.914 [J]

ISBN 0 340 51779 4

Printed and bound in Great Britain for Hodder and Stoughton Paperbacks, a division of Hodder and Stoughton Ltd., Mill Road, Dunton Green, Sevenoaks, Kent TN13 2YA. (Editorial Office: 47 Bedford Square, London WC1B 3DP) by Cox & Wyman Ltd., Reading, Berks.

*To my family and friends,
with thanks for their unfailing
support and encouragement.*

And to Peter Welford, endlessly tolerant.

A wet sheet and a flowing sea,
    A wind that follows fast
And fills the white and rustling sail
    And bends the gallant mast;
And bends the gallant mast, my boys,
    While like an eagle free
Away the good ship flies and leaves
    Old England on the lee.

O for a soft and gentle wind!
    I heard a fair one cry;
But give to me the snoring breeze
    And white waves heaving high;
And white waves heaving high, my lads,
    The good ship tight and free –
The world of waters is our home,
    And merry men are we.

There's tempest in yon hornéd moon,
    And lightning in yon cloud;
But hark the music, mariners!
    The wind is piping loud;
The wind is piping loud, my boys,
    The lightning flashes free –
While the hollow oak our palace is,
    Our heritage the sea.

                              A. Cunningham

PART ONE: 1814–1815

The Poacher

CHAPTER ONE

In the room which his parents liked to call the parlour Tom Elderfield stood, tense and silent, listening to the shouts and catcalls that were closer with every flicker of the candle flame, every breath of icy wind under the door. The men must have left the alehouse much earlier than usual; it was not yet ten o'clock. Did that mean the ringleaders were now goading them to fresh purpose, fresh hatred?

Tightening his grip on the brass candlestick Tom moved to the window. The metal-rimmed soles of his boots clacked on the flagstones. He peered outside, leaning close to the panes to blot out his reflection. There was nothing to see, only the night with its dimly etched clouds and the creaking silhouettes of elms.

Tom realised he was shaking from more than the cold, and at once he despised his cowardice but, at fifteen years old, the responsibility for his mother's safety as well as his own lay heavily on him. Damn it, why couldn't his father have missed chapel for once? The Andover meeting house was three miles off – a long ride home to Hatchley village in the dark.

Being the blacksmith's son set Tom apart in some ways – the craft was more lucrative than most, less dependent on each year's harvest – but Hatchley was his home and he knew its folk. The wars with France had brought high prices and low wages; men were restless and bitter, looking for scapegoats. True, they were more full of talk than action, but in the next parish a dissenting chapel-goer had been attacked and nearly killed. This was bad enough, but for a Dissenter like his father, who also had a French wife . . .

His mother's voice from upstairs, weary and anxious, made him jump.

"*Tom, qu'est-ce que tu fais?*"

"*Rien, maman. Je viens.*"

The words of her native tongue came to him naturally, without thought. With her he spoke French; with his father, English. It was the way things had always been.

He checked that the doors at front and back were secured, left the candle at hand in case of emergency, and climbed the stairs two at a time. At the top he paused, took a deep breath, and entered his parents' bedchamber.

"I was just locking up," he said cheerfully in fluent French. "Are you all right? Warm enough?"

Marie Elderfield turned her head on the pillow and he saw how pale she was. The baby which had arrived two days ago was her third stillborn child. The midwife had told him, when questioned in private, that there would be no more children.

He sat on the bed and took her hand. His mother liked to be told nothing and to believe that she had been told everything; a weakness which he humoured out of compassion and to avoid tearful scenes, and he did not know himself which motive was the stronger.

"The men are just letting off steam," he said. "They won't hurt us. At least . . ." He grinned. "They might black Pa's eye for him, given half a chance."

Marie Elderfield's hand jerked, her fingers tightened around his with surprising strength. "I am not a child, Tom, to be shielded from the truth. Englishmen are very patriotic these days. They hate my French blood, and they choose to believe that a man who is not of the established Church is also a traitor, a supporter of Napoleon Buonaparte."

"They must tell it to Boney, then. I don't reckon he knows."

"My dear, can you not be sensible?"

"Seriously, those men out there are my mates – well, some of them. That's why they haven't turned nasty up to now." He glanced wryly at the miniature of his father which stood on the dressing chest. "Not that Pa would believe it."

"Is that why you drink with them, and ride foolish races with the Tandy brothers? To win them to our side?"

"No," he laughed. "What am I, a saint? And the Tandys have been on our side all along. Listen to me, *maman*, you've lived in England twenty years or more – eleven of them here in Hatchley. And *grand-père* was a royalist. If you hadn't left France, the revolutionaries would have sent you all to the guillotine."

"We know this, of course." Marie Elderfield let go of his hand and patted it gently. "But here men are less well informed and this winter has been so hard; their families are hungry. What can we say to them? I am French."

She was right and Tom knew it. The folk of an inland village would not remember how Marie's father, along with many of his compatriots, had once been welcomed by the people of Lymington on Hampshire's coast; or that he and hundreds of others had joined the doomed Quiberon expedition and died fighting the revolutionaries. Now, in the frostbound February of 1814, the men of Hatchley cared only that William Elderfield was a non-conformist who would not work on a Sunday, whatever his obligations, and that Elderfield's wife sent and received letters in her own language. More than once Tom had noticed that when such a letter arrived from the Vaillants, their Lymington friends, the seal had been broken and badly repaired.

A wordless shout from outside, followed by angry laughter, made Tom glance involuntarily at the window. "Never mind them," he said, "I'm with you, and the doors are bolted."

He thought she was willing to be reassured, until her head turned restlessly and he saw the tears on her cheeks glisten in the candlelight. "People were different in Lymington," she said. "Not bitter and full of hate. Oh my dear, we were such fools to leave."

Tom thought otherwise. In Lymington William Elderfield had been out of work, with the press gangs growing more active after a brief lull in the war. When he heard that Hatchley needed a blacksmith, bringing his wife and four-year-old son to the village had been by far the most sensible course. Tom's memories of Lymington were dim, and he had only a vague, yearning curiosity to smell the salt breeze and see tall ships again.

"Wouldn't you like to go back?" he asked. "Stay with the

Vaillants, just until things are quieter?"

"What about you – and your father?"

"Oh . . ." He slanted her a rueful look. "I'd be here to keep Pa out of trouble."

Marie Elderfield reached up to stroke her son's tousled blond hair, and he sensed that she was seeing his father twenty years ago, before time and a stern outlook had hardened William Elderfield's brilliant blue eyes and streaked his hair with grey. "We stay or leave together," she said. "The three of us –"

Her words were cut off by the crash of a breaking window downstairs, followed by a thud and the tinkle of falling glass. In the lane, cheers were mingled with hoarse obscenities. Marie Elderfield gasped, and Tom squeezed her hand before running for the stairs, muttering a very Anglo-Saxon oath.

It turned out to be the parlour window that was broken. A brick lay on the floor and must have been hurled with considerable force; the window frame had cracked down one side.

"Where are you, then, *madame*? Let's see your pretty French face." Tom recognised the voice of Rob Hanson, the usual ringleader and a man whose company he rarely sought. "What news have you got for Boney this week? That we can't buy bread to feed our children? That your man is out praying we soon starve?"

Tom was too angry to be afraid. Flicking back the bolts he opened the door wide and stood facing a score of Hatchley labourers.

"You're a bloody liar, Rob Hanson, and you'll let my mother alone!"

Astonishment caused a momentary hush among the men. Then someone said, "Oh, aye? Thrash us one at a time, will you?" And there were jeers of contempt and sour humour.

Tom stood his ground. "Drink has addled your brains, the lot of you. I don't see eye to eye with Pa over some things, but I know for bloody sure that he's a loyal Englishman, and so should you, and I'll fight any bastard who says different."

"Your fight's with me, then."

Rob Hanson moved forward, a powerfully built man whose loose-fitting smock emphasized the breadth of his shoulders. As self-appointed spokesman he had talked of

14

'our children', but in fact he was not yet married and there-fore suffered less hardship than most from the pitiful wage rates. A couple of paces from the cottage doorway he stopped.

"Come on out, Elderfield, and shut the door behind you. I wouldn't want your poor mother to see this."

Tom stepped into the lane and began warily circling his opponent, fists raised in the manner of a prize-fighter. The crowd was growing uneasy. From the back a man shouted, "Why not call it a day, Rob? The constable ain't abed yet, and there's no sense in killing the lad."

There were several murmurs of agreement. Tom called back, "Isn't this what you came to see, Dan? Or do you only like chucking bricks and threatening women?" And Hanson growled over his shoulder, "I'm for killing no one, but he needs a lesson in –"

The much-needed lesson was to remain undefined, for as Hanson's eyes left his opponent, Tom bounded forward and punched him on the jaw.

The blow was a hard one. Two years working alongside his father at the smithy, wielding a nine pound sledge-hammer as often as not, had given Tom an efficient set of muscles. Rob Hanson was taken completely off guard and would have fallen if his companions had not steadied him in time.

Now the murmurs were those of nervous laughter. Rob Hanson rubbed his jaw and looked at Tom, who had backed off and resumed his former stance. The expression in Hanson's eyes twisted Tom's stomach with dread; the man stood a head taller than him and the discrepancy in weight must make any contest a one-sided affair. Well, wasn't his Pa forever saying he had the luck of the devil? He was going to need it.

Even as he finished the thought Hanson came at him with a roar. Tom saw the heavy fist swing and he ducked fast beneath it, getting in a short left jab to Hanson's back before the labourer's second punch caught him a glancing blow on the temple.

He fell across the doorstep, the night around him bright with coloured sparks. A booted foot drove into his side and he curled up defensively. So much for fighting fair – but two

15

could play that game! The next time Hanson lashed out Tom grabbed his ankle and tried to tug him off balance – with the result that the man kicked out savagely and slammed Tom's fingers against the edge of the doorpost.

With a cry of pain the boy rolled to avoid another kick, starting to clamber to his feet. Hanson almost nonchalantly drove a fist into his stomach.

Tom doubled over and sank to his knees, gasping for air. He heard voices raised in protest. There was a burst of shouting and, looking up, he saw Rob Hanson dragged back.

"It's not the boy that's at fault –"

"Let him alone, Rob –"

Through the general din came Hanson's loud oaths, gradually subsiding as the men's words penetrated. Rob Hanson knew his mates were a set of boot-licking disciples and nervous hangers-on, but many of them liked the Elderfield brat, in spite of him being half Frog and the son of a joyless Bible-preaching traitor, and bloody arrogant besides. Giving him the beating he deserved would cause Hanson to lose face. Shrugging off the restraining arms he stood quite still, regarding Tom.

"What's the matter, boy? Had enough already, have you?"

Tom would have yelled defiance, if only he could have found the breath. After a moment the labourer spat directly into his face and turned away, giving the man nearest to him a clap on the back.

"Cringing cowards," he said gruffly. "Like father, like son."

When they had gone, Tom sat down and wiped away the spittle. His right hand throbbed unmercifully, swamping all the other aches. He bit back a groan as he tried to straighten his fingers. At least they were not broken. There was no excuse for sitting in the lane feeling sorry for himself.

He went upstairs slowly, nursing his swollen, bleeding fingers, uttering a stream of obscenities in a breathless undertone. He slid the hand gingerly into his breeches pocket before going into the bedroom. His mother was sitting up, the covers thrown aside as if she would have rescued him herself.

"Tom – oh, my darling, I was so afraid. I heard them shouting. I thought –"

"That I couldn't take care of myself? *Maman*, you know better than that. Don't cry, it's all over, they've gone away."

He rearranged her pillows and made her lie down, drawing the blankets up to cover her thin shoulders. When he bent to kiss her she stopped him; her hand trembled as she smoothed the hair back from his temple.

"Your head . . . Tom, you're bleeding."

"Only a graze. It doesn't hurt now." He would have to clean up before his father came home. Time enough in the morning to confess to brawling on the doorstep and to endure contempt for his inept handling of the situation. "Hush now," he said, "You mustn't think about it any more."

"Stay here, Tom. Sit with me. Just for a while."

When she slept at last, he went down to tidy the debris of battle from the parlour floor. Afterwards he took the candle through to the kitchen; the stone sink contained water drawn from the well that afternoon, and he bathed his hand and washed the blood out of his hair and furtively relieved himself outside the back door. A walk to the privy beyond the vegetable patch would have required too much energy.

It was after eleven when he settled himself in the hard armchair beside the kitchen hearth and turnspit, to wait for his father. The ticking of the clock was sombre, monotonous, out of time with the beat of pain through his swollen fingers. His breath turned to mist on the air, and he made the effort to build a fire before the candle burned low and died.

William Elderfield did not come home.

At first Tom thought he might have stayed with acquaintances in Andover for, after all, wouldn't the mare have trotted back to her own stable if there had been trouble on the road? It took a lot to keep old Belladonna from her feed. But Tom decided to wait a while longer, just in case. He curled up on the hard chair and dozed through the night.

By dawn he had acknowledged that his father would not have stayed away from home deliberately, the times being what they were. Straightening his cramped limbs he rose stiffly and went to the writing table in the parlour – a proud purchase years ago, when business had been brisk in spite of the war. He penned a note of explanation for his mother, the need to write left-handed making the message brief and nearly illegible, then crept up to her room and propped the slip of paper against the rosewood dressing box which had belonged to his wealthy French grandmother.

Then he let himself silently out of the cottage, and sprinted along the lane that would take him through Hatchley and on to the Andover road.

CHAPTER TWO

After the events of the previous night Tom did not expect to pass through Hatchley unchallenged, but the few people he met were intent on their own business; deliberately so, it seemed. The driver of a dung-cart gave him a sullen, side-long glance and then ignored him; and the shoemaker's wife, taking her husband his breakfast in the workshop, looked at Tom with something like compassion before turning silently away.

Tom began to see guilt in their silence, to imagine eyes watching him from behind frost-patterned windows. Surely the village had never been as quiet as this?

He raced past the deserted green, dodging a startled flurry of geese crossing the lane, and struggled to maintain his pace up the long incline out of Hatchley. He needed transport, and there was only one person he felt able to ask.

Reaching the farmhouse at the top of the hill, he leaned on the gate, panting and called to the man who stood in the porch, quietly smoking.

"Sir . . . Mr Tandy . . ."

The man shifted the pipe from one corner of his mouth to the other, and strolled to the gate. "Fine time of day to come visiting, lad. Something wrong?"

Sacheverell Tandy, a man of liberal but atheistic views, was one of the most talked-about people in the village. Moving to Hatchley as a youngish man, he had bought some land and commissioned the building of an eight-roomed house for his wife and himself. Now a widower, he lived impossibly well on the profits of eighteen acres of sheep pasture. Gossip whispered of a fortune made in youth – by smuggling or highway robbery, no doubt – but whatever the source of Mr Tandy's wealth, he kept no servants. His four children received board and lodging, and personal tuition in every subject, but were obliged to look elsewhere for their spending money. Remarkably only the eldest, Obadiah, resented this, and even he worked on the farm for a labourer's wage rather than leave home altogether.

Yet Mr Tandy was generous, less formidable than he looked, and intolerant only of treachery and injustice. Over the years his home had been Tom's frequent refuge; a haven of sanity, companionship and boisterous fun.

Now Tom said jerkily, still breathing hard, "Pa didn't come home from chapel. Some of the men – with Rob Hanson – I reckon Hanson could kill a man if he was provoked enough – and you know what Pa's like for scorning folk that don't share his views –" He choked, close to tears and furious with himself for the weakness.

Sacheverell Tandy opened the gate and dropped a heavy arm across his shoulders. "We'll take the haycart, you and me together. Come along, now, no time to be lost."

The man's kindness might have caused Tom to break down, but just then a girl emerged from behind the house and, catching sight of the visitor, hitched her skirts above her ankles and ran to greet him.

"Tom! Tom Elderfield! Our pond is frozen again. I'll have to go skating before I can think of starting any chores at all. Will you come?"

"Now then, Jessica." Sacheverell Tandy lowered his black brows at his daughter. "Tom wants none of your nonsense. He has more urgent matters to attend to than skating on our pond."

Jessica skipped round to Tom's other side, almost running to keep up as they headed for the stables. She was a year younger than he, with the dark eyes and curling black hair of all the Tandy brood, and a promise of heart-stopping beauty.

Also her figure was no longer that of a child, and lately Tom had felt a shyness in her presence sometimes, as if she might read his thoughts and despise him – but today he had too much else on his mind.

Jessica, running again to draw level, straightened her

straw bonnet and pushed a lock of hair out of her eyes. "Has something bad happened, Tom? Is your Ma worse? Oh!" Catching sight of his injured hand. "Oh, Tom, that must be sore. Did you fall off Belladonna?"

Able to trust his voice again, Tom outlined the story briefly. Jessica was both horrified and fiercely indignant that such things could happen in their own village. She raced back to the house for a bandage and cobwebs, and insisted on binding his hand while Sacheverell Tandy harnessed the workhorse. Tom could not contain his impatience, when the smallest delay might prove fatal. Tying the ends of the bandage with his teeth and one hand, he bounded up on the cart beside Mr Tandy. The girl would have joined them, had her father not growled that no passengers were required.

Jessica stood glaring up at him, hands firmly on her hips. "Passengers, is it? I'm useful enough in a crisis, Pa, as you know quite well and have said more than once."

This was true; since her mother's death four years ago Jessica had cooked and cared for her father and three high-spirited, unpredictable brothers and, very often, Tom Elderfield as well. She was accustomed to taking crises in her stride.

Sacheverell Tandy shook his head, glowering to silence any new protest. "You'll stay and prepare a fine breakfast for our return, my girl. If Mr Elderfield has been hiding out in some barn all night, he'll be half frozen and as hungry as any of us."

Tom might have taken offence at this interpretation of his father's absence, but he knew that Mr Tandy did not believe in it. As the cart trundled into the lane he looked back to see Jessica swinging on the gate, her solemn face reflecting his own anxiety.

It was in a ditch not half a mile from the village that they found William Elderfield. The blacksmith lay on his face in ice-crusted water, his clothes and hair white with frost. The loyal, ageing Belladonna was still nosing his head as if to rouse him from sleep.

Tom jumped from the moving cart and slid down the bank to reach his father. Stooping in the ditch he punched through the ice, breaking it up until he could grasp his father's arm and roll him over.

The delays had been unimportant, after all. William Elderfield had not suffered an obvious beating; the bruise on his head suggested that he might have fallen from his horse, knocked himself out and drowned in a few inches of water. His eyes were open, blind, and runnels of muddy water streaked his face like tears.

Tom stood up slowly. Strange; now that the imagined horror had become reality, he felt only emptiness. The whole structure of his life had been ripped away.

Sacheverell Tandy gripped his shoulder. "Come on, lad. Let's get him up in the cart."

"I should have warned him," he whispered. "I owed him that."

"Did you, indeed!" The farmer's voice rose in explosive anger. "Are you a fortune-teller, now? Could you read Hanson's intention before he knew it himself? Stop your nonsense, boy, and give me a hand!"

Between them they heaved William Elderfield's body into the cart, and Sacheverell Tandy drove rapidly back to Hatchley. Tom followed at a slower pace on Belladonna, gazing straight ahead but seeing nothing, and thinking of the night before.

Several chapel-goers from Andover came to the funeral, as did the Tandys. Tom guessed it was mostly shame that kept the rest of Hatchley's folk away; there had been no trouble of any sort since the tragedy, and none of his ale-house acquaintants would have wanted murder on his conscience. He despised them, these men who were accessories through silence and inaction; following Hanson's lead because they feared to cross him, or passing by, like the Levite, on the other side.

And yet, although Tom grieved for his father – for the injustice of his death, for words unsaid between them and opportunities missed – he was not devastated by the loss. There had never been any real point of contact, the boy understanding neither his father's values nor his father's God.

As an only child, faced with suffocating affection from one parent, and well-meant but often brutal discipline from the other, Tom had spent most of his childhood escaping from both. At the age of six, when his mother began tutoring him, the hours closeted with her patient, cloying tenderness had been too much to bear. He had fled to share the Tandys' lessons whenever possible, in defiance of the beatings he received for it at home. Finally Sacheverell Tandy had taken him as a regular pupil, on equal footing with his own children, pointing out to an enraged William Elderfield that this was apparently the only way to ensure that his son got an education. The clannish Tandy brood, perhaps because of Tom's refugee status, had welcomed him unreservedly, an honour they allowed to few outsiders.

Now, Tom was a half trained apprentice in sole charge of the village smithy. The future scared him; but its challenge set his blood coursing fast, like the fear before going out poaching, or climbing the church steeple for a wager, or racing Amos Tandy across rough ground on an ill-tempered horse.

In the meantime, one problem needed an immediate solution. When the funeral service was over, Tom left his mother in Jessica's care for a few moments while he drew Sacheverell Tandy aside.

"I was wondering, sir, if you'd do me a great favour."

The man nodded, frowning, and answered as to an equal. "If I can help in any way, Tom, I certainly shall."

"I'm going to watch the grave for a couple of nights, and I, er – I don't want to leave Ma alone in the cottage after dark. I know it's short notice, but if she could stay with you, just until –"

"Good God, is that all? We'll be glad to have her, and that's the truth."

Tom's hand was grasped in a warm, hard grip and he thanked Sacheverell Tandy with a feeling of tremendous relief. Hospitals paid well for fresh cadavers for dissection and research, and no question asked, so that one had to keep an eye on new graves. The professional bodysnatchers – the so-called Resurrection Men who sometimes murdered to help supply meet demand – had become active in most neighbourhoods.

Having seen his mother safe in her temporary lodgings, Tom worked at the smithy for the rest of the day, and returned to the churchyard at dusk. He was met by no less

23

than three of the young Tandys. Amos, the same age as Tom and his partner in most escapades, volunteered to share sentry duty. Ten-year-old Thomas – invariably known as Mace – was there to prove he was not afraid of ghosts, and Jessica insisted she had only come to see that Mace behaved himself.

The eldest of the brothers, Obadiah, had business elsewhere. He had gone to Andover with Hanson, to see a cockfight; and, as Jessica said, at seventeen he was old enough to keep company with whoever he liked, even a bullying, murdering pig.

The girl had brought blankets, and supper in a covered basket. They chose a grassy hollow over some long forgotten villager's grave and ate chicken and new bread in the twilight, talking in low voices as befitted the place. Mace scampered off afterwards to watch for owls, but when full darkness came he strolled back, humming, pretending nonchalance, and sat rather close to Jessica, his eyes round and his whole body taut with unconfessed terror.

Jessica whispered, "Want to go home, Macey?" But he shook his head, affronted, and clenched his chattering teeth.

A rota was agreed. Tom and Amos would take alternate two hour stints, Amos having borrowed his father's pocket watch for the purpose. Jessica and Mace were reserve troops who could sleep when they pleased.

The night passed without incident, though it was colder than any of them had anticipated, in spite of the thaw having set in some days before. By morning, Tom and Amos were bleary-eyed and less than eager to start the working day. Amos had lately become one of the Squire's new 'watchers', assisting Sir Charles Gullifer's head gamekeeper in laying the hated man-traps and spring-guns along tracks frequented by poachers, or else working the night shift to patrol the estate. The number of men willing to risk injury and perhaps death, either from the keepers or the traps, had increased in proportion to their poverty and they were not deterred by the threat of capture and a summary trial. The recent Enclosure Acts had deprived them of their common, used as grazing land by generations of cottagers. Sir Charles considered himself a fair-minded and honourable man, but he had small patience with the labourers' grievances, excepting those which could be laid at Buonaparte's door. Were their wages not supplemented from the Poor Relief Fund, to which he subscribed more generously than duty demanded? He had been quick to recruit more watchers to protect his game.

As Tom trudged back with the Tandys for an early breakfast, he voiced his thoughts reluctantly. "Best not stand duty with me any more, Amos, or you'll be falling down asleep on your own traps. It's not likely the Resurrection Men will bother us hereabouts."

"You're a bigger fool than you look, Tom Elderfield." This was Jessica, running beside Mace to catch up with the older boys. "You'll be telling us next that Hampshire surgeons don't need corpses. Why, I believe the cold dew has turned your brain, if you have one."

Tom had quarrelled often with this bold, vital, fiery-natured girl whose dark eyes missed nothing and who apparently spoke each thought as it occurred to her. And now he was cold and weary, disinclined to swallow the insult just because she was female. He said rudely, "You can stay out of it. You weren't invited last night and needn't come again, so keep your opinions to yourself."

Jessica drew breath to deliver her current opinion of Tom Elderfield; but one look at his face stopped her. To Tom's lasting bewilderment she linked her arm through his and sent Mace ahead with Amos. Having thus established herself as Tom's ally against all comers, she walked beside him with her head high, not saying a word, and ignoring the winks and grins of her brothers.

Tom was glad to have lost the argument; Amos and Jess knew how he would have hated to continue the dismal, freezing, eerie vigil alone. Making plans for the future was all very fine and exhilarating, but with the Tandys he could be himself, without being required to bear his new responsibilities like a man, with a man's strength of mind and purpose. He was sorry to have snapped at Jessica.

He waited to tell her so until breakfast was over, and the girl had shut herself in the kitchen to wash the dishes. Tom heard her singing; her voice was sweet and clear, but the ballad was a sad one. With the menfolk gone from the house, and his mother in bed, Tom sauntered into the kitchen and leaned on the door jamb, hands in his pockets. Jessica was scrubbing each item of crockery with savage concentration, the violent movements of her arm at odds with her gentle singing.

"That's a pretty tune, Jess."

"I learned it last Michaelmas, from a balladeer at Weyhill Fair." She glanced round, half smiling. "You don't have to say sorry. I was unkind to you."

He grinned sheepishly and advanced to peer over her shoulder. "I'll choose my own punishment, then. Want some help with that?"

"And have our best plates all in pieces on the floor? Get away with you, Tom."

He picked up a clean plate, set it rolling the length of the dresser, and leapt to catch it three inches above the floor.

"There – how's that?"

Jessica clicked her tongue as if exasperated, moving to the long table to fuss with the arrangement of some snowdrops in a vase. Tom lounged against the dresser and watched her narrowly.

"Still angry with me?" he asked.

"You're putting me off my work." Her voice sounded odd, and when she turned he saw her eyes brimming with tears. "Oh, Tom, I keep thinking about Rob Hanson. If it was my Pa that was killed, I know I'd go after Rob to murder him. You wouldn't try anything like that on your own, would you, without telling any of us? He'd kill you if you did, Tom, you're no match for him yet –"

"I'm not going to murder Rob Hanson."

The girl caught her breath. "You mean you don't even want to?" Clearly this was worse than that he should risk his life in the attempt.

He answered seriously, aware that this was something he would tell no one but her. "Hanson is a day-labourer, out of work most winters. He gets his glory leading a gang of thugs, and winning the county championship for singlestick-playing. All right, let him."

"Tom!"

"I shan't swing for him, he's not bloody worth it. But I'll beat him, Jess, by God I will. This time next year I swear I'll be earning as much every week as Hanson could in a month

– and I'll take the championship from him too, soon as I'm old enough to qualify." He stopped, with a breath of ironical laughter. "Here endeth today's lesson."

Jessica came to him and placed her hands on his shoulders; her hands were still damp and he felt their warmth through his shirt. Last year she had been the same height as himself, but already he was at least three inches the taller. She stood so close that he noticed how thick and long her eyelashes were, and discovered with a flicker of surprise that she had borrowed his mother's French perfume. On Jessica it smelt different; fresher, more elusive, wholly enticing. The nearness of her sent a heat through his body and quickened his blood.

The girl leaned forward on tiptoe and kissed him on the mouth, her lips just touching his before she stood back to look solemnly into his eyes.

"You'll show them, Tom," she said. "I know you will."

Tom had never kissed a girl before, but no girl had ever looked up at him with that shining confidence, as if she would take his side against a thousand Rob Hansons. Hesitantly and awkwardly he pulled her close and returned her kiss, with much gentleness at first, and then with certainty and hunger as all the stresses of the past week found unexpected release, and her need seemed as great as his own.

At last she struggled free of his arms and backed away, smoothing her hair and dress, although neither was disarranged. "If that's your idea of an apology, Tom Elderfield," she said breathlessly, "I'd as soon have it in plain ordinary words next time." But her eyes lifted to his and she smiled, and Tom's grin in return made them at once conspirators. "Well," she said, "I'll see you in the churchyard, I suppose."

"Oh, bet on it, Jess," he said, and retreated from the kitchen in awe and wonder, hardly aware of the ground under his feet. He ran most of the way home, and all that day derived a ridiculous amount of pleasure from whistling the tune that Jessica Tandy had learned at Weyhill Fair.

CHAPTER THREE

After that first night in the churchyard, young Mace Tandy stayed at home unprotesting, having proved himself sufficiently a man. Amos and Jessica continued as loyal sentries. The girl shared Tom's hours on watch, huddling inside the same blanket for warmth, her back against the same chill headstone. If an owl hooted nearby, or some small creature screeched its death cry, she would clasp Tom's hand and nestle closer still.

This show of fear was a convenient pretence. There was Irish blood in the Tandys, inherited from their mother; they were wild and fearless and in love with life, and the daughter of the house would have faced any danger – ghosts and Resurrection Men alike – rather than be seen to play the coward. But she loved Tom Elderfield with all the naive, obsessive sentimentality of the very young, and these nights were her secret joy. She would even behave like any silly nervous female, just for an excuse to hold his hand.

The Resurrection Men did not appear, and on the fourth night the vigil was ended by mutual agreement. There was a sharp frost, the first for a week; also the corpse was no longer quite fresh. As Jessica remarked, there would be little point in them all freezing to death and joining Mr Elderfield.

"You must come back with us, and take your Ma home in the morning," she told Tom, her manner easy and casual, so that he would not guess at her reluctance to part with him so soon. "There's the spare bed in Mace's room."

Tom had occupied this bed many times; mornings in the Tandys' house were hectic and riotous, a delicious contrast to the repressive atmosphere at home. Even with his mother there, the prospect was tempting. He accepted the invitation gratefully, and in the dim light from cottage windows Jessica caught his smile, mischievous and faintly arrogant, not meant for Amos to see.

Turf or log fires burned in every hearth tonight; the smoke drifted high, its resinous fragrance sharp and sweet on the icy air. Jessica was filled with a swift, illogical merriment, and only respect for William Elderfield's memory kept her from running and dancing up the hill towards home.

The house was welcoming; the parlour fire burned, and the kitchen range was lit, and the smell of mutton stew overlaid that of woodsmoke. Jessica ran to her father and hugged him, begging food and shelter for three poor frozen sentries. He swung her high off the floor, so that she squealed for mercy, while Obadiah returned from the stables and started a good-natured sparring match with Amos. In spite of her happiness, the girl was embarrassed for herself and her menfolk; until a glance at Tom showed him looking relaxed and amazingly cheerful, already sampling the stew from the end of a ladle.

As the evening progressed, even Marie Elderfield seemed less careworn than usual. Jessica grew confident, eager to excel as a hostess. Having tempted her guests with elderberry wine and downed two glasses herself, she gathered everyone around the piano. Her mother had taught her to play, but Jessica had no patience with Mozart and the like; tunes with words were more entertaining. Tonight she chose the old songs of the Scottish Jacobites, and the least bawdy of the sea shanties from her father's youth. The house being Tom's second home – if not his first – he had learned these long ago, and joined in as loudly as her brothers and rather out of tune.

The wine was making her bold. She looked up at the young blacksmith and sang of Bonnie Prince Charlie with laughter in her voice. Tom, who was on his fourth glass, clearly found this romantic parallel both absurd and hilarious, and threatened to 'carry her over the sea to Skye' and leave her there if she didn't stop acting daft.

"Do you know what tomorrow is, Tom Elderfield?" she asked.

"Monday. What else?"

"Oh, nothing. Nothing at all," she said, and would not have confessed for anything that she had hoped he would remember Valentine's day this year. Amos was grinning and nudging Obadiah, but she pretended not to notice. The next moment brought a diversion. Mace's overgrown hound charged into the room, pursuing his equally excitable owner across a card table, the chaise-longue, and a plateful of cakes, and Jessica could be sure that her foolishness was forgotten.

Later, lying awake in bed, she told herself that Tom Elderfield was nothing to her. Less than nothing. A thoughtless, heartless, insensitive . . . well, she could do better. There were other admirers to send her Valentine gifts.

But in the morning she rose early and ran downstairs, remembering the superstition that the first man she saw would be her future husband; and the sight of Tom loitering aimlessly in the hall made her stomach tighten and her heart beat light and fast.

Seeing her, he pushed away from the wall, his expression an odd mixture of wickedness and embarassment. "Good morning to you, Jess."

"And to you, Tom. My, but it's cold! Let's bring some logs in –"

"Jessie . . ." He blocked her way to the kitchen. "I bought – well, I bought you these, in Andover, on Friday." He pressed a small bundle of lace into her hand. "Happy Valentine's Day."

They were a pair of garters, frivolous and exquisite, threaded with yellow ribbon. Blushing with pleasure, Jessica wanted to ask boldly whether he hoped to see them again; but that would be too cruel.

"They're beautiful," she said. "Thank you – oh, thank you."

He said awkwardly, still seeking reassurance, "You don't reckon they're too . . . familiar? I had the devil's own job thinking what to buy."

She shook her head, laughing, and the relief in his face was a compliment that needed no words. This time he kissed her with as much assurance as passion, and Jessica responded eagerly, wanting only to prolong the moment, to feel his hands tentatively exploring . . .

A door slammed upstairs and they jumped apart. On the landing above, a dog padded from one bedroom to the next. Jessica made a wry face, expecting a similar reaction from Tom; but he was looking unbearably smug and his eyes were merry, as if nothing in the world could hurt him now.

Jessica scooped her long hair back from her face, trying hard to behave as though this were still just an ordinary day. "The men will be down clamouring for breakfast in five minutes."

"Well, if we've got five minutes . . ."

Jessica stopped pretending that the day was in any way ordinary. When Sacheverell Tandy and his sons came downstairs soon afterwards, they were greeted with innocent smiles and a plate of yesterday's bread and cheese. If the older boys had their suspicions, they were wise enough not to give them voice.

That morning, Marie Elderfield returned to the smithy cottage. Jessica promised to help with the housework there every Sunday, until Tom's mother had regained her strength. She would have found any excuse to visit him, but without a legitimate reason these visits would have caused trouble at home. Obadiah was inclined to be over-protective – much more so than their father – and he had lost no time in telling Jessica that she was too young to be looking for a sweetheart, and that Tom should watch his step. Jessica had refrained from answering that she would lose her virginity to Tom Elderfield as soon as he cared to ask her.

He did not ask, but Jessica had a great capacity for patience. She found it expedient to be known as wilful, head-strong, one of the wild Tandys who fought for themselves or each other and the devil take the consequences. Such a reputation was useful. Even Tom believed her to be naive and tactless, incapable of any sort of subterfuge.

So she was content to bide her time, and as the weeks passed she saw a new side to the boy she had known from infancy. Business at the forge was bad; many folk took their custom elsewhere, encouraged by the action of Sir Charles, who now sent to Andover for a smith rather than trust his horses to a fifteen-year-old apprentice. Tom received some orders for tools and repair work, but not enough. Jessica feared he might react as her brothers would have done in

31

such circumstances, getting drunk and running up debts and rushing headlong into danger to forget his troubles. Instead, he stopped visiting The King's Head, took no dares, laid no bets, and applied himself to the matter of survival with a proud and single-minded determination.

It was over a month before Jessica learned at second hand that he was out most nights, bagging hares, rabbits and partridges to sell to Harry Colbourne, landlord at The King's Head, who as the local middle man sold the game to the London outlets. Hurt that he had not chosen to confide in her, Jessica would not have betrayed to Tom that she knew of these activities; but when she arrived at the cottage one Sunday morning he was seated alone at the kitchen table, head low over a closely written accounts book, a kettle steaming unheeded above the fire.

He started violently at her first greeting. His face, pale with fatigue, lit up, and he rose and embraced her with an enthusiasm which took her breath. She struggled against him. "Don't! Tom, your mother –"

"– is still asleep. Jess, I'm going to be rich, but you're not to tell a soul except Amos – not a soul, you hear?"

Seeing how his eyes shone, Jessica felt a twinge of apprehension. She said dryly, "In that case it must be either illegal or dangerous, and probably both. Is it connected with the poaching, this idea of yours?"

"You know about that?"

Jessica gave an unladylike snort of contempt. "Doesn't everyone, except your Ma?" She drew away from him, to make tea from the jar of used tea leaves bought from Sir Charles' cook. "You could have told me a month ago, if you'd wanted to. Why now?"

"Because I've only been testing the ground. Now I'm going into it seriously."

"Like the Farminer brothers? They've been poachers for ten years, served four gaol sentences between them, and Ned has been caught twice in man-traps. The next conviction will get one of them transported. They're not rich yet."

"Harry Colbourne is."

Jessica set the kettle down, gripping it so that he would not see how her hand shook. "Is that the scheme, then? To compete with Mr Colbourne for business?"

"He's milking me of half what I'd earn by selling direct to the London markets. Have you seen his new carriage, and the strain on his waistcoat buttons?"

"A fat man with gold in his pockets. Do you think he'll just sit by and let you undercut him?"

"Jessie . . . I'll be an independent operator, not running a gang. What the others do is up to them." Tom sighed, and slumped back into his chair with a tired resignation that hurt the girl as much as his next words. "I thought you'd understand. I don't like . . . I don't want us to have secrets."

Jessica swallowed every reproach she had meant to utter, and placed a mug of hot tea in front of him. "When was the last time you had a proper night's sleep?"

"You sound like my mother," he said.

"That's just what I'm not." She sat opposite him, reaching for his hands. "I can stand the truth. You don't have to shut me out. Not ever. Tell me the plan."

"You mean for after I've saved a few guineas and thrashed Hanson too?" A smile glimmered. "In two or three years I'll take Ma back to Lymington, where I was born. It's a prosperous town and I've been educated, same as you. I intend doing well there."

Jessica nodded slowly. His heart was not with the forge; she had always known it. Not even the apprenticeship with his father would have made him a dedicated blacksmith for long, any more than the beatings had turned him into a pious chapel-goer.

"I think about the sea sometimes," he said. "Don't you? When the gulls fly inland, or seeing all those prints covering your walls at home – the ships in full sail? Jess, don't you ever feel stifled, living among folk who'll call a man foreign if he was born ten miles away?"

Jessica could not deny it. The sea was in the Tandys' blood, too; little Mace had taken to copying the seascapes, drawing the ships' lines with a loving and skilful hand. But whereas Mace's dreams were harmless, Tom's were liable to get him killed; and he had not even considered taking her with him to Lymington.

"Jonah Wooldridge is a good head keeper," she said. "The traps are moved every week. I wonder you haven't been caught in one already, a novice like you."

"I nearly was, last night." He frowned into the mug. "It made me think. Amos does work for Wooldridge –"

"So that's it!" Now, at last, Jessica lost her temper; for this was beneath contempt, this was unforgiveable. "Amos will keep you up to date, will he? Warn you of all Wooldridge's tricks? Never mind if he loses his job or ends up in prison –?"

"It's not exactly likely –"

"Hah! I suppose Sir Charles will be pleased to have one of his men in league with a poacher!"

"Who'd tell him? And I haven't even asked Amos yet."

"When did he ever refuse a dare? Oh, and to think I was *sorry* for you!" She was on her feet now, shouting at him across the table. "We mustn't have secrets – oh, no. You filthy, stinking hypocrite, I bet you've planned this all along –"

"That's not bloody true!"

"Don't you swear at me, you – you *worm*. Go and get yourself shot, then, or hanged if you want to, and you needn't think I'll be shedding tears over it, but don't you dare involve my brother in your stupid scheme! Don't you bloody well dare!"

She fled towards the door, and when Tom leapt to grab her arm she blazed at him, "Leave me alone! Leave all of us alone!"

In the parlour, with a closed door between herself and Tom, Jessica dusted the furniture vigorously, blinking back tears of anger and frustration, aware that few of them were for the minimal risks to Amos. Tom Elderfield was a fool; an occasional poaching foray was one thing – Jessica had netted a partridge once or twice for a dare – but no one could beat the odds indefinitely. He would be caught, or shot . . .

A sound from the doorway made her turn. Tom stood there, looking grim and obstinate, braced for further battle.

"I've got to ask him," he said. "I know it's irresponsible, and self-seeking, and maybe worse things besides –"

"Much worse," she whispered; but without Amos' help he would be lost. She must be his ally now, or condemn herself for ever afterwards as a whimpering coward.

Tom was watching her, squinting slightly like a man

turning to face a storm wind. "Wouldn't you really care if I was hanged, Jess?" he said.

She folded the duster neatly and set it down, and went to him in silence, twining her arms about his waist. He looked down at her with such incredulous joy that she thought: how young he is. He doesn't even know what a man might achieve with smiles like that, and those blue, blue eyes. Perhaps he will break my heart and not know it.

"Poaching is one thing," she said, and kissed his mouth. "But if you're hanged I'll never forgive you."

CHAPTER FOUR

Persuading Amos was easy. Working for Jonah Woold-ridge made a man unpopular if he carried out his duties too zealously, and it was a short step from this laxity to giving active assistance to a friend.

Obadiah proved less amenable. He picked a fight the next time Tom entered the farmhouse, and a violent free-for-all developed to include Amos, with Jessica struggling to part the three boys and Mace dodging in and out of the fray and throwing punches at random.

Into this scene came Sacheverell Tandy, sour and irritable after a row with the parson over bringing up his children outside the guidance of the Church. Having separated the main antagonists, and ordered the furniture set to rights, he occupied his favourite chair and mutely held out his hand for a brandy, which Jessica quietly supplied.

"Now," he said ominously, "I'm waiting."

Explanations took some time, and more than once Mr Tandy shook his head in apparent despair. But instead of condemning Tom's actions he said briskly, "You must take your chances, then, the pair of you, just as usual. I'm in no position to lecture on morality. Don't you ever wonder how we live like this, or how I made my fortune?"

Only Obadiah looked as if he knew what to expect, and he was still glaring from Tom to his father and back again, obviously incensed by Sacheverell Tandy's mild reaction.

The farmer continued, "I lived in Mudeford, west of Lymington. I became a lander, a beachmaster. You know what that is? I organised the landing of cargoes, and the distribution of goods inland, sometimes as far away as London Town."

Tom whistled through his teeth, enormously impressed. "You really were a smuggler?"

"Just like the gossips say."

It was Jessica who asked, wide-eyed, "What cargoes, Pa? French brandy?"

"And a lot of tea, in those days. The list of commodities in demand is endless. You would be yawning before I reached the end of it. Although I might be prevailed upon, after supper . . ."

This was all the encouragement Tom needed to stay well into the evening. He was less concerned, nowadays, about leaving his mother alone after dark; folk were more tolerant, with Napoleon's once formidable army demoralised and disintegrating. He listened entranced to stories of sea and land smugglers; of fast purpose-built ships which the Revenue Service could not catch; of fierce battles, and women whose charms had distracted the attention of the Customs men at appropriate moments. It was a glimpse of another world. He understood now why men on the coast were neither poor nor embittered. Sacheverell Tandy stressed that promotion often took years, but Tom made no secret of the fact that the business attracted him.

Much later, when he set out for home, the ex-smuggler hurried after him. "Wait, lad – wait a minute."

Tom allowed Sacheverell Tandy to fall into step beside him; but the man gripped his arm and forced him to a halt.

"You haven't understood yet, have you?" his voice a hiss, his expression unreadable in the dark. "You've no idea why I chose tonight to tell you those yarns. Why do you think I left the Free Trade, eh?"

"Because of the risks?"

"Risks! By God . . . I left while I still could. My wife was carrying Obadiah, I had a family to think of. The gang was taking all my loyalty. If I told you the things that were done to informers – the things *I've* done, on suspicion alone, and sold what was left of their corpses to the Resurrection Men, just to be rid of the evidence –"

"No!" The denial was wrenched from Tom; he respected and loved this man more than he had his own father. "No, sir, I won't believe it."

"I was the beachmaster. It goes with the job. The men

under my command were too scared to give up the Trade, in case I got to thinking they might turn informer. I made enemies. And I was sick of it all, of seeing hate and terror in men's eyes. So I came inland with the money I'd made, and I've never regretted it. The parson complains that I don't give my children proper moral instruction, but I've no right, Tom. No right. You hope to make your fortune and then set up a legitimate business in Lymington. Don't do it, lad. They'd find a use for you, sure enough, but believe me, it's not worth the cost."

"What about Jess?" Tom's voice shook; he felt betrayed, somehow a victim of deception, and the knowledge that this was both childish and unreasonable made him angry. "If you tell Jess any of this, sir, I'll fight you over it, and I won't care who knows the reason."

"My God, Tom, if I thought for one moment that Jessica would ever find out, or the boys either –"

"Goodnight, then, Mr Tandy."

Tom walked quickly away, and this time he was not followed. He kept his eyes fixed on the dark road, his mood as black as the moonless night. There was no one left to admire, or turn to for advice. Amos was a good mate, but his habitual loud exuberance was offset by deep insecurity and a tendency to pessimism, which in Tom's opinion made his judgement as unreliable as his temper. Even Jess . . . Jess was marvellous, a girl in a million, but she was only four-teen.

Well, he thought, trying desperately to laugh at his tears, wasn't this what he had always wanted? Total independence, sole responsibility for his actions and his fate? Maybe he was wrong to put Amos at risk, and maybe he would never be able to thrash Rob Hanson at singlestick or anything else. Maybe he would move to Lymington and regret it for the rest of his life. Too bloody bad. He was not about to change his plans on the recommendation of a murderer. He did not need Sacheverell Tandy's advice.

But he felt he had lost a father twice over. Nothing else which had happened that evening seemed important by comparison; not even the fact that he had made an enemy of Obadiah.

During the following week Tom passed several evenings

at The King's Head. It was well known that Colbourne sold to agents who came and went furtively; the so-called 'higglers', members of a city-spawned underworld, who arranged for the secret transport of game to London from all the counties within easy travelling distance. Tales of the higglers were numerous and often chilling, but Tom was resolved to deal with them direct, relying on local grapevines to spread the word that a new operator was looking for outlets.

His fellow poachers were against the project, mainly from a conviction that no good could come of meddling with 'foreigners'. Tom remained politely aloof; these men, the Farminers included, had been with Hanson the night his father died. He cared no more for their opinion than for Mr Tandy's.

Then came news which diverted nearly everyone's attention for a week or two. Jogging home at dawn from a successful foray into the heart of Sir Charles's estate, Tom vaulted over the last gate to find the lane through Hatchley crowded and children dancing in circles on the green. He left a brace of partridges out of sight, and concealed the net, wire and cudgel in the deep pockets of his poachers' smock before running to question the nearest child.

"Have we won a battle, then, Hannah? Or is Boney dead?"

"It's peace! Peace! The allies are in Paris! Boney is defeated."

It had to be impossible. Buonaparte was the arch enemy, the ogre of his childhood. Tom had never known a time when Britain was not fighting the Emperor; life without the background of war could scarcely be imagined. And yet the news was true.

After twenty years of war, the fall of Paris was incredible to old and young alike. In church on Easter Sunday men jostled for standing room in the aisles, and the parson, beaming with delight, had to delay his sermon of thanksgiving until the clatter of hob-nailed boots had subsided.

Even before Easter came, the distant boom of a triumphant salute, fired from Winchester, was barely heard through the pealing of bells from every church for miles around. Harry Colbourne at The King's Head enjoyed record profits, while outside the young folk danced to Ned Farminer's fiddle as darkness fell and the stars went reeling.

In honour of the occasion, Sir Charles organised a single-stick tournament on the green. The result in the men's category was as forecast; Hanson beat four tough opponents and ended the day two guineas the richer. The youths were more evenly matched. Each was armed with the standard weapon, a cudgel three feet long and an inch and a half thick, and inevitably the boys wielded these with less punishing force than their elders. There were only three cases of concussion. Tom beat Amos in six rounds, lost his chance of the ten shilling purse to the wheelwright's son, and retired from the ring dizzy but undismayed; but the thought that in a year's time he would be eligible to face Rob Hanson was a sobering one.

In the afternoon there was a feast, Sir Charles presenting the singlestick prizes while his wife actually waited upon the villagers, with plenty of roast beef and plum pudding to go around, and ale for everyone old enough to lift a mug.

Jessica nudged Tom in the ribs, whispering, "The Queen of Hearts she made some tarts, and gave them to all the grateful little poachers. What price your revolution now, Frenchie?"

Tom made a face, gazing at Lady Gullifer's extravagantly feathered hat. "The one that got away," he said gravely. "Didn't you bring the partridge net?" And Jessica had to smother her laughter against his shirt.

When the day's celebrations were over, and folk had sung 'God Save the King' to the accompaniment of the church bells which would ring all night, the villagers took their benches and tables home, with full bellies and a sense of euphoria induced by victory and alcohol. But the excitement had wearied Marie Elderfield to a degree which worried Tom. She had been stronger last spring. He helped her upstairs and made sure she was asleep before he slipped out into the night.

There were some stragglers still lurching home, singing 'God Save Great Wellington' to the tune of the national anthem. From The King's Head came cheers and raucous yelling, muffled by the thickness of the tavern walls. Harry Colbourne was holding a cockfight there.

Tom sauntered along the lane, kicking at stones, and sat down on the low churchyard wall. He would not be poaching tonight. He had drunk less than most, staying fairly sober for the singlestick matches, but all the same he felt light-headed and his reactions would be slower than usual.

From here he could see the Tandys' farmhouse on the hill, black against the twilight. A lamp burned in Jessica's window. Maybe she would lie awake thinking of him, wishing she could have stayed all night at the smithy cottage.

Tom moved restlessly, and pulled a tuft of moss from between the stones of the wall. He wanted Jess so much; God, how he wanted her! But if they were lovers there would be a child, most likely, and a wedding, and years of struggle and hardship. Jess deserved better than that. He would take her as well as his mother to Lymington, make a home for them all . . .

His thoughts were cut off abruptly by the consciousness of being watched. There was no one else in the lane now; no one but himself, and the figure which stood in the shadow of the churchyard yew, cloaked by darkness and the loud pealing of bells.

Tom stood up, saying loudly, "If it's you, Hanson, come out and show yourself."

The figure laughed; a low giggle which jarred with the sound of bells and lifted the hairs at Tom's nape. Emphatically this was not Rob Hanson.

Before he could act on the thought, the apparition darted forward with a speed and suddenness that caught him unawares. Tom swore and lashed out, an instinctive impulse, and the man dodged sideways out of reach.

"No call to get personal, Mr Elderfield," he purred.

Seen more clearly, the man was shorter and not much older than Tom, with a mouth that in the dark seemed grotesquely widened by the sores at either side. A leap of intuition told Tom what this encounter must be about.

"Are you Colbourne's higgler?"

The young man giggled again, and Tom decided this was a nervous affliction, having little to do with mirth. "A higgler I am, Mr Elderfield, and Higgler you'll call me. I don't use no other name hereabouts. To business, then. I'll pay a

41

shilling for a hare, two for a plump pheasant, ninepence for a brace of partridges. Guaranteed."

Tom regarded Higgler steadily, then turned his back and strolled homeward along the deserted lane, whistling softly.

Footsteps hurried after him. Imagining a slit throat or a knife in the back, Tom gritted his teeth and waited until the last possible moment before swinging round to face the other man.

Higgler squeaked in surprise and retreated a few paces. "I ain't meaning no 'arm, Mr Elderfield. We should talk. Friendly, like."

"You must think me very green, Mr Higgler." Tom fervently hoped that the bells' melodious din hid the tremor in his voice. He had not expected to make contact like this; to have to bargain in the dark with this sly, greedy, malevolent creature. "I'll have the same rates as Colbourne. No more, no less. I wouldn't like you to be paying me one amount and telling your boss another, and pocketing the difference. Six months of that, and you'd be setting up as another Harry Colbourne yourself. Not very fair on me, Mr Higgler."

The effect of this speech was dramatic. For the second time the speed of the little man took Tom by surprise. Higgler snatched an unsheathed knife from his breeches pocket and thrust it close to Tom's face. Tom backed hastily and Higgler laughed, fingering the naked blade.

"Green as the sweet Hampshire grass, ain't you, Mr Elderfield? I could've had you then, and both of us the loser. We'd best reach an agreement. You want a guaranteed market and I want my chance of a decent living."

"If you need charity, try the w_rkhouse. My hares are two shillings, pheasants three-and-sixpence, partridges half a crown a brace."

Higgler's eyes narrowed; he emitted his low, nervous giggle. "Now, Mr Elderfield –"

"Take it or leave it."

Higgler sucked his teeth; the knife gleamed as he took an uncertain step forward.

"The point is," said Tom evenly, "wounded men don't set snares, and dead men are no use to anybody." He paused to let the words register, then added, "Which days could you pick up the goods?"

Higgler blinked. After an interval he said grudgingly, "Mondays and Thursdays. An hour after sunset. You'll find my cart behind the alehouse." The knife flashed. "And don't you go setting no keepers on me. I dare say you're fond of that clever tongue of yours, and men in our business don't peach on their mates. Understand me, Mr Elderfield?"

"Well enough, Mr Higgler."

This time Tom did not care to turn his back until the man was out of sight. Then he walked slowly home, and by the time he reached the cottage he was shaking uncontrollably with reaction. Latching the door quietly, not to wake his mother, he leaned against it and shut his eyes. He was still alive, he had dealt with the higgler on his own terms – and he was working for the same percentage as Harry Colbourne.

Tom opened his eyes and grinned, triumphant, the sick feeling in the pit of his stomach forgotten as the significance of the victory came home to him. This was the first step towards buying the home that he and Jessica would share.

He had become a professional poacher.

CHAPTER FIVE

During the whole of that summer of 1814, the national joy was shared even by those who had faced acute poverty in the long years of war. For a while, grievances were forgotten. Even the French could be tolerated since Boney's abdication and exile to the island of Elba. It seemed that the only person in all England who took no part in the celebrations was His Majesty King George III. The old King, quite mad, did not know the war was over.

For Tom it was the best summer he had known; despite the death of the beloved and ancient Belladonna, and his inability to afford a new mount. Free to channel his formidable energies in whatever direction he chose, he worked at the forge, kept a few chickens, tended the vegetable garden – and retired early each night to wake refreshed at three in the morning. A poaching expedition might take a couple of hours, and he seldom came home empty-handed.

He visited Jessica nearly every morning. Amos always worked at night now, and over breakfast the two boys would discuss any changes in the deadly pattern of traps and spring-guns. More than once this saved Tom's life, and he admitted to owing Amos a greater debt than he could ever repay.

In all respects except one, Tom was happy with his lot; but his determination not to sleep with Jessica was severely undermined by the girl's attitude. She would assert, with that shining look which both bewildered and delighted him, that as Tom would be rich some day it could not matter if they were obliged to be married tomorrow. She was not afraid of a few years of poverty.

"That's because you're not afraid of anything," he said once, panting slightly, watching an iron bar change from red to white hot as he pumped the massive forge bellows. "It'll only be a year or two."

"In the meantime," she said, not quite joking, "you might show me you'll be a husband worth waiting for."

He cuffed the sweat out of his eyes and attended to his work, but after this day Jessica seemed different towards him. Though she was still loving and eager to share his dreams, Tom sometimes caught her studying him with sadness or anxious doubt. This was usually when a poaching trip was mentioned, and he told himself that Jess was only concerned for his safety.

At Michaelmas he drove with her to the annual fair on Weyhill Down, buying her ribbons and lace until she cried out in despair, protesting that they would never save enough to be wed.

"Well, I like buying you things," he said jauntily. "And I'll work extra hard tonight to make up for it."

This pleased her even less; for with the coming of autumn, the silent pursuit of hares and partridges had given place to more hazardous work. On cold nights the pheasants roosted high in almost leafless trees, clear targets in the moonlight. Borrowing Mr Tandy's shotgun, Tom could hit up to six birds with a single shot, making off fast with a full sack before the keepers came running. But whatever Jessica said about the risks, she did not try to pressure him into choosing another career. Of course not, he thought; how could she? She would have been out there with him, given the chance.

December came, with gales that penetrated every chink in door and window frames. Marie Elderfield spent most of her time huddled by the parlour fire, and as the winter progressed she developed a persistent cough and sore throat which nothing would cure. Jessica again regularly kept house at the smithy. Often, sleeping in Tom's bed while he gallantly occupied the parlour settle for a few hours, she rose before dawn to cook eggs and toast and crisp bacon for when he returned shivering with a sack of pheasants, his hair white with frost and his fingers almost too numb to hold a knife and fork.

On one such morning in February, an Andover physician

called on Sacheverell Tandy to treat him for an attack of gout. Tom jumped at the chance to ask professional advice for a minimal fee, and escorted the doctor to visit his mother.

"He says she ought to go away somewhere," Tom confided later to Jessica, as they went out to inspect his latest acquisition among the hens. "I thought of writing to the Vaillants, sending her to them for the winter. Sea air is reckoned to be healthy."

"Easier for you, too," Jessica teased him. "No one to deceive."

"I can do that standing on my head anyway." He bent to catch the new chicken and stood examining her bedraggled feathers. "Been in a scrap again, haven't you, little lady?" A swift glance at Jessica. "What the doctor actually said is that it might be an early stage of consumption."

"Oh Tom. Oh no."

"Ma refuses to go to Lymington without me, and I can't miss the pheasant season here. Besides, she doesn't need me with her. Just thinks she does. What the hell am I to do, Jessie?"

Jessica felt an odd jump of the heart; he had never asked her for advice before, was always totally self-reliant, too stubborn to reach out for help.

"I think," she said, "that you should invite the Vaillants here for a week or two. And I don't care how frightfully grand they are – if they're real friends they won't mind the cottage. It will be a novelty. And when they ask your Ma to go back with them, I'd lay bets she won't feel able to refuse."

For some seconds Tom said nothing at all. Then he gave her the dazzling smile which as usual made her weak with longing. "Come here, partner," he said, carelessly tossing the prized hen in the direction of the henhouse; and while he was kissing her Jessica forgot all her problems, and thought herself the happiest woman alive.

That night, unable to sleep for thinking of Jess alone in his bed upstairs, Tom lay on the settle listening to the rain. Perfect weather for netting partridges; the roosting pheasants might not be such easy game. He rose before eleven and donned the working clothes kept in a chest by the door. Inside the thick smock, below his right armpit, a loop of material held Mr Tandy's gun butt securely. He damped the fire and went out into the night.

Black nights had long ceased to unnerve him. Choosing a strong stick, he beat the ground ahead in case of tripwires, moving fast with a confidence born of experience and superb physical condition. The wind and drenching rain were a bore, but not a hindrance. Having made such an early start, he calculated there would be time to shoot some birds, make his escape, and still net a few partridges into the bargain.

The trees he sought were close to Hatchley Hall itself, and the area was intensively guarded. Jonah Wooldridge was as protective of his lovingly reared pheasants as one of Tom's hens clucking over her chicks. Here the traps were moved frequently, and there were more spring-guns than on any other part of the estate. Tom slowed down and felt ahead carefully.

It occurred to him that he hardly felt tired at all. Why shouldn't he work like this every night, going to bed early and rising before midnight, to return home at dawn and sleep for a while before breakfast? A quick way to make a fortune . . .

The stick hit something that could have been a briar. Tom struck it aside – and the spring-gun beside the track clicked, swivelled, and fired its charge of shot with a flash and a terrifying report.

Tom's reaction was faster than his thought. That first click had been his only warning, but as the mechanism designed to shoot a poacher through the head swung the barrel upwards, Tom threw himself down flat on the wet, muddy track.

Winded by the fall, he sat up slowly. The black, squat shape of the spring-gun was only just visible even to his night-adjusted eyes. He could not see the tripwire. Dear God, if he had ducked a split second later . . .

This horror, narrowly avoided and now vividly imagined, forced him into action of a sort. He struggled to his knees and retched violently.

Then he was scrambling up, cursing his dull wits; for the woods were suddenly alive with the yells of keepers alerted by the shot. Their voices came from nearer the village. If

Tom sprinted for home, he would run straight into Wooldridge's men.

He left the woods and raced along the edge of a turnip field. Behind him a shout came clearly on the wind, "Halt, villain, or take the consequences!" The voice of Wooldridge himself.

Tom ignored him. The chance of the head keeper hitting a moving target in the dark was mercifully slim. The report from Wooldridge's gun set his heart pounding, but the shot ploughed harmlessly into the undergrowth on his left. Sacheverell Tandy's shotgun bounced against his hip as he ran. The thought of using it did not occur to him. If he did so, he would swing for it.

Wooldridge fired again; the shot went wide as Tom dived through a gap in a hedgerow. There were a couple more random shots, but Tom's zig-zagging route across the next field defeated the marksmen. He was in more danger of breaking an ankle than of being hit.

Even when the shooting ceased he kept running. Another five broad fields, a stretch of rough pasture. Rain blew hard in his face. His lungs hurt, his legs were like jelly; but he heard the men still, far off, in half-hearted pursuit.

Blinded by wind and rain, he stumbled at last into a barred gate, scrambled over it and dropped to the ground, boots squelching in the mud. Close at hand loomed Weyhill Down, and Tom groaned with mingled relief and frustration. He was outside Sir Charles's estate and way beyond the lands of the local tenant farmers – but he was miles from home.

He chose the circuitous route along the lanes. Nothing would induce him to cross the estate again that night. For a time he jogged to keep warm, but his leg muscles were quivering from the long chase and he walked most of the way, drenched and cold, lashed by the stinging rain. By the time he reached Hatchley, he was longing to crawl into a warm, dry bed. The recollection that he must sleep on the settle, which was lumpy and about five feet long, did nothing to raise his spirits.

The cottage was not in darkness. An unsteady glow showed under the door and through the parlour window.

Damn it to hell, he thought. He could have done without his mother's tears and recriminations.

The hearthfire was lit and blazing, but it was not his mother who waited to greet him. Jessica Tandy, fully dressed and wide awake, uncoiled herself from a chair and stood up. Her huge eyes were very dark, her face impassive.

"I heard you go out," she said, with all the emotion of someone passing the time of day with a stranger. "That was four hours ago. You walked into trouble, I suppose."

"A spring-gun that Amos didn't know about. I'm all right," he added quickly, dragging the wet smock over his head and tossing it on to the chest, beside the gun. "Wooldridge chased me nearly to Weyhill. Surprised he didn't burst a blood vessel."

Jessica retrieved the smock and hung it nearer the fire. "You'd better take off those wet clothes," she said.

Tom stripped off his jerkin, neckcloth and shirt, then sat down and began tugging at one boot, laughing ruefully as his efforts failed to budge it. Jessica knelt, unsmiling, and removed the boots with a good tug at each.

"Come on, Jessie." He leaned forward to ruffle her hair. "We're not dead yet. Just one little smile, eh?"

Still kneeling at his feet, Jessica raised her eyes slowly, her solemn gaze lingering on his bare chest with its covering of fine blond down; then moving up to the broad shoulders, and the new, hard lines of cheek and jaw, and the way his hair was darkened to brown by the rain. She saw his discomfiture, too, knowing that habit he had of crinkling his eyes as though against rough weather or some less tangible foe. At sixteen, Tom Elderfield was a very attractive youth; in a couple of years he would be magnificent.

His hand was stroking her cheek. "Poor little girl, you've been really scared tonight, haven't you? I won't let them catch me, Jessie."

"I'm not a little girl. The worst you can get for a first offence is to be shot dead, or given a one-way trip to Australia or Van Diemen's Land. It couldn't happen to you, could it? Because everyone knows you were born to be hanged."

"Aw, Jess, don't talk of sad times that might never come –"

"It's *now* I'm talking about. It's *us*." Gripping his hands she stood up. "I don't want to change you, Tom. Just say the word and I'll be out there at your side. But if I lose you tomorrow or next week or next year, I don't want to spend the rest of my life thinking I never even loved you properly."

She stepped back, unfastening the copper hooks down the front of her bodice, her fingers deft and quick. Tom recovered from his initial astonishment and leapt up, really intending to stop her – but Jessica kicked off her slippers and shrugged out of the gown and thin petticoats, letting them fall crumpled about her feet. Her body, naked and softly curved, glowed golden in the firelight.

"Now say you don't want me, Tom Elderfield," she whispered, "and I'll leave this house and not trouble you again."

Tom hardly knew she had spoken. He stood helpless, awed, entranced, all his fine resolutions meaningless and lost. He had escaped out of danger tonight; he was free and alive and Jess was his girl. He loved her beyond bearing. Nothing else was real.

In the same instant that he moved, she stepped clear of the discarded dress. He bore her carefully down on to the settle, and peeled off the rest of his clothes while Jessica encouraged him with growing boldness and smiled into his eyes.

His exploration of her body was tentative at first, half shy; mouth and hands seeking confirmation of everything which had haunted his dreams at night and his imagination by day. Finally it was the knowledge of her pleasure that gave him confidence, making all shyness between them no more than a memory of childhood. When he thrust into her she gasped, but her body strained to welcome him, her hands dug into his back, urging him deeper until their bodies moved together and her soft cries were breathless with incredulous delight.

Afterwards they slept, until the fire died unnoticed and they woke shivering in each other's arms. Tom gathered up their clothes and led her upstairs, both of them laughing silently like guilty children. They made love again in the warmth of his narrow bed, and would gladly have stayed there all day, content just to sleep and to savour each new journey of discovery. After a leisurely, experimental interlude which Jessica had found particularly satisfying, the girl leaned on one elbow and pushed back her trailing curls. He gazed drowsily up at her.

"I haven't been good to you, have I?" he said.

"Oh, I wouldn't say that." Her mouth curved in a smile of delicious wickedness, while her fingers traced invisible patterns on his chest. "But if you think we need more practice . . ."

Tom refused to be distracted. He caught her hand and held it fast. "All these months," he said, "I thought you were just impatient. I thought we wanted the same things."

"How lucky that we do."

He grinned, and they nestled closer. "You realise," he said, "that if I get you pregnant we'll have to marry at once and live mostly on the Poor Relief?"

"Somehow I can't see you living on the Overseers' charity, my darling. Your natural dishonesty would get the better of you."

"Ouch. And I'll have you know," he continued archly, "that poaching isn't a real crime, according to Ned Farminer, any more than smuggling is. Unless there's murder done, of course."

"Your nasty little friend Higgler would know all about that, I suppose." Jessica wrinkled her nose as if the very thought of Higgler was offensive. Then she smiled again, and freed her hand to place a finger to his lips. "Hush your silly talk, my darling. What does it matter? What does any of it matter? Together we're a match for the best and the worst of them."

"So we are," he said. He thought of his father dead beside the Andover road; of his mother huddled in her chair, dreaming of the town where she had been young and happy. So much goodness wasted, so many dreams thrown away in useless moralising and the fear of grasping what life could offer. He remembered the spring-gun, the flash and the deafening report, the sudden stark awareness that life became doubly sweet through having been so nearly lost.

Jess was right, together they could fight and win. Wasn't she born to it, after all? The daughter of a Mudeford beach-master and a wild Irish girl, living by her father's heathen yet

51

liberal creed, thumbing her nose at the conventions of polite society?

And besides, a life without the spice of danger would be no life at all.

CHAPTER SIX

Tom's narrow escape from the keepers had disturbing repercussions. The morning after the incident, as he was starting a letter to the Vaillants, Jonah Wooldridge arrived, quoting his legal right to search the cottage without a warrant. He covered every inch of floor space and peered into every cupboard, while Tom with difficult nonchalance finished his letter and commiserated with Marie Elderfield over the gamekeeper's want of manners.

There was nothing conclusive for Wooldridge to find. Last night's mission had yielded only one prize, as Tom thought with inward laughter; and that was none of the gamekeeper's business. As Tom saw him politely to the door, the man said for his ears alone, "You've been lucky, Elderfield, and we both know it. Sir Charles says to bear in mind that you pay rent like the rest of us, and he's lost too many pheasants this season. If you're the man we're after, you'll be out. Homeless. How would that affect your mother's health, eh?" Jonah Wooldridge raised his brows at Tom's impassive expression, and doffed his hat. "Good day to you," he said.

Tom was shaken as much by the man's complacency as by his threats. Wooldridge could afford to play a waiting game, for no poacher working night after night could evade capture indefinitely.

But though Wooldridge's threats made him careful, he was far more deeply concerned by Gaspard Vaillant's reply to his letter. The Frenchman, eight years older than Tom and the agent for a Lymington saltern owner, regretted that winter was his busiest time and he could not be spared; however he and his mother would be delighted to visit during the summer, and Madame Elderfield would naturally be most welcome to return with them.

This was all rubbish, since Tom knew quite well that the salterns only operated during the summer months. Thwarted and seething, he lost his temper at his mother's peevishness for the first time in years, slammed out of the house, and left Jessica to cope. After a reckless hour-long ride across country on the girl's new chestnut gelding, he apologised to his womenfolk with reluctant contrition; but his plans were no further forward.

Jessica stayed most nights at the cottage now, her only worry being that she was neglecting Mace; but the boy started turning up there at all hours, offering his services as man of all work. Tom let him take care of the hens for a shilling a week.

"I couldn't be a farmer, though," Mace told him once, "I'm going to be a shipwright. The bloody best."

"What, twenty-five miles inland? You've been at Jess's elderberry again."

"Hellfire – I'm nearly twelve! I've decided – I'll move south one day, like you, and design a ship grander than *Victory*."

"In that case," Tom said, making an effort to take the boy's ambition seriously, "give us all tickets for the maiden voyage."

In fact he was very fond of Mace, liking the boy's bravado and irrepressible gaiety. At the beginning of March, when Boney escaped from Elba meaning to regain his lost empire, Mace had had to be physically restrained from running away to embark with Wellington's troops. Tom suspected that Mace would one day give Mr Tandy more trouble than all the rest of his offspring together.

Buonaparte's renewed quest for glory was short-lived. In July the British and Prussian victory at Waterloo provided fresh cause for merrymaking, and Boney was sent into final exile on the island fortress of St. Helena.

With the disbandment of Wellington's army came disillusionment. Ex-soldiers came home looking for work, the new Corn Bill kept prices high, and the numbers claiming Poor Relief rose steadily.

National problems could not affect Tom deeply. The warmer weather brought some improvement in his mother's health, and he had Jess. Life was precious, the world was beautiful. Sometimes, waking in the dark to feel Jessica curled warmly against him, her body moulded to his, he was so overcome with love that he felt he would burst for sheer joy. Even when, around the time of Waterloo, the girl lost their first child only seven weeks after its conception, his sorrow was for her sake, and was tempered by guilty relief.

Towards the end of July, Tom wrote again to Gaspard Vaillant, reminding him of his promise. This time the answer came promptly; and the Frenchman and his widowed mother arrived the day after their letter.

The carriage alone – a gleaming, hooded, green and black affair, drawn by two high-stepping horses – drew Hatchley folk from their homes to stare. Jessica and Mace, involved in a frenzied spring-cleaning of the cottage, followed Tom outside to greet his guests; and with disbelief saw him kiss not only Madame Vaillant but also her son – on both cheeks.

Tom stood back to inspect his childhood friend, who had taught him to ride, box and swim, all before Tom's fourth birthday. In the three years since their last meeting, Gaspard had not changed. Tom guessed in amusement that the padded chest, beringed hands and rouged cheeks must place his manhood in doubt for the simple villagers. There were no dandies in Hatchley.

"*Mon cher*, but you are taller than I," said Gaspard, studying him with the aid of a glinting monocle. "Insupportable. I declare I shall feel quite inferior."

Tom was prevented from replying by the force of a second embrace from Madame Angélique Vaillant, whose huge bosom butted him in the stomach. "My little Thomas, it is so good to see you." Then, in a stage whisper, "So distressing about last winter, but Gaspard will explain, indeed he will, in his own good time. Do not be angry with us."

"Me? Angry?" he said, grinning, and hugged her with affection.

The visitors were conducted to their rooms to unpack. Jessica had been right; Madame seemed not to mind sharing a bedchamber with her long-time friend and Gaspard chuckled at the prospect of sharing with Tom. "How diverting. I have acquaintances who will be green, truly green with jealousy when I tell them," he drawled, and then smirked at Tom's outraged look. "Only teasing, *mon cher*. Forgive me, or I shall be wretched."

Tom warned Jessica not to take seriously anything that Gaspard might say, but she struck up an easy, bantering camaraderie with the Frenchman, and spent only the nights at her own home.

"Alas for me," he told her in private, "Thomas has snared the most exquisite creature I have yet seen on either side of the Channel."

"Second only to yourself, I assume," she countered.

"And I am to be married in November," he added, with a sigh. "How fortunate for my fiancée, and for Thomas, that we did not meet a year ago."

"And how fortunate for you, *m'sieur*, that these eggs are needed for lunch, or I would certainly break one over your head."

Tom kept a tolerant if wary eye on Gaspard, but he had schemes of his own afoot. In a recent county singlestick match, the prize for Hampshire had been won by a gypsy called Ayres. Rob Hanson had been unfit to compete due to a concussion suffered in a tavern brawl, and was now eager to challenge Ayres for the championship. Mr William Cobbett, locally as famous for his patronage of the sport as for his radical journalism, would permit the title to be contested in the grounds of his house at Botley, in the south-east of the county. The purse would be fifteen guineas plus a gold-laced hat.

"Sir Charles is allowing everyone the day off work, Hanson being a Hatchley man," Tom told Gaspard. "It's a fair distance, we'd be up at dawn, but I reckon it'll be a good day out. Jess will be coming, and maybe her brothers."

Gaspard was remarkably keen. It would make a change, he said, from betting on duels and prize-fights. In the event, the three were joined by Amos and Mace, borrowing the Tandys' haycart to accommodate everybody. Obadiah, declining to travel with "Elderfield and that painted Frog," rode with Hanson's cronies.

The journey was long, hot, and – since the carts drove in convoy – tediously slow.

"I imagine you will advise me to bet on this Hanson fellow," said Gaspard, taking his turn delicately with the ale flagon.

"He can't lose," said Amos sourly, giving the horse an unnecessary flick of the whip. "Been champion for four years running."

Tom said nothing; but when Jessica realised that he was drinking only water she eyed him suspiciously, and he wondered how much she guessed.

They reached Botley House to find a splendid feast laid out on long tables by the river. The ring was already roped off, in the centre of a wide, sloping lawn, above which the red brick farmhouse and walled garden gave the Cobbetts some privacy.

The man who stood to welcome the visitors was tall and broad-shouldered, rather stout from recent prosperity, and clearly pleased by the arrival of so many spectators. Tom returned his greeting with respect; he had read Mr Cobbett's weekly news-sheet, and knew that the farmer had spent two years in Newgate gaol for his outspoken opinions.

The match between Hanson and Ayres began at noon, by which time the stables were full, the road lined with carts, and the crush of spectators at the ringside meant that only those squashed against the ropes had a decent view. Tom hoisted Mace on to his shoulders and the boy relayed loudly every detail of the action.

Ayres was young, skilful and agile, but Hanson had ten years' experience behind him and he was heavier and basically stronger than the gypsy. Within fifteen minutes, after only four rounds, Hanson was being presented with the purse and hat by a beaming William Cobbett. The veteran singlestick player was not even out of breath.

Aware of the crowd's disappointment at this anticlimax, Mr Cobbett injected some drama into the proceedings. He lifted Rob Hanson's arm above his head and declared triumphantly, "Gentlemen – ladies – I give you Mr Robert Hanson, undisputed Champion of the County!"

Now that the moment had come, Tom found he was sweating from more than the heat. Hanson's strength, and his tendency to bend the unwritten rules of fair combat, were legendary. Setting Mace down, Tom pushed his way to the ringside and ducked under the rope to address William Cobbett.

"I dispute it, sir! I challenge his right to the title."

"Great heavens! Your name, sir?"

Tom enlightened him.

"Mr Elderfield, I owe you an apology." Cobbett pumped his hand with enthusiasm. "I doubted there was a man present who would prove his mettle against Mr Hanson here."

The crowd agreed with him; there were murmurs of growing interest. Tom shot Hanson a look of calculated arrogance. "Rob won the purse fair and square. Maybe he wouldn't like to risk losing it so soon."

Hanson took the bait. "Risk?" he asked softly. "What risk is that? Though I can't promise you the sport of an equal match, Mr Cobbett. When a boy pits himself against a man . . ."

William Cobbett narrowed his eyes at the champion. "We will commence immediately, Mr Hanson, unless you require time in which to recover your strength."

By way of reply Hanson kicked Ayres' discarded weapon across the grass towards Tom, who beckoned Amos and a dubious Gaspard to act as his seconds. Following Hanson's example he stripped to the waist, and Cobbett signalled for play to begin.

If the discrepancy in weight between the players was due partly to Hanson's massive shoulders and two inches' extra height, it also owed something to a thickening waistline. Tom, as nimble as Ayres and less predictable, won the first two rounds with comparative ease, and was grinning as he strode back to his corner.

"Where's Jess? Did she see me knock him down?"

"She's watching, don't you worry," said Amos. "Just don't get over-confident. That bastard is playing cat and mouse."

Tom swilled ale round his mouth and turned to spit, taking care to miss the spectators leaning on the ropes. One good blow to his opponent's head would make the blood run an inch and give him the victory. He might have the advantage of surprise, too, for Hanson under-estimated him. Amos was being a pessimist.

The veteran player was ready with a few surprises of his own. Well into the third round, as Tom aimed a swing at Hanson's left ear, the man ducked and sidestepped, and his cudgel landed with vicious, sickening force across Tom's right shoulder-blade and upper arm. There were a good many cheers and a few mutters of disapproval. Tom made a weakened effort to parry the next blow, then stumbled to his knees as Hanson's stave thudded again into his throbbing arm.

Some of the crowd were booing and yelling obscenities at Hanson. The sport was to 'break' a man's head, not to inflict maximum pain while prolonging the battle.

Clutching his arm Tom hissed through shut teeth, "What's the matter? Too scared to play fair, are you?" And Hanson in response dealt him a crippling blow on the thigh, before Cobbett could intervene to declare the round over and warn Hanson to change his tactics.

The pattern was set for the next five rounds. Fighting mostly left-handed, and with a badly bruised leg to slow him down, Tom felt he was living out a nightmare as his upper body took an almost continuous battering. Like being flogged, he thought, recoiling from a stroke that raised a new scorching weal across his back. God help all seamen! Whenever Hanson, for the sake of appearances, aimed at his head, the intention was so clearly signalled that the merest child could have dodged in time.

At the end of the eighth round, Tom was felled by a blow that left him gasping and hugging his ribs in agony. Gaspard, unexpectedly strong, hauled him up and supported him back to the corner, where he perched shakily on the knees of his seconds. Jessica was there as well, which was not allowed but no one seemed to care. The crowd was yelling for Tom; it was rare for anyone to last so long against Hanson in this mood, and they were enjoying taking the side of the underdog.

Jessica leaned over him, close to tears as her brother and Gaspard set to work with dripping cloths and sun-warmed water.

"Don't do this, Tom. Oh, please, please don't. You haven't got anything to prove. Not any more."

Tom blinked sweat out of his eyes and tried to control his

ragged breathing. So tempting, just to sit quietly and concede the match. Everything would hurt much worse when he moved.

But he could admit to himself, now, that the battle was not to avenge his father's murder. Hanson had thrashed him when he was a boy with inadequate defences; now he was a man, and needed to pay off a score that was entirely personal.

He grimaced at Jessica. "Wish me luck," he said.

As Cobbett called 'time' she squeezed his hand. "Kill the bastard, then," she said; and Tom limped to meet Hanson wondering if he could have heard correctly.

Stooping forward, the players circled each other. Hanson was the first to lash out; a fast, slicing stroke, aimed with precision, caught Tom on the knee and brought him down hard, his own singlestick trapped beneath him. The fall hurt his leg and gave the cracked ribs an appalling jolt; but as Hanson's cudgel whirred again through the air Tom flung up his right hand in a desperate attempt to shield his body.

The stick slammed against his hand, wrenching it cruelly, and in rage and pain and almost despair Tom rolled and swung his own stave left-handed.

He felt it connect solidly with Hanson's belly.

Unlike his opponent, Rob Hanson had not spat out all the beer he had been offered. It was a hot day. Clutching his abdomen he doubled over, his face grey-green.

In agonised slow motion Tom struggled to one knee, then summoned his remaining strength for a final, decisive blow. Hanson toppled forward and lay face down, blood trickling from behind his ear.

The roars of delight came even from those who had lost a few pence on the wager. For Hatchley folk, the notorious young poacher had achieved new glory. He had also given them half an hour's first class entertainment.

Tom made no attempt to get up. Letting the cudgel drop he knelt hunched over, nursing his sprained wrist and trying not to breathe. Several people had leapt over or scrambled under the ropes, eager to congratulate the new champion; but Jessica reached him first. She turned on the yelling, jostling, boisterous throng,

"Let him alone! Can't you see he's badly hurt?"

William Cobbett was already shouting for order, his voice carrying such authority that Jessica's efforts were unnecessary. The crowd backed off a few feet, their attention still riveted.

Cobbett turned to the victor. "Mr Elderfield, that was the finest display of courage I have seen for many a summer."

Tom barely heard the compliment. He was being assailed on all sides by solicitous questions from Gaspard and the three Tandys. Glancing up at their worried faces, he said painfully, "Christ . . . you needn't look like mourners round a death bed."

"Hark who's talking – the bloody corpse!" said Amos. "D'you need a hand, mate?"

"Mm. Careful . . . Agh! Mind my ribs, damn it."

"Highly stoical. Whatever happened to the hero of the hour?"

"Do you want a black eye?"

"When? Next month? I reckon you should see a quack."

"Of course he should!" Jessica exclaimed hotly. She rounded on their host, too incensed to think of showing him respect. "Are you just going to stand there and *watch*? I think you might at least have had a doctor standing by at the ringside –"

"Young lady, our local physician is an invited guest who is presently attending Mr Ayres. He will doubtless be with you shortly." William Cobbett's dark eyes twinkled as he added sternly, "And I really must insist on being treated with courtesy on my own land, if nowhere else."

Jessica turned pink, and made a business of smoothing Tom's shirt, which he had thrown down in the corner. Neither Tom nor Amos had ever seen her so thoroughly embarrassed or so effectively silenced.

The physician arrived, offering nothing in the way of a bedside manner to young men who beat each other half to death for fun; but his field dressings were neat and comprehensive. When he had finished, Tom felt constricted, just as sore, and – with his shirt draped carefully over the bandages – slightly ridiculous.

By the time the purse and hat had been presented he was also feeling really ill, shivering with reaction in spite of the heat. It was a relief to let Jessica take him to a sunny area of the riverbank for their private picnic. Lowering himself inch by excruciating inch on to the grass, he saw the girl's expression mirror his own in anguished sympathy.

He said, not knowing whether to laugh or groan, "God, Jessie, I waited a year and a half for this. Don't you want to say it serves me right?"

Jessica regarded him, the peace around them disturbed only by the birds and the quiet river, and the sounds of merriment further along the bank.

She stooped and kissed him briefly and very tenderly, and almost smiled when she drew back to find him studying her in wry amusement.

"I'm proud of you, Tom Elderfield," she said.

CHAPTER SEVEN

After six bone-jarring hours on the road, with Amos unable to avoid the potholes as daylight faded, Tom was past caring what his reception at home might be. In fact, Marie Elderfield said very little. She left Madame Vaillant downstairs interrogating Gaspard, and stood wringing her hands and uttering the occasional moan of shocked pity, while Jessica helped her son out of his clothes and into bed.

At last she said in real distress, "Oh Tom, why must you do such things to worry me?"

"Nothing for you to worry about," he muttered, lying down carefully. "I'm all right, *maman* . . . Please go to bed."

But she sat down on the edge of the coverlet. Jessica at once protested, "He's worn out, Mrs Elderfield. It was a horrible journey. He simply can't take any more tonight."

"I am leaving for Lymington with our guests in the morning," she said quietly. "Angélique has been helping me to pack."

Tom blinked; the sudden capitulation was hard to believe. "Do you really mean it?"

His mother smiled sadly. "I have been wilfully blind for too long. I thought: my son is very young, he lacks judgement and caution and, without my influence, who knows what he might dare to become? But Angélique has enabled me to see . . . My son is not a child. He breaks the law and deals with London game-higglers, and I have lived in adequate comfort on the proceeds. It appears that now he is also a county champion. I cannot influence him. I never could. Yes, my dear, I shall go to Lymington, and at Christmas you may fetch me home."

Tom was so shamed by this speech that he could not bring himself to answer any of it except the last sentence. He patted his mother's hand. "I'm glad you're going," he said.

"Such exquisite tact." She bent and kissed him; a dry, light touch, like a blessing. "Sleep well, my dear."

But he passed a sleepless, wickedly uncomfortable night, and in the morning wasted half an hour listening to the sounds of frantic activity, taking almost as long again to dress before finally easing his way downstairs.

Jessica, not having expected him to surface, thrust a glass of golden liquid into his hand and told him to go back to bed. He shook his head, amused by her bossy manner.

"Been there all night, Jess. Very boring. What's this stuff?"

"French brandy. Gaspard is leaving us the bottle."

Tom was not aware that his face gave anything away, until she added, "If you still feel like that about last year, darling, you should tell him. Hear his side of the story."

He acknowledged the sense in this with a rueful grimace. "You've really fallen for our M'sieur Vaillant, haven't you?"

"Well . . . you could have taken your Ma south, but you didn't, because of the pheasant-shooting. It's too easy to blame Gaspard."

He knew she was right; but for curiosity's sake alone, there was a question he wanted answered. Just before the carriage left, he managed to draw Gaspard aside for a moment, and said civilly enough, "Not so fast with the goodbyes, *mon cher*. I thought you were going to explain about last winter. That's the season for smugglers, not saltern agents. Get a promotion did you, in one of the big gangs?"

Gaspard arched his brows, and adjusted the points of his green swansdown waistcoat. "There are good prospects on the coast, Thomas, for ambitious young men fluent in two languages."

"Tell me again in a year or two." He watched Jessica climb into the carriage and arrange a blanket across his mother's knees. "When I've built up some capital here, that'll be the time to get wed and move south."

Gaspard looked unconvinced, but as they crossed to the waiting carriage he was already assuming a tragic expression and begging the ladies to hurry with their farewells, lest he should be totally unmanned at being parted from the beautiful Miss Tandy.

Until this moment, Tom had felt only an immense relief at his mother's decision to go with the Vaillants, convinced that a few months of sea air and amiable company, in the town she loved, would restore her health for the winter. Now he was suddenly in doubt, feeling her thinness and fragility as he gingerly embraced her, and seeing the aching sorrow in her eyes as the carriage drove away.

She called to Jessica, who ran alongside for a short distance, "Take care of him!" – and Tom hung his head and limped back to the cottage. His mother's final words stayed with him like an echo, and he knew that she did not expect to return.

Marie Elderfield's departure caused a change in routine at the smithy cottage. Jessica had lost her chaperone, and neither Sacheverell Tandy nor Obadiah would consent to her staying overnight there, alone with Tom. Making the best of the situation, the girl rode to the forge every day on one pretext or another. Mace seldom accompanied her these days. Still keenly in pursuit of a shipbuilding career, he had switched his loyalty to the village carpenter in the hope of securing an apprenticeship.

The trip to Botley had given Mace an additional interest. He and Jessica took to spending Sunday evenings at The King's Head, reading aloud from their father's copy of Mr Cobbett's weekly news-sheet. The locals held that meddling in politics was a strange pastime for a girl and a twelve-year-old child, but Harry Colbourne was glad to give the new ideas a hearing. They brought him custom from neighbouring villages.

For Tom's part, beating Hanson had exorcised more than one ghost; and having become friendly with Ned Farminer and his young wife, he was ready to forget the past and admire Jessica for her 'meddling'. It was time that labourers found a public voice; and William Cobbett, with his blistering eloquence, was one of the loudest, most aggressive voices in all England. Often Tom went to hear the readings, making use of the time to catch up on Amos's news; for he had started poaching again a fortnight after the singlestick match. Amos was anxious over recent changes in Wooldridge's attitude and policy, and he tried frequently to persuade Tom that the risks inherent in the trade were beginning to outweigh its advantages.

"I'll tell you straight," he said one December evening, scowling into his beer, "I wouldn't get panicky at the first whiff of shot, as we both know, but Wooldridge is playing his hand close. He doesn't tell us things like he used to – not until it's too late to leak information. You're bagging more game than all the rest put together, and Sir Charles knows it. He's out for your blood."

"Sir Charles mustn't count his conies before the traps are sprung."

"That's another thing – the traps are moved twice a week now, and there are more guns. A lot more. The tenant farmers are being encouraged to set them, too – especially Scadding, his woods being a haunt of yours. For God's sake, Tom, you used to be the one with a brain in your head. Can't you ease off for a month or two?"

But the allowance Tom sent to his mother was already a serious drain on his savings. With a smaller income from Higgler he would be lost.

He started work early that night, having arranged to meet Jess at her own house by midnight, a ruse they sometimes employed when Amos was on duty and the family asleep. Tom grinned smugly in the dark, increasing his pace alongside a hedgerow to combat the penetrating cold. The moon was up tonight, glistening on the frost. Perhaps this winter would be as bad as two years ago, and there would be skating again on the Tandys' pond.

He shifted the gun to hang more comfortably inside his smock, and ducked among the trees that bordered Scadding's land. There were voices beyond the next clearing; this was a favourite spot for the keepers' sentry-go. Brushes with them were common nowadays, but Tom suspected Amos of over-reacting to Wooldridge's supposed change of tactics. What could the head gamekeeper do, that he had not tried a dozen times already?

Within seconds, Tom had his answer. The trap was set full in the path; the stick which he held in front of him snapped in two as the great jaws clanged shut. A couple of small, unseen creatures scuttled off through the undergrowth – and the keepers' low conversation ceased.

Tom began to run, ducking wildly past briars and the sharp ends of branches that tore at his face and hands. Someone fired; a signal only, for now the yells of excited pursuit came from all around him. No direction promised safety. Amos was right; there had never been so many watchers in Scadding's woods.

They had moved the traps. The guns too, maybe. No time for caution, or the fear which he had believed conquered. But fear was present, waiting in shadow, a darkness at his back urging him onward faster, ever faster through the brambles and the slanting, inconstant moonlight which might save or kill him now.

He leapt and dodged the shots, running until the blood pounded in his ears. The older men tired quickly but the young ones kept after him, enjoying the chase, maybe guessing his identity. Maybe shooting to miss.

He could not take that chance. Glimpsing the wicked teeth of a second trap he leapt high and clear and landed neatly, only to stagger off-balance as his shoulder caught a lopped bough. He turned to see three shadows following; one paused to aim and fire, and the shot slammed into the tree where Tom's hand had rested a second earlier.

Another hundred yards and it seemed the men were losing him. Bounding across a frozen stream he slipped and trod through the thin crust, icy water gushing inside his boot as he scrambled for purchase on the far bank.

A fourth man came racing out of the deep shadows under the trees.

Tom doubled back along the stream, the new pursuer sprinting to intercept him; and the man launched himself at Tom with a howl that, even in his fear, he recognised as a terrified warning.

In the instant their bodies collided, Tom's foot caught a length of stretched twine. As he fell beneath his captor, the report of a shotgun only inches from his head shattered the night and rang in his ears long after the sound had died.

Silence lay thickly on the woods. Momentarily dazed by the fall, he thought the blast had made him deaf. Then, in the distance, a keeper shouted, and Tom knew the unnatural quiet around him was real. There was no sound but that of his own laboured breathing, and the calls of the hunters as they raced towards the noise of the shot.

The shot, fired at point-blank range, from a spring-gun whose barrel would swivel up to kill a falling man. And the watcher who now lay so quiet, almost stifling him; this man had pushed Tom out of the firing line in time to save his life.

Tom shoved the body aside and knelt up. The moonlight filtering between the branches was merciless, leaving nothing hidden. The young man must have died instantly; and the shock to Tom was such that he forgot the keepers, forgot everything as grief and horror overcame his initial sick revulsion. For he knew the youth too well not to recognise him now, even lying in bleak moonlight with half his face blown away.

It was Amos Tandy.

Tom stood up, slowly, as in a nightmare, his stricken gaze never leaving the mess of blood and brains and shattered bone. The keepers' voices were drawing nearer; they jolted him into a realisation of his own imminent danger, and with a sobbing breath he turned and blundered among the trees. The frozen stream shone with a luminous and uncanny brightness, threading between the willows. Tom cleared it successfully, then fooled his pursuers with a sharp change of direction. The voices were fainter, dying in the night.

A moment later, sounding far away, someone yelled in rising horror, "Mr Wooldridge! Oh Jesus Christ . . . Here! Over here!"

Amos had been found. Tom forced his way through a net of brambles, clawed up a steep bank on to a path he knew, and ran without looking back.

In the Tandys' parlour Jessica sat huddled over a tattered copy of 'Mansfield Park', with no light but that of the hearthfire. Having read the same page five times without taking in a word, she glanced again at the clock. Another hour to waste until midnight.

She had accepted long ago that loving Tom meant choosing to endure heartache, anxiety, nail-biting hours alone. She had learned to cope with fear and had little patience with his mother's whining; for Mrs Elderfield had tried to possess and subtly cage her son and had won only his pity.

But tonight . . . tonight Jessica felt close to panic. She told herself not to be a fool; Tom was not even late.

And yet, suppose Jonah Wooldridge had moved the traps again. Suppose Tom was hurrying, thinking of her, not guessing his danger . . .

She would go out to meet him, just this once. After all, who was to know or care? The household slept.

Even as she crossed the hall she heard it; not the usual furtive scratching at the door, but the heavier, more urgent thud of a fist. Jessica ran and opened the door wide, and Tom pushed past her, with so little regard for secrecy that she whispered, "Hush, what are you thinking of?" And then, seeing his white, scratched face, and the dark smock blotched and spattered with dreadful stains, "You're hurt! Tom!"

"It's not . . . my blood ." He stumbled on the words, his voice breaking, "There's been . . . an accident, Jess." He was taking her into the parlour, pushing her gently into a chair, squatting before her to clasp her hands. His body shook as if with ague.

She cried out in terror, "Not Amos? Oh, say it's not that! Not our Amos."

"Jessie. . ."

"No, oh no," she whispered. If Tom had killed her brother she could not bear it; she would have lost them both. Better to die than face that. "Was it you? Was it?"

"They were after me, I – I didn't know about the gun. They never set one there before. They can't have told . . . told Amos till he came on duty. I'd have been killed for sure if he hadn't brought me down –"

"Oh God." Jessica also was trembling uncontrollably, choking back the sobs that might wake her menfolk. "You left him . . . like that?"

"I couldn't help him, Jessie."

She must not think about it; not about Amos lying dead in the cold woods.

"Obadiah will raise a hue-and-cry," she said. "With Rob

and the others. They won't be looking for evidence. If they catch you, they'll kill you."

"I'm not scared of Obadiah, nor Rob Hanson. But Sir Charles, he'd get me transported for this. I'd never see you again. Oh Jessie, Jessie . . ." His hands enveloped hers, crushing them. "I could stand anything except losing you. If you'll only come with me now, to Lymington, we'll get wed, buy a place, just like we always planned. If you'll only come . . ."

Seeing the pain in his eyes, the terrible uncertainty, Jessica wondered how he could doubt her. She loved him, she would have gone anywhere – to Van Diemen's Land itself – just to be with him.

She stretched out her arms, and when Tom with a groan of relief drew her close she clung to him, as though his youth and pride and stubborn optimism were the source from which her own courage must spring.

But every moment now was precious. Jessica climbed the stairs alone, and by candlelight wrote to reassure her father, clearing Tom of any blame for Amos's death and mentioning London as their most likely destination. To Mace, who could be trusted, she told the truth, writing with great neatness so that he would have no trouble in deciphering the Vaillants' address. She crept into the child's room and slipped this very private note under his pillow. Mace did not stir. Jessica kissed him lightly on the forehead, and left him sleeping.

She had no idea whether she would ever see him again.

CHAPTER EIGHT

Two miles north of Lymington, where the main road from Brockenhurst was overhung by bare and dripping trees, a solitary caravan presented a spot of incongruous gaiety. Muslin curtains were stirred by the van's leisurely progress southward; scarlet and yellow paint was outshone only by the brass trim of the horse's tack. The man leading the horse had the unmistakable aspect of a gypsy, from his battered high-crowned hat and spotted neckerchief to the soles of his much-mended boots.

His younger companion carried a girl of about seven perched on one shoulder, like a sailor with a monkey, and would occasionally smile at her chatter, in a way that suggested absent-minded courtesy rather than amusement. The child was teaching him the Romany tongue. After two days in her company – twenty-five miles in all – he could volunteer such phrases as, "your mother is kind", "the night is cold" and "I eat the nice hedgehog . . . later," with passable accuracy.

In fact Tom's lessons were a diversion, not a necessity, for Vinnie Wells and her parents spoke good English. He and Jessica had been overtaken by the caravan as they trudged along the road south of Andover, tired and footsore; for although Tom had chanced a return to the smithy for money and clothes, they had walked all night just to keep warm. The gypsies might not have offered a lift but he had asked outright, and it turned out they were headed for the coast anyway.

To explain Jessica's bleak, unnatural silence, Tom had given a brief account of the circumstances of his flight, and at once the Wells' attitude had softened. Othi, it seemed, was a poacher of repute, and knew well how accidents could occur. His wife Meg had hugged Jessica impulsively to her thin bosom, rocking her like a child; and, taken off guard, Jessica had sobbed out her grief. Afterwards she had been better, subdued but no longer withdrawn. That night Tom had made love to her, swathed in blankets in a corner of the van, and she had come to him with a violent and desperate passion which awoke an answering need in himself. For the first time there was neither fun nor tenderness in their union. As if, thought Tom, remembering, they had both needed confirmation that a part of their youth had not died with Amos in Scadding's woods. But on the whole, he thought perhaps it had.

Vinnie wriggled in annoyance, and rapped her bare heels against his chest. "You're not listening, Tom. Let me down. I'll catch some snails."

He swung her to the ground, and Vinnie skipped on to the verge and began prodding the concealing grasses with a stick. Othi ignored her, but his black eyes narrowed at the road ahead and a smile of complacent pride touched his lips.

"She's a good girl, that one," Tom said, to please him but also because it was true. "A credit to you both. Pretty, too."

"Like her mother. I used to want sons, but we started late. Doesn't matter like it once did. Vinnie doesn't leave room in a man's heart for regrets."

A sound from the back of the caravan made them turn, and Jessica jumped from the step and came to walk beside Tom, linking her arm through his. Her hair was blacker than Vinnie's and nearly as tangled, her cheeks were flushed from sleep.

"And here's another," said Othi with soft emphasis, "who wouldn't leave a man room for brooding on the past. The youngster took his chances same as you, and wherever he is now, he won't be holding you to account."

Jessica squeezed Tom's arm, and he glanced down to see her eyes bright with tears. "Meg says guilt is like a canker," she said. "It will grow inside us, if we let it, and eat away everything that's good. She says you blame yourself and I must help you not to, because you and I belong where there's hope and laughter. Other people will need that from us, she

72

says, because even jewels can't shine without the sun on them."

"December, Jess. Not much sun any more."

"But we're alive," she said in deep distress. "We're together. Isn't that what matters now?"

He hugged her close to his side, offering reassurance and comfort; but he had never felt so distant from her, so unbearably alone. Almost worse than the guilt was the knowledge that he had fled from danger, played the coward, and all through loving a girl too much to give her up. For the past two years he had seen himself as independent, proud of his lifestyle, fired by the challenge of risking his life night after night; and yet Jess had always been there, his anchorage, his safe harbour.

He had forsaken honour for love, just like the despicable Paris for Helen of Troy. It was too bloody contemptible. And this was the one thing he could not tell Jess, the one thing she would not forgive; that he could so loathe himself for having chosen not to let her go.

With Meg at the reins the caravan bowled at last into Lymington, passing several private carriages, and drawing outraged glances and abuse from the smart pedestrians whose skirts or polished boots it spattered with muddy water.

The Wells' destination was the Saturday market which congested the lower part of the High Street. Business promised to be good; the approach to Christmas meant an increased demand for meat skewers and holly, along with the exquisite imitation moss roses, fashioned from the pith of rushes, which were Vinnie's pride and delight. Othi stood on the tailboard, exchanging sardonic greetings with the owners of stalls and handcarts; but finally they parked in a lane on the far side of town, where there was less chance of being moved on before tomorrow.

Tom and Jessica gathered their few belongings. While Meg was embracing Jessica, Vinnie presented Tom with a cluster of the precious moss roses.

"We're in the Forest all winter," she said. "Up round Fordingbridge, mostly. You'll come and visit us, won't you?"

"I hope so. We'll see," he said; and then, as Vinnie's mournful eyes reproached him, "Well . . . for you, Lavinia Wells, of course I will."

Arm in arm with Jessica he walked back into town, keeping in mind Othi's directions for the Vaillants' street; but Nelson Place was easy to find. The terrace of expensive town houses ran down close to the river, and Tom quickened his stride, hurrying Jessica along beside him. The prospect of living among the gentry did not intimidate him; the place stirred a faint but welcome memory, and to his four-year-old self everything had appeared larger than it actually was. He had no hesitation in bounding up the front steps and rapping on the door.

It was opened by a manservant, immaculate with gleaming buttons, who twitched his sparse grey eyebrows and said scathingly, "There is a tradesman's entrance. Be good enough to use it."

Before Tom could formulate a reply, Gaspard's voice came to them, muted but with a distinct edge to it, "Do send them packing, Hodges, we really cannot – *Thomas*!"

Gaspard thrust past the silently indignant Hodges. "Thank God you came so fast! I was afraid you would not be in time – though indeed my letter was posted only two days ago –"

"What letter? Time for what?"

The Frenchman drew in his breath with a hiss. "You don't know? But I assumed that was why . . . Thomas, your mother is very ill. An attack of fever, most sudden, and the doctor insisted on a blood-letting. He is with her now. We are told it might only be a matter of hours, and yet she has held on . . ."

He did not finish, for Tom rushed up the stairs and through the only open doorway. The doctor, a dried-up, black-clad stick of a man, more like an undertaker than a physician, fixed him with an icy glare.

"Since when do servants have the run of the house? This is a sick-room – be off with you!"

Tom strode to the bed and knelt beside it, lifting his mother's hand which lay limp and cold on the coverlet. Marie Elderfield opened her eyes. Her hair was quite grey, her cheeks and eye sockets sunken like those of an old woman; but she smiled at her son.

"Gaspard said . . . you would come."

"You should have written that you were ill," he said in anguish. "It can't be so sudden, you must have known."

"No. Worried you enough. All these years." Her eyes focused on the doctor, who seemed caught between distaste for Tom's uncouth appearance, and embarrassment at having addressed him so rudely. "Would you be so kind . . . as to leave us alone for a moment?"

When he had gone, she reached up to stroke Tom's cheek. "My darling, don't take it to heart so. We always knew . . ."

Her voice was weaker already, her eyelids quivered shut, and lifted again with an effort. Tom could not bear it; first Amos and now this. He gripped his mother's hand as though his own longing to save her could give her life.

"Don't die," he whispered. "Please don't."

"My poor Tom. Forever trying . . . hoping . . . to beat the odds. Not this time, *mon p'tit*. I waited . . . only to see you . . ."

Her head slid sideways, her breath was expelled in a long, rattling sigh. Tom put a hand to her face, turning it towards him, but the eyes which stared through him were blank and dead. His hand shook as he closed them.

Behind him the door creaked. Without looking round he said, "She guessed about the poaching, you know. All along. She was scared to leave Hatchley, thinking I might be killed or transported and she'd never see me again. That's why she wouldn't come here last year. Because of me."

Gaspard's hand rested on his shoulder. "Thomas, come away now. The doctor will attend to everything."

"Has Jess told you –"

"About Amos? Yes. That was not your fault, either."

"I know that. Of course I do. People keep telling me. I know it, but – I can't – I can't believe it –"

"Oh, my dear boy," Gaspard said with infinite pity; and Tom groaned, stumbling blindly to his feet. He meant to head for the door, but somehow ended by leaning against the wall with his face turned to its cool surface, his body shaken by sobs of grief and bitter guilt.

Gaspard went on patting his shoulder and murmuring,

"My dear boy," at intervals; and not until Tom had regained a degree of shaky self-command did the Frenchman guide him from the bedchamber and up the next flight of stairs, into what he termed his retreat. The room was small, firelit and cosy, furnished as an office and personal library, and Tom once again found himself being plied with French brandy.

"I'm sorry, Gaspard," he said at last, unable to meet the Frenchman's eyes. "I couldn't have . . . I didn't expect . . ."

Gaspard sighed, and leaned his hip on a table spread with charts of the Solent and the coastline of South Hampshire. "Thomas, this is a French household, not an English one. You are not required to be more than human."

"I'll have to make arrangements for the funeral. If you could advise me . . ."

"My dear fellow, the least I can do."

Tom crossed to the window. One could see the ships' masts from here, beyond the mews rooftops sloping down towards the river. He had money to pay for a decent funeral, but not enough to marry Jess and buy a place, or to set up in business on his own. In the past he had considered everything from running an alehouse to starting a bookshop. It would not happen now. Luck had abandoned him too soon.

Holding the brandy glass rather tightly, he faced Gaspard, who was running his fingers along the rim of an uncomfortably starched cravat.

"You said once there'd be opportunities for me in this town. Is that still true?"

The Frenchman's hand paused, moved on, played with his emerald cravat pin. "Most certainly, Thomas. My own employer would be happy to find a use for a man like you."

His words echoed Sacheverell Tandy's of long ago: *"They'd find a use for you, but believe me, it's not worth the cost . . ."*

Tom shrugged off the memory. If luck had deserted him for the moment, he must cajole her back to his side; for that temptress, like God, often helped those who helped themselves. A man had to make the best of his talents and his fate.

He raised his glass in a solemn toast. "To the future, then," he said, and Gaspard acknowledged the decision with sardonic and glinting approval. "The future, *mon cher*," he said.

PART TWO: 1816–1822

The Venturer's Agent

CHAPTER ONE

Christmas passed quietly at the house in Nelson Place. Out of respect for their friend's memory, the Vaillants refused all invitations to local balls and routs. Gaspard's wife Sophie, ever mindful of appearances, frowned on the servants if they showed a spark of festive spirit.

Tom had no leisure to find the sombre atmosphere oppressive, nor to let his mind dwell on the past. He was encouraged to spend each morning closeted with Gaspard in the 'retreat'. Here they pored over maps and charts, the Frenchman marking lightly the route out of Lymington River and across ninety miles of sea, to where the Channel Islands lay amid their deadly scatter of rocks.

"This is our usual port of call." Gaspard rapped the island of Guernsey with a pencil. "As you know, my employer is Captain Hicks, owner of the Pennington Creek Saltern. He operates a fleet of four smallish vessels, ostensibly for the sole purpose of exporting salt, which remains a profitable sideline. This town on Guernsey's east coast is St Peter Port. Note the proximity of the little isles of Herm and Jethou. This mark indicates a cave . . ."

In that lamplit, firelit room, secluded from the womenfolk and all domestic trivia, Tom felt like a magician's apprentice, bewitched by the ancient lore of the sea. He told Gaspard this, mocking his own foolishness; but the Frenchman answered seriously.

"I am obliged to bewitch you, Thomas. If you are to succeed, the sea and the Free Trade must rule your heart. At Sophie's insistence I have agreed to resign from the Captain's employ within two years – "

"What! I thought you loved the life."

"Ah, but Thomas, I always intended giving it up when I took a wife. Sea-smugglers are the worst husbands in the world, never at home when they are wanted, and liable to be arrested or shot at a moment's notice. I do pine, you know, for the years before the Peace – the Golden Age, we called it. Preventive officers were few and ineffective then, the Government having better things to do with its men than send them chasing after the likes of us. I rather fancy myself as a timber merchant. What think you?"

"But you're implying . . . Am I being trained as your successor? As Captain Hicks' new agent?"

"I am certain that both you and the lovely Jessica will be equal to the challenge. I have approached the Captain; he is prepared to consider you for the post."

"Without ever meeting me?"

"All in good time. You used to keep chickens, did you not? One must allow the egg to hatch, before deciding that the chick might grow into a fine cockerel."

With this cryptic reply Tom had to be content; but he needed paid employment, and soon. Staying with the Vaillants for a month or two was acceptable, but to remain any longer might be awkward, since Gaspard would be outraged by an offer of money. Besides, though Tom saw Jessica every day, the entire family was usually present, whether the occasion was an afternoon drive into the Forest or an evening around the piano. The young couple could seldom snatch more than five minutes alone, and this irked them both; the difference was that whereas Tom could lose himself in study, being given the freedom of the 'retreat' even during Gaspard's absences, Jessica was offered pastimes such as sketching the view from a window, or embroidering a rosebud on a handkerchief.

"I'd sooner run through those streets than draw them," she confided to Tom with a sigh, in a rare moment of privacy. "We used to go skating, do you remember? Every time our feet grew too big, your Pa would hammer us out another pair of skates to strap on to our new boots. Oh, don't fashionable people have any fun? Must I be dull and ladylike forever?"

The next day Tom ordered two pairs of ice-skates from

the local blacksmith, and after this they would often creep from the house after luncheon, to find a frozen stream or creek, and later a barn with a warm hayloft. Before their return to Nelson Place, Tom would pick every tell-tale wisp from Jessica's hair, though she fussed and wriggled, claiming not to care one jot what Sophie Vaillant might think.

Having thus solved the main problem, Tom wondered if perhaps, just perhaps, they could go on like this; postpone the wedding until next year, reach some financial agreement with Gaspard . . .

One afternoon, snug in their favourite loft, he murmured into Jessica's hair, "How would you like to be a smuggler's mistress, and sail with me on every trip across the Channel?"

He heard her draw breath sharply, but her face was turned from him. "You don't have to feel trapped," she said, "just because we left home together. I know Gaspard is showing you a new world, and you've never been truly free before, with no one to provide for and worry about. We can wait another year or two, if you like."

He was shamed by her perception, and overwhelmed by the knowledge of how he had wronged her. His imagination had made her into a burden; something that Jess, of all women, would never willingly become.

He kissed her shoulder. "Marry me, Jess. Would you like a summer wedding? We could be wed on Midsummer's Day." And then, as she kept her head silently averted, "Being free wouldn't count for much, darling, if I didn't have you."

"Damn you, Tom Elderfield," she said, her voice breaking. "Damn your wretched conscience. It'll be the ruin of us both."

Thinking the words fanciful he stroked her arm, not knowing how best to comfort her, distressed only for her sake. But when he announced their news over dinner, Jessica accepted the Vaillant's congratulations with glowing happiness. Tom was relieved, and yet uneasy; it seemed that ever since the flight from Hatchley they were less close in spirit, less honest perhaps, and that he was the one who had changed.

Gaspard sailed next day with Hicks' fleet, and was away

for three days. Immediately upon his return, he declared that all was arranged; Captain Hicks had summoned Tom to an interview at Pennington Creek.

"An engaged couple should not be penniless," the Frenchman said, "We must presume the chick ready to hatch."

He drove Tom along lanes blackened by the coal ash of generations, leaving the river behind. This was a landscape which awoke in Tom only the faintest memory: the lattice-work of square, shallow ponds, drained now for the winter; the little windmills; the sheds and cisterns and boiling-houses. A few of the latter still spewed out smoke, the refining of Epsom salts giving work to a handful of men, but the place had a desolate aspect. It was only in summer that wind and sun could evaporate water from the brine-ponds.

Gaspard left the carriage in Hicks' coach-house, the habit of secrecy being natural to him, and Tom gazed with longing at the bramble-covered bank which cut off the view of the sea.

"Look sharp, Thomas," the Frenchman said. "No time now for ogling the scenery."

Hicks' office was a cottage nestling in the lee of the wind-mills. Gaspard knocked once, opened the door without receiving an answer, and gave his protégé an encouraging push across the threshold. "The Captain is expecting you. I shall be in the boiling-house, when you are ready to leave."

Inside, the room literally shone. On every possible surface, wan sunlight through the window struck gleams from a hoard of brass and bronze, dominated by an astonishing collection of ships' bells.

The man seated behind the desk fixed him with a narrow stare, and began abstractedly to rub one corner of a bronze cigar box with a handkerchief. The top of his bald head shone as if he had polished that too. His eyes were the bleak grey-green of the winter sea.

"*Asseyez-vous,*" he said. "*M'sieur Vaillant dire à moi vous parlez très bon français. Bien, donc? Est-il droit?*"

One could not call it French. Tom blinked, and obeyed the instruction to sit down. He answered the rest politely and in his mother's language.

"Gaspard was generous, sir, if he told you that. My

vocabulary must be poor compared to his – and he says that Guernsey folk have a dialect very unlike the French spoken around Paris."

For measurable seconds, the handkerchief remained poised over the cigar box. Then it was crumpled, enveloped in one brown, scarred fist, and tucked into a greatcoat pocket. Its owner said in English, his voice smooth as oil on water, "Vaillant also informs me that you're barely seventeen years old."

"Old enough, sir, for any task you'd set a man to do. I'm used to being out in all weathers and taking what comes."

The Captain stroked his chin, with an air of missing a once familiar beard. "You're recently betrothed. A pity. I don't doubt the girl will adopt Mrs Sophie Vaillant's view."

"No, sir, she won't."

"Knows you too well, eh? You'll go your own road, and to hell with the woman you claim to love."

The shaft was well aimed. Tom caught his breath; but too much depended on this interview. Leaning back on the hard chair he crossed his knees and said evenly, "With respect, sir, I've told you what I'm willing to do."

"Ah yes. You take what comes." The Captain's brows twitched; the set of his mouth hinted at cruelty. "Everything in your stride, eh? Does that include getting your sweetheart's brother shot through the head? Seeing your mother die of consumption three days later? Well, does it?"

"No, sir." Tom spoke with white intensity. "No, it didn't include that."

"Past tense. So these were episodes to be endured and then dismissed from the mind – "

"No, sir!"

"– with some lingering regret, of course, but finally with a shrug and a smile. Your sort, Elderfield, are two a penny."

Tom uncrossed his legs and leaned forward, elbows on his knees. Not daring to look at Hicks he stared down at his own clenched hands; what bloody right had this smug, self-important crook to put him through such a wringer? He was after a job, not a seat among the angels!

He said softly, "Amos was my best mate. If I hadn't gone out poaching that night, he'd still be alive – and yes, I can live with that, because I must. But not with shrugs or smiles, as you reckon. Every day I'm alive is Amos' gift. I don't take that lightly . . . sir. Would you?"

"If I was your age," said Hicks, in quite a different voice, "and sitting where you are now, I'd have leapt straight up and knocked my prospective employer's teeth out."

Tom raised his eyes slowly. "No, Captain," he said, "because then he wouldn't employ you, and you'd lose your best chance of a decent living. And then how would you justify having fled from home like a coward, bringing your girl with you?"

Hicks' impassive gaze did not waver, but his mouth twitched, and a muscle moved in his cheek.

"Vaillant is right," he said. "You show great promise. Would you be willing to inherit his position, a year or two from now?"

Tom stared back at him, speechless; and Captain Benjamin Hicks threw up his head and guffawed, tilting his chair so that it creaked precariously on two legs. Finally, recovering a little, he brought the suspended chair-legs to the floor with a crash.

"Now, Elderfield," he said. "Let's finish with play-acting. You'll be bound to me for five years, and since I'm giving you an apprenticeship on full pay, I call that bloody reasonable. But this first year I'll be forever at your back, by Christ I will, and in a month I guarantee you'll wish me dead." He paused, and chuckled. "If you don't already. Here, shake hands on the deal, Elderfield, and forgive me the rest, if you can. If you can't – well, I'm bound to say in that case you won't last long, working for a crafty old seaman who'll bring you naught but toil and danger, and heartache for your girl."

For long moments Tom regarded his new employer. The Captain must be nearing sixty; the administration of his personal empire was being entrusted gradually, inevitably, into youthful and perhaps irresponsible hands. He needed to be very sure of the new generation – and in this case, on the strength of a few minutes' acquaintance, he was taking quite a risk. Only a fool or a born gambler would offer a contract on such terms, and Tom did not believe that Benjamin Hicks was a fool.

Acknowledging a kindred soul, Tom smiled, and rose to grasp the Captain's hand.

"To be your agent, sir, I'd forgive anything," he said, not quite joking; and he would remember that easy promise, years later when its implications would at last be recognised and understood.

CHAPTER TWO

Tom had assumed that much of his time would be spent at sea, even at the start of his apprenticeship; but Hicks had other ideas. The Captain believed that an ambitious young man should gain experience in every aspect of his chosen profession. Tom was hired first as a tub-carrier.

The gang was accustomed to meet at the Angel Inn. When the Preventive men were busy elsewhere, Hicks' little fleet could sail upriver to the Quay itself; and from here the tubmen could carry the goods uphill via a tunnel dug for that purpose, and emerge in the Angel. What more innocent store for contraband, as Hicks remarked, than a public house with an amenable landlord?

Since the Peace, however, the Trade was becoming as dangerous as Gaspard had suggested. Returning ex-servicemen, finding other work scarce, were eager to join the ranks of either the smugglers or the Revenue Service. It was now more usual for the cargoes to be dropped at Pennington Creek or nearby Keyhaven; but the inn remained a favourite meeting place for men living in town.

Gaspard was at sea when Tom visited the Angel for his first briefing. He climbed the High Street alone, making for the sounds of raucous merriment. As he entered the taproom, the smells of tobacco smoke and strong beer were as comfortingly familiar as an old coat drawn close against the cold, windy night.

Benjamin Hicks strode to greet him, ushering him through the odorous fog to a crowded table. "Gentlemen, our newest recruit. Elderfield, meet some of my best men on land. Boxer Corrigan, Navvy O'Rourke, Trekker Verity..."

Trekker, the youngest and least formidable, sarcastically doffed his cap. "I be hearing your Ma's folk were French aristos, and lucky to escape Madame Guillotine. What d'you say to that?"

"That you're right," Tom said amiably, with a faint and Gallic shrug, "if a town house and a bad choice of friends can turn a vine-grower into a Vicomte."

Trekker grinned broadly, and handed him a pint of ale. "Welcome aboard, Aristo," he said.

"And this," said Hicks, "is Mr Jack Bezant, my beach-master. You will be answerable to him for as long as you're a tubman."

The man half rose, his expression blank as a shuttered window. Tom shook the proffered hand – and Bezant's grip squashed his knuckles, while a fleeting look of satisfaction twisted the man's heavy features.

"Well, now," said the beachmaster. "I'm glad to make your acquaintance."

By a considerable effort Tom kept his smile in place as Bezant increased the pressure. "Likewise, sir," he said. A minute ago it would have been true.

Unable legitimately to prolong the moment of pleasure, Jack Bezant withdrew his hand and sat down. Tom breathed a carefully inaudible sigh, and sat flexing his fingers under the table while Hicks outlined the evening's plan of campaign.

When they left the Angel, heading for Pennington Creek on foot, Captain Hicks did not go with them. The furtive company was joined by forty other men along the road, and Tom found himself paired with Trekker Verity near the back of the ragged column.

With Bezant out of earshot, the young tubman muttered, "What did you do? Rape his daughter?"

"Wasn't he just showing me who's boss?"

"That bastard's got nothin' to prove to nobody. He used to be a prizefighter. Killed a man once, in the ring. Be you, er . . ."

"Am I what?"

"Promised Vaillant's job?"

Tom's wary, startled silence was answer enough.

"Jesus," said Trekker, "I wouldn't be in your shoes.

Bezant's been chasing that post since he were our age, and he didn't think to lose his chance this time round."

Tom whistled through his teeth, watching the broad back of Hicks' beachmaster trudging ahead.

"Course, his French be terrible good," said Trekker judiciously. "Comes of being taken prisoner-o'-war in '13. But I wouldn't hire he, if I was the Captain. Buggered if I would. First Frog to speak out of turn would be a dead Frog – er, no offence."

"None taken," said Tom; but he resolved to treat Bezant with caution. It would be perilous indeed to make an enemy within the gang.

Among Hicks' numerous outbuildings at Pennington Creek was a boathouse, containing a dozen gigs with two pairs of oars apiece. The tubmen were ordered to carry these solid little craft to the beach; and Tom had his first glimpse of the Solent in thirteen years. The tide was full, covering the marshes seaward of the dyke, only a strip of shingle remaining. Away to the south-west, at the end of a mile-long shingle spit curving out into darkness, the two lighthouses of Hurst Castle burned steadily through an advancing sheet of rain. The more distant coastline of the Isle of Wight was to be guessed at rather than seen.

The wind here was squally and cruel, penetrating the thickest garments. Trekker yelled across it, "Bezant be needing three men to a boat, this weather. Two to row, one to bail. You see up there?" He pointed to Hurst Spit, where, in fitful moonlight, a figure crouched on top of the shingle bank. "One o' the Keyhaven boys. Soon as he sights the fleet, he'll signal *Bold Intent* that the coast be clear, and she'll lead the three luggers in like a swan wi' her cygnets."

"Have we got a long wait, d'you reckon?"

"Should be any minute. They'll want to pass Hurst afore the tide ebbs. A terrible bloody bottle-neck for currents, that be."

The words were hardly out, when the figure on the Spit moved sharply, his lantern showing a pin-point beam. There were soft cheers from the men on the beach. Trekker pulled his cap down low and grinned at Tom.

"A right thorough christening you'll get tonight, Aristo."

Bezant gave orders to launch the gigs. With Trekker and

the big ex-Navy man, Boxer Corrigan, Tom dragged a boat into the water. The storming surf drenched them instantly, the colour of new milk in the darkness. More than once Tom was almost knocked off his feet by waves breaking waist high. When he clambered aboard the gig, it was already half full of water.

He found a bucket roped to the stern thwart, and started bailing fast while Trekker and Boxer took the oars. Only a hundred yards from shore the waves grew steep; their crests curled and whitened. Each time the prow hit a trough it plunged below the surface, giving the crew a comprehensive soaking and making a joke of Tom's efforts to empty the boat.

He squinted ahead, at the four unlit vessels now sailing into view from behind the manned fortress of Hurst Castle. The wind was sou'westerly, helping the fleet but making progress nearly impossible for the gigs. Tom doubted they would reach the rendezvous point alive. He shouted to Boxer, above the noise of wind and rain, and the crash and withdrawing rattle of the surf along Hurst Spit, "We're shipping too much water!"

The veteran of Trafalgar laughed, his toothless gums witness to the fact that he had survived worse perils, scurvy included.

"Then don't spend your breath whining, Aristo," he yelled back. "Keep bloody bailing!"

There followed the most frantic, terrifying, exhilarating hours of Tom's life; or so he thought at the time. Deluged by great gouts of water which threatened to swamp the tiny craft, he bailed with a speed born of fear – but gradually they neared *Bold Intent*, converging with a few other gigs, while the half dozen remaining crews chose the small luggers: Hicks' own favourite, *Escapade*, or one of the new sister-ships *Marshlight* and *Winter Witch*.

Closing with the tall square-rigger, Tom saw men 'laying out' along the yards, furling topsails, while others leaned precariously from the rigging to watch the gigs' approach. He gazed up at masts that raked the sky, at sails that tugged and bellied with each fearsome gust. He heard the moving timbers creak . . . and he was filled with a sudden climbing elation, a surge of pure joy that banished even the memory of fear.

He caught a rope's end flung from the deck of *Bold Intent*, and the Master bellowed, "Make ready to take on cargo!"

Tom stared, for the Master was Gaspard Vaillant; but in place of the rouged and corsetted dandy stood a wiry rogue, complete with a gold-braided hat, an incisive manner, and no time for fools.

"Elderfield! We haven't got all confounded night."

The oilskin packs of tea, coffee and tobacco were handed down. Last came the brandy kegs, to be strung out behind the gig; ten in all. Boxer gave his oars to Tom for the row ashore, and the reason was soon clear – it was hard work, for the extra weight was considerable. Trekker, though small and slight, had no trouble; but after rowing ashore five times from *Bold Intent* Tom's hands were blistered, his shoulders aching, and his mind too preoccupied with these discomforts to worry about Preventive men.

But no one interfered with the tubmen's duties that night. The lightened fleet sailed for Lymington. On the beach at Pennington Creek, eager knives slashed the ropes linking a hundred kegs, while the rest were stored in the boathouse for later collection. Tom, following Trekker's example, hung a forty-five pound keg against his chest and another against his back, shivering in wet clothes in the clawing wind.

"This be what she's all about, Aristo," said Trekker, sounding jaunty. "Not glory and romance, like all they pictures and prints do tell 'ee. I'll be looking to retire at fifty wi' broken-down lungs and a crooked spine."

Tom glanced sharply at him, but Trekker shook his head. "No joke. I get the longest treks 'cause I ask for they, 'cause there the money do be. But we all come to the same end." The young tubman put his head on one side. "I know your business, Aristo. Want to know mine? Eddie Verity, footman to Mr Walter Fordyce, one of our best customers."

Bezant reformed the marching column of fifty men. Navvy O'Rourke and Boxer Corrigan, armed with holly clubs, took up the rear, while Bezant with whip and cudgel lumbered ahead. Several tubmen wore knives in their belts.

Tom whispered to Trekker Verity, "Any of this crowd ever killed an Exciseman?"

"Not this lot. But Hicks has got four hundred men, all told, land and sea."

Tom gave a low whistle of astonishment.

"And," continued Trekker, "folk like old Nell and her girls, who do put the colour in."

"Who *what*?"

"Brandy comes in looking like water. Stuff won't sell in England. So we lug he straight to Nell, who doses he with burnt sugar. Nice little moneyspinner for the daft old bat."

Nell's cottage stood beside a dark and rutted lane, within sight of the glimmering windows of Keyhaven. The newly imported barrels were lowered into the cellar, and the tubmen trudged onward with the 'dosed' kegs. They passed the outskirts of Lymington, and Trekker pointed to a white, porticoed mansion set back from the road.

"Fordyce residence. Home sweet bloody home."

"Aren't they good to you?"

"The maids," said Trekker, "be terrible plain."

Tom's smothered laugh ended in a curse; the ropes were already sawing at his shoulders, and the night's work had scarcely begun.

They left the town, treading deeper into the Forest. Sometimes the column would halt at a farm or village, to deliver a few barrels and bid goodnight to a handful of tubmen. Bezant's whip, usually employed only to encourage stragglers, curled too often around Tom's legs, stinging even through thick trousers.

In the dripping quiet of a Forest bridleway, six miles from the coast, Bezant stopped the four remaining tubmen. Even Navvy and Boxer had long ago been dismissed.

"Dipper – Ace – make your drop, lads. You an' all, Trekker. This'll be the last port of call tonight."

Tom's chin jerked up. "What about me?"

Bezant's eyes glittered in fleeting moonlight. "You, Aristo? Seems you've misunderstood the orders. Slow-witted, maybe. Is that what I should tell the Captain?"

Tom waited, unmoving, watching Bezant's face.

"Your tubs are for Mr Fordyce," the beachmaster said, "You should have dropped 'em off when we passed the house. Now you'll have to carry 'em back again, won't you?"

It was Trekker who gasped audibly. Tom held Bezant's challenging stare, thinking that he couldn't do it; it wasn't bloody well possible, and not even Captain Hicks could blame him for refusing to try.

He showed promise, Hicks had said. If he conceded the fight now, Bezant would have won in the first round.

Without a word he turned and walked slowly back the way they had come.

Only Trekker and Jack Bezant accompanied him on the homeward journey, the beachmaster setting a pace that made the kegs bounce unmercifully against Tom's back and chest. The difficulty in breathing was almost worse than the ropes cutting into his shoulders, or the protests from the straining muscles of his back.

It was six o'clock when Bezant left the two young men outside the Fordyces' house. Glaring at the beachmaster's departing figure, Trekker swore with such prolonged obscenity that Tom nearly laughed.

"Motion seconded," he said. "Help me off with these, will you?"

Trekker willingly obliged. "You'll not be working tomorrow night," he said, watching Tom straighten up.

"Fancy a small bet?" Tom gingerly touched one shoulder, investigating the frayed jacket. His hand came away sticky with blood.

"Jesus," said Trekker, "I wish you'd have dared take a swing at he."

"Um . . . Hicks knows what Bezant is like. That means he wants to find out how much I can take. If I crack, and end up in a brawl with the beachmaster, I'll never be Hicks' agent."

Trekker's mouth fell open; then he rolled his eyes and said with callous glee, "Eighth wonder o' the world – a tubman not scared o' Jack Bezant. This'll be a bloody enlivening winter, Aristo. You need a jerkin that be leather, not cloth. Want to borrow one?"

"Please. And, er, Trekker . . . Who'll be Master of *Bold Intent*, when Gaspard Vaillant quits the Trade? One of the other skippers?"

"So 'tis whispered. Gospel Deacon. Why?"

"That'll leave the skipper's berth vacant aboard *Marshlight*. I'm being taught navigation, and other things

92

that agents and ordinary seamen wouldn't need. She's not a big vessel. Crew of – what? Ten? Twelve? Would Hicks hire a youngster for the job, if I'd gained enough experience by then?"

"There ain't never yet been an agent, who weren't a skipper too."

Tom smiled slowly, and stood rather more upright. "Well, thank God for that," he said.

"Riddles afore sunrise, Aristo, be unsociable things."

"Bezant can't afford to have an enemy among the skippers. He needs their cooperation too badly. So when he's made life unpleasant for a while, and I've shown no signs of ducking out of the Trade, he'll have to swallow his fury and make amends. In other words, he won't risk doing anything much worse than tonight's little effort, even if he's ninety-nine percent sure of breaking me . . . because if by some tiny chance I'm not the type to give in to bullying, then maybe I'm not the type to forgive and forget."

Trekker stared, laughed, spun on his heel, and vaulted to the top of the garden wall. He stood up, a small black figure against the brightening eastern sky; and his soggy cap, flung with vigour, sailed in a high, triumphant arc over the Fordyces' lawns.

"Poor old Bezant." He grinned down at Tom. "First time I ever felt sorry for the bastard."

CHAPTER THREE

Jessica clung to the dream of her wedding day as to a life-line. She loved Tom, knew him better than he knew himself; yet this lay at the root of her fear. Rising sometimes before dawn, she would see him come in exhausted, drenched and aching; but whereas in the old poaching days he would have been ready for a hug and a cooked breakfast, now he merely suggested she go back to bed, or stated abruptly that he could manage well enough alone.

Jessica had started to believe him. He no longer appeared to need her. Working for Bezant most nights, he slept for much of the day, and studied – with or without Gaspard – in the evenings. The afternoon outings grew less frequent; and although Tom was kindest to her on these occasions, she felt that their lovemaking had become for him just a means to satisfy his own sexual hunger, and that even when concentrating on her pleasure he was merely performing a fairly enjoyable duty.

He was uncharacteristically snappish and quick to anger, even with the servants. Jessica recalled that he had been the same in the months before his father died, when, instead of simply escaping from Mr Elderfield, he had begun to question the very basis of his father's stern morality. He could not bear to be chained; and if the chains now were forged by his own conscience, then he was beyond her help. She could only hope that, once they were married, he would realise how little the ceremony need alter his life. It would be a bowing to convention, for the sake of any children they might have, and that was all.

At times Jessica managed to stifle her doubts. She knew

that Jack Bezant was sometimes brutal. Tom did not tell her all that happened on the tub-runs, but he could not hide the evidence of cuts and weals and dreadful bruises. Wouldn't such persecution dampen anyone's spirits?

And then there was Sophie Vaillant. A tiny English-woman of deep maternal instincts, she had at first over-whelmed the 'poor orphaned boy' with gushing sentiment; until, faced with a tough and capable young man almost six feet tall, who treated her with courtesy and an amused, rather wary affection – and, moreover, developed a habit of patting her on the head – Sophie had felt her sympathy spurned. Tom's disappearances with Jessica, unchaper-oned, for hours at a time, had been the final affront. Sophie now took every opportunity to comment on Tom's low origins and lower morals. The confiscation of his grand-father's Paris house and the vineyards in the Loire Valley, followed by the family's flight into near-penniless exile in England, had been no excuse for the young Marie to marry a blacksmith.

More than once, filled with remorse after an unprovoked flash of temper, Tom had told Jessica that nothing was wrong; it was just Sophie's attitude making him edgy, and he would feel better about the situation when they had found somewhere to live.

In April, this problem was solved. Among the many small salterns which had closed in recent years, due to cheaper rock salt from Cheshire stealing the markets, had been one belonging to Hicks; a site called West Mills, adjacent to Pennington Creek. The cottage was still in good repair, and Hicks offered to let it to his newest recruit for the stagger-ingly low rent of two pounds a year.

"We can move in straight after the wedding," Tom said, brimming with enthusiasm. "The Forest ponies come down there to graze, and it's right by the Creek. We'll have our own jetty – Hicks is even giving us the old boat moored there. One of the barns is not too derelict, and I could actually turn the windmill into a chicken-house – "

"But darling," Jessica interrupted, laughing, "why on earth is it so cheap?"

"Hicks is getting old. Spending time at the Creek saltern gives him rheumatics. He'd rather be at home. But he likes the thought of someone being around there, keeping an eye on the boathouse and so on, in case the Riding Officer starts sneaking about."

"So for two pounds we can get rheumatics instead of him."

Tom was undaunted. "Sweetheart, you'll love the place."

For Jessica, it was indeed love at first sight. She did not care that the cottage was squat and neglected, the windows too small, the interior damp and dark.

"I'll whitewash all this," she cried out, whirling to indicate every one of the living-room walls. "Which bedroom shall we have?"

"This one," he said, scooping her up to carry her through the doorway. "With the biggest bed."

Yet the acquisition of West Mills Cottage did not improve his temper for longer than a week or two. When they visited the gypsies at Fordingbridge – which shocked even Madame Angélique, and brought Sophie near to apoplexy – Jessica was anxious enough to ask Meg Wells to tell their fortune, and even more worried by her calm refusal.

"I have little skill in the art," the gypsy woman said, "but I think, Jessica, that soon you will have to make a choice, between one destiny and another. I'll help you then, if I can."

Tom paid no heed to Meg's words. Jessica had made her choice, just as he had; but the tub-runs with Trekker Verity remained, in spite of Bezant, his only sure escape from the interminable wedding talk and preparations. To prolong the time spent away from Nelson Place, he often stayed for a drink with Trekker in the Fordyces' kitchen, after the deliveries had all been made. The footman held a back-door key, to save waking the other servants in the small hours, on the understanding that he would not sample too often the liquor which his own efforts had provided; but that Spring had been the coldest and wettest in memory, and Trekker considered that he had earned his perks.

On the night of May 2nd, when the celebrations for Princess Charlotte's wedding had caused the postponement of the tub-run until law-abiding folk were abed, the two young men drank their contraband coffee and brandy so late that Trekker began glancing over his shoulder and jumping at the slightest sound, convinced that the cook would bustle in to start the day's work and catch them red-handed.

Tom was amused by his friend's jittery nerves. Though quick to criticise the foibles of master or servant, Eddie Verity was not at heart a rebel. He flourished under a firm but benevolent thumb, and would have been as helpless as flotsam if turned out to fend for himself.

"I'd best be off," Tom said, finishing his coffee at a gulp. "We've survived being half drowned every night for three months. I'd hate to see you die of fright at this late stage."

Taking the joke in good part, Trekker saw him out. A grey, sullen dawn promised more rain to come; the first drops were already falling. Leaving the noisy gravel drive Tom kept to the grass, moving silently and without haste, glancing to right and left only from habit.

A figure stood, white-clad and ghostly, in the shadows under a cherry tree. Catching sight of this apparition suddenly, and at close quarters, Tom's heart jumped with the shock and he stopped dead; but it was just a girl, thin and shivering in a gown more appropriate to a hot July afternoon. He recognised her; had seen her sitting with downcast eyes in her parents' carriage. A strange little creature, by Trekker's account, and an only child, shy as a mouse and curious as a kitten; Miss Louisa Fordyce, aged fourteen.

The child had backed against the tree, her eyes wide with terror. He said gently, afraid she might scream, "It's all right, Miss Fordyce, I'm not going to hurt you. I'm not a burglar."

"I know what you are," she whispered. "A Gentleman of the Night."

Tom's brows rose at the romantic epithet. "Miss Fordyce, you shouldn't be out here. You'll catch cold."

"You won't tell . . . my mother . . . that you saw me?"

"Of course not," he said, puzzled, for the girl seemed more scared of her mother than of this encounter with a 'Gentleman'. "How could I, anyway? Look, run along inside, go on. There's no one in the kitchen except Trekker – er, Edward – and he won't tell tales either. Go on. I won't touch you."

She gazed up at him in fascination; then cautiously she smiled. Elfin, he thought, was the word to describe her, with her thin arms and her pinched, delicate features, and that mass of crimped, pale brown hair barely controlled by the lacy cap.

"I'm not cold," she said, very timidly. "I often come out to the garden, if I wake early."

"At first light? And in the rain?"

"I like the rain."

Tom regarded her in some perplexity. He could not just leave her wandering about the place. Maybe she was lacking a few wits.

"But usually I come out," she said, "to see the Gentlemen of the Night."

This put the matter beyond a joke. He stepped purposefully forward. "Give me your hand, Miss Fordyce."

Louisa stared.

"Come along, I bet your mother is asleep and snoring, and your father too. We won't disturb them."

Like a sleepwalker, or a person spellbound, Louisa slid her hand into his. The kitchen door was still unlocked, though Trekker was nowhere in sight as they went inside. The door to the cellar stood open.

"Your footman," said Tom lightly, releasing her cold hand, "is finding room for the old *aqua vitae*. Water of life."

This comment brought colour to the girl's face and even a spark of fire to the huge green eyes. "You mean brandy, I suppose. And I do understand Latin, sir."

"Much better than I do, probably." Tom leaned against the table, crossed his ankles and folded his arms. "All right, since you're not a half-wit, and if I can trust you not to throw a fit of the vapours, I'll tell you straight. Our beachmaster is no gentleman, in any sense of the word. He arranges for spies to be systematically beaten up. It's said that informers have been killed before now – only on suspicion, mind – "

"But he cannot suspect me." Louisa's blush had faded; she looked white as death. "I'm not an informer."

"Of course you're not. But we aren't playing games for your amusement. I want you to promise that you will never, ever spy on us again."

"I don't think it's a game, I know how brave you all are, and how dangerous smuggling is nowadays. Have you . . . have you ever been wounded by a Preventive Officer?"

Tom raised his eyes briefly heavenward. He said, sighing, "Miss Fordyce, I've hardly ever seen a Preventive Officer, let alone stared down the barrel of his musket. I'm a tub-carrier, that's all. It's risky, now and then, but what job isn't? I could be a farmhand and drive a pitchfork through my foot."

"But if the sea is rough – "

"Yes, sometimes there's a sort of excitement, the thrill of beating the elements, or staying one step ahead of the dragoons." He shrugged ruefully. "I reckon that's what makes the life bearable. Mostly it's just hard work and a few extra shillings in your pocket. We're not heroes."

Louisa was again studying his face, but this time with alert, intelligent curiosity. She was growing bolder by the moment.

"I don't believe you are just an ordinary tubman," she said.

"Well . . . define an ordinary tubman."

"There – you have proved it! You talk as though – as though more words go through your mind than come out of your mouth. And yet Mama's and Papa's friends, who are so fashionable, and accomplished, and frightfully witty, seem to give exactly the opposite impression nearly all of the time."

Tom shook with laughter. "Miss Fordyce, will you please promise to stop spying, so that I can go home?"

Louisa swallowed, her cheeks flaming. "If you – if you will tell me your name. I wouldn't tell anyone else. Not a soul."

"Thomas Elderfield." He bowed, with an extravagant flourish. "I'm sure we'll be formally introduced at some function or other."

"Will we?" The shy, oddly touching smile returned. "You see, I knew you were a gentleman in disguise."

"No," he protested, laughing. "A villain, born to be hanged."

"You have my promise, then, Mr Elderfield. And I'll not be afraid of Mama tonight, because I would rather endure her tongue than – than a musket ball. You make me ashamed to be a coward."

"Cowards live to grow old." On impulse he patted her

bony shoulder. "Take better care of yourself in future," he said; and then, with a final, sparkling look as he turned to go, "I'm sorry to have destroyed your illusions about smugglers."

"You haven't," she whispered; and the words were repeated, more softly still, following like an echo. "Oh, you haven't."

He noticed her often after that, driving through town with her ageing father, or promenading on the Quay in the company of her strikingly beautiful mother. The girl always looked abstracted, never happy, her mind far removed from the subject of her mother's shrill, vivacious chatter. Tom could not manage to catch her eye.

Four weeks before Midsummer, he forgot Louisa Fordyce. At breakfast time, only two hours after dropping exhausted into bed, he was woken by Jessica shaking his arm.

"Tom! Oh darling, please wake up. Please!"

He sat up, groaning at the intrusion, rubbing a hand over his face. "What the bloody hell . . ."

"I've had a letter from our Macey."

The anguish in her voice brought Tom fully awake. Jessica laid the crumpled sheet of paper on the coverlet.

"Read it," she said.

Drawn curtains shut out the daylight, and Tom squinted to decipher the flamboyantly atrocious handwriting.

> *Jess – I am sorry to write but things are so bad here, we think Pa will die very soon – maybe in a week or less – he keeps wishing you will come home before it is too late – Jess please come back, please hurry – your affectionate brother, Mace.*

Tom said, frowning, "He lost your Ma, and then Amos, and you. He might be worrying over some trivial ailment. Your Pa was never ill, except for the gout."

Jessica shook her head, in such hopeless grief that Tom's throat constricted. He was offering false hope and they both knew it. Mace, for all his soaring imagination, had a ruthless capacity for meeting the facts head-on.

Tom leapt out of bed and started dressing. "There must be a coach to Southampton today," he said. "Maybe even to

100

Andover, in which case we should make it to Hatchley by dusk – "

"No!" She stood to face him. "I'd rather go alone, truly I would."

"Out of luck, then, aren't you?" he said, preoccupied, hardly aware of his own careless cruelty. "You must be daft if you think I'd – "

"Let me do this, Tom. Let me go."

Shrugging into a jerkin he sent her a flashing, angry glance. "I said we'll go together."

"It's too dangerous."

"We'll arrive after dark. Anyway, I don't care a damn about Sir Charles Gullifer. He's most likely forgotten me months ago."

"And if he hasn't?"

"I'll be shipped out to Van Diemen's Land, won't I?"

"Maybe you wouldn't be sorry."

The accusation stung. He turned on her furiously. "What is this, a bloody inquisition? You're scared I'll leave you standing at the altar, is that it? Afraid I'll fail in my duty?"

"Duty! Is that all our wedding means to you?"

"Oh, I might have known we'd get on to the bloody wedding. No one in this house ever talks about anything else."

"You brought it up!"

"Christ, I'd need to be desperate though, wouldn't I, to get myself transported just for the pleasure of staying a bachelor."

"Tom!" His name broke from her like a cry of pain.

He stood motionless, appalled by what he had said, his anger killed by her tears. "God, Jessie . . . I'm sorry."

"I want to go home, Tom. I want to see Pa again . . . and Macey. And I don't want you with me."

"I love you." He could not hide his despair; the thought of losing her was a physical agony as though a knife had been driven between his ribs. "I didn't mean those things, it's just . . . Jessie, I'll make it up to you, I swear on my life. Sweetheart, don't leave me."

"Only for a week or two," she said. "Perhaps all we need is a little time apart. When I come back, we'll both know better how we feel." She took his hands. "I'll write every day. And if I'm not back in a fortnight . . . well, you must come and fetch me, that's all."

She kissed him on the cheek, drawing away when he would have held her close. As she reached the door he cried out, "You said once – you said that together we'd be a match for the best and worst."

"Tell me that in two weeks' time," she said, "and I'll never doubt you again."

CHAPTER FOUR

Tom saw Jessica board the mail coach in the Angel Inn yard, and returned to Nelson Place so downcast that even the imminent prospect of a trip to Guernsey could not raise his spirits.

But once *Bold Intent* weighed anchor, there was no leisure for brooding. The three luggers had sailed on the previous ebb, but a fine blow was expected, and Gaspard Vaillant planned to make up for lost time. He was not disappointed. At dusk, as they left the Solent and passed the westernmost point of the Isle of Wight, giving the Needles rocks a wide berth, the wind approached gale force. It whipped streaming froth from the crests of impossible waves, into which the bows crashed with the juddering impact of hammer on anvil.

Tom, ordered aloft with the rest of the Second Mate's watch to reef topsails, found that the higher one climbed above the deck, the more violent the rolling, pitching motion became. Edging out along the topsail-yard, surrounded by the flap and crack of billowing sailcloth, his feet rocking on the foot-ropes, Tom made himself as useful as an ignorant landsman could. He tried to ignore his stomach's reaction to each lurching forward plunge.

Seasickness, however, could not be conquered by determination. He passed most of those first four hours on deck hanging over the side, too wretched to care if the next wave swept him overboard. The order at eight bells to "Go below the watch!" seemed the sweetest words ever uttered; and he collapsed into the newly vacated hammock shared with a man from the alternate watch. The derisory comments of several shipmates washed over him, unheeded and unanswered.

By four o'clock the gale had abated. Commanded to 'tumble up' on deck for the next spell of duty, Tom discovered that rising from a prone position no longer made his head spin and his stomach heave. Even the smell of bilgewater could be tolerated.

Dawn had broken, dismal and reluctant. Gaspard had taken the helm, to steer *Bold Intent* through a labyrinth of rocks. The Guernsey coastline to starboard was very close; away to port lay the isles of Herm and little, hump-backed Jethou. Tom knew that these waters were as deadly as a coppice full of man-traps. Only his faith in Gaspard's skill enabled him to keep his mind on the tasks of scrubbing the deck and polishing salt-tarnished brass, ready for a proud entry into St Peter Port.

They tied up alongside a pier beyond the inner harbour, and were allowed shore leave once the cargo of Epsom salts had been unloaded. The crews of *Marshlight* and *Winter Witch* greeted them noisily; but when Tom looked around for Gaspard, he saw the Frenchman rowing out to *Escapade*, anchored offshore near the island fortress of Castle Cornet.

"Bound for the cliffs above Fermain Bay again, one must suppose." The speaker was Jeremy Lomer, the bespectacled ship's boy from *Bold Intent*. "Monsieur does not appear to take his marriage vows altogether seriously."

Tom had never thought of Gaspard keeping a mistress, and was slightly shocked. All the same, Jem's earnest disapproval amused him. "*Escapade's* crew want to get ashore, same as us," he said. "Gaspard could hardly commandeer the ship for that sort of . . . escapade."

"Perhaps," said Jem, with a scornful glimmer, "the entire crew will take the bluebell path along the cliffs. Although, of course, it's rather late in the year if one is looking only for bluebells."

Tom grinned; Jem Lomer was very young, and not intentionally a prig. The son of a bankrupt shipbuilder, he despised his current lifestyle, and was engaged in a verse translation of The Odyssey; yet this in itself was a symptom of his fascination with the sea. He was also inclined to recite great chunks from Coleridge's 'Ancient Mariner'. The crew of *Bold Intent*, addicted like all sailors to songs and rambling yarns, would have forgiven him these eccentricities, if he had not remained so piously aloof, seeming to hold them all in contempt.

"Do you fancy," Tom said, "showing me the finest alehouse in St Peter Port?"

The pleasure in Jem's face surprised him. "As a matter of fact, I've yet to see the inside of one here. I'm sure it would be an educational experience."

Tom threw a comradely arm across the youth's narrow shoulders. "Get ready to further your education," he said.

They were soon joined by half a dozen men from Tom's watch, plus some English lads from the Southampton mailpacket – a circumstance which amazed Jeremy Lomer, used to being left alone. They saw, too, the insides of a good many inns, before their companions began dragging a couple of giggling, squealing girls upstairs. Tom had no intention of being unfaithful to Jessica, now or ever; and when Jem backed out of the mêlée, round-eyed, Tom strolled with him back to the ship.

Gaspard was the last to rejoin *Bold Intent*. *Escapade*, it transpired, had indeed taken him south along the coast. Until his promotion last year he had skippered the lugger, and he and others had formed lasting relationships with women in the area. There had once been a brush with a Revenue cutter; and when the troop of desperate young smugglers had rowed ashore to seek help for their wounded, under the very noses of the soldiers at Fort George, many of the cottagers' menfolk had been away fighting Napoleon. *Escapade* had returned for her missing crew members two weeks later; and more than one pair of sorrowful eyes had watched her sail away.

Tom heard all this at second-hand. He would not question Gaspard, aware that the less he knew, the less he would have to conceal from Sophie.

Hicks' fleet sailed from the crowded port in daylight, their departure causing little stir. They dropped anchor on the far side of Jethou, beside the islet of Fauconniere, where a cave showed deep and black. Here the contraband had been left by Guernsey fishermen, for collection by the English smugglers. The days had passed when such cargoes could be loaded aboard quite openly in St Peter Port. During the last fifteen years British Excisemen, stationed in Guernsey, had clamped down on the illicit trade which had helped to transform St Peter Port into a seething, brilliant concourse of wealth and fashion; but overlooking the harbour, the maze of Georgian terraces and mansions told their own story. The Free Trade was not yet ready to die.

After a detour via St Malo on the French coast, picking up tobacco with which to fill the hollow spars of *Marshlight* and *Winter Witch*, the fleet set sail for home. They arrived five days after setting out; and though the Revenue cutter *Vigilant* was sighted off the Needles, the luggers were fast, weatherly vessels, and Gaspard boasted that *Bold Intent* could outrun any ship on the Solent coast.

Tom expected to find at least one letter from Jessica awaiting him. He was wrong. By the time he had made another trip across the Channel, Midsummer was only ten days ahead, and still no word came from his bride-to-be.

"My dear boy," Gaspard said, as they stretched their legs before the drawing-room fire, drinking good port until midnight, "If Jessica's father is dying, the poor girl will scarcely want to apply her mind to letter-writing."

Tom swirled the liquor morosely around his glass. "She promised. And she's been gone more than two weeks."

"Would she desert you now, having remained loyal even after her brother was killed so tragically? Hardly likely, dear boy."

But Tom remembered how Jessica had leaned from the coach window to kiss him with lingering tenderness, drawing whistles from a gang of sailors; and how, as the coach rattled away, she had gazed back at him with desolate longing, as if to imprint every line of his face on her memory.

The next day, he borrowed Conqueror, the fastest horse in Gaspard's stable, and covered the miles to Hatchley by nightfall. The Tandys' house was in darkness, curtains drawn back to reveal rooms empty of life. Tom had not anticipated this, but it was a fair bet that the family were keeping vigil beside a hospital bed. He rode down to Ned Farminer's cottage; and though the poacher could not have been more astounded to see him, he insisted that Tom share a rabbit stew with himself and his pretty wife Emma.

Over dinner, abandoning awkward formalities, Tom

steered the conversation to his reason for being in Hatchley. Ned shrugged, evidently bewildered.

"We did think," he said, "that you'd know what became of 'em."

"The Tandys? But surely—"

"Folk don't just vanish overnight. 'Tain't natural."

"Ned! Are you saying they've gone? Packed up and left?"

"Mr Tandy was ailing, so 'twas said, and then young Jess turns up. Next thing you know, we wake up one morning and they're gone. Like the earth swallowed 'em. Although," Ned added thoughtfully, "there'd been some odd fellows creeping about. Camping out, like, near the house. Just two or three. They weren't seen no more, though, after the Tandys disappeared."

Tom felt the blood draining from his face. He heard again Sacheverell Tandy's words: "I had a family to think of . . . I made enemies . . . it's not worth the cost . . ."

Emma said sharply, "Stop it, Ned! Anyone would think the Tandys were murdered in their beds and thrown down the well, the way you carry on. Here, Tom," she added, handing him a mug of weak tea, "Take no notice. If truth be told, Obadiah and young Mace had been preparing all week, even afore Jessie came home – settling little debts, like, and no one thinking nothing of it, till we all got talking after the event. But all the clothes are missing, and some paintings off the walls. Now, thieves might pinch paintings, but not breeches and worsted stockings."

"Why not?" Tom muttered. "If they could sell them . . ."

"Now, I'm sure that's nonsense," said Emma.

But it was bound to seem that way to her. She could not know that a motive for murder existed.

That night Tom rode to Andover and called at every inn and public house, including the hedgerow alehouses along the road. No one recalled a party of travellers answering the Tandys' description.

He could not give up hope of picking up their trail, nor allow his mind to dwell on horrific possibilities. Having brought little money, he lived for a week like any wandering vagabond, breaking into outbuildings to feed Conqueror, and drawing on his old skills to snare rabbits and hares. He filled his pockets from the shops and market stalls, while distracting their owners with questions that grew increasingly desperate. A trip to Fordingbridge yielded no clues; the gypsies' summer circuit had taken them far away.

Yet he clung to the belief that if Jess was alive, she would contact him somehow before Midsummer's Day. Unshaven and hollow-eyed, exhausted by sleepless nights and waking nightmares, he came home at last to Lymington.

Hodges the butler greeted him with unaccustomed warmth, and even with sympathy. "M'sieur is in the drawing-room, sir. He has a letter which arrived for you by this morning's post . . ."

As Tom rushed into the room, his eyes wild, Gaspard rose. "Thomas, my dear fellow, I have not read it. The seal was already broken."

Tom snatched the note, his hands shaking.

My darling -- Mace told the truth. Pa will die if he stays in Hatchley, though not of any illness, and we have learned how a beachmaster makes his fortune. Pa and my brothers talk of leaving England, to start a new life where the past can't touch them. I shall go with them, for the same reason. Please try to understand and forgive me. I know you used to love me, before Amos died. Be careful, my dearest love, and explain to the Vaillants. I have arranged for this to reach you long after our ship has sailed, and I shan't write again. It's for the best, Tom.

With affection always,
Jessica

So the Farminers had been right to a degree. Sacheverell Tandy's past had caught up with him; though how, and why, Tom would probably never know. But he had lost Jess, and reasons did not count for much.

White-faced, he handed the letter back to Gaspard, and walked from the room in silence.

Gaspard's reaction to his friend's misfortune was to give him a permanent berth aboard *Bold Intent*, so that officially his time with Jack Bezant was over. Tom made a tremendous effort to keep up an appearance of good humour, for the sailors would have laughed to scorn any mention of broken hearts. The daily routine of a seaman's life, which made discomfort habitual, and narrow escapes from death commonplace, nurtured the philosophy that a man should not go to sea unless he could take a joke. Sentiment was expressed only in haunting ballads sung during the two-hour 'dog-watches' at twilight, when the entire crew would be on deck, smoking and idling a little before the night watches were set.

It was the custom for Hicks to cease all illegal activities in summer, and use the fleet solely for the export of salt; but this year summer never came. Rain and cold winds, week after week with hardly any respite, did not allow sea-water to evaporate from the brine ponds at Pennington Creek Saltern. To keep his pockets full and his men employed, Hicks intensified his illicit trading, instructing Gaspard to approach the owners of several purpose-built warehouses on the French coast. These would supply any goods not available from Guernsey or the usual French sources.

One damp August evening, after calling at St Peter Port for the first time in three weeks, Gaspard dropped anchor in Fermain Bay, shrugging his shoulders at the ominous presence of Fort George on the cliff-top.

"The ship lives up to her name tonight, *mon cher*," he said, "Will you come ashore, Thomas, and meet my friend?"

"Your mistress?" Tom shook his head. "No business of mine."

Gaspard persisted. "Do come, dear boy. The lady is afire to meet you."

Tom rowed ashore with Gaspard, three of the crew from *Escapade*, and severe misgivings. Despite the clashes of temperament between Sophie and himself, and his fear that she would stifle Gaspard's adventurous spirit, he was sorry for the way her husband deceived her. However, Gaspard was still a mate. Tom would meet the mysterious lady, not from curiosity alone, but for friendship's sake, and to avoid being thought a prig like Jeremy Lomer.

Parting from the others, Gaspard led him up a steep cliff path edged with gorse, into a wood where bluebell leaves rustled underfoot. Here, in an artificial glade overlooking the bay, a house stood alone, whitewashed and faintly luminous in the dusk. Not a mansion, but no fisherman's hovel either.

Gaspard had his own key. Pausing in the hallway he called out, "*Hélène! Ma belle, où es-tu?*"

The reply came, amused and abrasive, in the same tongue. "What are you thinking of, *m'sieur*, to arrive at such an hour? Have you no respect for a widow's reputation?"

The widow herself glided into view; tall, self-possessed and magnificent. With brown hair piled unfashionably high, she was not much shorter than Tom. He guessed her age at around twenty-five.

Her winged brows rose at the sight of him. "*Alors.*" The word expressed appreciation as well as surprise. "Gaspard, may we perhaps be introduced?"

Her lover obliged, with smiling apologies. Tom bowed over the hand of Madame Hélène de l'Erée. "*Enchanté de faire votre connaissance,*" he said smoothly; and he could see, in fairness, why Gaspard had not kept his marriage vows.

"On the contrary, it is I who am charmed," said Hélène. Her voice was low and thrumming, like the echo of a plucked string. "You must stay for dinner, of course. I shall advise Cook."

Dinner was candlelit and sumptuous. No one could have guessed that their visit had been unplanned. Nor was Tom made to feel like an interloper. Hélène de l'Erée was the perfect hostess, giving equal attention to both her guests.

Only when the meal was over did Tom discover why. Hélène raised her glass. "A toast to your marriage, Gaspard," she said, without irony. "To your firstborn child – due, I believe, quite soon – and to your newborn conscience. We have had pleasant times together. I am sorry there will be no more." She looked steadily at Tom, and the candlelight flickered in her eyes. "Perhaps I can bear the pain, since Mr Elderfield has elected to comfort me."

Tom could not mistake her meaning; and now he understood Gaspard's eagerness to entice him ashore.

He surged to his feet. "So," he grated at Gaspard, "I'm to replace you, am I, while this – this lady plays substitute for Jess?"

Gaspard rose, his face stony. "Take care, Thomas – "

"Go to hell! Next time you want to pimp for a whore – "

"Thomas!"

"Count me out of your list of customers!"

"You ignorant, pompous lout – this is not a brothel. You have insulted a lady of integrity and breeding."

"Keep her, then!" Tom could not hold on to his anger; it was swamped by other emotions beyond his control. Tears coursed down his face as he wrenched the door open. "I don't need her, you hear? I don't need anyone."

He ran blindly out into the night, stumbling downhill through the bluebell woods, not caring enough to search for the path. Twice he slipped on the wet ground and fell, rolling several feet before scrambling up again to continue the reckless descent; until a final slithering fall brought him to the cliff edge.

His progress baulked, Tom sat staring down at the bay and the four anchored, restless ships; and the night that hid his tears was vast, uncaring and cold. The future had always offered a challenge, the greatest dare of all. Now he felt only its immensity, the decades to be faced alone. For more than two years Jess had loved him literally with all her heart: he had seen her skip and dance for the joy of knowing he was happy; had seen her weep for his sorrow, groan for his pain. Without her, he would go on playing for the highest stakes, because that was his talent and the only life he understood. But the fun had gone out of the game.

Hearing footsteps behind him he took no notice, until Gaspard sat beside him. It was the Frenchman who broke the silence, speaking softly, his own fury having died also.

"Thomas, you did Madame de l'Erée a great wrong."

Tom gazed at the dark sea, unable to speak.

"Though I am as much to blame, for having led her to believe . . . Thomas, I made an error of judgement. I thought – Sophie and my mother were so certain – it seemed that Jessica's departure had wounded your pride more deeply than your heart."

Tom caught his breath; then abruptly he laughed, a brief, hard sound without mirth. "Christ, I deserved that." And then, scarcely trusting his voice, "Is that really how I treated her? As a – a diversion, like your Hélène?"

"Dear boy, Jessica believed, as we all did, that you had fallen out of love. Such things happen; they cannot be helped."

"It wasn't true," he whispered. "It was never true."

Gaspard sighed. "If there is anything I can do, Thomas," he said. "Money, or . . ."

"Just one thing. Don't tempt me to think of your house as home. Sophie hoped to be rid of me two months ago, and now with the baby coming . . . it's my fault, not hers." He hesitated, and added more firmly, "I'm moving into West Mills Cottage next week."

Gaspard's silence betrayed his embarrassed relief more obviously than any false protestations could have done.

CHAPTER FIVE

Tom put everything he had – all his enthusiasm and energy – into the pursuit of professional success. He lived for the Free Trade; belonged to it, heart, mind and spirit. It was only during nights ashore that he dreamed of Jess; and if sometimes, waking in the dark at West Mills, he would bite his knuckles to keep from groaning aloud in anguish, no one was there to mock him for it.

He spent less time at the cottage than Hicks would perhaps have liked, using it as a base rather than a home. Having been a guest of the Vaillants for so long, he was often included in invitations addressed to them, and attended a fair number of society functions and dinner parties. One evening around the piano at Nelson Place, Sophie, amid much hilarity, taught him to waltz. The birth of a son, Raoul, had proved a sufficient outlet for her maternal urges; her gibes at Tom had ceased, and were readily forgotten; and he, learning from his initial mistake, was careful not to patronise her.

He continued to see a good deal of Trekker Verity. The two young men, opposites in more ways than one could count, were mates in a way that Tom and Gaspard could never be; for the Frenchman could not quite discard the role of tutor, whereas Trekker was content to follow rather than lead.

In the autumn of 1817, Gaspard resigned as Hicks' agent. There had already been one serious encounter with a Revenue cutter that season, three men from *Winter Witch* having been wounded by cannon and musket-fire at close range. The smuggling vessel had been lucky to reach

Keyhaven, where she had been laid up for repairs ever since. Only the prompt jettisoning of her cargo had saved the crew from arrest. This incident, closely followed by the trial and imprisonment of six of Bezant's tubmen, intercepted during a trek inland, had silenced the last of Gaspard's doubts. He was ready to enjoy his new career as a timber merchant.

As everyone had known would happen, Skipper Deacon of *Marshlight* became master of *Bold Intent*, and Aristo Elderfield, then serving as second mate aboard the larger vessel, was appointed as *Marshlight's* new skipper, and as venturer's agent in Gaspard's stead.

Tom had been a well-liked second mate – something few men achieved. Being counted neither as an officer nor one of the ordinary seamen, it was easy to become isolated and despised by all. Yet, in spite of his popularity, there was a strong feeling in Hicks's fleet that someone so young, after only eighteen months' experience at sea, and with his head stuffed full of book-learning, was not fit to take command of a ship crewed by twelve men.

But *Marshlight*, alone of the three luggers, had a young crew: four were not yet twenty-one. Of the rest, only two voiced their resentment publicly. One of these requested, and was granted, a transfer to *Bold Intent*. The other, an old sailor of sixty winters, took the opportunity to retire from the Trade.

This could hardly have suited Tom better. Permitted by Hicks to choose replacements, he signed up Jeremy Lomer at once. Against all odds the youth had turned out to be a bold and capable seaman, and his loyalty to Tom was unquestionable. No one else aboard *Bold Intent* had shown Jem much kindness, nor taken such a genuine interest in his studies.

To fill the last berth, Tom went to Eddie Verity. Trekker had grown disillusioned with a tubman's life; the merciless weather of 1816, with no summer break, had given him a taste of the aches and pains he could expect in middle age if he continued in the job. He had also fallen out with the Fordyces' butler, over his regular sampling of the household's contraband.

He looked askance, however, at Tom's suggestion, put to him one night over a drink at the Angel.

"If you be claiming, Aristo, that sailors don't get wet – "

"At least you'd have oilskins. Besides, you wouldn't have to traipse around night after night with those bloody kegs strapped round your neck. That's got to make a difference. Christ, I worked long enough hours in rain and frost before I came to the coast, but those six months with Bezant were killers."

Trekker was still looking for problems. "Don't know if I can take orders from 'ee. And what if I don't like he?"

Tom sorted out the pronouns and said with conviction, "If you really couldn't stand working for me, I'd get you a transfer. But if you hated the life . . . well, there's that risk. Could be difficult to find another law-abiding job ashore, with so many men out of work. Bezant might take you back, though – and you can move into the spare room at West Mills, and stay as long as you like."

Trekker had been orphaned at the age of five, spent the next ten years in the workhouse, and served six months' hard labour for stealing a dozen eggs, though Mr Fordyce did not know it. Tom believed it was the fear of being homeless and alone that made him so wary of change.

His assessment of Trekker's character was accurate. The young tubman pushed his cap to the back of his head, and beamed.

"Aye, aye, skipper," he said.

Eddie Verity took to life on shipboard like a born seaman; and if he followed orders with an occasionally satirical grin, or even a tug at his forelock, Tom had no complaints. Trekker had settled into his new family, with curses and venomous humour which barely disguised his readiness to learn from every member of the crew.

The men accepted Tom more willingly than he had expected. Though quieter than Gospel Deacon, he was more decisive and less capricious, so that they knew where they stood. Discipline was strictly enforced, and offenders would find themselves kept busy at such futile tasks as scraping the anchor chain; but Tom used the whip only once. Just before Christmas, while *Marshlight* lay at anchor off the Brittany coast, he rowed back to the ship sooner than anticipated, after negotiating a thorny deal with a tightfisted tobacco merchant. Two of the youths were keel-hauling Jeremy

Lomer through the icy water – "all in fun, like, skip, and no harm meant."

He gave each of them six heartfelt strokes, trembling with fury; and he came to understand how dangerous power could be. For if he had surrendered to his anger then, he would have flogged them until their bones showed white.

When the punishment had been inflicted, he gave them salve to cool the weals; but they looked at his face, and they never touched Jem Lomer again.

The Christmas festivities in England were muted and apologetic, the whole country mourning the death of the Princess Charlotte in childbed. The streets of Lymington were dismal with the daily ebb and flow of black coats and gowns. George Ward, landowner and man of business, dubbed by many the 'Island King', celebrated the bright return of spring with a ball at his Cowes home. Tom was sent a personal invitation, on the strength of his close friendship with the families of Hicks and Vaillant; and he crossed the Solent with them aboard *Escapade*, the one vessel in Hicks' fleet with cabins fit for passengers.

They tied up alongside the new Fountain Quay at West Cowes, and sauntered uphill. The night was fine and warm, so that even Sophie was not tempted to hire a carriage. Benjamin Hicks, who had powdered his head as a sign of respect for their distinguished host, was still abstractedly shining a waistcoat button as the party threaded a path among the carriages on the drive.

Northwood House was imposing; but Tom had been there twice before, and he was accustomed, by now, to hearing his entrance announced in grand houses. The ballroom was hot and crowded, humming beneath the dazzle of chandeliers.

"These damned functions would be twice the fun," he muttered to Gaspard, "if half the invitations were lost in the post."

Sophie, overhearing, gave him a reproving tap on the chest with her fan. Her cheeks were flushed with excitement; she loved these glittering occasions. "Now, Thomas, we are here to enjoy ourselves. Let me see . . ." Her gaze roamed the ballroom as the orchestra, having paused for refreshment, began playing a waltz. "There must be someone you have not met. Why, of course! Miss Fordyce came out this season, and you have been away so much, I am certain you were never introduced. Come with me – come, Thomas."

Tom grimaced over her head at Gaspard, who was trying not to laugh. But he allowed Sophie to lead him around the edge of the dance floor, interested to see how Miss Louisa Fordyce would have changed in two years. He had not looked for her in the street since the summer of '16.

Tonight the family was not easy to ignore. Mrs Elizabeth Fordyce was holding court. Surrounded by a group of young officers, who served aboard one of the vessels attached to the new Yacht Club, the lady was conducting an animated monologue on the state of the country.

"So I told him, naturally, that the fellows are idle from birth, and their wives no better. One only has to look at them, for surely one need not be dirty just because one is poor? How can they expect decent people to employ them? Naturally, one does what one can, but . . ."

Mrs Fordyce's words, Tom reflected, exactly matched her voice and manner. Poisonous effervescence. Champagne laced with arsenic.

Louisa Fordyce stood apart from her mother and bemused father, her gloved hands fingering a chair-back as though she would have liked to sit down, but did not dare. She had grown tall, and her figure was no longer thin, but slender and narrow-hipped. Attractive if one liked boyish waifs, which Tom did not, particularly. But her pale, freckled prettiness showed up well, he thought, beside her mother's painted beauty.

"Louisa, my dear, how are you?" Sophie was saying. "I've been wanting for so long to introduce you to Mr Elderfield . . ."

The girl had raised her head at Sophie's first words, and she saw Tom before she heard his name. Her lips parted slightly; the green, guileless eyes widened. He acknowledged the moment of recognition with a smile in which mischief vied with courtesy, and won.

"I'm very glad to meet you at last, Miss Fordyce," he said.

"And I, you," she murmured.

The introductions continued; but Tom had met most of

the young men before, and Mrs Elizabeth Fordyce was determined to secure his whole attention. Her fund of coy looks and pert smiles was inexhaustible; it seemed that every new male acquaintance must be treated as a likely conquest.

"And you are Captain Hicks' agent at the saltern, I believe," she said. "And the skipper of *Marshlight*. Do you not find it a terrifying responsibility?"

"Challenging, perhaps."

"Dear heaven, how coolly you say it – just as if we did not all know, Mr Elderfield, what the position entails. Louisa," she called to her daughter, who had shrunk back against the wall, "why, whatever is the matter, child? Did you not hear, Mr Elderfield works for Captain Hicks?"

"Yes, Mama. I know."

"Well, heavens, you finally meet a brave and splendid young man, who might have stepped straight out of one of those novels you so adore, and you cannot say two words to him."

Louisa gazed at her mother in speechless horror, her face scarlet.

Elizabeth Fordyce sighed, and fluttered her fan, smiling ruefully at Tom. "My apologies, sir. One could tolerate a daughter being plain, if only she were endowed with an ounce of intellect – or, indeed, spirit. Whatever have I done to deserve such a dreary creature?"

This was too much. Tom spoke directly to Louisa. "Would you like to dance, Miss Fordyce, or is your card already full?"

"No. That is, yes . . ."

Elizabeth Fordyce said, smiling, "How gallant you are, sir. The poor child so rarely has the opportunity."

He steered Louisa on to the dance floor. When he drew her against him, in the embrace which had originally made the waltz such a scandal, a tremor went through her. He wondered if she was still afraid of him; and yet, guiding her through the first steps, he felt her start to relax.

"You dance beautifully," he said.

"You did not have to . . . just because we had met once. My mother would have danced with you."

He looked away from her upturned face, for his thoughts were not fit for her to read. At last he said, "The French make little mannequins – dolls, dressed in the latest Paris fashions, for seamstresses all over Europe to copy. We import them sometimes." In command of his features now, he smiled down at Louisa. "Have you ever seen one?"

The girl shook her head.

"Their faces are wax," he said, "too perfect to be real, with painted cheeks and lips."

Louisa cast a glance in her mother's direction, as though fearful of being overheard. "You must not say such things."

"Such things as what? That dolls are only scraps of soulless frippery?"

Louisa gave a breathless little laugh, half in shocked delight, half in awe.

"Miss Fordyce," he said, "you are far prettier than your mother, if only you'd believe it."

She did not believe it; he saw the doubt in her eyes, the terror of being mocked and taunted. It was something outside his experience, that anyone could be so utterly without self-esteem. However harshly Tom had judged himself for his behaviour at times, he had never felt basically inferior to the next fellow.

But then, all his life he had accepted as natural that a smile from him would usually bring a warm response; had taken for granted, too, the physical toughness which had allowed him to return insult for insult, taunt for taunt, dare for dare, and survive the consequences. He had been luckier than this despised and fragile girl.

Damn Mrs Fordyce, he thought fiercely, and damn her feeble milksop of a husband! It was time someone came down on their daughter's side.

"Have you got a horse of your own?" he asked her.

"Yes . . . I don't ride very often."

"Would your parents let you come riding in the Forest?"

She forgot the steps of the waltz, and stood motionless before him, amid the whirling dancers. "Sir, do you mean . . . with you alone?"

"Captain Hicks," he said solemnly, "would vouch for my character. But I thought the Vaillants might come too."

"I don't understand," she said. "I told you, Mr Elderfield, you need not feel under any obligation.

"Miss Fordyce," he said, grinning and rolling his eyes

heavenward. "I want you to come riding. Would you like to? Yes or no."

"Yes," she said, almost in a whisper. "I would like it very much."

CHAPTER SIX

They rode out at noon, slightly hungover and not too wideawake. *Escapade* had not reached Lymington until dawn.

Before they had gone a mile, Tom was reassured on one point. However little time Louisa Fordyce had spent in the saddle lately, she was more at home there than Sophie. Gaspard's wife had a deep mistrust of horses, and Tom suspected that she had only come in the hope of playing matchmaker.

They galloped across heathland aflame with gorse, taking care to avoid the bogs, and then down into damp woodland. Tom was riding Conqueror, bought from Gaspard the previous year, and he and Louisa left the others far behind.

"Shouldn't we . . . don't you think we should wait?" the girl asked.

"We'll explore, then, while they catch us up."

They led the horses to a river shaded by beeches, with great knotted roots groping the banks. There was a grassy place, smooth and springy with moss, and Tom threw himself down, leaning on one elbow and beckoning. Louisa knelt, cautiously in her best riding habit, aware that the grass was damp and would probably stain.

"There," he said, turning to point down into the sun-dappled water. "See the fish?"

They were only minnows; a flickering, darting shoal. Louisa smiled, enchanted; until he grabbed her arm, squinting intently upriver, compelling her attention. Louisa glimpsed a dark, sleek back, streaming ripples, before the animal swam out of sight.

Tom turned over and gazed up into the maze of young leaves, hands clasped behind his head. "Otter," he said, with satisfaction. "First one I've seen in years."

Studying him shyly, Louisa thought how extraordinarily brown he was, darkly tanned by hours at sea in wind and April sun. She knew very little about him; although for two years he had inhabited her dreams, cast as the hero in every novel she had read.

Gathering all her courage, she said, "Sophie told me . . . last night . . . that your mother died, the day you came to Lymington. Is your father dead, too?"

"Mm. Four years last February. Seems longer."

"You're an only child, like me, Sophie says."

He turned his face towards her, drowsily amused. "Sophie has been very talkative."

Louisa felt her cheeks burning. "I'm sorry – I did not know you would mind, it was just –"

"That you're a busybody," he said, grinning, "like the rest of us. Don't look so stricken, Miss Fordyce, I don't care what you ask me. Besides, I've heard a bit about you, now and then, from Eddie Verity. Might as well even the score. What d'you want to know, then?"

"Well . . . everything."

He clapped a hand dramatically over his eyes, then parted the fingers cautiously. A blue eye glimmered. "My child," he said piously, "Think what happened to Eve."

But he did tell her, in the end; the barest facts, flippant and unembellished. Louisa had heard of his broken engagement, of course, jilted bridegrooms being a rare treat for the gossipmongers. The news had lent a pale gleam of hope to her lonely existence; but inwardly she had condemned Miss Tandy, whom she had never met. The passage of time had not altered that opinion.

Louisa was not yet practised at concealing her thoughts. Tom said, frowning, "Listen, you mustn't think badly of Jess. I don't know how she put up with me for so long."

"I don't believe," Louisa murmured, "that you could be unkind to anyone."

"Oh, Miss Fordyce." His voice held reproach, regret, a touch of irony. He sat up, hugging his knees. "So smugglers are not heroes any more. Just saints."

Louisa was silent, not knowing how to reply.

"Jess . . . Miss Tandy and I were partners," he said, "until I lost faith in the 'marriage of true minds'. Wiser than Shakespeare – how's that for arrogance, eh?"

Louisa was not sure that she understood him; but she thought her heart must break with knowing that he loved Miss Tandy still.

"Well," he said, with a grin to dismiss the past, "So much for my sins. Do you like forest rides, Miss Fordyce, or would you rather be at home reading *The Mysteries of Udolpho*?"

"No," she said, blushing helplessly. "I would rather be here, sir, with you."

The look in the girl's eyes gave Tom a severe jolt. Met at last by Gaspard and Sophie, he made certain not to wander off alone with Louisa Fordyce again. It would not do to let her imagine any romantic inclinations on his part.

And yet, riding home that evening, he felt a sense of achievement; for he and the Vaillants had begun to show Miss Fordyce that real life need not always be lonely, dull or cruel. She would not be so shy with them, next time.

Gaspard, heavily involved in his new business venture, could not give much time to chaperoning Louisa Fordyce; but Sophie was glad to oblige, delegating the care of Raoul to her mother-in-law and a nanny. As a result, Tom saw the girl every fortnight or so, taking pleasure in the gradual change in her; the awakening of self-confidence, as Louisa found that neither he nor Sophie Vaillant would scorn her opinions or treat her with contempt.

The three of them sailed to Yarmouth once, on the packet-boat, for this was the closest Isle of Wight town to Lymington. Louisa, leaning on the guardrail to watch a distant fleet of yachts, confessed to a secret terror of the sea.

"No shame in that," said Tom. "She commands respect, that's for sure."

"We are all afraid of something," said Sophie.

"But such power . . . and you all love her so much. I've seen it in your eyes, Mr Elderfield, when you turn your face to the wind and say, 'We'll have a rough crossing tonight,' or 'the breeze is set fair for *Vigilant*, and if this weather holds it'll be the worse for us.' The sea and the weather govern your lives."

He nodded, thinking of Jessica. Perhaps Louisa Fordyce was right; perhaps a man who lived by the sea's bounty was never free of her, but was shackled as securely as any land-bound farmer to a domineering wife.

"What governs our lives is the Government," he said wryly. "The Navy is releasing God knows how many warships to stamp out smuggling for good. The garrisons aren't in venturers' pay these days. Hurst was taken over by coast-guards who couldn't be bribed, even before I moved down here."

"If the Free Trade dies, whatever will become of you?"

"Well, fashionable folk have started coming here for entertainment and the good of their health, what with the spas and bathing machines, and the Regent joining the Yacht Club. There's talk, too, of a steamboat company to compete with the Southampton sailing packets. Plenty of opportunities for seamen. Don't you worry, Miss Fordyce, I won't starve."

"No, indeed," put in Sophie, with caustic humour. "Be assured, Louisa, here is a rogue who will set a course for the sunrise."

"No," he said, laughing. "One has to move with the times, that's all."

Louisa seemed relieved, and Tom was amused, as often before, by her ambivalent attitude. She took delight in being acquainted with a high-ranking smuggler, but hated to think he might go on risking his life indefinitely – or until he lost it. Her parents' view was in a way similar. Walter Fordyce bowed to his wife's judgement, and that lady wanted to see her daughter married to a man of ambition, who might advance the family's position in society. Elizabeth Fordyce would overlook the means by which Mr Elderfield was making a fortune and a name. Venturers' agents had, in the past, become venturers themselves, and influential in the community.

Tom could not bring himself to make allowances for Mrs Fordyce. He was embarrassed by her habit of flirting with him, in front of her husband and daughter. It appeared that, having married a man of independent means, some twenty years older than herself, Elizabeth Fordyce needed constant reassurance that she was still attractive to younger men.

Clearly she was jealous of Louisa, and resented having to be seen in public with a grown-up daughter. Tom gritted his teeth, was unfailingly polite, and concentrated on showing Louisa that she was worthy of someone's regard, whatever her mother might say or do.

At sea, he was obliged to forget the girl's troubles. The Revenue Service was trouble enough. Summer arrived, yet the smuggling runs continued. Short, moonlit nights, calm seas, soft breezes; all were guaranteed to help the men of Hurst garrison, and the look-outs aboard *Vigilant* and *Rose*. Hicks was under pressure from Jack Bezant and Gospel Deacon to maintain a year-round service; for since the arrests and the clash with *Vigilant*, Nell's cellar, full of 'dosed' liquor, had been raided. The old woman had pleaded senile ignorance, and been let off with a warning; but the wages of the beachmaster and all four skippers varied according to the profits. Tom had noted before that Hicks seemed half afraid of Bezant and Deacon. A compromise had been reached: the ships would operate throughout the summer, but not as a convoy to attract unwelcome attention. The cannons of *Bold Intent* were obsolete; pitched sea battles belonged to the vanished Golden Age, and could only enrage the new breed of coastguards, Preventive men and judges.

At two o'clock one June morning, in dense fog, *Marshlight* crept past the Needles without a glimpse of the lighthouse. Sliding in towards Pennington Creek, none of the crew had seen Bezant's signal; but the coast was clear, the gigs launched and waiting. The beachmaster had not let them down. *Marshlight's* anchor chain was let out quietly, muffled with rags. The men whispered, aware of how their voices might carry through the fog. Tom moved among them, softly giving commands.

"Cargo at the ready. Gigs on port bow, two hundred yards."

The tiny craft came alongside. The goods were passed down from hand to hand, the operation smooth and hushed. For men used to winter storms, this was a picnic by comparison.

As the gigs made their second trip ashore, the fog began rolling gently away eastward, the sky brightening towards dawn. The sea was flat calm, reflective as a lake. The lugger was as exposed as a fly crawling on a window pane.

It was Jem Lomer who spotted *Vigilant* sailing from behind Hurst Spit. The tubmen had seen her, too; but they were already beached. Only *Marshlight*, with a third of her illicit cargo still on board, was in danger. The Excisemen knew their quarry; they only wanted evidence.

Tom rapped out orders, swiftly obeyed. *Marshlight* weighed anchor and trimmed her sails for Lymington – but there was no hope of outrunning *Vigilant*. The flood-tide through the Hurst bottle-neck carried her towards them at four knots, with the merest breath of wind.

Tom spoke softly to his crew. "Jettison cargo. On the lee side, where you won't be seen. Use lead ballast if there's time." He glanced up at the hollow spars, now stuffed full. "Forget the tobacco. They won't find that."

Working with his men, Tom did not notice at first that Trekker was missing. The discovery surprised him, for Eddie Verity was no shirker. He looked up – and saw his friend standing in the bows, gazing back at *Vigilant*.

Tom strolled casually across to him. "We need another pair of hands," he said.

Eddie Verity chewed at his lip. "You be a first offender, in the eyes o' law. I got six months afore. What d'you think he'll be, for this? Transportation?"

"Not if we get the cargo overboard."

"No time to weight he. They'll see the stuff floating, and add two and two. They'll take I away from *Marshlight* . . . from all this." He looked at Tom with haunted eyes. "I hate gaols."

The captain of *Vigilant*, within hailing distance now, shouted, "In the King's name . . ." And Tom glanced at the advancing ship.

Eddie Verity vaulted over the rail and into the tranquil sea.

Tom whipped round, but too late. On *Vigilant* a man yelled in anger and frustration, sure of the crew's guilt, "Sir – in the water – look there!" Several muskets were raised.

Tom shouted. "We're not your prisoners. Hold fire! *Hold fire!*"

His words were drowned in a volley of musket fire – aimed

not at *Marshlight*, but at the young man swimming strongly for the beach. The smugglers heard no cry; but they saw Trekker fling up an arm in dreadful parody of a carefree farewell, before he sank beneath the calm surface.

Aboard both ships, there was a moment's tense silence. *Vigilant's* captain had a hand across the muzzle of his lieutenant's gun, as if regretting the command to fire on an unarmed and possibly innocent man.

Into the hush, Tom said loudly, "Search my ship, and welcome!" Then he dived overboard and struck out for the place where Trekker Verity had disappeared.

This time, no gunfire. The captain, it seemed, was unwilling to repeat his initial mistake. Easier to justify one murder than two, maybe. Tom was too anxious about Trekker to feel more than fleeting relief.

The jettisoned barrels, designed with air pockets and false bottoms to enable them to float behind a gig, bumped against him; the linking ropes tangling with his legs. He paused to tread water, yelling hoarsely, "Trekker!"

Twenty yards away, a hand clawed the top of a keg, and slid helplessly out of sight.

Within seconds Tom reached the barrel, and dragged at the limp figure clinging to a section of rope below the surface. Eddie Verity lay face down, only his shoulders and the back of his head visible. "Trekker, help yourself, for Christ's sake . . ."

No reaction; but when Tom pulled his friends's head up, Trekker gave a choking cry of pain and started swearing and coughing up salt water.

"Where are you hit?" Tom asked urgently.

"Straight . . . through the heart," said Trekker, vaguely indicating a ragged hole in his jerkin, above the left breast. "Mortal."

"Doubt it," said Tom; but the position of the wound worried him a great deal. "Reckon you can swim?"

"Not . . . to bloody *Marshlight*."

"No. To West Mills. Come on, mate, it's not far."

It took half an hour, with Tom doing most of the work, before they staggered up the beach at last and collapsed on the shingle. Trekker lay like a dead man. Tom, panting for breath, dragged at his arm.

"Come on. Just over the bank. No distance."

By the time they reached the cottage, Trekker seemed barely conscious; but having been dropped on to his own creaking mattress he revived to some extent.

"We be rats," he said groggily, "deserting the sinking ship."

"No solid evidence. The tide will take the kegs." Tom's hands were busy, ripping his friend's shirt to expose the wound. "If there's trouble for the men, I'll sort it out. The Excisemen might be interested in whether you're dead though, and what sort of guilty conscience made you jump ship like an idiot."

"D'you think . . . the others'll tell my name?"

"Your name's Trekker. They'll look innocent, and say they never heard you called anything else. Long live nicknames."

He rolled the remains of the shirt into a wad, and gingerly mopped the area above the hole where the ball had entered. The wound was still seeping thinly.

"You must have lost a fair amount of blood," he said, "but it looks as if the ball has gone in slantwise, and lodged up by your collar-bone. That accounts for you not being dead."

Trekker squinted downwards. "Can you dig he out?"

Tom paused. "Do you really want me to try?"

"You ain't fetching no quack, I'll tell 'ee that much!"

Tom was saved from an immediate decision. Into the silence came the sound of galloping hooves, brought sliding to a halt near Conqueror's stable.

Trekker looked for the first time close to panic. "Land-sharks," he muttered, using the tubmen's name for Preventive men.

"Only one, and he can't arrest us," Tom said firmly, though his heart was thudding. "There's no evidence. Remember that."

Trekker nodded, biting his lip.

The cottage faced eastward. As Tom opened the front door, blinking into the risen sun, a cloaked figure came running and stumbling across the wet grass to the doorstep, her face screwed up in breathless anguish.

"Oh Mr Elderfield, thank God – I heard someone was killed –"

Tom leaned against the door jamb, exasperated as much as relieved. News, it seemed, travelled fast; the Fordyces' new footman worked for Jack Bezant.

"Miss Fordyce, it's five o'clock in the morning. Do your parents know you're here?"

"No, I – I woke early. I heard a sort of commotion by the kitchen door, and went down to see, and our footman said that a man from *Marshlight* had been shot and perhaps killed."

"No one has been killed." Tom hesitated, unsure what to do with her, and then sighed. "All right, you may as well come in. I don't suppose you know how to get a fire going?"

"I've seen the maids do it." Louisa followed him into the parlour. "Your clothes are all wet."

"A fire," he agreed, "would be nice."

"Where is Edward?"

Tom inclined his head towards the bedroom doorway. "In there, with a musket ball in his shoulder." He smiled sourly at Louisa's gasp of shock. "Your footman got the story half right."

"Shall I go for a doctor? I could make up some excuse to bring him here. I would be most convincing."

Tom grimaced. "Trekker wants me to do the surgery. Actually it wouldn't be difficult. I can see where the ball is lodged – it can't be more than an inch below the skin."

"*An inch*? . . ." Louisa swallowed, and straightened her back. "I will stay to help, Mr Elderfield, if you need an assistant."

"Well . . . have you got a strong stomach?"

"Quite strong, thank you." The girl lifted her chin somewhat resentfully, her pride touched. "I have never fainted, either."

"Good," he said dryly. "All right, then, you're always wishing to play the heroine. Now's your chance."

The operation was as straightforward as Tom had hoped: one clean incision with a sharp knife, and he was able to hook out the ball with finger and thumb. All the same, though he managed somehow to keep his hand steady, he was sweating more than his friend as Trekker uttered sobbing curses and writhed under Louisa's restraining hands. Glancing at the girl's pale but calm features, Tom was astonished at her resolve.

When the job was done, and Eddie Verity was sleeping off the effects of the brandy which had been poured down his throat beforehand, Tom left Louisa tidying up. Outside the bedroom, he leaned back against the wall for a moment; then gradually slid down, hugging his stomach, to sit with bent knees and closed eyes, his head tipped back. The hearthfire spat and crackled with resin.

Louisa said uncertainly, from directly above him, "Mr Elderfield."

He looked up. "All finished? Good girl."

"What are you doing? Are you ill?"

"Not really." He drew a deep breath. "It'll pass. Will you get into trouble, riding home for breakfast?"

"I'll use the kitchen door. Never mind that." She squatted beside him, full of puzzled concern. "Edward is weak from loss of blood, but he will recover. You said so yourself."

"Yes. A few days' rest . . ."

"Then what is the matter?"

"Maybe," he said, "I'm just not used to putting my best mate through agony."

It was clearly a revelation to her. Tom did not know whether to feel flattered or insulted, that she had assumed he could face such an ordeal with equanimity. The nausea was passing, though.

"You're a remarkable young lady, Miss Fordyce," he said, "and you made my task a lot easier, but now I really do think you ought to go home."

"Remarkable?" she asked, wide-eyed.

"Beyond doubt. And if I ever hear you call yourself a coward again, there will be serious trouble."

"Then I shan't," said Louisa, glowing with pleasure. "Not ever again."

CHAPTER SEVEN

The crew of *Marshlight* were given a week's shore leave, to let the fuss die away; but in fact the enquiries made by the Revenue men were brief and unenthusiastic. If the murdered man's corpse had vanished, so much the better; and if the witnesses aboard *Marshlight* had apparently been struck deaf, blind and stupid, better still. The Riding Officer who called at West Mills was vague and courteous, and never advanced beyond the doorstep.

The day after Trekker was shot, Captain Hicks paid him a visit. Not to commiserate, but to point out, loudly and with many expletives, that the next man to jump ship in such a manner would find himself out of a job.

Tom, knowing the influence wielded by Deacon and Bezant, thought it time to put a suggestion of his own.

"Have you heard, sir, that a few other gangs are floating their cargoes? Weighting them offshore, just below the surface, for their tubmen to retrieve in their own good time?"

Hicks scowled. "Not a method I like. Chancy in rough weather. Easy enough to lose a whole consignment, and many's the time that *Vigilant* or *Rose* have pounced on a floated cargo."

"*Vigilant* did a neat job of pouncing on us yesterday." Tom glanced at Eddie Verity, who was sitting on the new Grecian couch with his feet up. "We dumped a lot of brandy."

"Thank you, Elderfield, I didn't need reminding." Hicks stood at the parlour window, watching Tom's lately restored sailing gig rocking beside the jetty. A cigar twitched between his lips. "You've done a fancy job on that old wreck."

"Sir, if we didn't have to liaise with Jack Bezant in advance, we could pick our moment to sail past Hurst."

The Captain pivoted on his heel; gracefully for a man so rotund. "Have you been talking mutiny, Verity?"

Both young men denied this heatedly, and Trekker added, "We'd follow the skipper to hell if need be, sir – but we ain't in no hurry to get there."

Benjamin Hicks removed the cigar and turned it back and forth between his fingers, studying it with close attention. Then he gave a bark of laughter, and looked straight at Tom. "We'll try it. Just with *Marshlight* and *Winter Witch*. The first cargo we lose, I'll think again. Is that justice?"

"Yes sir," said Tom, with gratitude and relief. "You've got yourself a couple of happy ships."

That evening Tom uncorked a bottle of cognac, and Eddie Verity said with a faint sneer, "If we be celebrating the new policy, don't look so gloomy about he."

"Not celebrating," Tom said, handing him a full glass. "Drowning sorrows. Today should have been my second wedding anniversary."

" 'Tis my experience that sorrows can swim. And narrow escapes from wedlock, Aristo, be terrible enlivening things. Viewed in the right spirit, o' course."

Tom raised his glass. "Here's to the right spirit."

They drank to it, with all the appreciation of connoisseurs. Tom sat on a Chippendale chair acquired at auction, stretched out his legs and crossed his ankles.

"Why don't you wed our little mouse?" asked Trekker.

"Don't talk daft."

"She bloody loves 'ee."

"Miss Fordyce," said Tom, "will fall for every smuggler under thirty, who is moderately presentable –"

"Hah! Meaning I ain't!"

" – and speaks a dozen kind words to her. Anyway, what's this sudden haste to get me down the aisle?"

"I be worried about 'ee," said Trekker, looking totally unworried. "Tavern wenches don't be good enough, seemingly. Society girls want marriage or nothin'. Two years . . . 'tis a long while. And don't tell I, mate, that nothin' rises no more except the price o' bread!"

"Er . . . drink your cognac."

"You been chasing a ghost long enough."

"I'm not chasing anything," Tom said mildly. "That's what is worrying you, remember?"

All the same, Trekker's words had struck home. Tom felt strongly that he could not exist for ever on stubborn pride and devotion to duty. And yet it was true that he would not be content to tumble a giggling wench now and then, knowing little about her and caring less. It would seem a betrayal, somehow, of all that he and Jessica had shared.

Perhaps, in the end, marriage would be the answer. West Mills had been lonely before his friend came to live there, and sooner or later some determined young woman would drag Eddie Verity to the altar. Tom liked his solitude in small doses, and prized his independence less highly than of old.

When *Marshlight* sailed at last for Guernsey, Eddie Verity refused to be left behind. Tom would not send him aloft, but Trekker made himself pretty useful, though it was evident that the wound still hurt him. When they tied up in St Peter Port he volunteered to stay aboard, while Tom had lunch in town with a wine merchant and the rest of the crew took shore leave.

"Bring I back a duckling wi' orange sauce," he told Tom. "You privileged bloody shirker."

"What?" said Tom sharply. A week ashore had done nothing for his friend's sense of discipline.

"Orange sauce," said Trekker, with an evil glint. "Wash your ears out, skip."

"Lend me the soap when you've washed your mouth."

They parted, however, in perfect accord, the inequality of the relationship suiting them both.

The wine merchant rushed his lunch and talked with his mouth full, allowing no time for pleasantries. His waistcoat was stained with the mementoes of similar meals. Tom, unimpressed and hypocritically smiling, bargained more ruthlessly than he had intended, took an unplanned gamble in threatening to withdraw Hicks' custom altogether, and came away with a deal that put a spring in his stride.

The bewildering maze of streets was interlaced with alleyways dark as tunnels, and flights of steps descending steeply to the sea beneath overhanging walls. Tom ran and bounded down the Quay Steps and from there to the market place, swinging his short jacket from one hand, and whistling a popular ballad between his teeth. He sauntered among the stalls, enjoying the competitive yells of the street vendors. The place smelled overwhelmingly of freshly caught fish.

He bought Sophie Vaillant a set of fancy silver buttons, and for Miss Fordyce a rosewood book carrier, small enough to stand on a bedside table and still leave room for a lamp. Clutching these wares, he wandered in search of knitted guernseys, which could be picked up cheaply during the summer.

A voice behind him, low and melodious, said in French, "So, my Englishman, you walk the streets of our town in sunlight, and spend your dishonest gold on a lady. I hope she deserves it."

He turned, hardly knowing what to expect – and looked into the long, grey eyes of Madame Hélène de l'Erée.

Tom had not known that he was capable of blushing at the sight of a beautiful woman, but now hot colour suffused his face and throat. He could think of nothing whatever to say.

Her expression was amused and mocking. "I see that you have not forgotten our little dinner party."

Tom found his voice. "*Madame* . . . the things I said . . . it's too late for apologies but . . . I was very young. There's no other excuse."

"Ah, the follies of youth. One may be forgiven ten or twenty of those, I hope, or how would any of us live to come of age?"

Her skin was pale as cream, her hair more chestnut than brown in the sunlight. She was like a ship's figurehead, he thought: sculptured, lovely, statuesque; slightly larger than life.

"We're not sailing until tomorrow morning," he said, very diffidently, his self-assurance in tatters. "Will you at least let me give you supper aboard *Marshlight*? I – well, I can't think of any other way to –"

"You would cook this meal yourself?"

"It won't be a banquet, I'm afraid. Will you come, *madame*?"

"When you call me that, I feel a hundred years old. My name is Hélène – and yes, my Englishman, I shall be

134

honoured to take supper aboard your ship. I shall see you at nine, *m'sieur*."

Tom was the only member of the crew with a private cabin. There was nothing splendid about it, but he did some more shopping after leaving Hélène de l'Erée, and set to work immediately on his return to *Marshlight*.

Trekker Verity, strolling into the cabin half an hour later, promptly collapsed against the bunk, convulsed with helpless mirth.

"I don't see," Tom said, grinning, "what's so funny."

The chart table was covered with a lace-edged table-cloth; and a vase of red roses, lovingly arranged, stood in the centre. There were candles in brass candlesticks; and on the clothes chest, displayed upon a napkin, a bowl of strawberries and a jug of cream.

Trekker waved an arm vaguely and said, trying between small explosions of hilarity to mimic his friend's accent, "I'm not . . . chasing anything. Not chasing anything." He abandoned the attempt. "Not bloody much, you ain't!"

Tom threw a duster at him. "If it's any of your business, Madame de l'Erée is a lady, and I want to treat her like one, and that is absolutely all. So drag your mind above your belt and go and annoy someone else."

"Ooh, hoity-toity," said Trekker, and went, still chuckling.

Hélène arrived exactly on time, being driven to the end of the pier in a hired carriage. Tom, standing on deck to welcome his guest, heard her instruct the cabbie to collect her at midnight. There was no evasion, no subterfuge.

"Good evening, skipper," she said, descending the gangplank, and surveying his unstarched cravat and the cut of his best jacket. "I wondered whether to dress for dinner. Now, I am glad that I did."

Tom had prepared a chicken salad, to avoid the need for last-minute organisation. He was concerned to appear unflustered; for having made a fool of himself once in front of the lady, he was in no hurry to do so a second time.

The evening was a success in every way. Hélène made it clear that she had dismissed their last encounter from her mind, and would not judge him for it. Yet it was only at midnight, when she rose to leave, that he summoned courage to ask the question which most intrigued him.

Helping his guest with her cloak, he said, with some lingering embarrassment, "I never understood, you know, that night . . ."

"Well?" she said.

"Why did you agree – without ever having met me –"

"To become your mistress? I did not." Hélène shrugged, but her eyes held warmth. "Gaspard said he had a friend who had been forsaken. A young man seeking forgetfulness in pleasure. I was furious, of course, that Gaspard should think me so . . ." Another shrug. "I do not like to have my lovers chosen for me."

"Neither do I," he said.

They smiled at one another, acknowledging Gaspard's foolishness.

"What changed your mind?" Tom asked her.

"I had imagined," she said, "when Gaspard spoke of you, that you would be a gauche and pimply youth."

"Well yes. I was only seventeen."

She looked at him wonderingly. "You really do not know. Would it astonish you, then, my Englishman, to hear that when I first saw you, I thought: yes, in spite of the idiot Gaspard, this is a man whose face I would gladly see on the pillow beside me, and whose body I would gladly embrace in the lonely nights?"

He was young enough to be astonished indeed, that a mature and sophisticated beauty like Hélène de l'Erée should have wanted him, for surely an older, more experienced lover would know better how to please her?

She said, with emphasis, "I have not repented of those thoughts."

He was acutely aware of her nearness to him; aware, too, of the visible rise and fall of her breasts, the neckline of her gown cut tantalisingly low. He wanted her badly, but needed her more.

She would not make the first move. Knowing this, he reached out tentatively and unfastened her cloak, tossing it aside. Hélène smiled, and her hands moved up inside his open jacket.

"*Mon Dieu*," she said, with laughter, "A man who

requires neither padding nor corsets. My prayers are answered."

He meant to begin slowly, with tenderness; but Hélène pressed herself against him, eager and responsive, and with ungovernable urgency he mouthed her bare shoulders and the base of her throat, fumbling at the hooks of her gown like a clumsy boy making his first conquest.

"Have a care," she gasped. "Give yourself time, my Englishman. The cabbie must wait."

She undressed quickly, though, and with composure lay down on the narrow bunk. Tom, breathing fast, his blood racing, nevertheless stood for long seconds looking down at her, his body tall and naked in smoky candlelight, the sudden doubt in his heart at odds with his proudly jutting masculinity.

"What is wrong?" she murmured, playing at petulance.

"Ghosts," he said huskily. "Lost summers. Nothing."

"Then remember nothing," she said, "and come here."

Thus their affair began, and only Tom was surprised, for unknown to him the crew had been laying bets on how long it would take their skipper to choose himself a Guernsey mistress. Jem Lomer won the pot, and kept both the money and his disapproval to himself.

Tom visited the house above Fermain Bay whenever *Marshlight* called at St Peter Port. Most often he took a hired cab from the town, for Hélène de l'Erée was not shy of public opinion. She had been married very young, to a soldier, her first love, the youngest son of a landowning family on the west coast. Serving under the Duke of Wellington, he had been killed in 1812. Since then his widow, living comfortably on an allowance from the family, had taken several lovers. Tom did not delude himself that she was faithful; he saw their relationship as delightful and highly instructive, but not as a long-term solution.

Sometimes, seeking a novel change from Hélène's four-poster bed, he cajoled her into walking southward along the coast; and she would sit resignedly on the cliff-top, shielding her complexion with a parasol that the wind tugged inside out, while her lover clambered down endless rough-hewn steps to investigate some sandy and secluded bay.

"Perfect," he would say, returning flushed and out of breath, his shirt snagged by gorse and blackthorn. "Plenty of shade, and very private. Come on, it's an easy path. You can manage."

"You are an infant," she said once, as he guided her down a particularly steep and difficult descent. "Why do I indulge these ridiculous whims of yours?"

On the beach, he settled down to illustrate thoroughly the answer to that question; but afterwards, not content to lie beside her, he sat fully clothed against a boulder in the sand, while the autumn shadows lengthened and the sun dipped behind the cliffs.

Hélène joined him finally, twirling the parasol, her pelisse flapping in the chilly breeze. Leaning on the boulder, she stroked his hair.

"You are very pensive," she said, inviting confidences.

"Do you ever think of marrying again?" he asked. "Raising a family?"

Her hand paused briefly. "I am barren. No, I shall not marry again . . . or not for twenty years or so. This life holds too many attractions." She moved from the rock to see his expression. "Was that a proposal?"

"No," he said, smiling, "I think we understand each other better than that."

"Yet marriage was in your mind." She sat at his feet, shivering slightly and hugging the pelisse around her. "You are thinking, perhaps, of the little girl in Lymington?"

He nodded.

"Are you in love with her, then?"

"Miss Fordyce is a sweet girl. Patient, gentle . . . Brave, in a way. She's scared of any number of things, but put her in a situation that most ordinary folk would find horrifying, and she'll outface dragons, just to be a part of it all."

"Naturally I believe you. But that is not what I asked."

Tom was silent, tracing spirals in the sand with one finger. After a while he said, "What I had with Jess . . . I reckon a man is lucky to find a love like that, even once in his life. If she came walking across the beach this minute, I'd see that nothing this side of the grave ever parted us again."

"And yet, knowing this, you would marry the Lymington girl?"

"Jess isn't coming back. If I went on alone, it would be – well, like saying that the best of my life was over."

"When in fact it is only beginning."

"Yes. Besides," he added, mocking his own seriousness, "Miss Fordyce has changed, these past six months. I feel . . . responsible."

"Vanity," said Hélène, teasing him. "Arrogance."

"Mm. But in a way it's true. I did set out to give her confidence to face the world – from pity, at first, and then because it seemed worthwhile. At least she's learnt to enjoy life – even if she does still want to turn it into a Radcliffe romance. I'd be good to her, Hélène. I do love her."

"As you would love a puppy that you had saved from drowning."

Tom winced at the analogy; but he could not deny the truth of it. "She'll want for nothing," he said.

"After you are married, I suppose we will not meet again."

"No . . . we'll have a few months, though, even if Miss Fordyce says yes. No point in rushing things. I want to rent a town house, go to some more furniture auctions, scout around the mop fairs for servants. I've got the money to do it, anyway, and there'll be a small dowry. Making the time is the only problem."

"And we are wasting the little time we have, you and I. Come, my bed is warmer and more comfortable than this uncivilised spot."

They walked up the beach together, in mutual respect and understanding; but Tom felt more then a twinge of regret at his decision to end the affair so soon.

On his return to Lymington, he took Louisa Fordyce riding, without a chaperone for once. His murmured hints a to the purpose of the outing, while waiting for Louisa come downstairs, had silenced her mother's protests.

They rode several miles inland, up on to heathland purple under a lowering sky, the pools of standing throwing back a sullen gleam. The wild ponies lifte heads to stare, and some would follow the horses fo with friendly interest.

Accustomed to discussing marriage, if at all, i

surroundings, Tom was not sure how a formal proposal should be made. It would have been farcical to leap from his horse and kneel in the wet heather; Louisa's unreliable thoroughbred would probably take fright and bolt.

The girl solved the problem for him. She said abruptly, across Tom's idle comments on the weather, "I hear that you are to be married, Mr Elderfield. I'm afraid our footman could not keep the news to himself, and then I heard you whispering to Mama this morning. It is quite all right." Louisa lifted her chin, and injected some false gaiety into her tone. "You need not break it to me gently. I'm a grown woman, you know."

Tom drew rein, obliging Louisa to do the same.

"Who is to be my bride, exactly?" he asked, feeling his way. "According, that is, to the tubmen's grapevine."

Louisa spoke easily the name which had obviously been branded on her heart. "Madame Hélène de l'Erée."

"Madame de l'Erée is a friend, but that's all. Your footman is misinformed, as usual." He took a couple of deep breaths, studying the horizon as though he might find inspiration there. But there was only one way, really, to propose to Louisa Fordyce.

Swinging one leg over Conqueror's withers he dropped neatly to the ground, and held up his arms to Louisa. Frowning, perhaps suspecting a joke at her expense, the girl dismounted, allowing him to steady her on landing; and instead of letting her go, Tom kissed her with slow tenderness, knowing she would like it best that way, leaving leisure for dreaming.

When he drew back at last, her tears were wet on his face, salty on his tongue. She was gazing up at him as if she had never seen him before.

He could say it easily, after all. "Will you marry me, Miss Fordyce?"

"Yes," she whispered. No smallest hesitation.

"You know what you'll be taking on?"

"A rich brigand, who will carry me off to his cave full of reasures untold, and leave me alone and weeping."

"Sophie Vaillant couldn't take the life, and that's partly hy Gaspard gave it up. But it's still the life I love, and any-ing else is a long way into the future. I'll be with the Trade for another ten years, at least. Maybe longer than that. If you can't accept it, Miss Fordyce, you'd be wise to turn me down."

The girl hunted in vain for a handkerchief, and wiped her eyes on her sleeve. "Mr Elderfield," she said, "If you had murdered ten men and were promising to butcher another fifty, I would still want to marry you."

He laughed out loud, immeasurably relieved. He had not known, until this moment, how much her answer would mean to him.

"We must do some serious talking, in that case," he said, "I want to set a date for the wedding before I take you home."

Louisa smiled up at him, her shyness swamped by incredulous exultation. She was going to marry Mr Elderfield; and ever since she was fourteen years old, no other dream had really mattered to her at all.

CHAPTER EIGHT

In the ballroom at Northwood, Louisa Elderfield stood at her husband's side, poised and smiling amid the encompassing din of music and animated chatter. Tom had been cornered by their host, and though Louisa was impatient to dance she forgave them both. Old Mr Ward was invariably charming, and reminiscent of an underfed spaniel, so that, as always, she had to resist the urge to offer him something from his own buffet.

Inevitably their talk was of steamers: for this was July 24th, 1821, one year to the day since the maiden voyage of Messrs Ward & Fitzhugh's *Prince of Coburg*, the first steam packet to run between Cowes and Southampton. This year, a rival company had launched a vessel in competition, and Mr Ward's anniversary ball was to some extent a publicity exercise.

"Is *Thames* really a threat?" Tom was asking boldly, totally at ease with the 'Island King'. "There might actually be enough passengers to fill both packets, with the city folk trooping south for the yachting."

"There may." George Ward's deceptively sorrowful eyes gleamed suddenly with humour, and Louisa was permitted a glimpse of the shrewd mind behind the façade of innocuous courtesy. "I'm a local man, however. I prefer to remain one jump ahead of an owners' consortium with members scattered from here to Stamford Hill. What would you think, Mr Elderfield, of a steamer built here in Cowes – built sturdy enough to make the Channel crossing, and offering summer excursions to Devon or Sussex? Perhaps even a trip around the Wight?"

Tom whistled. "A special service for the summer crowds? It's an intriguing idea. Have you got a builder in mind?"

"Ratsey. It's no secret."

Tom put an arm around his wife, drawing her close to his side. "What do you reckon, darling? Would your friends welcome the chance to see Torquay Regatta?"

He habitually referred to their wide circle of acquaintances as her friends; and in fact there were many whom he barely knew. Louisa would hold dinner parties in his absence, to pass the time, and when he came home she seldom felt the need to socialize.

She said now, with a faint grimace, "We ladies have some doubts, Mr Ward, as to the safety of steam packets. Are your passengers not for ever falling under the paddles, or being blown to heaven by an exploding boiler?"

"*My* passengers? No, indeed. My dear Mrs Elderfield, you are speaking of the age when steam engines were in their infancy. Our British engineers are the best in the world."

"In that case," she said, tapping her glass against that of the Island magnate, "let us drink to the venture, which certainly cannot fail, Mr Ward, with yourself and Mr Fitzhugh at the helm."

Some minutes later, as Tom guided Louisa on to the dance floor, he murmured, "I think George Ward is a tiny bit in love with you."

"Nonsense," she said, blushing.

"Can't say I blame him."

Hearing the pride in his voice, Louisa thought for the hundredth time that being Tom's wife was worth all the heartache of the empty days when she longed only to see his face, or to know that he was safe in some foreign harbour. Having been married for two years, four months and three days, she was still deeply in love with him – despite the unavoidable nuisance of sharing his bed.

Louisa recalled her horror on their wedding night; not at her husband's tender, conscientious lovemaking, but at his hope that she would participate actively and even enjoy doing so. He was a skilful lover, and certainly a patient one, whose perseverance often achieved results for Louisa; and yet she chose to remain the passive recipient of pleasure, contributing only a resolute willingness to be loved. She felt that the whole earthy, undignified business somehow demeaned their spiritual love for one another; and in secret guilt she wished they might dispense with it entirely, and return to the romantic days of courtship.

After their first six months of marriage, Tom had started to request his marital rights less often, and Louisa put this down to his thoughtfulness. When she had questioned him timidly, concerned not to neglect her duty, he had said, with a crooked smile, that he did not want a dutiful wife; and the girl, taking his words at face value, had been grateful and reassured.

The music stopped, bringing Louisa back to the present, and between dances she had leisure to notice several late arrivals, and listen idly to a pair of ladies gossiping behind their fans.

"And see who is down from London! The Earl of Wickham – no, my dear, no relation to the Marquis of Lansdowne, and I'm sure the Marquis is glad of it –"

"Hush, he will hear you – but do look at that extraordinary young man beside him! Did you catch his name? One cannot hear half the announcements with this infernal clamour . . . But if *that* attire is an example of London fashions . . . One cannot credit that *anyone* would be seen in a green tail-coat and striped scarlet waistcoat. Just like a travelling tinker – and my dear, what *is* he doing?"

Glancing in curiosity at the party under discussion, Louisa saw that the youth in scarlet and green was fast attracting every eye in the room. It was not just his odd colour sense, nor his being half a head taller than any other man present. He was attempting to balance a small chair on his head, to the delight of his companions, holding one of its clawed feet precariously amid his unruly black curls.

Louisa, though disapproving, was reluctantly amused, and found herself wondering if the young man would be ejected forcibly from the house, and whether she had seen him among the Earl's friends before. Almost certainly not: she would have remembered that narrow, fresh-complexioned face; the widely curving mouth; the long nose which had been broken once or twice and had set awry – quite apart from the gangling height of the rogue.

A battered, clever, mobile face, with nothing handsome

144

about it except the dark eyes which now glinted to and fro, assessing their owner's effect on his gaping public.

Tom gripped Louisa's arm, making her jump. He said in an undertone, sounding unaccountably breathless, "Come and meet somebody."

"Tom, not that absurd young giant! I'm sure he must be drunk. Please don't say that you know him." But looking sideways up at her husband, she grew uneasy, seeing his pallor under the deep tan. "Darling, who is he?"

Tom was already steering her towards the raucous group. The unknown youth, for the moment concentrating on his prank, paid them no heed.

Tom said softly through the din, "So you're still making trouble, then, after all these years."

The chair swayed, toppled, was neatly caught. Setting it down, the youth bounded to grip Tom's hand and punch his arm, saying with awkwardness and forced laughter, "It's good to see you looking so fit, Tom Elderfield – though I swear you've shrunk."

Tom shook his head, making a valiant but too obvious effort to retain a degree of *sang froid*. "Louisa, darling," he said, "you must have heard me talk of little Mace Tandy."

Now she understood, for the name of Tandy had haunted her since she was fourteen, and in love with a betrothed tub-man. She suppressed a perverse, self-destructive urge to ask Mace Tandy what had become of his sister, and said only, "I believe that you have been living abroad, Mr Tandy. Did the life not suit you, after all? We would love to hear of your adventures."

"Abroad?" Mace hunched his wide, bony shoulders, looking as apprehensive as a small child guessing its punishment. "No, we, haven't – but Jess had better – that is –"

He glanced in confusion at some point behind Tom, and Louisa saw her husband whirl, his face impassive, frighteningly shuttered.

The woman approaching them around the edge of the crowded dance floor paused once, and then advanced boldly, unsurprised, showing only pleasure at the meeting.

"Why, Mr Elderfield," she said, "how delightful. We knew that you had been invited, of course. I suppose you had no idea that we were moving down from London."

If the words implied a question, Tom was not aware of it; his eyes had not left her face.

"So this is your lovely wife," Jessica said. "Mrs Elderfield, you've won a prize which I'm sure you appreciate. I'd have married him myself," she added, with a guileless and glowing smile, "but Fate was against me. And life moves on, doesn't it? We are none of us the children that we were five years ago – my little brother especially. Don't you agree, Mr Elderfield? Did you ever see a scrawny little sprat grow so tall in so short a time?"

"No, Miss Tandy," he murmured, "I never did."

"Yes, I am still Miss Tandy." Again that brilliant smile. "I haven't been so lucky as you, Mrs Elderfield. I am destined to die an old maid."

Louisa could think of nothing less likely. It seemed to the girl that Jessica Tandy, with her cropped curls and bright vivacity, was far more beautiful than Louisa's mother had ever been.

The conversation drifted to more general matters, as the Earl of Wickham and several others joined them. The Earl was clearly entranced by Jessica, appearing as interested as Tom to learn that the Tandys were living in a rented house in Keyhaven. Tom was still behaving with formal courtesy, taking his cue from Jessica; but Louisa began to feel desperate, knowing that Keyhaven was less than a mile from West Mills. Edward Verity and his bride now rented the cottage, since Tom had moved to Lymington, and they would undoubtedly give Edward's skipper an alibi if he needed one. Oh God, what could she do? How could she hope to compete with Jessica Tandy?

As if sensing her despair, Tom suddenly turned to her. Astonishing that blue eyes could burn with such scorching intensity!

"Darling, you're my wife," he whispered. "You. Not Jess. But I must know . . . will you help me? Will you do as Mace says?"

"Yes," she said, not understanding what he meant, and yet feeling some of the burden lifted, because he was strong and had never let her down.

Tom murmured something to Mace Tandy, who at once

bowed to Louisa. "Mrs Elderfield, can I please claim this dance, if I absolutely swear not to trample on your feet?"

And she allowed him to lead her on to the floor, her tall figure dwarfed by his.

The Earl of Wickham, laconic and distinguished, drawled, "You appear to have forgotten, my dear Miss Tandy, that you promised this dance to me."

"The stars are out, Miss Tandy," said Tom.

"So they are – and this room is so hot. Do please excuse us, Lord Wickham."

She walked ahead of Tom, out to the cool terrace and down on to a lawn lit by clusters of tall candles and lanterns set amid the shrubs.

"Jessie . . ."

She waited for him. "So I'm Jessie again, am I? And you a married man, Tom Elderfield."

"I rode from one end of Hampshire to the other, bribing every ostler and farm boy for news of you." His smile was bitter. "Well, almost. You broke my heart, you know."

"But it mended." She touched the lace at his wrist, her expression desolate and mocking. "And such prosperity . . ."

"Can't you tell me what happened, Jess? Even now?"

For answer she took his arm, and together they strolled across the candlelit lawns. She told him the story, then; how three skippers from the old Mudeford gang had been brought to trial twenty-five years ago; how they had served a few years' hard labour and then, like many ex-convicts, been impressed into the Navy and Army. This much Sacheverell Tandy had made it his business to find out; for when he had fled to Hatchley as a young man, his fortunes had included his colleagues' share of the loot.

With the disbandment of Wellington's troops after Waterloo, the three men had come home to Mudeford and had used the county's vast underworld network of tubmen, waggoners and game-higglers to trace the Tandys at last to Hatchley.

The hirelings seen by Ned Farminer had lurked about the village for days, presumably awaiting orders from Mudeford. Then the letter had arrived: unsigned, forthright, stating that until the gold had been returned, and Tandy lay in his grave, not one of his children would be safe. He was given one week to raise or unearth the money; and Jessica, unsuspecting, her whereabouts noted, would be the first to suffer for any delay.

Mace had written to bring her home, and in the small hours the Tandys had left Hatchley village, the gold having been placed conspicuously for any burglar to find, in the hope that the hunters would take it and abandon the chase. Jessica's friendship with the gypsies proved useful: the Tandys sought refuge with the Wells family, one of the few to possess a caravan as well as a tent, and travelled some distance with them, to settle at last in Deptford. Here, Obadiah took unskilled work in a shipyard, while Mace became an apprenticed shipwright.

"Why did you write that you were leaving the country?" Tom asked her. "And that you'd left me from choice? You couldn't – Jess, you couldn't have thought me capable of betraying you out of spite?"

She stopped walking, and gave his arm a little shake, her eyes meeting his with helpless pain. "As though I could ever think that! Oh Tom, if you had guessed that I was still in England, still wanting you, still ready to believe you loved me, wouldn't you have moved heaven and earth to find me?"

"You know I would," he whispered.

"But you didn't suspect, any more than I had, that the Vaillants' house was watched. You would have traced the gypsies first, they were the obvious refuge – and the link that our enemies wouldn't find without your unwitting help. You would have killed us, Tom, and probably yourself too."

"The seal was broken," he said, remembering. "On your letter."

"I'd hoped they would read it. That was another reason for writing what I did."

They walked on, no longer touching. After a time she said, "My father died two weeks ago. A sudden seizure – I think the constant uncertainty, of not knowing where death might lie in wait for any one of us, had weakened his heart."

He gave no insincere condolences. Jess was free again; his Jess, the one woman to whom he would have offered his independence, not as a sacrifice, but gladly, as a gift; for she was his equal, his match in courage and passion, and they would have drawn strength from their dependence on one another.

She was free again, and it was too late.

"Mace is a qualified shipwright now," she said. "That's why he came south. We've been living in the West End of London for some months; moving in high society. The Earl of Wickham has offered to use his influence, to get Macey into one of the yards building for the Royal Yacht Club."

The Regent had bestowed this title on the Cowes Yacht Club the previous year, when he was crowned King George IV. Tom frowned.

"I'd sooner pull some strings for Mace myself," he said grimly. "Lord Wickham charges his debtors high interest, from what I've heard."

"Whatever do you mean? He has shown us nothing but kindness."

"Mm. Watch him, though, Jess. And how did Mace serve his apprenticeship in only five years?"

"Oh, in typical fashion. Quite unplanned. He started an affair with his employer's daughter, who was also jumping in and out of bed with her rich fiancé. The girl is now pregnant by one of them or the other. Mace was willing enough to forget her and move to West London with Pa and me, in return for having two years knocked off his apprenticeship and the deeds falsified."

"You're joking. I'll give him full marks for cheek, if nothing else. Can he get away with it?"

"Of course. He's worked so hard to learn the shipwright's craft, Tom, and he's a clever designer too."

"What about Obadiah? Is he here?"

"No, just Mace, and Amos's children –"

"*Amos* . . ." He had halted abruptly, and was staring at her.

Jessica sighed. "About four months after Amos died, a girl from Andover came to see Pa. Pretty, Mace says, with red hair and blue eyes. Jane somebody. Maybe you'd met her."

"Don't think so. And she was carrying Amos' child?"

"Worse. The babies were two weeks old – twins, a boy and girl. Jet black hair, very curly . . . Pa couldn't deny they looked like Tandys. The girl said they'd end in the workhouse if he couldn't give them a home, so of course he did, and sent the girl away with a full purse. He might not have kept them long, but then I came home. I made him take the babies with us to London. I suppose I've become their foster-mother, and they adore Mace – and I couldn't exactly have sent them to Obadiah in Deptford. Oh Tom . . ." She was standing before him, gloved hands on his shoulders, her eyes brilliant in the candlelight. "We've been in Keyhaven a week. I haven't been idle. I've spoken with Trekker Verity. He thinks you're unhappy – that you need something more from marriage than Louisa can give you."

"No," he said roughly. "He had no right to say such a thing. I haven't complained, nor had cause either."

Jessica smiled a little. "You're such an accomplished liar," she said. "You learned it young. Why is it that you cannot lie convincingly to me?"

Tom drew a shaky breath, turning away from her. He had not bargained on how deeply the sight of her in that ballroom would affect him; nor on what he might feel when she gazed up at him with those great dark eyes, and asked if his wife made him unhappy.

"Tom," she said, "I came back to find out what had become of you. I didn't know you would be married. Please believe me. I don't want to hurt you, or spoil whatever you have with your wife. But if . . . if it's not like that . . ."

He shook his head. He could not bear to look at her. "You'd best make your own life, Jessie," he said painfully. "I've made mine without you."

"If I can't marry you, I'm not looking for a husband. I won't share you with her, Tom, I couldn't do that – but if you leave her –"

"Jessie, don't," he groaned; and she came to him, reaching up to turn his face towards her.

"There's been no one else," she said. "No other lovers. Come back to me, Tom Elderfield, and I'll show you a marriage without the need for vows in church."

"No, Jess!" He held her away from him. "I'm already married. I'm not claiming it's perfect – sea-smugglers aren't reckoned to be model husbands, are they? But I love Louisa – that's the truth. You and I belong to the past. We can't go back. I don't want to try."

She stood looking up at him, the girl to whom he could not tell a convincing lie. The girl he had tried so hard to forget, and would love for always.

At last she smiled, and linked her arm again through his.

"Come, then, Mr Elderfield," she said, "we'll show your wife she has nothing to fear. We'll silence the gossips. Don't you remember? Together we're a match for the best and the worst of them."

"So we are," he said, struggling to imitate her cheerful tone, proud of her as never before.

And she would never know, he thought, what it was costing him to turn her away.

CHAPTER NINE

A fortnight after the Northwood ball, the Elderfields' first quiet evening for some time was disturbed by a visit from Mace Tandy.

Brandishing a magnum of duty-paid champagne, Mace loped with speed and jubilation into the parlour. He wound his arms around the maidservant who was announcing his arrival, kissed her hard to silence a squeak of protest, and deposited her outside the door. "Wait, for me, little witch," he said, with an overt wink, and kicked the door shut.

He turned to see Louisa looking shocked, clutching a circle of embroidered silk in a tambour-frame. Tom was on his feet and laughing.

"Do you mind keeping your hands off our servants? And what's the idea of bursting in here like –"

"A bucketful of firecrackers?" Mace could not contain his joy, could barely stand still; this was the greatest day of his life. "It was you, wasn't it? You've sweet-talked Thomas White –"

"Into what?"

"You know damn well!"

"Don't swear," said Tom mildly, "in front of my wife."

"Oh . . ." Mace felt vaguely sheepish and, with difficulty pulled himself down to earth. "I beg your pardon, Mrs Elderfield."

"Would you like to sit down?" said Tom, in a tone that brooked no refusal. He waited until Mace perched on the edge of a chair before adding, "You've been offered a job, then, have you?"

"At White's yard. White's of Cowes! Only the best bloody – er –"

"Pardon granted."

"He's the best employer on the Island – the most prestigious yard – really gives his men the chance to use their talents. His son is experimenting all the time with new designs – there's even a pool for testing scale models –"

"When do you start work?"

"He said Monday. Tom, did you know the Yacht Club are beginning to look for speed as well as comfort? There have been races."

"There have always been races."

"Yes, by a few harebrained types. But Mr White says it'll change everything when fashionable folk expect thrills, excitement, competition, not just the annual parade –"

"Racing is frowned upon by respectable people." Tom flicked a finger at the Chronicle, which lay on the card table. "You only have to read the local papers. Dangerous, indecorous . . ."

"To hell with the bloody press!" Mace yelled; and then froze, hearing what he had said. Glancing at Louisa, he was amazed to see the warmth in her eyes.

"My husband is teasing you," she said. "He told me last week that racing was bound to become popular, for people of all classes prefer sport to pageantry."

"And when it does catch on," said Tom, "the most successful designers and builders will be those with experience – those who've been constructing fast, weatherly ships for the Revenue Service and the smuggling venturers for years. Mr White fits the bill."

"I didn't even realise you knew him," said Mace.

"Only as a nodding acquaintance. But I spoke to George Ward. He introduced me to Lord Yarborough, the Club's Commodore, whose own yacht was built at White's . . . *et voilà*. No trouble, honestly. Just a case of joining the right links in the right chain."

Mace was stunned: Tom spoke as if it was an everyday occurrence to help a man achieve his dearest ambition – but Tom, of course, was not aware of all the circumstances. Sacheverell Tandy had not left his children a penny; settling the Mudeford debt had bled him almost dry. In the months

153

just before his death – following the abrupt termination of Mace's apprenticeship – the remainder had been spent on moving to the West End, and cultivating rich friends. Only Obadiah had chosen to remain in Deptford. So many years had elapsed since the flight from Hatchley that the risk of discovery was slight; especially since the Mudeford gang believed they had fled the country. Mace had joked that his father was hoping to marry them off to dukes and duchesses, and it now seemed that perhaps Sacheverell Tandy had known that his heart was failing, and had tried in some fashion to provide for his offspring. At any rate, when he died, the young Tandys could not have paid off his most recent debts and moved south without the willingly offered loan from the Earl of Wickham.

Mace was not too proud to use his own contacts to secure a position. Good jobs were scarce, and a nagging distrust of Wickham's motives made him eager to repay the loan quickly. His usually happy-go-lucky attitude towards money – irresponsible, his sister called it – had taken a sharp turnabout, when he saw how the married and notoriously amoral Lord Wickham smirked at Jess. Mace was doubly overjoyed to have been hired by Mr White, for it left him beholden to Tom Elderfield instead of to the Earl.

"I just – I don't know how to thank you," he said.

"I do. Are you going to wave that bottle around all evening, or can we sample the contents before it explodes?"

Some three hours later, when even the self-disciplined Louisa had been prevailed upon to down a few glasses, it became obvious that Mace was incapable of returning to Keyhaven that night. At Tom's insistence he stumbled and finally crawled up the stairs, allowing himself to be ushered into a spare room, where he collapsed fully clothed on the bed and lay in a happy stupor, uttering little purring snores.

"Like the cat that stole the cream," Tom murmured, sliding an arm around Louisa as they stood looking down at their guest.

"You're very fond of him, aren't you?" she said.

Tom shook his head, not in denial but in helpless acknowledgement. "Mace has been designing boats since he was ten years old. Being a shipwright is probably the only thing in his life that he has ever planned for. I'm glad I knew

154

the right people to help him." Tom squeezed his wife's waist. "He's a bit lacking in drawing-room manners, I'm afraid."

"Goodness, if that were all! He has done worse things."

"Who says so? Give them a punch on the nose from me, next time."

"Oh, I don't take much notice. Mr Tandy – Mace – really cares . . . about life, people, ships. Everything. Or that is how it seems to me. One must forgive a man for being totally irresponsible, when he is so innocent and sincere about it."

And that, Tom thought, was the most generous summing-up of Mace's character that the young man was ever likely to receive.

Turning to Louisa, he kissed her mouth very lightly and briefly. "Are you tired," he asked, "or shall we go to bed?"

He felt her body tense, but she looked up into his eyes and smiled. "That would be nice," she said.

It would have meant so much to him if she had asked for his loving, even once in two years of marriage; or if she had once consented without seeming to say, "I would do anything to please you." But he had long ago resigned himself to the fact that, for Louisa, sex was the antithesis to romantic love and would therefore always be repugnant to her; just as he had learned to live with the knowledge that, whenever he took her, he must feel guilty for taking unfair advantage of the vow of obedience she had made at the altar.

This burden, however, was having its effect. That night Tom found himself impotent, as on one or two recent occasions. Louisa was kind and consoling, telling him that she did not mind at all, that truly it did not matter.

For Tom, what really hurt was knowing that she meant every word.

Tom had assumed that Jessica and the twins would move to Cowes with Mace; but a week later he saw Jess in Lymington High Street, walking with the Earl of Wickham. The Earl also paid court to her at various social functions attended by the Elderfields. Hearing the gossip that travelled along the tubmen's grapevine, relating to Lord Wickham's lifestyle when not in Lymington, Tom felt a growing certainty that Jess could not know the kind of man he was.

One afternoon, breaking his firm resolve to meet her only in the most public places, Tom rode to Keyhaven. He had told Louisa – merely for her peace of mind – that he was visiting West Mills to talk business with Eddie Verity.

No enquiries were needed to locate the house rented by Jessica. Beside a lane leading from the harbour, in a cottage garden hemmed by rosebeds and apple trees, two children of four or five years were playing 'tag'. He sat for a moment watching them; and the twins, becoming aware of the horseman's scrutiny, stopped their game and ran to the low garden wall, leaning on their folded arms and lifting their feet off the ground.

"Have you come to see Mama?" the girl asked.

The question was bewildering; until Tom recalled Jess saying that she was virtually their foster-mother.

"If you meant your Aunt Jess," he said, dismounting to lead Conqueror through the gateway, "then yes, I have."

"Sometimes she's Auntie Jess, and sometimes Mama." The girl skipped in front of the horse and held the gate open, closing it behind him. "It's a game we play."

The boy patted Conqueror's leg, which was all he could reach. "I want to ride your horse," he said.

"No. He's too big, for one thing, and he's got a temper."

"Has he? We have, too. We're twins. I'm Luke."

The boy spoke with confidence, throwing out each phrase like a challenge. There was none of the shyness which so often afflicted small children; but these were Tandys, after all.

The girl, having clambered unnoticed on to the gatepost, suddenly patted Tom's hair, making him jump. He spun on his heel with mock outrage, and she giggled in delight.

"It's sort of yellow," she said. "You're Mr Elderfield the smuggler, and we know all about you. Uncle Macey tells us stories, and he drew a picture of you once. It was in pencil, but he said pretend the hair was sort of yellow, so we did. I'm Honor. I'm twins with Luke, of course. Hello."

"I'm very glad to meet you both." Tom lifted Honor Tandy and set her on the ground. "Will you run and tell Auntie Jess that I'm here."

"We'll both go," said Luke. "That's best."

"And it's not rude of us," Honor gravely pointed out, "because Uncle Macey says we work best as a team."

Tom watched their departing figures. Nice-looking children, straight-limbed and sturdy, with eyes as blue as forget-me-nots, and only the mop of black curls marking them as Tandys. They probably kept Jess on her toes; for they were not the kind, those two, to sit with folded hands in a drawing room, listening in silence to adult conversation.

Jessica came towards him across the lawn, with the twins scampering and dodging around her, having resumed their game of 'tag'.

"Go and change your clothes," she told them. "Luke, remember you're older than Honor, and make sure her bootlaces are tied. Old James is down at the harbour. He's said he'll take you both fishing."

Luke gave a shout of joy, and his sister asked eagerly, "May I wear breeches?"

"If you must. Go on, don't keep him waiting."

Having thus dismissed her charges, Jessica stood with hands on hips, head slightly tilted, looking Tom up and down as he knotted Conqueror's reins around the gatepost.

"Is this a social call?" she asked.

Tom realised that no amount of diplomacy would help him. Jess expected honesty; but she was not going to like it. He paced restlessly in front of her, hands thrust in his pockets.

"I came to put you on your guard," he said, "against Lord Wickham."

Her head reared back; the dark eyes kindled, blazed. "He's old enough to be my father, is that it?"

"Of course not."

"Should I enter a nunnery, since you don't want me?"

Tom fought down his anger, hardly believing that she could so misjudge him. "Look, I know it sounds like jealousy –"

"That's exactly what it sounds like. As a matter of fact, if it's any of your damned business, I might indeed agree to become his mistress. I could do a great deal worse."

The thought of her in Wickham's bed acted like a spark to a powder keg; now Tom was jealous in truth. He stopped pacing and rounded on her, gripping her shoulders. "Damn it, will you listen! Do you know that Wickham and his cronies give parties that don't include their wives?"

"Take your hands off me!"

"They've adopted the motto the Hell-Fire Club used. *'Fais ce que voudras'*. Or in plain English – Do what you bloody well like!"

"How dare you." She struggled to loosen his grip, and stumbled back when he let her go. "Lord Wickham is a fine man. You don't know the first thing about him."

"I know he enjoys revels with a Roman flavour. The more the merrier –"

"*What?*"

"D'you like crowds, Jess?"

"You vicious –"

"Guests welcomed over the age of ten?"

"Lying bastard!"

"And if the girls don't suit a man's fancy, maybe the boys will."

Jessica slapped his face so hard that he staggered.

Recovering his balance, he stood still, regarding her with narrowed eyes, while her boiling fury died to a simmer. She put a hand to her cheek as if the blow had stung her, too.

"Apologise," she said.

"I'm sorry, then – but only for shouting at you. Wickham is well known for being absolutely ruthless with folk that cross him, and as for the rest – well, I don't believe it's all idle gossip. Please, Jess, don't assume he's innocent until proven guilty."

Jessica bit her lip, but did not defend Wickham. "It's my life, Tom. You have no right to decide whose bed I may share."

And she had no right, Tom thought, to imply that he himself was at fault, for having refused to desert his wife in favour of the girl who had jilted him practically at the altar.

He had not the heart to say it aloud. Jessica's life since the summer of 1816 had been far more empty than his; and she was the one, now, who was left with nothing to show for all the grief.

"All right," he said quietly, "you win. But if you're ever in any sort of trouble . . . well, whenever *Marshlight* sails up the Solent, you can guarantee I'll be home for a day or two. I'll always help, you know. You only have to ask."

"I'll remember," she said.

Tom hoped that she would; but he rode away dissatisfied. The visit had not relieved his anxiety in the slightest.

CHAPTER TEN

Whether or not Jessica had taken any of Tom's words to heart, she made no effort to discourage the Earl of Wickham. Tom's one consolation was that she was not yet his mistress; for the smugglers would have been the first to know. Her neighbour was the son of *Escapade*'s skipper, and many Keyhaven folk worked for Jack Bezant.

But the grapevine worked both ways. From remarks that Trekker's wife let slip, Jessica and the twins were frequent visitors to West Mills – and there were other clues. Tom still kept his restored sailing gig there, in the derelict windmill or moored beside the jetty, and often he would discover in the boat an apple core or plum stone, or see the muddy prints of booted five-year-old feet on the windmill floor. He had an uncomfortable notion that, in spite of his meeting Jess in society now and then, she was also keeping track of his less public activities. If he had not known her to be incapable of low cunning, he might have suspected her motives.

Autumn passed, and the worst of the winter. Hicks was arrested, politely interrogated, and released for lack of evidence. Nell, the sugar-burner, died, leaving her daughters to continue without her. Otherwise, business was as usual. Storms were weathered, cargoes beached, fortunes made by a lucky few, among whom Tom Elderfield was reckoned one of the luckiest.

One dull February afternoon, when the wind was dying, *Marshlight* left her precious brandy kegs floating a foot below the surface of the sea, in the lee of Hurst Spit. They were strapped to an anchored, weighted raft, whose position was marked by an inconspicuous black buoy. Tom was certain that the weather was set fair, until dawn at least, for Bezant's tubmen to retrieve the cargo at a time to suit the beachmaster.

By the time *Marshlight* had tied up at Lymington, and been subjected to a thorough search by His Majesty's Customs, the wind was freshening from the south-west. Tom squinted at the steep, mountainous clouds veiling the sunset; and he thought of the kegs afloat near the treacherous overfalls and currents around Hurst. In four years he had never misjudged weather signals so badly. If the anchor dragged, or the raft broke up, he would lose the entire cargo. Then would come the row with Hicks, the Captain's insistence on a return to traditional, dangerous methods . . .

He called at home briefly, to warn Louisa not to expect him for some hours, and to reassure her smoothly that no risks whatever were involved. Having greeted him – quite uncharacteristically – with impassioned elation, she grew unreasonably anxious at his news. Tom could not stay to offer more than fleeting comfort. Instead he rode hard for West Mills, and ran from the stable to the cottage.

Eddie Verity and his wife were arguing on the doorstep. Rachel had been crying, and her hand lay protectively across her swollen stomach. Both young people turned at once to Tom.

"I been telling she, *someone*'s got to haul the bloody kegs in!"

"Aristo," Rachel wailed. "Tell he, 'tis too rough, there be a bad storm coming. He wants to take your gig out all alone."

Tom enfolded her in his arms. "We can't avoid putting to sea tonight, little girl," he said, meeting his friend's troubled eyes over Rachel's head. "But Eddie won't be going out alone. Hush now . . . Trekker, can you round everyone up? Just our own crew, and any tubmen who are handy and willing?"

"Tubmen? That be for Jack Bezant to decide," said Trekker doubtfully.

"Bezant can go to hell. Will you do it?"

"What'll you be up to, in the meantime?"

"It was my order that floated those kegs. I'll take the gig

161

out now, and beach as many as I can before you arrive with reinforcements. That way, one trip each for the rest of you might be enough."

The Veritys protested loudly, but there was no time left for discussion. When Trekker had galloped off towards Keyhaven, Tom instructed Rachel to stay indoors, keep warm, and stop worrying. Then he strode down to the jetty to check the single-masted gig and prepare her for sea.

Darkness fell quickly, and the first spots of rain pattered down. Satisfied that the craft was still seaworthy, Tom leaped ashore to untie the last mooring line.

Someone was running towards him; a small figure in a baggy oilcloth coat and trousers, with a sou'wester pulled down low.

Tom paused beside the mooring cleat. "Rachel? Have you taken leave of your senses, girl?"

"Maybe I have, Tom Elderfield." Jessica Tandy laughed at him from under the brim of the sou'wester. "I've left the twins with Rachel, and borrowed Trekker's oilskins. He's still in Keyhaven, rushing round like a one-man press-gang, trying to bully or shame a few tubmen into action. So I'm your first volunteer."

"Don't be daft, Jess. You don't even know how to sail."

"And how else do you think we amused ourselves in London, Mr High-and-Mighty, Know-it-all –"

"The Thames is a river."

"And this is a sturdy little boat with an experienced skipper, who would be very glad of an extra pair of hands aboard, if only he wasn't too stubborn to admit it." She stepped past him, letting herself nimbly down into the gig. "Cast off, skip. Where are the oars?"

Tom was annoyed, worried, and grateful; and he would have loved her then just for her gaiety in the face of discomfort and danger, and for risking her life to save a cargo of contraband in which she had no stake and no real interest.

He would not let her row, remembering how his own hands used to blister before they hardened. Besides, the boat was wide and heavy, the oars barely long enough for use by one person. He rowed out to open water beyond the mouth of the creek, and saw the apprehension in Jessica's face at the violence of the gusting wind. The rain was falling faster now. Tom was wet and bone-cold, and relieved that Jess had worn oilskins.

He yelled to make himself heard, "D'you want to hoist the mains'l? I'll take us round, eye into wind. Watch the sail doesn't knock you over the side."

Jessica knew what she was about; her hands were strong and sure on the halyard. Tom stowed the oars and ducked aft to man the tiller; but the sail jammed half way up, flapping and cracking like a bullwhip. Lashing the helm again he leapt on to the centre thwart and climbed the mast, clinging like a monkey, to free the head of the sail with one efficient jerk.

As Jess hoisted the sail, the gig swung to catch the wind, heeling perilously. Tom landed on his feet beside her, and she laughed again, the sou'wester pushed back, wet curls stuck to her cheeks and forehead; united with him in victory, challenging the elements and winning for a time at least.

"Take the helm, Jess," he yelled. "We'll stay on this tack for a while."

She held the gig on course, close-hauled on the wind, while Tom flew the storm-jib and reefed the mainsail for battle, and they surged forward with racing, prancing speed.

On the final tack towards Hurst Spit the wind approached gale force, each fearful gust laying the gig over on her beam ends. Tom bailed in a furious, back-breaking rhythm.

He called over his shoulder, breathless from the prolonged exertion, "The buoy . . . should be dead ahead . . . Any sign?"

"Not a bloody thing, skip."

It came to Tom that she was playing a game out there, even as he was. They were children again, engaged in a daring prank while the adults' backs were turned. For this hour, grief and bitterness were forgotten. The communion of a danger shared had set them free.

They could not have located the buoy in that black, heaving seaway, had the edges of the raft not been visible, breaking the surface. Tom's anxiety had been justified, for three long planks had splintered away. Thirty of the two hundred kegs were gone.

Tom furled the sails quickly from long practice, and hooked the buoy inboard to hold the gig against the raft, tying on fenders to absorb the constant minor collision shocks.

Lying across the gunwhale, he cut the nearest barrels adrift and began heaving them aboard, grunting with the effort of raising each forty-five pound keg from sea-level.

Jessica squatted beside him. "What should I do?"

"Nothing," he said, grimacing as he lifted the next keg and brought it down in the boat with a thud. "Too heavy for a woman. See that the fenders are doing their job."

Jessica silently counted to ten; but perhaps he should be forgiven. Very likely his wife could manage nothing more strenuous than lifting a needle and thread; and perhaps Louisa did not mind being considered a fragile, useless ornament.

Struggling to stay on her feet, Jessica began moving the barrels into rows, tightly packed and lashed into position. For all her determination, she grew progressively more weary from dragging and rolling the kegs. She marvelled that Tom could persevere with such grim energy, when his back must be aching more than hers.

They were joined at last by a fleet of six gigs, each rowed by four men tonight. Trekker was there, and nearly all of *Marshlight*'s crew, and those tubmen who had been lured by the promise of a fat bonus.

Not until forty barrels were stowed aboard Tom's gig, did he set sail for the creek and West Mills. Though the gig wallowed slightly, labouring under the extra weight, the wind and tide were in their favour. In the creek itself, the current took them neatly alongside the jetty. Jessica bounded ashore with the stern mooring line and stumbled to her knees from sheer weakness, scrambling up again to secure the rope.

Tom, occupied in tying off the other line, called through the rain and wind, "I'm not unloading tonight. A sheet of tarpaulin will keep her dry. D'you fancy making tea while I see to it?"

The thought alone gave Jessica's steps some buoyancy as she trod the squelching path to the cottage.

The fire was still glowing in the room which served as both kitchen and parlour. There was no sign of Rachel, and Jessica drew a breath of mingled satisfaction and stomach-churning dread. It seemed that Eddie's wife had obeyed instructions.

Jessica hung her oilskins behind the door, and snatched a towel from the linen basket to wrap around her nakedness, pleased to find that the makeshift garment reached her ankles. She tiptoed to the door of the main bedroom, and lifted the latch. Rachel lay on the wide mattress with an arm across the twins, who slept in frowning concentration, heads together, blankets up to their chins.

Rachel was still awake. "Is Eddie . . ."

"Quite safe," Jessica whispered. "He'll have beached the gig by now. We salvaged most of the cargo." She hesitated. "I asked Eddie to delay one hour, before coming home. Will you mind?"

The girl shook her head, looking at the twins, and stroking Luke's tousled curls. "Will you tell Aristo tonight?"

"No."

"But he'd come back to 'ee for sure, if he did know."

"Oh yes. His conscience would bring him running. I don't want to trap him, Rachel. I want his love, freely given . . . or nothing at all."

The girl sighed, and went on stroking Luke's hair.

"And if I lose him," Jessica whispered, with intensity, "he must never know – not from you, nor Eddie. Mace has already sworn not to tell. Will you do the same, Rachel?"

Silence.

"Rachel?"

"I do swear, and Eddie too. But I don't understand 'ee."

"Well . . . never mind."

Crossing to the bed she stood looking down at Luke and Honor, whose eyes since birth had been the same brilliant blue as Tom Elderfield's, and whose hair was as black and curly as her own. Born eight months after the breaking of her engagement, they were almost a year younger than Tom believed.

Jessica kissed her children softly, not to wake them, and then squeezed Rachel's hand. "Thank you," she said.

"I wish 'ee luck," said Rachel Verity.

It took Tom several minutes to remove the mast sections

and tie down the tarpaulin; and when he came in, stripping off the soaked guernsey and shaking water out of his hair, Jessica was ready. She sat on the hearthrug sipping tea, the towel firmly knotted.

"Yours is made," she said, indicating a mug on the hearth beside her, and seeing how the firelight played across his bare torso.

"Wonderful." He glanced at her, and blinked. "Where are your clothes?"

"Wet," she lied. "The oilskins sprang a leak. But the twins are fast asleep, so . . ." A shrug, an innocent smile. "Rachel says I must stay the night. The spare room is empty."

"Good idea." Kneeling, he reached stiffly for the mug, and sat down close to her in order to lean back against a chair. He stretched his legs in front of the now blazing fire, and groaned with luxurious relief. "Oh, Jessie. I don't think I'll ever move again. Will you make tea every half an hour?"

"I'm sure a chair would be more comfortable," she said.

"Mm. Warmer down here." He shot her a rueful look. "You shouldn't have done all that, you know. Are you all right?"

"I'll tell you tomorrow morning."

He grinned, but said seriously, "I'm glad you were with me."

Until this moment, something had remained of their easy comradeship aboard the gig. But now their eyes met and held, the sudden contact like a spark falling into a tinder box; and he said in anguish, "God, Jessie . . . I can't pretend for ever."

She made no answer, but in silence took the mug from his hand, and placed it beside hers on the hearth. She had waited months for an opportunity to set this choice before him, but the decision now was for him to take alone.

He still gazed at her in tormented doubt; and then he drew her into his arms, crushing her in a desperate embrace as though his fervour could blot out guilt and shame, kissing her like a man starved of love. The chair scraped backwards, so that Jessica lay beneath him on icy flagstones, and she said, gasping for breath, "Not like this . . . Tom, please!"

He scooped her up in his arms and carried her into the empty bedroom.

It was the start of the wedding night they had never had; the affirmation of all their long-ago nights together, and the love which had survived all the wasted years. When Jessica made clear that her need was as urgent as his, he surged up inside her with such relentless power that she cried out like a virgin, half fearing the strength of this man who was not the boy-smuggler she had left behind; but she twined her legs around him, moulded her hands to his taut buttocks, while he drove her to heights of unbelievable ecstasy whose existence Jessica had almost forgotten.

When he was spent, they lay quiet for a time, listening to Eddie Verity damping the parlour fire and preparing for bed. Though neither would remind the other that minutes were precious, they both knew that Tom must ride home before the night was over. Jessica reached for him, caressing him; and this time he took her with as much tenderness as passion. Together they embarked on a voyage of redis-covery, delighting in the subtleties and nuances which their first frenzied union had left no leisure to explore; and being gentle, too, with more consideration now for sore and aching muscles.

They came only gradually to the understanding, and sworn agreement, that as from this night they were married in their hearts if not in law, and would not part again.

In the small hours, woken from sleep by the rain lashing the window panes, Jessica rose to struggle with the tinder box and light the candle on the dressing-chest. Tom opened his eyes, frowning, roused by the scrape of the flints, and looking, despite the blond hair, so like his son that Jessica's heart turned over; but she would not tell him yet.

"Is it morning, love?" he said.

"It's four o'clock, my darling, and your wife will think you have drowned."

"She might wish I had," he said; and then, his voice breaking, "God, Jess, if only she was different. If only she'd ever been spiteful, or nagging, or unfaithful. She's never done me any wrong, except to love me for the sort of white knight I don't know how to be."

It tallied with what Jessica had gleaned from the Veritys in recent months. Eddie believed that Tom's wife was an ice-maiden whose favourite bedmate was a novel by Mrs Radcliffe; drawing mainly on servants' gossip, of course. But there was something badly wrong, he said, when a man three years married did not speak of his wife if he could help it.

Jessica had been confirmed in her opinion that Louisa Elderfield did not need a husband, but only a fantasy. Such a girl could not possibly make Tom happy.

Jessica lay down again beside her lover, nestling close to him, offering the comfort of her body's warmth and intimacy. "We'll go away from this coast, if you like," she murmured. "You needn't ask Louisa to divorce you. Why put all of us through such an ordeal?"

"Because I want to marry you," he said. "What if we have children?"

"They would take your name, as I would. Nothing could be simpler."

He kissed her forehead. "I suppose," he said, "Louisa might even be happier without me, in the end."

Hearing the pain in his voice, Jessica experienced a qualm of doubt. Louisa had been his foundling child, his protégé. Jessica wondered if Tom knew himself what it would cost him to leave her.

"You must do this with full knowledge, my love," she said. "Are you ready to live with regrets, and perhaps disillusionment?"

"Disillusionment? Not with you, Jessie. Not ever that."

"Be very sure."

"Darling Jess," he said, "let me be the one to worry about Louisa. I'll see that she never wants for anything."

Except the man she loves, Jessica thought, but could not say it. She had too much at stake to risk probing his conscience too deeply.

Tom dressed reluctantly, flexing his stiff shoulders and shuddering at the touch of cold, sodden clothes. The salvage trip to Hurst Spit seemed a lifetime ago.

He lingered to kiss Jessica once more, and could hardly bear to leave her, even for so few hours. They had agreed that from tomorrow he would live with her in Keyhaven, giving Hicks a month to find an agent who would need no training in seamanship. After that, Tom would be free to move away from the area; perhaps only as far as Southampton, or to a smuggling town like Poole or Christchurch. It was too soon to decide which direction his career should take next, but he had a small amount of capital, and did not fear the challenge.

Though he would miss his friends – Trekker especially – and all the crew of *Marshlight*, Jess was worth the sacrifice. It was only the thought of Louisa that filled him with guilt and grief.

When he arrived home, though it was still dark, Louisa was sitting up in bed, reading by lamplight. Tom was more conscience-stricken than ever, thinking that she must have been awake all night worrying about him; but Louisa denied this with a glowing smile.

"Edward Verity came last night, to put my mind at rest. He told me that when the job was done, you would stay at West Mills."

Since Trekker could not have known this when he rode to round up the men, Tom entertained just for a second the idea of a conspiracy between Jess and the Veritys; and then dismissed the notion as absurd.

Louisa laid aside her book, watching her husband change into dry clothes. "Did you manage to save the cargo, after all?"

"Most of it. Louisa . . ." He sat on the bed and took her hand, meeting her level, unaccountably joyful gaze with difficulty. "There's something . . . something we've got to talk about. Something I want to tell you . . ."

"And *I* have something to tell *you*! I was so excited yesterday, I believe the servants thought me a little mad. But now you see I am quite composed."

The counter-attack threw him for the moment. He said, with a sigh, "More gossip?"

"Not at all. I have suspected for some weeks – but now it has been confirmed. Tom, my dear husband," she said, her eyes shining, "we are going to have a child."

And then, because he stared at her so wildly, as if she had warned him of her own imminent death, or that the world would end tomorrow, she said with a breath of happy laughter, "Darling, you mustn't worry so. Women have babies all the time. And now, I have told you my news. Can yours really be just as important?"

But he turned from her, and blundered out of the room like a man struck suddenly blind. Louisa heard the front door slam, and jumping out of bed to look down from the window, she saw her husband pause to lean against the railings in the deserted, twilit street, his head bowed as though in grief. As she watched, he slammed his fist with frightening violence against the wrought iron gate, so that Louisa flinched; and then slowly he walked towards the alleyway which led to Conqueror's stable.

Louisa climbed into bed and, lying down, she turned her face to the pillow to muffle her sobs, for the servants must not think that her husband was cruel to her, or had ever made her unhappy.

CHAPTER ELEVEN

Jessica took breakfast with the Veritys, but would not answer their unspoken questions, not caring to boast of success until Tom proved it by his actions. Yet this was mere superstition; she trusted him completely, and sang to herself as she went outside to hunt for Luke and Honor among the outbuildings. Calling them would not bring a response; they heard what they chose to hear.

She saw Tom when he was still half a mile away, riding hard along the lane from Lymington across the flat marshlands. He had come, most probably, to help Trekker unload the kegs into Hicks' boathouse.

The wind was fiercely cold, flattening the salt-grass. Jessica shivered and did not mind, for he was hers at last, and neither of them need ever be lonely again.

He reined in beside her, dragging at the horse's mouth with unwonted savagery; and she knew then, before he said a word, that her bright plans for their future together had not survived the dawn.

"You didn't tell her," she cried out. "You didn't tell her!"

He slid to the ground, his face haggard from a long inward battle. "Louisa is carrying my child. In God's name, Jess, how can I leave her now?"

She wanted to scream at him: *You have a son and daughter who need you. Will you give them up for your wife's whey-faced brat?*

But no woman would keep Tom's love by holding him in chains. Neither he nor the twins would ever learn the truth from her lips.

"So we've finally lost the game," she said, "and Louisa

has won. I should be grateful, shouldn't I, that we had last night?"

"Jess . . ." He reached out to her, and then dropped his hand. "I love you," he said, his voice cracking, "I love you."

"That's not enough, is it? You must keep your precious honour too."

"You must see that I can't leave her."

"And you must see," she said, "that I can't wait for you any more, Tom Elderfield. I've had my fill of that."

His despair was overlaid by appalled comprehension. "Jess, don't go to Wickham because of this. God knows I've no right to say it, but –"

"No, you have no right. You forfeited that."

"He's a bastard. He'll break you –"

"And you wouldn't, I suppose, with your conscience and your honour. Lord Wickham may have his faults, but he puts my interests above those of any other woman, and that's a virtue I rate highly."

"You said . . . you wouldn't share me with Louisa. But Wickham is married, and you'd be his mistress."

"His, yes. Not yours."

His face contorted. "Jessie, *why*?"

Jessica could have told him that she would not be jealous of Wickham's wife, for the Earl was nothing to Jess; only a handsome face, and the promise of a fine house, where her children might grow up with all the advantages that were seldom laid in the path of penniless bastards.

She could have asked him, also, how he dared to offer her second best, after his vow to make her his bride in all but law.

But she said only, "Last night I would have died with you, out there by Hurst Castle, and died happy. I loved you more than life. Women are such fools."

"You can't mean that," he whispered, "You can't just stop . . ."

"Stop loving you?" She raised a mocking smile and lifted her chin, daring him to doubt her word. "Just watch me."

And she turned her back on him, not in hatred but because pride alone had goaded her to inflict such a wound, and she could not relish his suffering.

"Watch me, Tom Elderfield," she murmured, too low for

him to hear, as she walked straight-shouldered to the windmill that was the twins' usual hiding-place. "Just you watch me."

Three weeks later, Tom learned from Rachel Verity that Jessica and the twins had moved to Cowes; not to her brother's modest rooms above a bakery, but to a large house overlooking the Solent. Officially, she was receiving financial aid from the Earl of Wickham, a friend of the family. Unofficially, the air fizzed with scandal at the mere mention of Jessica Tandy's name. Tom knew she would not care; the front of respectability would be mainly for the children's sake.

With Louisa, Tom tried desperately to behave as if nothing had happened. He did not refer to his conduct on the morning after the storm, and Louisa seemed deliberately to avoid doing so, as though her suspicions could have no basis in truth while they remained unspoken. She became more and more withdrawn. Perhaps, Tom thought, one could blame her pregnancy, for she had no inclination for anything much except reclining listlessly on sofas. Even conversation tired her. She read a great deal, as she had done as a young girl. Sometimes when he spoke to her, it appeared to Tom that she dragged herself by an effort of will from the unreal world she inhabited, where nothing could hurt her.

Yet at other times, Louisa would sit smiling to herself in secret, and once when he came into the room she said, folding her hands over the small mound of her stomach, "Isn't it wonderful, Tom? We're going to be so happy, aren't we, the three of us?"

"Of course we are," he said, and patted her head in passing.

"You do want this baby, don't you?"

"Darling, what a question! Doesn't every man want a son? Though a daughter will do just as well, to be going on with."

"Oh please, let us see this one into the world before we think about the next!"

He had made her laugh, however, which few things did nowadays, and he was relieved to find her content with his answer.

She became more nervous than ever before about his trips abroad, and less wary of admitting it, saying tentatively but often that smuggling was no profession for a family man.

"Darling, how can I afford to give it up?" he protested on one occasion. "Look at the things you buy without consulting me? That new curtain material for the nursery, for example."

"You always say you don't mind what I spend," she said, her lip quivering ominously, "so long as I tell you about it. And I'm hardly ever extravagant. It's only for the baby."

He sat on the couch, moving her feet to give himself room. "I don't mind in the least," he said gently. "I'm only pointing out that we have to pay a landlord, a butler, a cook and two maids, not to mention the lad who looks after the horses when I'm away. Working for Hicks makes it possible, but saving for a house of our own is still a slow business."

"It's my fault," she said. "You only keep servants for my sake, and live in this house because I have been used to comfort all my life."

"That's nonsense," he said, squeezing her hand. "And you know it."

"I do so hate you being away so much. Especially now. Tom, you don't really mean it, do you, when you talk of staying with Captain Hicks until you are thirty?"

"We'll see. In another year or two, who knows? I might even go into partnership with Mace Tandy, and build racing yachts."

"No need, Tom. No need for that." She was suddenly agitated, trembling. "We don't have to associate with the Tandys any more. I've heard that Mr Ward will want recruits for his new steamer."

"Well, I doubt if he'd consider a notorious sea-smuggler for a job cosseting the *Medina*'s passengers."

Tom did not inform her that he was crossing to Cowes that very day, for an interview with George Ward and William Fitzhugh. He could guess why the Island King had summoned him to an audience.

He was not mistaken. Meeting at the Fountain Inn for an opulent luncheon, the three men were joined by Captain Knight, who was to command *Medina* following her launch in June. The interview gave Tom much to think about. He was glad of the three hour sail back to West Mills, with his sturdy gig fighting the floodtide.

William Fitzhugh's words came back to him. "Your career with Captain Hicks has been impressive, Mr Elderfield, if slightly – shall we say, colourful? We would like to offer you the position of Mate aboard our new vessel."

"To be frank, sir," said George Ward, doleful eyes showing the merest glint of humour, "We have taken into account more than the suitability of your background and character. We feel that this appointment would do much to, er . . ." He paused, and coughed delicately. "To win the ladies to our cause. To encourage them, in short, to embrace the new age with affection."

Tom could not help grinning, "You forget, Mr Ward, that I'm a married man."

"On the contrary. The life of a saltern agent is precarious, if you understand me. I hold Mrs Elderfield in high esteem, and should not like to see her widowed."

"You must be aware that our first child will be born in four months."

"Is a secure profession, with solid prospects for advancement, not worth more than a quick fortune and a premature funeral?"

Tom had answered, smiling, "I very much appreciate your offer, but I haven't yet begun to crave security before variety."

Messrs Ward and Fitzhugh were obliged to accept his refusal as final. Tom's main worry was how to break the news to Louisa.

The news that awaited him at home that evening drove everything else from his mind. In the hall he was assailed by the youngest of the maidservants.

"Oh, sir, you be home at last." The girl was close to tears. "Mrs Elderfield have been terrible poorly, and none of us knowing where to look for 'ee."

"Poorly? But she seemed all right this morning. Has someone called the doctor?"

"He's been and gone, sir. Mr Elderfield," the girl added, sniffing, "There were no warning, truly. Madam didn't fall, or nothing like that. She's lost the baby, sir."

When Tom entered the bedroom, Louisa appeared to be

175

sleeping. He would have tiptoed out again, but his wife opened her eyes and stretched out a hand to him. He sat on the bed and held her hand tight, almost overcome by pity; but his grief was for Louisa's loss, not his own. The baby had not yet become real to him; and because of it he had lost Jess.

"You should have been here," she whispered. "Tom, I was so afraid. Where have you been?"

"With Captain Hicks." The lie came easily. "The waggoners on the inland routes are demanding higher wages. Louisa, darling, I'm so sorry."

"I used to think we could be a team," she said. "Like you and Jessica Tandy –"

"Darling, don't."

"But we can't. I'm not brave, or strong. Every day and night I'm frightened for you. And now . . . I couldn't even give you a son."

"You're safe, that's what counts. We're young, there'll be other chances."

"What's the use? What's the use any more?" Louisa moaned, turning her head restlessly as if to escape the secret thoughts that tortured her. "I thought this baby would bring you back to me –"

"I'm here, darling. I'm not going away."

But she moaned and wept, clutching his hand, so that he feared she was delirious; until gradually her sobs quietened, and she fell into an exhausted sleep. For Tom, sleep was far away that night. He loved Louisa as he always had, with protective tenderness, and was racked by the knowledge that she no longer believed it. He had convinced himself once that she would happily survive without him; now, he saw his mistake. Perhaps it was fortunate, after all, that his folly had not been tested; for he and Jess were strong enough to continue their lives apart.

Tom made up his mind to be more attentive to his wife in future, and let her see how much she meant to him.

This resolution was to call on all his reserves of patience. Louisa recovered physically from the miscarriage, but her mental state began to worry Tom. She read avidly whatever she could find, from Scott's novels to the weekly Hampshire Chronicle. This was nothing new; except that for days at a time she seemed wrapped in dreams, and at night, deprived of fantasy, she would groan and mutter in her sleep. She accepted Tom's many small kindnesses with smiles that gave no clue to her thoughts, and only reproached him if he suggested a ride in the Forest, or a visit to friends. She seemed childlike, and somehow lost; and he had not the heart to make love to her.

After a month of this, Tom paid a surreptitious visit to her physician. The man was concerned, but reassuring. "These fits of melancholy are quite common after a miscarriage, and you wife, sir, is a lady of delicate sensibilities. You must be persistent, and ensure that Mrs Elderfield has a full social life. Time, I fear, is the only sure healer – but congenial company may be very beneficial. Indeed it may."

Though Tom followed the doctor's advice, and noticed some improvement in Louisa's awareness of reality, he did not take her to see the Veritys' new baby. Instead he rode alone to West Mills, offered his congratulations to the young couple, and insisted that Trekker must not join *Marshlight* when she sailed next day for Guernsey.

"Your place is here," he told his friend. "God knows, I've taken enough shore leave these past few weeks, when I didn't want to trust Louisa to the servants' care. Now it's your turn."

"Aye, but you can afford to lose a week's money here and there. 'Tis more than I can manage, just now."

"Then take your wages from me, for a change. And I won't hear any arguments. Call it a birthday present for the baby."

Over dinner that night, Tom casually mentioned that Rachel had given birth to a daughter, looking anxiously at his wife to gauge her reaction.

"And Edward sails with you tomorrow," she said wanly. "Poor Rachel will be all alone."

"No, Trekker is staying with her. Won't you try to eat something, darling? The lamb is very tender."

"When will you return?" Louisa asked, pushing aside her full plate.

"Oh . . . within three days. Tuesday morning, probably."

"*Winter Witch* sailed into port today. I saw her from the window. I suppose the cargo has been floated somewhere offshore."

It was unlike her, nowadays, to show curiosity about such details, and Tom felt a lift of hope. Was it possible that at last she was beginning to take an interest in his profession again?

"Mr Bezant must be dreadfully annoyed," she said, "now that the ships arrive separately, instead of in convoy. He has to send his tubmen out four times as often."

"I haven't asked his opinion. Actually it doesn't always work quite like that."

Louisa was obviously awaiting enlightenment, so he went on, "*Winter Witch* has dumped her cargo offshore, right? Fine summer weather, no foreseeable problems. *Escapade* is due in on Monday afternoon, and Bezant has planned to beach both cargoes at once, on Monday night."

"I see," she said. "Yes, it sounds very sensible."

After dinner, Tom stood at the table poring over the chart, calculating the tides and plotting a course to and from St Peter Port. To evade the warships and Revenue cutters, he tried to vary the homeward route with each voyage.

Louisa read the Chronicle, taking a pencil to mark a paragraph now and then. She often underlined or cut out reports of local weddings, or the season's new fashions; even though she seldom attended the former, and never nagged Tom to spend money on having the latter sewn for her. She had not forgotten his plea for frugality.

When the Elderfields retired for the night, the newspaper lay abandoned on Louisa's chair. If Tom had glanced that way, he would have seen the page uppermost which dealt with Southampton and Lymington news, and the editorial note which stated that any person giving information leading to the capture of smugglers would receive the customary reward of £20 per man, plus one half of the value of any contraband seized.

He would have seen that his wife had drawn a small asterisk beside the relevant paragraph; and he would perhaps have thought twice about setting sail the next day for St Peter Port.

CHAPTER TWELVE

Louisa sat alone in the parlour on the first floor, stitching at her embroidery, drawn curtains shutting out the warm night. She could not read, for tonight the real world pressed too close. Tom was not due home until tomorrow morning, but her day had been far from empty without him.

Images of the eventful afternoon crowded unbidden into her mind: the terror of walking along the busy High Street, imagining accusation in every face; the scent of newly cut grass in Mr Locke's cottage garden on the edge of town; the surprise of the maidservant at Louisa's appearance on the doorstep.

Mr Locke had made her welcome, especially when she explained the purpose of the visit. The dapper, eager little man rushed about the room, checking doors were locked and windows fastened. He had been sworn in as a Special Constable only a month ago, and took his duties seriously. Louisa had approached him in preference to a Riding Officer, or the men of Hurst garrison, simply because he knew her father. An observer would assume that she was paying a social call.

"You wish to say . . ." Mr Locke brimmed with excitement; fiddling with a snuff box, straightening a picture, returning a book to a wall-shelf. "You wish me to believe that some forty or fifty men will be on the beach tonight, near Pennington Creek Saltern?"

"I do." Louisa sat demurely, with folded hands, her nervousness well hidden.

"With some two hundred barrels?"

"Yes."

"And you will not tell me how you came by this information?"

"No, Mr Locke. I cannot. I'm sorry."

"And yet the Saltern there is owned by Captain Hicks, your husband's employer. Did Mr Elderfield send you here, to inform on the smugglers on his behalf?"

"No, indeed. He would not be a party to it, if he knew. Mr Locke, if you apprehend forty men tonight, you will owe me eight hundred pounds."

The prospect astounded him. "Madam, we can hardly hope for such a complete triumph."

"I understand that. Ten or fifteen would do, since I am to receive, by law, one half of the value of the cargo."

"By all means," he said faintly.

"My husband must not guess the source of this money. I plan to fabricate some tale of the death of a distant relative."

"You have my solemn assurance, he will never learn of this interview from my lips. Permit me to say, Mrs Elderfield, that you are a courageous lady."

"No," she said, "for don't you encourage the townsfolk to be public-spirited in these matters? Besides, I am merely passing the time of day with my father's friend."

Though Louisa's hand shook on the tambour-frame as she recalled this conversation, she was relieved to have acquitted herself well. She was helping Tom to quit the Trade, to start afresh. Had he not told her that it was really only his financial commitments that kept him tied to the Free Trade?

The ethics of what she had done did not trouble Louisa. She had gleaned something, over the years – mainly from Edward Verity – of how Jack Bezant had once treated Tom. Bezant was an evil man; and as for the rest, it was well known that sentences for smuggling offences were rarely harsh or long, except for the ringleaders.

The sound of distant musket-fire cracked the still night. Louisa froze, listening; and Lizzie the maid, entering the room with Mrs Elderfield's usual supper of strong tea and one oatmeal biscuit, gave a shriek and dropped the tray with a clatter.

Louisa said absently, watching the closed curtains, "Get a cloth, girl, and wipe it up."

"But ma'am – that was guns, ma'am."

"Yes." Louisa had hoped there would be no shooting. "The Preventive Men must be out in force."

"But ma'am, my Harry be out there wi' Mr Bezant tonight."

Louisa paled slightly, laying down her embroidery. "I'm sure that your Harry will come to no harm. The Excisemen do not intend murder, you know, unlike some of Mr Bezant's men. Come, Lizzie, fetch a cloth and clean up that mess at once."

But when she had gone, Louisa rose and crossed to the window, drawing back the curtain a fraction. She saw nothing but her own reflection, large-eyed, the lamplight making a halo around her crimped hair. She heard the muskets again, and shivered in the draught from the window. How often Tom had stood here, studying the clouds, hands deep in his pockets. Well, things would be different now. If her husband watched the weather in future, his concern would be for Mr Ward's new steamer, not for *Marshlight*, or *Bold Intent*, or *Escapade*.

She stood dreaming, hardly aware of the passage of time. The last of the twilight faded, and the night grew black. She turned away from the window at last; but at once there was a sort of commotion from the street below; running footsteps, someone's gasping breath, a hammering on the front door. She heard the butler, Robinson, utter a few startled words, and then Eddie Verity's voice in the hall, breathless and agonised.

"Get . . . Mrs Elderfield. I need to speak to she . . ."

Louisa guessed that he had come to tell her of the arrests. She hurried downstairs, to see Edward leaning exhausted against the door-jamb, and Robinson looking puzzled and irritated at the intrusion.

"Why, Edward," she said, "the hour is late for visiting. I hope your wife has not been taken ill."

"Miss Louisa, please." He had been calling her that ever since his days as the Fordyces' footman. Separated by class divisions, they had never become real friends. Now he stammered slightly, and his eyes were haunted by some nameless horror. "You've got to come wi' I. *Marshlight* . . .

made fine speed. Home early . . . sailed past Hurst an hour ago."

"Dear God," she whispered, clutching at the bannister for support, and knowing what his next words would be.

"Someone informed on the tubmen. There be three men dead, and Jack Bezant were wounded and escaped – he be dying, they say – and Aristo came ashore to help in the fighting, and so did the rest o' *Marshlight*'s crew –"

"Is Tom hurt? Has he been wounded?"

"A musket ball got he in the chest. They say he won't last another hour."

How odd it was, Louisa thought in some detached part of her mind, that she could remain calm, when her husband was dying and she had murdered him, as surely as if she had fired the gun herself.

"Robinson," she said, "I want both horses saddled –"

"The boy be seeing to that. I told he already," said Trekker; and then, despairingly, "Miss Louisa, there ain't much time.'

They rode hard along the dark lane towards Keyhaven and Pennington Creek. The marshes were eerie, with their mounds and ponds and the shells of windmills long disused. On the banks, bramble stems clawed the night sky, like the limbs of gigantic spiders crushed into the salt-grass.

At a barely discernible junction, Trekker said, "Turn off here."

Louisa drew rein. "Here? Is Tom at West Mills, then?"

"Where else be suitable for tending wounded men? Hicks' boathouse?"

His voice sounded wrong somehow, and false. Quite suddenly, Louisa felt the black loneliness of the place. If anyone but Edward had come for her, she would not have trusted them so readily, nor believed the tale of *Marshlight*'s unscheduled return.

"Edward," she said, "are you being honest with me?"

"Miss Louisa," he said, with an edge to his voice that made her heart knock against her ribs, "Why should a smuggler lie to 'ee tonight?"

Now she knew what was happening, and why he had lured her here. She said lightly, starting to guide her horse past him, "Your joke is in poor taste, if my husband is still in mid-Channel. I should like to go home now. Please let me pass."

"I be sorry," he said, "terrible sorry, 'cause I liked 'ee . . . but you ain't going home."

It was not the tone nor the words that frightened her most, but his use of the past tense when he spoke of having liked her. As though she were a memory, and dead long ago.

Louisa screamed, at the same time urging her horse forward; but all at once the lane was full of shadows, men leaping to grab the reins, while someone dragged her roughly to the ground and clamped a bruising hand over her mouth.

A whispered voice said, "Shut your noise, bitch!" And she saw above her a man's dreadful face, with a sabre slash across the forehead, and blood running down his cheeks and into his eyes. "Shall we make an end?" he grated over his shoulder. "The bitch won't stay quiet.'

Another voice, belonging to Nathan Street, her neighbour's butler, said, 'Kiss her with the holly, then. Bezant wants her at West Mills."

For a brief and terrifying instant she saw her captor raise above his head the holly club which was the standard weapon of the tubmen's armed escorts. Then the club fell, and Louisa had time to think that after all it was a quick and easy death, before the darkness took her.

But she had not died, for the gradual awakening brought no visions of either heaven or hell, only the worst headache she had ever known, and the realisation that she was lying on cold flagstones, hands tied behind her back, in a room alive with candlelight and shadows – the living-room at West Mills Cottage.

Men were talking in low voices. Louisa tried to sit up, and groaned as a piercing agony split her head in two. She saw blood on the floor where her head had lain. The voices ceased when she moved.

Eddie Verity knelt beside her, and she squinted up at him. "Edward, make them let me go." A plea without hope. "I won't tell . . . anyone about this . . . if you'll only let me go."

Nathan Street laughed unpleasantly. "Get up, bitch, and talk to Mr Bezant."

Trekker touched her face, his mouth twisting as she

shrank from him in fear. "Miss Louisa," he said, quite gently, "I'll see they don't hurt 'ee too much, if you do what we say. Can you stand?"

She let him help her up, a glimmer of hope born within her now. She would behave herself, and they would punish her and let her go. When Tom came home he would kill them, every one of them, and Edward Verity most of all, for his treachery when she had thought him an ally.

He said, with that haunted look in his eyes, "Do you know why I done this, Miss Louisa?"

She stared bleakly at him, without comprehension, and he held her arm as though afraid she would fall.

"Mr Bezant," he said, "wants 'ee to admit that Tom put 'ee up to it. But I don't believe that, and so I brought 'ee here. To hear 'ee let Mr Bezant know the truth."

Louisa said, trembling in spite of all her prayers for courage, "Tom doesn't know. I swear it – on my husband's life, which is more dear to me than anything in this world."

"Good," said Trekker. He glanced towards the hearth-rug, where a chair stood with its back to her. "She be ready to make confession, sir."

The occupant of the fireside chair said, "Then let her stand before me."

As Eddie Verity led her forward, she became aware that the room was full of men, lounging in corners or perched on the arms of chairs. She wondered inconsequentially where Rachel was; and then she faced Jack Bezant, and forgot all else.

The beachmaster sat hunched and grim, one hand gripping the arm of the chair as though to draw strength from its solidity. His face was not florid now, but grey and curiously waxen, with here and there a smudge of pink, as from a careless application of rouge. His right hand clutched his belly, and faint and sick with horror, Louisa saw that an Exciseman's cutlass or sabre had ripped him open, so that only the clutching hand held back his spilling entrails. So Edward had told one truth; Jack Bezant was indeed dying.

Seeing her, Bezant's mouth curved in a parody of amusement. "So you'd swear on your husband's life, would you? Swear, then . . . before these twelve good men and true . . . to tell the whole truth and nothing but."

Louisa heard rather than saw the men close in around her for a better view, and to acknowledge that the trial was beginning. Only Eddie Verity remained where he was, holding her arm, offering in this way a little of the comfort that he dared not give her in words.

Through and beyond the fear, Louisa knew clearly that whatever happened, she must not allow these evil and misguided men to convict Tom for her own crime.

With head high, she swore the oath. Edward's grip on her arm relaxed slightly, and Bezant watched her face, and waited.

Seeing that he would not interrupt her, she said softly, "My husband's loyalty is to Captain Hicks, and to you all – even you, Mr Bezant, in spite of your cruelty. He has too much honour, you see." Here, she ignored Bezant's sneering look. "He cannot afford to give up the Trade, and so I have acquired, for his sake, the money that will make us free of you, Mr Bezant, and your kind."

There were murmurs from eleven of the jurors. Trekker said nothing, but drew his breath in sharply, and his hand jerked on her arm.

Jack Bezant said, "Seems you were right, men, and I was wrong. I must recommend to the jury . . . against my wishes, and my hopes . . . you return a verdict of Not Guilty on Thomas Elderfield, in his absence . . . unless you find reason to doubt the testimony of this informer."

Nathan Street spoke up. "We were all of a mind with Trekker, sir, before the trial. There's not a man among us that thought Aristo guilty, nor wanted to, for 'tis well known he's more loyal to us than to this bitch."

"Then I must instruct you," said Bezant, in a loud, strained voice, "to find the female defendant guilty as charged. Retire, gentlemen, to consider your verdict."

"With respect, sir," said Nathan Street, "I don't reckon as any of us need to consider. She's guilty, out of her own mouth, of killing three of our men, two of them having wives and children to support, and . . ." He shuffled his feet. "And of causing your own injury, sir."

"My death, in fact."

"What's the sentence, then, sir?"

"The usual," said Bezant, smiling a terrible smile.

"Nothing fancy. Trekker has asked us for that favour, and I grant it willingly."

Louisa, who had stood quietly through all this, now turned to Eddie Verity, her courage momentarily leaving her. "You promised. You said they wouldn't hurt me."

"Nor will they. You'll not have time, Miss Louisa, to feel anything much."

"*No!*" Louisa screamed at him, tearing herself free, shrinking back against the mantelshelf because in every other direction the jurors stood implacable and grim. "I didn't mean it to happen like this. I didn't want anyone to be killed or hurt. If they'd caught you, it would have been enough. Oh God, I didn't mean it . . ."

Nathan Street said, "Want me to shut her mouth now, sir?"

Jack Bezant, smiling still, said, "Thank you, Nat . . . but the rest of her sentence must be carried out first."

These low words cut through Louisa's terror, and her sobbing ceased, hiccupping into precarious calm. She stared at Jack Bezant.

"For God's sake, I cannot bear it. What do you mean to do to me?"

"Do you remember," Bezant said, "a stormy night, this last winter? When your husband . . . took his boat out from here, to salvage a floating cargo? He had a woman to crew for him, and brought her back here afterwards."

"No," she said. "No, it's not true."

"Thought he was faithful, did you? So you've given your life for him, and nothing would please him better."

"You're lying," she whispered; though at his words, the suspicions she had buried since that February night rose like gibbering demons to mock her. "Tom loves me, he would never be unfaithful, and he'd never, never wish me harm."

"Loves you, you say? He was sorry for you, I'll allow that. You stupid whimpering little bitch, he married you because he wanted a woman to come home to, like we all do . . . But you weren't up to being a smuggler's wife. He doesn't stay in this game for the money . . . he loves it. Loves it better than any woman, except maybe one. The one who crewed for him . . . the night he saved the brandy."

Louisa leaned against the mantelshelf. Bezant was right,

of course; what she had done would only set Tom free, to go to Jessica Tandy, the woman he truly loved.

She knew then that she could bear whatever fate Bezant had chosen for her, and bear it with courage and a willing heart. She had told Edward the exact truth: Tom was everything in the world to her. Before he entered her life she had been nothing; he had taught her to face the world with her head high. Perhaps she had asked too much, in asking for his love as well; but without that love, she was still nothing. There was no use in living if loneliness was all she had left.

And what a gesture it would be, to die for his sake, setting him free at last. Bezant would feel no satisfaction in his supposed vengeance, if she showed no fear and did not mind.

She stood upright, tall and straight, and smiled down at Jack Bezant. "You had better kill me, then," she said quietly, "and have done with all this nonsense."

It left him at a loss; she saw the disbelief in his ravaged face; and then his glance slid sideways to Nathan Street, and he murmured, "Do as the lady says."

Eddie Verity, sidling out of the candlelight, saw Street step towards her, picking up a holly club. It seemed that judge and jury held their breath.

Trekker stumbled unnoticed into the bedroom, and shut the door behind him. His wife lay wide awake, round-eyed with horror at all she had heard, her arm around the baby girl.

He knelt beside the bed and leaned forward, pillowing his head on his arms, and then moving to clamp both hands over his ears, his face contorted in anguish as he heard Nathan Street bring the club down again and again, smashing Louisa's skull, continuing long after she must have died.

Rachel Verity watched him in helpless pity, offering no comfort. After what Eddie had done that night, she did not know what comfort she could give him.

CHAPTER THIRTEEN

As soon as *Marshlight* passed Hurst Castle in the light of early morning, the crew saw that West Mills was ablaze. Fearful for the Veritys' lives, Tom did not stay to supervise floating the cargo. He launched the ship's boat, and rowed ashore alone.

Running up the path from the jetty, ignoring the Keyhaven folk who rushed past him with buckets of sea-water, he realised that the cottage was beyond saving.

A figure detached itself from a small cluster of onlookers and came slowly to meet him.

"Trekker! Christ, mate, are you all safe? Rachel? And the baby?"

"Aye. Safe."

Tom felt deep sympathy for his friend. Trekker looked like a man bereaved.

"How did it happen?" he asked.

"I burned West Mills," said Eddie Verity, "and everything in he."

Tom could not believe that Trekker knew what he was saying; until he saw in his friend's smoke-reddened eyes the shadow of some remembered nightmare.

"Burned it?" he echoed, with a glance at the ruin.

"The tubmen were informed against, last night. Ambushed. Bezant and three others be dead. Boxer Corrigan, and a couple of lads from Hordle."

"Oh God. Poor old Boxer. Is it known who peached on them?"

"Aye." Trekker stared at the ground, and then back at the cottage. "The informer," he said, "went to see Locke. The person didn't be knowing, I reckon, that half they Special

188

Constables be smugglers theyselves . . . Not Locke, but when he spread the word around . . . Bezant didn't get no warning till he were down on the beach, and then it were too late . . . but at least he knew the culprit. Bezant sat as judge, afore he died."

Tom's mind made the obvious jump. "Christ, Trekker – you're saying they tried the man and executed him? Here at West Mills?"

"Not a man. A woman. They'd have sold the corpse to the Resurrection Men," said Trekker flatly, "but I wouldn't let they do that. She insisted, you see, that you had nothin' to do wi' peaching on Bezant, so they had to find 'ee not guilty. And she died as brave as anyone ever could."

"Who?" Though Trekker's words made no sense, fear clenched around Tom's heart. He gripped his friend's shoulder hard, and shook him. "Damn it, what's happened? Who's dead?"

Eddie Verity looked straight into his eyes. "Louisa," he said.

Tom stood like stone; then his nerveless hand dropped from Trekker's shoulder. "No," he said.

"She thought you'd leave the Trade once you had the money."

Tom shook his head; he could not accept it, could not believe that Bezant had killed her. When he got home she would be there, the same as ever, coming to greet him with that glad, quiet smile . . .

"I brought she to trial," said Trekker, " 'cause otherwise they'd have laid in wait and killed both of 'ee, for sure."

Looking dazedly at Eddie Verity, Tom saw that it was true; that his friend had led Louisa to her death, and Bezant was gone where no vengeance could reach him.

"You," he said, "I'll see you in hell!" And bounding forward he closed his hands around Trekker's throat. They fell together on to the charred grass, while Eddie Verity writhed and struggled, unable to cry out for mercy.

Two pairs of brutal hands dragged Tom to his feet. He shouted at the newcomers in frenzy, "Let me at him! He's mine! He's mine!"

One of the men, still holding him fast with one hand, used the other to punch him hard in the mouth.

Tom sagged, the world reeling. Through a haze he saw Eddie Verity scramble up and run, with many an agonised backward glance, towards the crowd and safety. A short, stout figure stood in front of Tom, saying tersely, "Bring him to his senses."

A bucketful of water was dashed in Tom's face. He gasped, choking, and Captain Benjamin Hicks, with a satisfied nod, spoke to his two henchmen. "Keep hold of him. Don't let him loose."

Tom stood still, fighting to recover his breath. "You . . . could have stopped Bezant," he said, with hatred. "You . . . could have saved her."

"No, Elderfield. Informers are executed. Those are the rules."

"I'll have your life for this!"

"No, Elderfield," Hicks repeated. "If you avenge your wife's just execution, you will be charged with murder. You know I've the contacts to arrange for that to happen, even in the event of my own death. If you're clever enough to engineer a convincing 'accident', for myself or Verity, someone you care for deeply will soon suffer the same fate. Miss Tandy, perhaps, or her brother, or one of the Vaillants. Take your revenge, if you think it's worth the cost."

"Damn you!" Tom said brokenly. "Damn your eyes!"

"You will appreciate, lad, that your employment with me must be terminated at once. I can't have an agent who hates me." Hicks paused, and said gruffly, with genuine emotion, "You're a good lad, Elderfield. You've done me proud. I'm more sorry than I can say – about your wife, and about everything."

"Go to hell, where you belong!"

Hicks sighed, and turned to the man gripping Tom's right arm. "He needs time to take in what I've said. Give him something to keep him peaceful until the Veritys and I are out of the way. Nothing too savage."

Tom had no chance to resist. He did not see what weapon the man used, and the blow to the back of his head felled him instantly.

He was unconscious before he hit the ground.

Benjamin Hicks walked away between his henchmen. The folk from Keyhaven, running to and fro with their buckets, parted around Tom's prone figure like water around a rock. No one stooped to help him, nor to make sure he was not badly hurt. No one dared.

When the smugglers took the law into their own hands, it did not pay ordinary folk to interfere.

The Men
of Enterprise

CHAPTER ONE

The woman in the pink bonnet clung with both hands to the *Medina's* gunwhale, her large bulk swayed by the motion of the steamer. Discreetly jostling her neighbours for a better view, she frowned at the host of skiffs and ketches that scampered across the waves in Cowes Roads or weaved among the larger yachts gathered off Cowes Castle for the first race. The number of fine folk who had put to sea in tiny, ill-equipped craft, merely to observe the vessels of the Royal Yacht Club at close quarters, was absurd. Few of these intrepid sailors showed any knowledge of seamanship, and many were apparently too drunk to care.

Unimpressed by the sparkling sea, the streamers and ensigns flying, and the discordant jollity of four bands playing at once – one ashore and three afloat – the woman glanced without pleasure at the ship which the *Medina* was towing out of Cowes Roads. *Falcon* mounted twenty-two guns, and her three masts stabbed the brilliant sky; but Lord Yarborough, the popular Club Commodore whose efforts had made this Regatta possible, was perhaps entitled to own the grandest and most luxurious yacht on the Solent.

The woman said loudly to her timid, tightly-corsetted female companion, "If we are to be no more than a tug-boat, and tossed like a salad into the bargain, Captain Knight really has no business charging us five shillings each for the privilege. I shall certainly demand that half the fare be refunded."

The *Medina's* Mate, hearing these words as he was meant to, broke off his conversation with a steward and approached the two ladies.

"Now then, Mrs Fearnehaugh," he said, with the dazzling smile that came easily from long practice, and was part of the job, "I did warn you that the sea would be choppy."

"Why, Mr Elderfield, you are incorrigible." Mrs Fearnehaugh blushed and simpered like a green girl, instead of a woman thirty years married. "I declare you said nothing whatever about it, but pocketed our money with a smile just like that one."

Tom decided against reminding the old harridan of her exact words: that a little breeze and a few silly waves would not prevent *her* from attending the Regatta.

He sketched a bow, and said in a conspiratorial whisper, "Madam, you have found me out. I'm a rogue and a villain, and if Captain Knight knew the lies I tell to attract custom, he would kick me overboard."

"Goodness, how perfectly unreasonable. In that case, Mr Elderfield, I shall perhaps save my complaints for our next excursion – but don't imagine that your dishonesty has passed unnoticed."

"Madam, I stand reproached," he said, and strolled with gritted teeth to the starboard side, exchanging courtesies with several less infuriating passengers along the way.

He had been in the job for two years. After Louisa died he had given up the house in Lymington, selling the contents at auction and banking the proceeds. He had kept only the little rosewood book-carrier, and a miniature of himself and Louisa together in all their wedding finery.

She had been twenty years old when she was killed. He tried to believe that for a time he had made her happy, before Jess came back; but it was the waste that he had grieved for most, and his own heartless folly. He learned then what nothing had ever brought home to him before: that however often he had shown compassion, even risked his life for the people he most loved, he had not once made a real sacrifice for any one of them. Expensive presents did not count; he liked giving them. Even his decision to stay with Louisa had been a pandering to his conscience, that was all.

Louisa had been his only family. He would have sacrificed anything – freedom, health, life itself – to have been able to bring her back. But she was gone, and would never know that he had loved her.

Wanting only to escape from everyone connected with the Free Trade, he had fled to Guernsey. Hélène de l'Erée greeted him warmly, providing physical comfort, a sympathetic ear, and a degree of companionship.

It was not Tom's nature to indulge in protracted self-pity, seeking nothing else to occupy his mind and energy. Before, he had always had the Trade. As a guest in Hélène's house, he took her walking or riding along every cliff path and inland lane south of St Peter Port. During these expeditions, he thought seriously and privately about the future.

Hélène, used to saving her powers of endurance for the bedroom, grew fretful and impatient. "If this is your idea of going into a decline, my Englishman," she said once, "how shall I bear it when you recover your strength?"

Within a month he came home – not to Lymington, but to Cowes. He moved in with Mace Tandy, keeping company with the young shipwright's friends rather than be drawn back into smart society. Whenever Jessica and the twins came visiting Uncle Mace, Tom treated Jess with cool civility, since she wanted nothing more. He did not enquire into her private life. The twins called him 'Mr Elderfield', but here their deference began and ended. Honor was affectionate and full of sparkling mischief. Luke was quieter, less trusting, a touch belligerent – and yet, alone with his twin, not guessing he was overheard, he was as lively and talkative as she.

Tom did not stay on the Island to be near Jess – or so he convinced himself. Yacht owners needed experienced skippers from spring through to autumn, since few of them knew or wanted to learn the first principles of sailing. In winter, he worked on the cross-channel packet boats. Yachts and ferries alike called often at Guernsey, and Tom did not lose touch with Hélène.

In the spring of 1824, *Medina* lost her Mate to a Club yacht, and this time Tom leapt at the chance of a permanent position. During the winters, when steamers did not run, he transferred to a Solent sailing packet.

Working on the *Medina* meant taking rooms in Southampton, where the Island ferry service was based. Though at first Tom missed Mace's noisy exuberance and bursts of intense romantic or political commitment, he made friends on the mainland. Of the fashionable set, he saw only the Vaillants – who now had four sons – and, as often as duty nudged him into it, Louisa's parents.

Now, in the summer of 1826, Tom was ready for change. A partnership with Mace Tandy had been a serious possibility ever since his soul-searching in Guernsey; and sharing rooms with the younger man had convinced Tom of three things. Firstly, that their friendship would withstand the inevitable stormy disputes; secondly, that Mace was as brilliant as Jessica believed – and thirdly, that he could not be trusted with any financial responsibility whatsoever.

Tom had been sure that he would grow up, but Mace was now twenty-three, and signs of responsible behaviour were not much in evidence. If Tom wanted to marry his own modest capital to Mace Tandy's genius, it would have to be soon – before Mace was reckless enough to set up in business on his own, or the likes of Mrs Fearnehaugh drove Tom mad.

During the past fortnight, and without Mace's knowledge, Tom had approached John Ekless, a landowner in Bursledon on the Hamble River. The house and land adjacent to Mr Ekless' own residence had once been leased as a boatyard to Jem Lomer's father, and the slips had not been used since Lomer went bankrupt and moved to Pennington. Now that the house's most recent tenant had died, the lease on the site was vacant, and Tom considered that such an opportunity might not occur again for some time.

An eddy of wind sent smoke swirling down around Tom and the other passengers standing aft of the tall, slender funnel. There was an exodus for'ard, and Tom casually followed the crowd.

In the bows, he stood beside Jem Lomer, the *Medina's* permanent steward. The earnest young scholar had given Hicks his notice after Louisa's death, in loyalty to his skipper. Last year, when Jem grew bored with the life of a lawyer's clerk, Tom had met him wandering on Southampton Quay, vaguely looking for employment, and he had been glad to put in a good word for Jem with Captain Knight.

"Look at that," Jem said, his spectacles glinting indignantly in the sun. "It is bad enough that half the crews of these small craft are inebriated, without allowing children to put to sea in this wind, in a rowing boat. It's iniquitous."

Tom looked where he pointed. A skiff was indeed being rowed across Cowes Roads. Its crew comprised two black-haired children of about nine or ten. They sat side by side, taking an oar each. The girl rowed as strongly as the boy.

From all appearances, they intended to cut across the *Medina's* bows with nothing to spare.

Tom said under his breath, "Bloody hell!"

"Utter folly," agreed Jem Lomer.

"I'll give them folly," Tom said. He shouted into the wind, "Luke Tandy! Honor! Get out of the way!"

They looked at him without alarm. Honor waved a hand, resting on her oar, while Luke steered the boat to starboard. As *Medina* passed them, Luke gave a masterly twitch at the oar to miss the paddle-box by inches. Then the twins' boat scraped along the steamer's hull. Honor scrambled into the bows of the skiff and flung a rope around *Medina's* flagpole, which rose from the stern close to the horizontal hawser towing the *Falcon.*

Tom sprinted aft, elbowing passengers aside in his haste. The last time someone had tried to board while *Medina* was under way, the damned idiots' boat had capsized and they had very nearly drowned.

Standing just for'ard of the flagpole to man the helm, Captain Knight bellowed down at the twins, only the presence of ladies moderating his language, "You little fools – get away from my ship! Mr Elderfield, see to it!"

There was not much that Tom could physically do. The rope attached to the skiff's bows – the painter – was looped neatly around the base of *Medina's* flagpole, and a knot tied where only Luke or Honor could reach it. The tiny craft was being towed helplessly and fast, close into the stern, the short painter stretched taut.

Tom said furiously, "You mustn't board now! Let go the line!"

Honor gazed innocently up at him. "We *are* coming aboard. We've got to. We can't even wait another single day."

"Don't be stupid! We're towing – we can't just stop the engine. Do you want to be killed?"

But it was clear to everyone, including Captain Knight and the passengers crowding aft to witness the drama, that the twins were now unstoppable. Honor Tandy was already climbing the painter. Her feet were against the *Medina's* stern, which overhung the skiff at a difficult angle and rose a good seven feet above the sea – and as the stern lifted and dropped sharply, Honor lost her footing.

She hung on grimly to the rope, feet dragging in the water. She began scrambling for purchase, but her skirts were sodden and heavy; nor would her wet, smooth soles grip the hull.

Luke yelled at her, "Try harder! Try!"

Tom realised that if Honor let go now, she would miss the skiff – and before anyone could help her, the *Falcon* would mow her down.

With a muttered oath he swung his legs over the stern. Grasping the flagpole with his right hand, he braced one knee on the gunwhale and the other foot against the outside of the stern. Mrs Fearnehaugh shrieked at him that she couldn't look, that he would be killed and the child with him. Captain Knight was swearing softly.

Tom leaned down far enough to clasp Honor's wrist. "All right, little one, I've got you." He used all his strength to hoist her up a few inches; his position was too awkward to do much more. "Come on now, climb! Hand over hand. That's my good girl."

As Honor obeyed orders, Tom shifted his grip to her waist.

A steep wave tipped the skiff almost on her beam ends, with Luke clinging to stay aboard. *Medina's* stern reared like an unbroken colt and smacked down, drenching Luke in spray.

The flagpole had not been designed to take such brutal and repeated stress. It splintered at the base, and snapped.

There was barely a split second's warning. Clasping Honor against him Tom let go of the breaking pole, grabbed for the gunwhale, missed; and snatched wildly at the thick hawser towing the *Falcon* as he somersaulted backwards. His right hand clenched on it, gained a momentary grip.

The combined weight of the sturdy little girl and his own tumbling twelve-stone frame jerked his arm straight at a wicked angle, and tore the shoulder out of joint.

He landed beneath Honor in the skiff, with his back twisted and rammed against the stern thwart. He did not even notice. Honor rolled off his chest and knelt up, untangling her legs from the painter and throwing the ensign and broken flagpole overboard. Through slitted eyes he saw her bend over him, her face white and shocked.

"Oh, no . . . Oh, Mr Elderfield."

He clutched the dislocated arm to his side, and clamped his jaw shut to keep from screaming as the skiff bucked and danced.

The gap between the skiff and the *Medina* was widening fast. Knight shouted above the general commotion on deck, "Elderfield! Are you badly injured?"

The *Falcon* bore down towards them. Tom tried to jam his good shoulder against the thwart and his feet against the bottom boards, but the frightful jolting went on and on. Dear God, how did society women manage to faint to order?

He squinted up at Honor. "*Falcon* . . ." He could hardly get the words out. "The Club surgeon . . ."

"Mr Day? Yes, he'll be on board. Have we got to tie up alongside *Falcon*, then?" She sounded both regretful and thoroughly apprehensive.

The skiff bounced over a foaming crest and Tom gave a choked cry of agony. His eyes were shut but he felt Honor pat his knee, heard her shaken, scared voice. "Mr Elderfield?"

"*Just do it!* Oh Christ . . ."

Luke pulled strongly on the oars to avoid being run down by the ship. Tom cradled his right arm in helpless pain, half sitting, half lying against the thwart. Honor wiped the sweat from his face with the hem of her petticoat.

"We're sorry," she said, blue eyes tragic.

"Makes . . . three of us."

"Mama and Lord Wickham were arguing, you see, because he's been telling Mr Ekless bad lies about you, because he doesn't want you to have a boatyard."

"We eavesdropped," put in Luke, glancing up at the faces

peering at them from the *Falcon's* deck. A rope ladder uncoiled itself from the high deck to the sea.

"Yes," said Honor, "and he was so angry, he said who we were. This is the first day we could escape since then, because today everyone was thinking about the Regatta, not watching us, and Lord Wickham is racing in the Gold Cup. We thought the steamer would drop people off at Cowes, but it didn't, because it was only a – only a –"

"Excursion trip," supplied Luke, sullenly.

"We had to see you, Mr Elderfield, to talk about things."

Tom leaned his head on the gunwhale. The child was talking nonsense. He could not bring himself to care much.

She said to Luke, "He doesn't know. He truly doesn't."

"We guessed that."

"Amos wasn't our father," Honor told Tom, with devastating simplicity. "You are."

"I . . . what?"

"And Auntie Jess is our Mama, but that wasn't odd. We've always called her that anyway, even though people in the South think she isn't. Oh, Mr Elderfield – are you fearfully angry? Do you wish it wasn't true?"

"No," he muttered.

He did not know what to think or feel. His children – his and Jessie's. And she had not told him, not even that night at West Mills.

Honor chewed at her lip; then bending forward she kissed his cheek, careful not to jar the injured shoulder. "We're glad it's you," she said, and sat down again very close to him, as if somehow that would make the pain bearable. Her mother's daughter, he thought, and groaned with an anguish that was physical and a lot more besides.

"Look there, we'll be alongside any minute," said Honor Tandy, with distress. "It's almost over, Mr Elderfield. You'll be all right now."

CHAPTER TWO

Their arrival alongside the *Falcon* was only the beginning. Although Mr Day descended to the skiff with alacrity, he pronounced himself unable to reduce the dislocation in such an unstable craft. Having strapped Tom's arm securely, and correctly deduced that the patient could not climb the ladder, he arranged for Tom to be winched aboard.

Tom would not have wanted to endure such an ordeal again. The ascent was far from smooth; but not until his helpless and suspended body swung against the hull did he achieve his wish and pass out.

When he drifted back to reluctant awareness, he was lying on his back, head pillowed on the lap of a woman in a lemon silk gown. He was surrounded by finely dressed folk and uniformed seamen. At his feet the twins stood pale and defiant beside Lord Canon, who was the Commodore's Chief Officer. Tom knew Canon, having served once as a steward aboard the previous *Falcon* in '23, on a short cruise to Lisbon.

"What is the diagnosis, Mr Day?" Lord Canon asked.

Day was kneeling to examine the injury as well as he could through Tom's jacket. Tom gasped in pain at his touch, and felt the silk-clad woman flinch.

"Straightforward displacement," said the surgeon. "No fracture, as far as one can tell."

The woman said, "Surely you'll at least give him brandy, Mr Day, before you set to work?"

Tom's heart jumped; for the woman was Jess.

"Liquor would not take effect immediately," said Day.

"The longer I delay, the more difficult my job will be. If I act now, before the muscles start to cramp, it should take only a few minutes." He looked down enquiringly at the patient.

Tom had no objection. He quailed at the prospect of waiting another twenty minutes or so, even for the sake of getting drunk.

With Day's necessary assistance he sat up and edged back against the steps leading to the foredeck. Better that way, the surgeon said, with a trace of humour. Less undignified than writhing about in front of ladies. Jessica sat above him, with her knee against his sound shoulder. She took his hand as the surgeon began.

Not long, Day had said. A few minutes. For Tom it seemed an eternity of impossible pain; and if hell existed, it was here and now aboard the Commodore's luxury yacht, with Jessica Tandy, whom he had lost forever, holding tightly to his left hand. Tom clenched his teeth and fought to control his ragged breathing; but he clutched Jessica's hand convulsively, and was glad when an officer ushered the twins below. Before the end he rolled his face against the folds of lemon silk, and drew more comfort from Jessica's nearness than he had thought ever to need again.

Day knew his job, however. The bone crunched finally into the socket; the agony receded to a throbbing ache. Tom relaxed with a sigh of inexpressible relief.

"Thank you, sir," he said, letting go of Jessica's hand and glancing up at her. There were tears on her face. "I'm sorry I squashed your fingers, Jess," he said.

"Don't be silly."

Luke and Honor, he thought. His own children.

It was nearly time for the first race, the Gold Cup. With the exception of Lord Canon, the crowd was drifting away to watch. Day, eager to join them, gave Tom a last perfunctory examination and a sling which he was forbidden to take off.

"Don't use that arm for at least two weeks," Day said sternly. "There's a considerable amount of damage to the ligaments and so forth. Give them a chance to heal. No more heroics, unless you want a repeat of today's trifling inconvenience."

After the surgeon had gone, Tom slowly picked himself

up. Now that the shoulder injury had stopped blotting out every other discomfort, he felt bruised all over; and when he stood upright his strained back muscles locked in an excruciating spasm.

It took his breath away. Jessica exclaimed in concern, and Lord Canon said dryly, "Since you are patently unfit to report for duty, Elderfield, I shall signal *Medina* to that effect. Lord Yarborough will be coming aboard shortly. I know I may speak for him in saying you have earned our hospitality." He regarded Tom's soiled and crumpled *Medina* uniform with disfavour. "You may borrow a spare Club uniform from one of my crew. Perhaps you would care to wear it when lunch is served." The suggestion came somewhere between a question and a command.

"I'll be honoured, sir. Thank you very much."

Canon paced in leisurely fashion to the port side. Jessica said coolly, "We must talk. I have a cabin reserved for my use today."

"A pity to miss the race," Tom said, and raised a lop-sided grin at her look of exasperated disbelief. "Marvellous inventions, yacht races, for occupying the mind."

The seven great yachts slipped their moorings at the second gun, fired by Lord Yarborough from a cutter lying off the Castle. Luke and Honor appeared from below decks, and sidled warily to the guardrail beside their mother. Jessica bent and whispered to Honor, who at once protested.

"I *have* said I'm sorry, and I am. I can't keep saying it all day, can I, Mr Elderfield?"

"Very boring," he agreed, meeting Jessica's eyes to silence her intended retort. "No real harm done, Jess. I've had worse backache lugging brandy kegs for Bezant." Which was not altogether true, but Honor had given herself a nasty experience and a bad fright, and her motives had not been mischievous. Maybe she had been punished enough.

"Mr Elderfield," said Luke fiercely, determined not to be left out, "I'll bet you twopence that Lord Wickham founders!"

His mother snapped, "Stop showing off!"

Tom kept his thoughts to himself and watched the race. The wind had dropped slightly; was light enough to ensure that the yachts made use of every square foot of canvas. The dipping, bounding hulls were dwarfed and at times invisible beneath shimmering acres of sailcloth. The 160-ton favourite ran temporarily aground near the start, and could not make up for lost time; but Wickham's ageing cutter *Xanadu* was still lying sixth.

Tom was awed by the beauty of the spectacle, but his nagging aches refused to be ignored. He felt more relief than disappointment when Jessica said, sounding tense and irritable, "All right, you've seen the start. I must speak to you, Tom, it's important. There will be races all week."

The twins were busy cheering *Xanadu* towards an inglorious defeat. Jessica warned them to bear in mind that they were already in disgrace before she led Tom below.

Falcon's interior decoration, discounting the gun deck, suggested not so much a yacht as a floating stately home. Jessica's allotted cabin was light and spacious. It came complete with a hearth, drawing room furniture as well as a wide bunk, and bulkheads adorned with framed maritime prints.

Tom sat on a crimson-striped chair without being invited. Jess leaned on the closed door, looking pale but determined, braced for battle.

"Are you seriously intending to lease that boatyard from Mr Ekless?" she said.

It was hardly the expected question, but Tom said with certainty, "Yes, if Mace is as keen as I am. I haven't mentioned it to him yet."

"Lord Wickham is an acquaintance of John Ekless. Not a close friend. Mr Ekless is a good man, he won't let his mind be poisoned against you. I've spoken to him. You'll get your boatyard, if you want it."

"Good! But I don't see why it matters to Wickham either way – nor to you, at this moment. You know, don't you, why the twins rowed out to *Medina*?"

"Oh, better than you do." There was no joy in her smile. "Luke confessed while I was shaking the daylights out of him, just before you were winched aboard unconscious. He said they would have asked you, as their father, to fight a duel with Lord Wickham, and kill him, because, of course, a famous smuggler was bound to be an excellent shot."

206

Tom was in no mood to laugh at the absurdity of the idea. "What has his precious lordship done to my children, to earn their hatred?"

Jessica moved from the door, hugging herself as though for warmth. She stood with her back to Tom, gazing through the closed porthole at *Xanadu* on the horizon.

"You were not totally wrong about him," she said. "In his youth he was dissolute, amoral. I'm sure he sampled every possible avenue of what he would term pleasure. He gave up those pursuits long before I met him. He's in love with me – I don't know how to make you understand. He doesn't care if I'm seen with another man in the street, or at a function like this. He's jealous of no one except you, because you are the only other man I ever loved, and once, before I knew him fully, I was honest enough to tell him so. He would prefer that Mr Ekless refuses you the lease. He would prefer to see you trodden underfoot, with nothing at all."

She paused, seeming to wait for some reaction; but Tom watched her averted profile, and said nothing.

"It took me a long while to see," she said, "that he hated Luke and Honor, simply for being a part of you and me. Many men beat their children – but the twins are not his. He beats them as if – as if he imagined they were you." A bleak silence, heavy with memories that Tom could not share. "He's too strong. I've fought him . . . but I can't stop him."

It was a minute or two before Tom could say, "Then how in God's name can you stay with him?"

"That's between Lord Wickham and me. It's no business of yours."

"No *business* –" Tom surged to his feet, and almost cried out with the pain in his back and shoulder. He leaned weakly against the bulkhead. "God damn it, Jessica Tandy, my son and daughter are my business! I've a right to know why their mother has shut me out of their lives all these years, and why she stands by and sees them ill-treated –"

Jessica whirled on him, shouting to drown his words. "Why else have I brought you down here? I'm sick of standing by – and I won't let you destroy us!"

"What the hell does that mean?"

"Nothing will keep you from our children now, will it? Lord Wickham will believe that you're using them as an excuse to enjoy my company. I don't know what he'd do to them if he believed that."

"If you've such a low opinion of me, that you think I'd let him lay another finger on them, you can bloody well think again!"

She was no longer angry. She said with a sort of hopelessness, "My opinion of you has not changed much, over the years. That's why I want you to take our son and daughter, and bring them up where Lord Wickham can't hurt them."

Now he was speechless; for surely no woman could give up her children to a father they hardly knew. Unless the alternatives were to live in fear, or flee into friendless exile for the second time in her life.

Suddenly Tom no longer cared about holding on to his pride, if there was the faintest hope of winning Jessica back.

He said quietly, "There's a house on the Bursledon site, Jess. The master bedroom is too big for one person. I never thought I'd ask you this again . . . Will you marry me, Jessie, and live with me in Bursledon?"

"No," she said, quite calm now. "I won't come back to you, Tom Elderfield. I'll never do that. My place is with Lord Wickham, and always will be. Won't your vanity let you accept that I'm not in love with you any more?"

"You cried for me, when Day put my shoulder back."

"Then give me credit for an ounce of common humanity! I'd have wept for the devil himself in such a plight." She drew breath as though taking in strength and courage from the air. "When you and Mace become partners, and move into that house, then you may snatch the twins. My only condition is that Lord Wickham must never know I was involved. Will you do it, Tom . . . for old times' sake, and for Luke and Honor?"

"Yes," he said, "as a short-term solution. I can't say more than that." He could not believe, in fact, that even his Jess was strong enough to give her children up for ever, in exchange for the love of a jealous and possessive man.

Her shoulders slumped, though whether in relief or wretched misery he could not tell.

"I'd better show my face on deck," she said. "Stay here, Tom, if you like. It might help to lie down for an hour or two."

He no longer felt that he knew her at all. How could she crucify him in one breath and mother him in the next?

"I think," he said, "I ought to spend the day getting to know my son and daughter."

At the Commodore's table, in a wardroom that buzzed with the conversation of more than forty guests, Tom found himself seated almost next to Lord Yarborough and opposite his elder son, the seventeen-year-old Charles Pelham. The Commodore had insisted that Tom join them, and he made a point of introducing him to everyone at the table. Most knew Tom already – either from the *Medina* or from society functions in the old days. There was evidently doubt in several minds as to the social standing of a steamer's Mate who had once been related to the Fordyces. To Tom's embarrassment, the problem was solved by his being treated simply as a hero, and a well-meaning lady next to him cut up his steak and vegetables.

It was Lord Yarborough himself who came to his rescue by changing the subject. "And what do you think of our Regatta this year, Mr Elderfield?"

Tom turned to him with grateful relief. Lord Yarborough's eyes shone with good humour; the day had so far been a total success and a personal triumph for the Commodore.

"I find the view from this ship rather . . . elevated," he said, with faint emphasis. "Luckily, my lord, I'm not afraid of heights."

Yarborough beamed appreciation, and smoothed his whiskers. "Lord Canon has been in communication with Captain Knight. You must report for duty when *Medina* docks at Cowes the day after tomorrow. Tonight you will be set ashore in the town, as will all my guests. These gentlemen have rooms at the hotel in East Cowes, and I'm sure would be happy to accommodate you –"

He was interrupted by murmurs of assent from the young men at the table, and glasses were raised in Tom's direction.

Tom said warmly, "It's very good of you – all of you – but I'll be staying with a friend tonight. Miss Tandy's brother."

"Ah, of course." Yarborough clicked his fingers at a sudden recollection. "You suggested once that I recommend that young rogue for employment. I hope you know that Mr White despairs of him. Calls him a drunken libertine and the bane of his life. Also a genius. Which do you call him, sir?"

"The most promising young designer on the Wight, my lord. I'm no expert on yacht construction, but I was weaned aboard vessels built for speed and manoeuvrability. Mace Tandy's ideas are practical and tremendously exciting." Tom drew a deep breath and added, on an inspired impulse, "That's why I'm going into business with him. My experience and capital, and Mace's talent. A winning partnership, wouldn't you say, my lord? Together we'll build the fastest yachts on the Solent."

"You are very sure of yourself, Mr Elderfield. Where is this famous yard to be situated?"

"Bursledon, my lord, where a bend in the river gives shelter from the sou'westerlies."

Yarborough grunted, apparently unimpressed. "Forget your grand notions, young man. These are bad days for local shipbuilders."

"Yes, if one depends on Navy contracts. But look around you." Tom waved his fork at a porthole. "The crowds must be three or four hundred per cent up on last year. A great many of those spectators are people with money to spend. Haven't I heard that you've a waiting list of gentlemen falling over themselves to join the Royal Yacht Club? It has to be the fastest growing sport in the country."

"Bravo!" This, rather surprisingly, came from young Charles. "I have been nagging my father all summer – have I not, Papa? – trying to convince him of exactly those facts. If I can only persuade him, you may build me a forty ton flyer for next year's Regatta. There, sir, your first commission!"

There was general laughter. Tom was disinclined to take the offer as a joke. His heart was beating against his ribs.

"After such a vote of confidence," he said lightly, eyeing Lord Yarborough, "perhaps you'd be interested to see Mace Tandy's designs. If your son is thinking of a racer, my lord, I'd guarantee he could not do better than commission it from the yard of – of Elderfield & Tandy."

The Commodore's eyes narrowed, almost disappearing among wrinkles. "You rant, Mr Elderfield, like a gypsy marketeer. Fast and fanciful words, as elusive as the breeze."

"The drawings, my lord, would vindicate me."

Yarborough hesitated, looking about to reply in caustic vein. Then he shrugged, and smiled broadly. "I shall expect both yourself and Mr Tandy in my main cabin tomorrow before lunch, at noon precisely."

Tom held the Commodore's twinkling gaze, trying to breathe slowly and naturally. Steady, mate, he thought with rueful mockery; this is just the start. You've no yard and no partner – and you're a long way yet from signing a contract with the Commodore of the RYC.

"My lord," he said, "we'll be there. You may stake your life on it."

"I'll not go so far as that, thank you, Mr Elderfield," said Yarborough, still smiling. "You are the risk-taker among us, after all."

CHAPTER THREE

Mace Tandy opened his door with one hand, while shrugging the other into the sleeve of a greatcoat; and he yelled with joyous relief at the sight of the visitor on the dark landing.

"Tom! Mrs Gribble said you'd been half killed, the blood-thirsty old crone! I'll tell her to her face –"

"Do you fancy letting me in?"

"What? Hell, yes – come and sit down, mate. I've just got home myself, only stayed for a bite. I was off out again to look for you. Is that arm broken?"

"No. I damaged my shoulder a bit."

"Mrs Gribble . . . I'll gag her with her best blue garters."

Mrs Gribble was the wife of the baker, Mace's landlord. She was plump and rosy and by no means a crone. For five years, in between his other pursuits and conquests, Mace had wooed her with unlikely compliments and astonishing insults, all of which made her laugh. If he knew the colour of her garters, he had been studying the washing line.

Tom walked slowly to sit on the nearest chair. Mace's two rooms with their shabby furniture, cluttered surfaces and pervading smell of new bread still felt more like home than Tom's Southampton lodgings.

"Orange walls?" he asked doubtfully, looking around.

"Subtle amber. Whitewash, carrot juice and rose-hip syrup."

"Breeding fruit-flies, then, are you?"

"Life is colour, mate. Colour is life." Mace threw his greatcoat on the table, narrowly missing a chunk of cheese. The lamplight quivered. A wooden vase rocked perilously, and dead rose petals wafted to the floor. "Black for mourning," he added. "White for shrouds."

"Also sails. Also the name of your employer."

"The best exceptions make the world go round."

"Only in a perfect world."

Mace laughed, and retrieved a bottle of geneva from beside the couch. "God, it's good to see you! Talking of perfect worlds, what about this morning? The big cutters, the first ever Gold Cup. White gave us an hour off. Power to the innovators, eh? Glory to the brave!"

"For ever and ever, amen." Tom shifted to ease his back, and got a vicious reaction from the injured shoulder.

"Ouch," said Mace. "Stay the night."

"I was going to ask. *Medina* sailed without me."

"Must have seen you coming. The ghost of Hamlet's father."

"Tandy the diplomat."

"So what's the story from the horse's mouth?"

Tom gave him a brief and wearily flippant version of the incident. Mace's imagination seemed to be filling in the details. He winced and poured Tom a full glass of geneva, saying with tolerance, "Those half-witted brats, I'll skin them alive. What's *Falcon* like, below decks? Sumptuous, I'll bet."

Tom said neutrally, "Why didn't you tell me they were mine?"

Mace froze, then groaned and ran a distracted hand through his hair. "Damn it, Jess made me promise. I never felt so bad about anything. How did you find out? Not from the twins?"

Tom was not unwilling to confide in Mace. The young man listened in frowning stillness, sitting backwards on a chair to face Tom across the table, with arms folded on the chair-back and chin resting on his knuckles.

At last he said, "Jess would have sent the twins away to school, if she didn't know how miserable they'd be, cooped up inland. And if she didn't need Wickham's money to do it. Still, she's been considering farming them out to a childless couple. She must think they'd be better off with their father, now they know who he is."

"Then why didn't she tell me months ago – years ago?

None of it makes sense. How can she go on loving that bastard Wickham?"

"You bloody fool," said Mace. Then, seeing Tom about to respond angrily, he leapt up with a muttered, "Hellfire!" and pushed the chair noisily under the table. "Time to break a promise. You're right – one imperfect world, one imperfect brother. Jess expects too damned much."

"What promise?"

Mace studied the ceiling, heels slightly off the floor, lanky frame stretched upward, hands clasped behind his head. After a couple of seconds he relaxed with a sigh, the decision made. He pulled out the chair and slumped on to it, reaching for his glass.

"I do know," he said, "what happened between you and Jess at West Mills – just the outcome, not the details, so don't turn volcanic. She was angry, bitter, let down. I, er . . . thought she was a bit hard on you, to be honest."

"None of your business, of course."

Mace grimaced. "Tandys stick together. You used to be like one of us – more than Obadiah. You should be glad Jess had someone to turn to, and trust. I'm on your side as much as hers. What bloody more do you want?"

A feather bed, Tom thought, would be nice. It had been a long day. He could feel his temper fraying like an old rope sawing on the edge of a pier, even though he knew Mace was in the right.

He took a gulp of geneva. "Sorry, mate. No excuses."

"Pax, then. Jess went to Wickham, but she didn't love him then, and she doesn't now. She forgave you bloody years ago."

"She didn't pull any punches this morning."

"Hellfire – can't you see it yet? Last time you fell foul of a man with influence, it cost you your wife, your career, your home, and the friendship of your best mate. When you sailed for Guernsey in '22, Jessie sobbed her heart out in this room, thinking you needed her and she couldn't go to you. She'd marry you tomorrow, you blind idiot, but Wickham would wait his chance and grind you into the dirt. He's virtually spelt it out to her, more than once."

Tom felt physically winded. Jessie still loved him, would be his wife tomorrow, if only . . .

"Mace," he said, his voice hoarse, "has Wickham ever threatened Jessie's life? Would she be in danger if she came back to me?"

"No. Not from the way Jess talks about him. He'd crack the opposition, namely you, and win her back with threats if all else failed." He regarded Tom with searching intensity. "She won't marry you. No matter what you say to her."

"What do you take me for?" Tom said softly; and even to his own ears his voice sounded dangerous. "You and Jess – do you think I'll let the woman I love sacrifice herself on Wickham's sodding altar? Just so that I can live in some fools' bloody paradise, with nothing to fear? My God, you must think I'm a craven bloody milksop if you've found it necessary to wrap me in cotton-wool ignorance for four years. I want a single-masted gig, Mace Tandy, about thirty feet overall length, and I want it in Cowes Roads tomorrow night by eleven o'clock."

Mace's initial gaping disbelief had been replaced by the beginnings of comprehension. An unholy light kindled in his dark eyes. He said with awe, "Consider it done."

"Jess and Wickham are invited to the Club dinner tomorrow evening, across the river in East Cowes. There'll be a firework display on this side of the river, on the Parade. I want the twins to see it with their Uncle Mace. Can you organise that?"

"Nothing easier. What happens then?"

Tom enlightened him, working it out as he went along.

"Long bloody odds," said Mace finally.

"Yes."

"You could be thrashed to a pulp . . . or worse."

"So could you, if we stand together."

"The difference being," said Mace, "that you're half pulped already."

"Bring on the violins."

Mace grinned wolfishly, and raised his glass. "Polish your boots and settle your debts. Here's to a fair wind for Southampton."

Tom said nothing that night about the forthcoming interview with Lord Yarborough, nor about the proposed partnership. He did not feel equal to a lengthy and excitable discussion.

The spare bed was a lot less comfortable than he remembered. He had ample time to finalise plans for abductions and boatyards.

In the morning he brought Mace up-to-date on the latter, while trying to dredge up the energy to get out of bed. Mace, tousleheaded and unshaven, his shirt untucked, stood with a shoe in one hand and a hunk of bread in the other, stunned into rare immobility.

"You'd really do that?" he asked. "Invest your money in me?"

"Equal partners, equal contribution. Different currency, that's all."

"What if I can't come up with the goods?"

"For Christ's sake, Mace, you've been aiming for a chance like this since you were old enough to lift a pencil. You've spent the last five years convincing us all that you're a genius."

Mace disconsolately dropped the shoe and rammed his foot into it. "Quite a cauldron brew, wasn't it? Hot air and hope, with a pinch of dedication. Hubble bubble. Serve to all comers. Induces faith in your friends, and indigestion in your enemies. The wizard had symptoms of both in childhood, and is now immune."

If there was one fact of life that Tom had thought proven beyond doubt, it had been Mace Tandy's invincible self-confidence.

A prone position was not ideal for exerting authority. Tom inched his way to a sitting position and gradually swung his feet to the floor. He wore only a pair of undertrousers, and his right shoulder was blue and purple and badly inflamed. Mace forgot his own troubles momentarily.

"I'll book those violins," he said.

The coming night seemed a long way off. "Finish dressing," Tom said. "Go to work. Don't say anything to White, except that you're invited aboard *Falcon* at twelve. Find the hull design you never showed him. I'll stay and do the figurework this morning – we'll need to quote a competitive cost per ton. Be back here at eleven to wash and change. Maybe you'd lend me a clean shirt."

Mace said fiercely, "What happened to equal partners?"

Tom stood up, holding on to a chair. "D'you trust my judgement?"

"Does the Free Trade turn all its sons into bloody autocrats?"

"I say we can succeed. I know that you're talented enough to scale the heights. Believe it, partner! We're going to win."

Mace hesitated, then tore at the dry bread with his teeth; a gesture of bravado, half angry. "Mount Olympus," he said with his mouth full, "Here I come."

The Commodore's main cabin was built high in the stern, with a row of sash windows giving a breathtaking panorama of the bustling Solent. Sunlight followed shadow across the great mahogany desk as the anchored *Falcon* swung gently with the tide.

Standing a little away from the desk, Tom regarded his prospective partner as Mace leaned on the spread drawing and prodded it with an eager finger. "This is what makes the difference," Mace was saying, with an upward glance at the intent faces of Lord Yarborough and his two young sons. "See how the stern slopes back slightly to the waterline? That's what creates the streamlined shape which –"

"Yes, of course," said Charles, with a shining look at his younger brother. "It is bound to cut down water resistance – and the whole shape of the hull is much –"

"In every other respect," said Yarborough, frowning, "there's a definite resemblance to the lines of the new *Vigilant* commissioned for the Revenue Service two years ago."

"Yes, my lord." Mace stood up straight. "She was built at White's, as you know. I threw in a few ideas – not many were used, and I don't think now they deserved to be. But I've tried to learn from *Vigilant's* success as a fast cutter – and her disadvantages."

Yarborough studied him narrowly, and Tom's stomach fluttered with nerves. He could not help wondering whether Mace in his best attire looked too theatrical to be taken seriously, with his russet tail-coat, pink waistcoat and blue glass cravat pin.

"I have heard of no disadvantages," said Yarborough mildly.

"*Vigilant* is clinker-built, with the planks of the hull overlapping and –"

"I am, in point of fact, aware of the definition."

Mace swallowed, and glanced at Tom. It was obvious that his voice had failed, along with his confidence.

"Mr Tandy believes," said Tom, "that a carvel-built hull, being smooth, would make better speed through the water. I skippered Captain Hicks' lugger *Marshlight* for nearly five years. She was carvel-built, and as nifty a vessel as any in those days. I agree wholeheartedly with Mr Tandy."

The Commodore stroked his whiskers. He looked directly at his elder son. "You've heard what Messrs Elderfield and Tandy have to say, Charles."

Charles and Dudley Pelham expressed their enthusiasm almost in unison.

"It does make sense, Papa –"

"Everyone who is anyone has a flyer nowadays –"

"Yes, yes. Spare me the rest." Yarborough sent Tom a twinkling look. "I've heard of nothing else but flyers since luncheon yesterday. For my part, I must confess that a cost of fifteen pounds per ton – though I have not enquired yet for other estimates – still sounds a trifle excessive. This vessel," he added, thumping an affectionate fist on the panelled bulkhead, "was contracted for ten shillings less."

"*Falcon's* construction costs were fixed two years ago, my lord." said Tom. "This summer, even second-hand yachts are fetching more than eleven pounds a ton."

Charles Pelham cleared his throat, and said nervously, "I, er . . . have asked for two other estimates, Papa. The lowest was fifteen pounds and five shillings."

Tom said quickly, "Wherever you enquire, my lord, I doubt that you'll find our price can be undercut by any competitor."

Yarborough nodded slowly. "Your timber will be supplied by Monsieur Vaillant of Lymington, you say?"

"Yes. M'sieur Vaillant and I are old friends. I know that he'll offer a good price. That's how I can afford to drop as low as fifteen pounds."

"Capital. Capital." Yarborough rubbed his hands, and beamed at Tom and Mace. "I may have misled you. I have made a few preliminary enquiries since yesterday. I suggest that we meet again, gentlemen, when you have leased a yard, made your intentions clear to Mr White and Mr Ward, and worked your notice. We will then draw up a contract. In the meantime, we are bound by a gentlemen's agreement, the single proviso being that the yacht must be completed in time for next year's season. Shall we look to a Mayday launching-party?"

Tom and Mace were not slow to accept the terms. They were invited to celebrate their first commission with another free lunch aboard *Falcon*; and it was only later, as a hired boatman rowed them back to Fountain Quay, that Tom's sense of euphoria began to die a little.

Seated next to him in the stern, Mace said, his eyes sparkling with elation and good wine, doubts temporarily abandoned, "This is it, then. The start of a new era. Hah!" He leaned back, stretching his arms up as though to reach literally for the sun. "Sweet existence! Sweetest day!"

"Pray to God and Lady Luck," said Tom, not quite in jest, "that we live to see sweet tomorrow."

CHAPTER FOUR

Luke and Honor Tandy sat facing their uncle, watching him pull hard on the oars to guide their precious skiff expertly through a dark maze of yachts and anchor chains. The twins had never seen so many boats anchored in Cowes Roads. The water glimmered with light from deck-mounted lanterns and sometimes a distant burst of laughter would carry clearly on the night air.

"How will you find your friend's boat?" Honor asked Mace.

"With consummate skill," he said.

Honor peered round him to where her father sat in the bows but Elderfield was gazing out across the Roads, his thoughts evidently far away. He had not said much since meeting them after the fireworks display on the Parade. She wondered if he was scared; but of course that was ridiculous. Mr Elderfield was not afraid of anything.

She nudged Luke and they grinned at one another, sharing their excitement without the need for words. They had been told the plan. Mr Elderfield was not going to let them down after all; and with a little luck, they would never see the horrible Earl of Wickham again.

The skiff approached an unlit sailing vessel with the name *Marianne* painted in yellow along her hull. Mace stowed the oars and reached for *Marianne's* gunwhale, holding the skiff firmly alongside, and the twins climbed nimbly aboard the gig.

Tom moved to the skiff's stern to correct the boat's balance. He frowned up at the twins, adopting a tone of grim authority. "You know your orders, don't you?"

"Make her ready for sea," said Honor, "and then wait."

"I want no nonsense, you understand? Never mind how long we're away, or whether you're afraid of missing the tide. You don't weigh anchor for any reason at all. Is that clear?"

"Yes, Mr Elderfield," they said.

"And try not to damage anything. Your uncle's mate wants his boat back in one piece."

Luke scowled but Honor said, with laughter and wickedness, "We don't damage boats. Only people!"

Mace was still chuckling as he pulled away from *Marianne* and headed for the East Cowes riverbank.

"What are you laughing at?" Tom said irritably. "She's old enough to have learned better manners."

Mace regarded his friend assessingly. He knew that Tom had spent much of the day working out finances, first for Yarborough and then for the new partnership, scribbling right-handed the figures which would make Elderfield & Tandy a reality. He no longer wore the sling but kept his right thumb hooked casually in his belt, preferring not to show Wickham an Achilles' heel.

Resting a moment on the oars, Mace drew a small leather flask from his waistcoat pocket and handed it to Tom. "Compliments of the best designer on the Island," he said.

The flask contained neat Hollands gin. Tom said with gratitude and reluctant amusement, "You are truly a genius."

"We can still turn back. You could set sail with the twins –"

"And what if Wickham finds out about yesterday? Jessie and me, alone together in a cabin on the *Falcon*."

"He won't hurt Jess."

"He won't get the chance!"

They moored the boat to a small jetty near a row of boat-houses and made their way towards the hotel, where members of the RYC would be gathered to see the week's prizes presented. The streets were not quite deserted; a few young folk still lingered in the hope of glimpsing more fireworks across the river.

As Tom and Mace climbed the steps outside the hotel, one of the two doormen barred their way.

"Members and guests only, gentlemen. Just for tonight."

"Come on, George," said Mace. "You know me. I need to talk to my sister and Lord Wickham. Desperately urgent. Life or death!"

George looked sceptical. "You're still not coming in – but I'll fetch them, as it's you."

While he was gone, Tom retreated to the foot of the steps. After some hesitation Mace joined him; this was not the night for provoking a physical attack.

The door swung open; the steps were bathed in light and music. Jessica rushed from the hotel ahead of Wickham and George, having taken her brother's dire message literally. "Macey, what has happened? Are the twins –"

She saw Tom then, and stopped dead. The shock in her face told him that she had guessed half the truth; that he was taking the twins away. Before he could speak, the Earl of Wickham stood beside her on the top step.

"Elderfield," he said dryly, "what a delightful surprise. I hope you can produce a good reason for having disturbed our evening."

He was a man whose looks had improved with the years, gaining distinction from silvered temples and side-whiskers. He was also tall, fit and trimly athletic. Tom hoped fervently that the encounter would be, as he intended, strictly a verbal battle.

"You might care to know," Tom said, "that I'm taking my children off the Island tonight. Will you sail with us, Jess?"

"No!" Her shock at losing the twins so suddenly was overlaid by horror. She clung to Wickham's arm as though to assure him of her loyalty. The two doormen were enthralled.

"We should have been wed ten years ago, Jess. Are you going to keep me waiting another ten?"

"Go away! If you have Luke and Honor, then I – I can't stop you taking them anywhere. Just go away and leave us alone!"

"Not very convincing, Jessie."

Wickham drawled, "We have nothing to discuss with you on that subject, Elderfield. Now, if you will excuse us . . ." He turned to steer Jessica into the hotel.

"I believe Lady Wickham suffers from a delicate constitution," said Tom, "and rarely leaves your Hampshire estate. I hope it wouldn't distress her to see your past made public in the local press – and among your fellow yachtsmen."

Wickham spun on his heel. He gripped Jessica's wrist as if she might flee at any moment, but she did not move. Her eyes were flickering in despair from Tom to her brother and back again.

"Oh Tom, don't do this," she moaned. "Macey, stop him –"

The Earl hissed, "If this is blackmail, Elderfield –"

"It's whatever you make of it."

In fact Tom knew nothing specific about Wickham's past, but the Earl could not be sure of that. The Yacht Club enjoyed considerable royal patronage, and a member who brought dishonour on the Club could expect neither protection nor mercy from Lord Yarborough. Keeping a mistress, however thinly disguised as a family friend, had done Wickham no harm; but his vices had not always been so innocuous . . . and the Earl valued his membership highly.

He said, with icy calm, "Mace, you and I have no quarrel. I advise you to leave, before you become involved in a matter which need not concern you."

Mace decisively shook his head. "I'll stay, thank you."

"I won't give up now, Wickham," Tom said. "I'm offering Jess marriage and a safe home for our children. What can you offer?"

Wickham said nothing for a long minute. Tom returned his stare, unwilling to be the first to look away. What he saw in Wickham's face made him shiver in the warm night. Surely Jess must realise that he had set her free; that he would never again be safe from Wickham's wrath, whatever path she chose. He had made certain of that.

"Elderfield . . ." Wickham spoke his name like a curse.

"My lord," Jessica interrupted him. "Please let me go."

Taking her literally, as perhaps she had meant, he dropped her arm. His gaze had not wavered from Tom.

Jessica did not speak to him again. She descended the steps quite slowly and gracefully and Tom blinked at her, not believing even now that he had won.

"You fool, Tom Elderfield," she said.

He smiled slightly and took her hand, not caring to show his feelings too much with the Earl of Wickham as audience.

"Welcome home, Jessie," he said.

The streets were emptying as they hurried back towards the river. Tom and Mace glanced over their shoulders often, anticipating trouble. The plan had gone almost too smoothly. Tom's instinct for danger had become highly developed during the years with Hicks and he was aware that he was slowing the others down. The injury to his back made running impossible.

As they turned into the alley between the boathouses, Mace said, "Want me to scout ahead?"

"Might be wise. I don't think we were followed, but –"

"Easy enough for his lordship to nip down another alley-way and cut us off."

"Be careful, Macey," said Jessica. When her brother was out of earshot she turned to Tom with more anxiety than joy. "You're both mad," she said. "Why do you think I never threatened to leave him? He'll break you, Tom, he'll find some way –"

"Say you love me, Jessie."

"Oh Tom, you don't know what you've done."

"Jessie . . . please say it."

She drew a shaky breath, and said, with a catch in her voice, "I grew up loving you, didn't I? Old habits are so hard to break."

From the darkness behind them a man said, "How very touching."

Tom swung round, holding Jessica close to his side, instinctively leaving his right hand free. Wickham strolled out of the shadows. Beside him walked a younger man whom Tom recognised as Sir Bevis Ponsonby, one of the Earl's London set.

Mace, striding into view from the direction of the river, swore aloud and ran to his partner's side, glaring at Wickham and Ponsonby.

"Need some help, mate?" he asked.

Tom sent him a warning look and said to Wickham, "Is there something you forgot to say?"

"Among gentlemen, it is customary for an affair of honour to be settled in private, not in front of a pair of gaping doormen. And discretion is of course vital, since duelling is illegal –"

Jessica cried out, "Duelling?" and Mace said, "Pistols at dawn? Don't be bloody stupid."

"I suggest," said Wickham, ignoring them, "that we meet tomorrow at first light. Sir Bevis will act as my second. Presumably Mace will be yours, Elderfield. Shall we agree upon a suitable spot?"

"For sweet hell's sake!" Mace shouted. "This is madness."

"Be quiet, Mace," Tom snapped. He studied the Earl with loathing. Wickham's air of complete confidence implied that he fancied himself as a marksman, and he could probably guess that Tom had never handled a duelling pistol in his life. It was also possible that Wickham had learned the extent of Tom's injuries, in which case he knew that Tom could not lift his right arm high enough to fire a pistol with any degree of accuracy. And this was the Earl's honourable solution!

Tom could feel Jessica trembling. Without looking at her, he said to Wickham, "If you kill me in a duel, the odds are that you'll escape the usual penalty for murder. If I so much as wound a peer of the realm, I'll hang for it. No, I will not fight a duel with you."

The Earl raised contemptuous brows. "I have heard much about you, Elderfield. I did not know until this moment that you are a coward as well as a villain."

"And I did not know until tonight," said Tom coolly, "that you are an unscrupulous killer as well as a vicious and perverted bully."

Wickham lost his temper. "By God," he said, "I'll settle this on your terms if I must." And he stepped quickly forward.

This action, as Mace said afterwards, had the same effect as a lighted candle dropped in a keg of gunpowder. Jessica tore herself free of Tom and rushed at the Earl, screaming to him to stop, and he swatted her aside with such furious brutality that she fell sprawling on the rough ground. Tom yelled and lashed out at Wickham, who blocked his punch easily; and as Mace leaped at the Earl with a howling battle-cry, Ponsonby dived for Mace's legs and brought him down, the two young men rolling over and over, gouging and clawing and kicking.

The Earl of Wickham was nearly twenty years older than Tom; but he was uninjured, and better informed than he had chosen to admit. Tom ducked sideways to avoid a well-aimed fist and the awkward movement twisted his back. As he tried to straighten up, the Earl's second punch crashed into his right shoulder with all the force of obsessive hatred and sent him reeling against a boathouse wall.

He slid down, clutching his shoulder. Through blurred and dancing moonlight he saw Wickham standing over him.

"That was for presuming to blackmail me, Elderfield," the Earl whispered. "This is for imagining you could steal what is mine . . .

Jessica shakily picked herself up; and beyond the grappling figures of Mace and Ponsonby she saw Tom stagger against the wall and crumple slowly to the ground. She saw the Earl murmur something inaudible and draw back his foot to kick his fallen enemy.

"*Wickham*!" she screamed at him. "You hurt him and I swear you'll regret it for the rest of your life!"

Wickham's head jerked. "My dear," he said, "do not attempt to threaten me!"

Jessica's hands clenched at her sides. She said with intensity, "If you hurt my Tom any more, I'll see that you pay for it – you and your fine friend here." She glanced briefly at Sir Bevis and Mace, who had abandoned their fight and now sat gaping at her. "I'll see that every newspaper in London and Hampshire prints the details of this night's work. And you know me well enough, my lord, to be sure that I don't make the threat idly and that I don't much care if scandal attaches to my name."

"You treacherous whore!" Wickham would have sprung at her but both Mace and Ponsonby were on their feet in an instant and Tom said between his teeth, "If you touch her . . . the same threat holds."

Ponsonby was growing increasingly nervous. He edged his way to Wickham's side and implored him, "My dear fellow . . . one must consider one's family, you know. The newspapers . . . I'm afraid we really must concede defeat. If we take things further, I fear . . . well, I should not like to see Miss Tandy hurt, you know."

Wickham was beaten, and he knew it. He turned to Tom, who was slowly pushing himself upright; using the wall as a support.

"Elderfield," he said, "you have won the first round. Not the match. Circumstances will not always be against me." And to Jessica he said, "I wish you joy. But happiness is so often snatched away, is it not, just when one is least prepared? Such a pity. Goodbye, my dear."

As he disappeared with Ponsonby into the dark, Jessica ran to Tom. She was crying, all the brave words forgotten. "Darling, has he hurt you? Your shoulder –"

"Intact . . . That's the main thing."

He moved cautiously away from the wall, nursing the injured arm. His shoulder was throbbing and the pain in his back made every step an excruciating effort. Jessica slid her arm gently around him.

Mace limped to join them, dabbing at a cut above one eye and grinning like an idiot. "Hell hath no fury like my sister on the battlefield," he said.

"Tom," said Jessica softly. "Was it worth it, love? You don't regret it, do you?"

He looked down at her; and the reality hit him then. He and Jess would be together for the rest of their lives; and Wickham, for all his threats, could never win her back.

He could have wept for happiness. "Will you marry me, Jessie?"

She gave a choking laugh. "Do you think I should let Honor be a bridesmaid?"

"What do we care about scandal?" he said.

CHAPTER FIVE

They were married in Southampton a month later. The
quiet ceremony was attended by a score of friends, and the
twins followed their mother down the aisle, their faces proud
and solemn. Obadiah had not answered Jessica's letter of invitation, and it was left to Mace to give the bride away.

That afternoon, in a newly acquired waggon laden with
baggage and furniture, Tom drove his family to Bursledon,
to the house known as Crosstrees which stood beside the
boatyard. Mace accompanied them; though he did say, with
a wink at Jess, that September was late in the year for goose-
berries, and maybe he should go home to Cowes and Mrs
Gribble.

In fact he was afire with excitement at the move; as
brimming with high spirits as the twins, and considerably
less manageable. In the space of four weeks he and Tom had
worked their notice – in Tom's case, as effectively as his
healing injuries allowed – signed a lease with Mr Ekless and
a contract with Lord Yarborough, and hired a team of carpenters and men-of-all-work to carry out repairs to the
neglected boatyard. In addition to all this, Mace had now
seen his sister wed to the man he liked and admired above all
others; the man who was also his partner in their glorious
new enterprise. Life, with all its lights and rainbow hues and
inescapable shadows, had never looked so rosy.

He sat between Luke and Honor in the back of the cart, on
a table recently bought by Tom at auction.

"You're not Tandys any more," he told the twins,
"You're Elderfields. Time to change the old songs." And he
began in a well-pitched baritone:

The Elderfield twins were bold and brave,
Their eyes a merry blue,
And they were full of mischief as
The devil and all his crew.

"Sing us some more," said Luke, when he stopped. "We want the verses about us slaying the Black Knight."

"Ask your Pa. He's the expert on heroic deeds."

"But he can't make up songs, Uncle Macey," protested Honor, "and he's got a voice like an old tomcat."

Their father let out a convincing yowl.

"That's why he was christened Tom," said Mace seriously; and at Honor's wondering expression he doubled up with mirth and nearly fell off the table.

In the end he gave them the requested ballad. Tom and Jessica added a few doggerel lines here and there, concocting them from the privacy of the high driving seat with shared whispers and smothered hilarity.

For the first time since the years in London, Mace felt part of a united family; and he sang out the nonsensical rhymes as though offering up a hymn to the blue heaven.

All the same, he was anxious about the twins. Having known Jess as their mother until they were four years old, they had accepted the idea of 'Auntie Jess' as simply a game, and of course had not been told that their father was Amos or anyone else. Mace was afraid they would see their new relationship with Tom as an extension of the same puzzling joke, and turn to each other as the one solid reality in a bewildering world.

His fears were somewhat allayed during the first months at Bursledon. Jess had brought the twins up to run wild – mainly, in latter years, to keep them out of Wickham's way – and they continued to do so; scrambling over piles of compass timber, their gleeful yells audible above the din from saw-pits and forge; or investigating the mould-loft, where Mace scaled up his drawings and carved the yacht's lines, life-sized, on walls and floor, thus to ensure the accurate measurement of the oak framework. At other times they distracted the thirty-strong workforce of itinerant ship-wrights, sawyers and carpenters with endless questions, and clambered on to the scaffolding to view the inside of the skeletal hull taking shape on one of the yard's two slipways. Charles Pelham had already chosen a name – *Spirit of the Wight* – but the company could not have survived if the relatively small *Spirit* had been the only source of income. Tom had advertised Elderfield & Tandy both in the local press and by word of mouth. As a result there were usually several fishing boats laid up for repairs, and the twins could always find something new to interest them.

They were undoubtedly happy; but whereas Honor loved everyone who was kind to her – Tom included – Luke remained uneasy with his father, and was often distant or sullen. Tom was partly to blame; he had seemed more comfortable with the twins when he believed them to be Amos' children.

Mace, who knew him pretty well, guessed that although Tom had no difficulty in worshipping his bride and his boatyard – definitely in that order – he could not instantly manufacture love for a pair of offspring thrust upon him almost a decade after their birth. Mace was also sure that Tom would never admit this to Jess, particularly if he thought the problem was caused by a weakness in his own character.

Though it was Mace's philosophy, unashamedly copied from Tom and often disregarded, that worrying was only useful if it resulted in action, a part of the solution fell almost literally into his path. Not long before Christmas, after a night of hard frost, he loped furtively into the house at dawn, with clothes crumpled, scarlet cravat askew, and coat enveloping an irregular bundle at about the level of his chest. Treading softly, and with sly glances to right and left, he sprang up the stairs three at a time and tapped on the door of Tom and Jessica's bedchamber.

The murmurs from within did not sound too friendly, but the bundle was starting to wriggle. Mace strode into the room, and sat heavily on the edge of the four-poster bed, the most expensive piece of furniture in the house.

"What the hell . . ." said Tom drowsily; and Jessica groaned, "Go away, little brother."

Mace grinned. "Look," he said, " at what I found in a ditch. Can't be more than a few months old." He drew out, with a conjuror's flourish, a bedraggled, small and sorrowful dog, with black bristling fur and no obvious pedigree. "Lucky he didn't freeze to death. I've given him a good rub down."

"Looks half starved," Tom muttered, opening one eye. "Take it away and give it some breakfast."

Jessica sat up, pulling the coverlet modestly about her. She was the only woman of Mace's wide acquaintance who habitually slept without a nightgown.

She put out a hand to stroke the quivering puppy. "He must be a stray. We'll have to keep him, I suppose. The twins will be pleased."

"Overjoyed. I did think," said Mace airily, "that Tom might like to give them the poor little scrap as an early Christmas present. You could pretend you found him, Tom, and help them with his training."

"That's a marvellous idea," said Jessica. "Tom, why don't you, darling?"

It was possible, Mace thought, that Jess saw a great deal more than her husband intended. He winked at her. Tom squinted from one to the other, still half asleep. Having trained himself, as poacher and smuggler, to operate at maximum efficiency during the hours of darkness, his body had never totally adapted to a law-abiding existence. Even after four years on yachts and steamers, he was not at his best early in the morning.

"Nagging bloody Tandys," he said, and took the dog from Mace. "Come here, you scrag-eared monster."

Mace, with a satisfied chuckle, leapt up and headed for the door.

Jessica said idly, "Macey, what were you doing, combing ditches for mongrels before sunrise?"

"Aren't you glad if your baby brother finds a warm bed on a cold night?"

Jessica smiled at the closing door, and nestled up against Tom, who was checking the dog for mange.

"I hope you know," she said, "that you've got a business partner worth having."

"Not to mention the best wife in the world," he said lightly, and kissed her forehead. "Whatever did I do to deserve such luck?"

"Earned it in East Cowes," she said.

The dog, which Luke named Smudge for no good reason, succeeded in bringing Tom closer to his children than he had hoped or expected. Every morning during that winter he and the twins would rise earlier than Tom liked, and romp through the yard and along the wooded banks upriver, leaping and prancing, chasing Smudge or each other, or tumbling in rowdy horseplay across tree roots and ice-hardened mud. Jessica stayed tactfully to cook breakfast, and Mace could rarely be found at such an hour. A basement room in one of the larger Bursledon residences was occupied by two maidservants – both young, pretty and accommodating – and neither chose to mention to their employers that the window catch was faulty.

After Christmas, at Tom's suggestion, he and Mace built a twelve foot dinghy for the twins, the hull being a scaled-down version of *Spirit*. It was ridiculous, as Tom pointed out, for children growing up in a boatyard not to have a boat of their own. The dinghy was launched at the end of January, not long after the twins' tenth birthday, and was christened *Gemini* by their mother.

It was a month or two later, when Luke and Honor had sailed upriver, and Tom had ridden to Lymington to discuss further timber supplies with Gaspard Vaillant, that Jessica ran from the front door of Crosstrees buttoning her pelisse and calling her brother's name gaily, skipping and turning on her heel like a young girl as she sought to glimpse his tousled head rising above all others.

Mace trod through thawing mud to meet her, her happiness lifting his own heart as usual. "What's to do, little girl?" he asked.

Jessica smacked his arm playfully. "That is one habit you needn't copy from my dear husband. I'm nobody's little girl these days."

"Where are you headed, then, foul misbegotten hag and ancient crone, witch of a thousand warts?"

The ensuing brief scuffle would have ended with Jessica falling on her behind in the mud, had Mace not scooped her up in time and set her on her feet.

"Pax, sweet sister?" he asked.

"Will you," she said, recovering her breath, "visit the gypsies with me?"

Mace gestured vaguely around the yard. "I ought to oversee the men, with Tom being away for two days."

"Nonsense, they've a reliable foreman. Meg and Othi Wells are camped in Salterns Lane. They've come especially to see us."

"To see *you*, maybe."

Since the Tandys' flight from Hatchley in 1816 Mace had not met the Wells family, though he was aware that his sister had kept in touch with them until her move to the Wight. He remembered only dimly the gypsy woman and her husband, and a pert, skinny child called Lavinia, who had tried to make him eat snails and hedgehogs, and had refused to lend him her blankets.

But he went with Jessica quite readily. The recent appearance of the first primroses had reminded him that spring was approaching fast, and with it the Mayday launch of *Spirit*. Before that date, Mace wanted to have ready an alternative hull design to show prospective customers; a design for a yacht that would perform well in heavy seas. Yachtsmen were making longer voyages than of old, and *Spirit* would be essentially a fair-weather flyer. Mace's newest ideas sprang from the performance of *Gemini* during the past month, but the work was not progressing as well as he had hoped. Tom suggested dryly that lack of sleep might have something to do with it, to which Mace had replied that he was a fine one to talk. Mace felt today that a change of scene might give him fresh inspiration.

The Wells' caravan and makeshift tent stood beneath dripping trees, set back from the lane. A tabby cat squatted morosely on the steps, and a mongrel twice the size of Smudge bounded to greet the two visitors, seeming to recognise Jessica even after a four year interval. Jess crooned over him and ruffled his fur, without regard for the paw-prints on her best pelisse.

A young woman emerged from under the trees, with a flat basket full of tied bunches of primroses, and came towards them, smiling a welcome.

Mace had always been attracted to gypsy girls, not least because they usually spurned his advances. It was heavily frowned upon by the tribe if such a girl consorted with a *gorgio*, a non-gypsy. Now, he stood transfixed; for Lavinia

Wells, velvet eyed and honey skinned, with her glinting chain necklace and moss-green shawl and skirt, was more exquisite than any fair complexioned, pastel clad lady of fashion, and far lovelier than the two plump maidservants whose bodies were white as winter.

Jessica hugged the girl. "Vinnie, where were you yesterday? I missed seeing you. Why, you've grown into a beauty, hasn't she, Macey?"

She must be eighteen, he realised; and gypsies married young. If Vinnie was married, Mace thought with a searing intensity that shocked him, then he would cover the walls at Crosstrees with portraits drawn from this one memory, and never look at another woman again.

He bowed. "Good morning, Miss Wells," he said, feeling breathless, dreading that she would deny her maiden name.

Vinnie was staring at him as though at a stranger; and no doubt he had changed a good deal in the intervening years. Jess always said he had been better-looking as a child.

"Mace . . ." said Vinnie.

He could not bear the suspense. "Vinnie, is your husband . . ."

Jessica laughed incredulously, but the Romany girl seemed unaware of her. She said softly, "I have no husband yet."

Did he imagine the subtle encouragement in those words? But he could not mistake her entranced gaze, nor the fizzing shock when their eyes met.

Jessica glanced from her brother to Vinnie Wells. She was no longer laughing. "I don't believe it," she said. "Mace, stop this! Vinnie, he's a *gorgio*."

Mace smiled at Vinnie. "Do you care about that?" he asked her.

"No," she said.

Jessica caught her breath. "Then your father will! For pity's sake, Vinnie Wells, tell my poor smitten brother that you will be gone to Fordingbridge before the end of the week, and will have left Hampshire altogether by the end of May."

"Will you, Vinnie?" said Mace.

She nodded, then half shook her head. Her eyes doubted him now, doubted herself, begged for his understanding. He saw that he was moving too fast, asking too much; she was only eighteen, and had not been parted from her parents before, nor been anything but a traveller.

"I . . . cannot tell," she said.

"Of course she can't," said Jess hotly. "Take no notice of my brother – he goes a little mad at the sight of a pretty face. Come along, both of you, I promised Meg yesterday that I would buy some clothes pegs and a new broom."

Mace could hardly credit his sister's lack of sensitivity. How could she let Vinnie believe that he fell in love with every girl he met? It was true that his affections in the past had been easily roused and often quick to die; but in all his life he had not felt this sudden, sweet, terrifying sense of communion. The fact that Jess could not know this, and wanted only to protect the young gypsy girl, did perhaps mitigate her offence – but not much.

He looked at Vinnie, and the girl said, with a note of confused and desperate apology that twisted his heart, "I don't even know you. How can I tell what I should do?"

"Do nothing," he said, very gently to reassure her, though a treacherous inner voice clamoured that he could not delay another minute, let alone a week, a month . . . "Only wait. Wait and see."

"And that," said Jessica, "is the first sensible thing you have said, Mace Tandy."

The three of them went into the caravan, which made it extremely crowded, and were greeted warmly by Meg and Othi Wells. Seated opposite Vinnie, Mace avoided her eyes whenever possible and addressed her with distant courtesy, fearful that a look or word might give away too much and frighten her again.

But when he left with Jessica, using the broom to strike unnecessarily at trailing brambles, Vinnie ran after him. He turned, and she stopped some few feet away, as if threatened by his proximity.

"Mace." No fear in her voice; just uncertainty. "Macey . . ."

She had heard Jess call him that. His mouth curved in delight. "I'll come again," he said.

"I hope you will, Macey."

A gypsy custom came into his mind. He had once known a

Romany woman who covered her hair with a neckerchief, a love token from her husband. Mace unwound his scarlet cravat and held it out to Vinnie.

"Will you wear it for me?" he asked.

"My parents will wonder how I came by it," she said. "No – worse than that – they will know quite well." But she was smiling. When she stepped forward to take the gift, her fingers touched his; and this time when their eyes met, it was to acknowledge a shared secret. For both of them, Jessica might not have been there.

Then the girl ran from him, back to the safety of her father's caravan, pausing only to knot the long red cravat in her hair.

Mace linked his arm through his sister's. "I think," he said. "I'll have to paint a portrait, and hang it above the fireplace in the parlour."

"You drive me to despair," Jessica said.

CHAPTER SIX

The drawing-room at Crosstrees was suffocatingly full, with guests spilling into the hall. Private carriages blocked the driveway outside, and the narrow lane. Hired cabs came and went. In a marquee on the lawn a buffet catered for thirty people, but more than a hundred had arrived so far. The cook brought in for the occasion was distraught; and the twins and Smudge, romping among the guy-ropes, were hopelessly over-excited.

Neither Tom nor Mace was complaining. If a launching party given for the Commodore and his sons could draw such crowds, it was excellent publicity for the company. None of the aristocratic gate-crashers had been turned away, and Jess was setting out to charm them all individually.

Tom stood on the front doorstep, welcoming late arrivals with a glass in his hand and a genuine smile on his lips. In the boatyard nothing moved except a curl of blue smoke rising from a pile of burning sawdust. The men had collected their fortnightly wages and been given the afternoon off. Tom was feeling relieved, exhausted and smug. Having overcome delays caused by everything from flooded or snow-covered roads that prevented the carting of timber, to having men laid off on half pay for weeks with a broken arm or leg, the boatbuilders Elderfield & Tandy had launched *Spirit of the Wight* on time and without a hitch.

Tom gazed with pride at the newly christened yacht moored at the boatyard's jetty. She was small enough to have been launched with masts and spars in position, and the Pelham boys had brought the sails and running rigging with them that day. A crew supervised by Charles Pelham was busy making the yacht ready for sea. A party of young bloods admired her lines from the jetty.

If *Spirit's* performance in the Solent this season were to bring in even one firm order for a similar yacht, the advance payment would take care of the company's overheads until the autumn; and Mace was both ecstatic and incredulous at the number of gentlemen interested in his newest design for a fast ocean-going vessel. True, most were probably just curious to compare his ideas with those of Joseph White and the famous owner-designer Mr Weld, as Mace was the first to admit in private – but in public no such doubts were visible. His personality and confidence either held prospective customers spellbound or inspired their total contempt; a state of affairs which suited Mace. Respect or scorn: he would return both with interest, whereas indifference would have cut him to the heart.

Tom had several times been obliged to smooth ruffled tempers and win back a valued customer by tact and subtle diplomacy; but already he was beginning to envisage himself and Mace as old men, toasting the company's fiftieth year. Perhaps their grandsons would take Elderfield & Tandy into the twentieth century.

It was quite a dream, he acknowledged wryly, to have grown out of eight months' struggle to survive, and the launch of one untried yacht and a score of repaired fishing boats.

Mace erupted from the hall behind him, flushed and agitated. "Quick – what time is it?"

Tom drew out his fob watch. "Where's the timepiece we bought you for Christmas?"

"Somewhere. I don't know." Mace was almost dancing with impatience. "What's the bloody time?"

"Nearly two o'clock."

"Agh! *No* – oh, *hell!*" he said; and clearing in one bound the six steps to the driveway, he dodged past the carriages, vaulted over the closed gates and sprinted out of sight. Tom gazed after him for a moment; most probably he was meeting some village girl or other. One had to take such dramatic outbursts with a pinch of salt.

Tom's guess was not wholly wrong. Just beyond the boatyard, Mace left the lane and pushed his way through prickly undergrowth to a clearing beside the river.

Vinnie Wells stood on the river bank. She was wearing her best blue skirt and lace-edged bodice, and his scarlet cravat held back her long hair. A tied bundle of clothes lay on the damp grass at her feet, along with a small loaf of bread and an unsheathed knife.

Her face lit at the sight of him. He ran and clasped her waist, lifting her off the ground to kiss her. She smelled of rosewater and lavender. Her arms twined around his neck. Tonight she would be his; Vinnie who had never before given herself to him, nor to any man, gypsy or *gorgio*.

He set her down, still holding her waist, and he wondered how a man could bear such happiness. "Darling love, I'm so late – can you forgive me? I was so afraid you'd be gone –"

"You are here now. That is what counts."

He laughed; Vinnie had a knack of grasping the essentials and discarding the dross. After their second or third meeting she had lost her shyness, and he had realised that she was not scared of men in general, but only of the one man who had inspired in her such violent and bewildering emotions.

"How did you come here?" he asked. "Did you really steal a New Forest pony?"

"I said I would."

"Sweet hell – you might have been arrested."

She touched a finger to his lips to silence him. "Foolish Macey," she said, and stooping, she picked up the knife and the bread. "We should do this in front of witnesses, but no matter. God sees."

She broke the bread, gave one piece to Mace, and handed him the knife.

Without hesitation he clenched his teeth and drew the blade firmly across the top of his thumb, wincing in spite of brave intentions.

"Oh Macey," she said, half laughing, "we are lovers, not warriors."

She pricked her own thumb lightly, and squeezed a drop of blood on to the bread she held, while Mace touched the other piece to his dripping cut. They ate each other's bread; tasted each other's blood. Later, he might laugh at the ritual;

but now he felt its ancient solemnity, as binding as vows in church.

When they had finished, Vinnie took his hands. "I pledge my love to thee, Mace Tandy," she said. "To go where thou goest, live wherever thou livest, and to share with thee all things . . . my body and heart to be thine alone, until the day of my death."

Smiling, he repeated the words, substituting her name for his. She nodded, satisfied.

"We are man and wife," she said.

They sealed the marriage with a single kiss, offering the faintest promise for the night to come. Then Mace picked up his bride's meagre luggage, and hand in hand, with more joy than apprehension, they made their way back to Crosstrees.

Among the carriages in the lane stood one that had not been there when Mace left. An opulent affair, crimson and gold, with a prim-faced coachman and a familiar coat of arms. The interior was empty.

Mace swore aloud. Thrusting Vinnie's bundle into her arms he said, "Follow, but not too close. All right, darling?"

He did not hear her reply. Vaulting for the second time over the gates he raced up the drive. The owner of the crimson carriage stood near the marquee, tapping a white-thorn cane against his boot as he conversed in low tones with Jessica. There was no sign of Tom or of the twins.

Mace bellowed, "Wickham – you bastard!"

Before the Earl could do more than face his assailant, Mace was upon him, bringing him hard to the ground. Mace straddled the prostrate and furious Earl and punched him in the mouth, then grabbed the end of Wickham's savagely wielded cane. Jessica was shouting for Tom, and trying to drag her brother off his helpless opponent.

Mace grated, "Don't worry, I've finished." He wrested the cane from Wickham's grasp and stood up. "Get off my property," he said. It sounded fine, though Mr Ekless might have argued the point.

Having been deprived of breath and dignity, Wickham struggled to sit up. He spat a tooth on to the lawn. A crowd of shocked and fascinated onlookers had gathered. The twins stood among them, frankly beaming. Tom shouldered his way to the front of the crowd and put his arm around

Jess. He looked as angry with Mace as with the Earl; but it was to Wickham that he spoke.

"If you've business with me, let us all hear it!"

"A vindictive man," said Wickham, still panting, "would press charges against Tandy here for unprovoked assault. I should like my many friends here to witness . . . I press no charges. I am not a vindictive man. I came, Elderfield, merely to congratulate you on your success, and to see *Spirit of the Wight* afloat."

Mace said through his teeth, "We'll do without your good wishes."

Wickham looked at him directly. "Yes, Tandy," he said. "You will indeed do without them in future."

To the spectators it must have seemed a very natural remark in the circumstances, and hardly constituted a threat. Mace was not so naive as to take that view, but he had made enemies before. Wickham could go and jump in the river. He shrugged his shoulders.

"You break my heart," he said.

A couple of gentlemen helped Wickham to his feet. He thanked them graciously. The guests muttered, sympathies about equally divided. Mace Tandy's behaviour had been outrageous; but everyone knew what Mrs Elderfield's relationship with the Earl had once been. During those years he had often spoken cruelly to her, even in public; and though many of the fashionable set despised Jess Elderfield, the Earl of Wickham was not universally admired.

Wickham wrenched open the gate and strode to his carriage, accompanied by half a dozen guests who seemed to be apologising on Tom's behalf, and certainly without his approval.

Tom hugged Jessica close to his side. "What did he want?" he asked in an undertone.

Mace waited to hear her answer.

"He will be spending less time in London from now on," she said. "When he's not sailing, he will be living at Durley Grange."

Wickham's Hampshire estate lay near Botley village, not five miles from Bursledon.

Tom frowned; his eyes glittered. "No reason given, I suppose."

"He's nervous about being an absentee landlord. Some of the tenant farmers are getting edgy, he says. There has been some unrest among the labourers."

Mace snorted. "It's about time. Have you spoken to farmhands around here? They're on the same wages now as before Waterloo – and they weren't happy with the rates then."

"As I've cause to remember," said Tom.

Mace knew that he was thinking of his father's murder; but if wages had not altered since those days, the labourers' motivation had. After some years of comparative docility among the men, last year's harvest had been disastrous; and in addition, people were starting to blame the new agricultural machinery for rising unemployment. Though the radical William Cobbett no longer lived at Botley House, his public meetings across the whole of Southern England during recent years had gradually fanned discontent to a dangerous heat. There was no telling, yet, how many folk might get themselves burnt, if something was not done soon to ease the plight of the poor.

"Wickham's labourers give him no trouble," said Jessica. "They are better paid and better treated than any others in the county. Mainly, I think, because the tenant farmers are charged a fair rent and can afford to pay decent wages."

Tom and Mace regarded her in disbelief, and Jessica sighed.

"You've only seen the worst side of Wickham," she said. "He's right, he *does* have friends – especially among the poor. He can be generous to those he cares little about. It's only the loved and the hated who are made to suffer."

This to Mace was incomprehensible; Wickham was obviously warped beyond redemption.

Tom's mouth twisted in sour understanding. "Thank God the yard is well insured. I don't reckon he'd risk causing actual damage, any more than he'd hurt any member of this family. He knows too well that if the law didn't punish him, the Commodore would, and so would I. Evidence or no evidence. But I think we should all watch our backs from now on."

At Tom's words, Mace suddenly remembered the most recent addition to their family. Clapping a hand to his fore-

242

head he spun round, to see his bride standing forlorn and uncertain by the gates, her belongings clutched to her breast.

"Vinnie! Darling – Oh, I should be hanged at dawn for forgetting you!" Running to the girl, he pulled her back to the newly riveted crowd. "Tom – Jess – twins and Smudge – gentlemen and ladies – I would like you to meet my wife, Mrs Lavinia Tandy!"

And seeing the expressions on the faces of his brother-in-law and sister, Mace laughed out loud, and in full view of the assembled guests he wound both arms about his bride and kissed her with scandalous enthusiasm.

Vinnie settled into life at Crosstrees more readily than her husband had expected. Mace's bedchamber, which he used also as a studio, was the largest of the upstairs rooms, and faced south-east towards the river and the morning sun. The gypsy girl liked its airy brightness, and the subtly pink walls. When they were rich, Mace said, he would afford some proper paint, instead of making do with whitewash and damson juice. Vinnie did not yearn for wealth or fine possessions. She had the man she loved, the freedom to come and go as she pleased, and could sleep under the stars sometimes in warm weather – a pastime which Mace willingly sampled, and found delightful.

He was constantly amazed by Vinnie. Demure and soft spoken in everyday life, with scarcely a hint of the boldness she had exhibited as a child, she became in bed an insatiable wildcat, calling upon all of his imagination, stamina and skill.

"I have heard," she said once, "that one girl at a time is not enough for you, my husband. It is my duty to make sure that you have no energy left for such nonsense."

"I think you're winning," he gasped; but the games they created together added some delectable wickedness to married life, and Mace was seldom short of new ideas.

Wickham's presence in Hampshire had no apparent effect on the fortunes of the company. That summer brought them two orders for small yachts like *Spirit,* following Charles Pelham's success in minor races in May. It was a pity that *Spirit* could not have taken part in the Cowes Regatta, but in June Lord Yarborough and his sons sailed to the Mediterranean aboard *Falcon,* and before their return home the twenty-two gun pleasure yacht and its mainly civilian crew became involved in the British, French and Russian victory over the Turkish fleet in Navarino Bay; a victory that secured independence for Greece, the cause for which the exiled Lord Byron had died in '24.

There were no orders at all for Mace's ocean-going yacht. Tom was unworried, his faith in Mace's ability undiminished. Give it time, he said. Let the R.Y.C. get used to seeing a new style of flyer on the Solent, and then maybe someone would risk an investment in a larger vessel.

Mace was not reassured, and his self-esteem plummeted lower than he would allow anyone outside the family to guess; but since his marriage he could not feel justified in totally despairing of the future.

The following summer, with three of their yachts now afloat, the company was commissioned to build a 120 ton luxury yacht, based on Mace's recent modifications to the original hull design of *Spirit.* Two more yachts were to be laid down at the same time, for different owners. Mace was suddenly gleeful, in love with all the world – except skinflint landlords. John Ekless, whom Mace liked and respected, was deeply concerned about the worsening condition of local farm labourers, and he had succeeded in stirring the consciences of both Mace and Jess. Having read aloud from Cobbett's newsheets in their youth, to an enthralled tavern audience in Hatchley, the Tandys had left politics alone since then; though it was true that Mace had gone once or twice to hear Cobbett speak. Now, however, it seemed to the brother and sister that the passage of time had made them selfish. They began regularly collecting copies of banned pamphlets – mostly Cobbett's – from a local publican, and distributing them among the yard's workforce and the villagers. Not that they agreed with many of Cobbett's notions, for the journalist was savagely opposed to progress of any sort, including the abolition of slavery; but Cobbett had taken up the labourers' cause as his first priority, and that was what counted at present.

At the end of October, Mace learned something that put politics and ships' lines temporarily out of his mind. Employed with the rest of the family in hollowing out turnip-heads for Hallowe'en, he paused to watch his sister stretching up to hang one in the window, and moved to help her.

"You're getting fat, Jess," he said. "Too much good living."

Tom and Jessica exchanged amused and shining looks, and Tom said idly, aware of the twins' presence, "That's what caused it, right enough."

Before Mace could speak, Vinnie said with intense satisfaction, "Good – I am glad. Jess and I will grow fat together."

She then had to suffer being caught in her husband's crushing embrace and whirled round the room, until she squealed for mercy and Honor told her Uncle Mace to please grow up.

After the initial excitement, though, he was all tenderness and consideration. Tom suggested, as tactfully as possible, that it might be a good idea to marry Vinnie legally, and have a legitimate son to inherit Mace's share of the company. Mace and Vinnie complied with resignation, the ceremony meaning little to either of them. According to Romany law they had been wed for eighteen months, and in their hearts for longer still.

As the weeks passed, Mace was relieved to see his wife suffering no ill-effects from her pregnancy; in fact she seemed to gain an added bloom, while Jess by contrast grew pale, tired, and short-tempered.

The reason for this was evident even to the love-struck Mace. Vinnie could neither cook nor sew properly, had no inclination for housekeeping, and habitually left everything to Jess. Crosstrees was a ten-roomed house, and they could not afford more than one maidservant. Tom was not averse to cooking and cleaning, and unlike his brother-in-law was proficient in both; but he had very little spare time. In the end he spoke quietly to Honor, who at once took charge. Meals, as a result, were experimental and often unpalatable; but no one complained, least of all Jess.

In April 1829, Jessica gave birth to a baby girl, efficiently delivered by Vinnie, and christened Annis. The gypsy girl had warned Tom against calling in the local 'quacks and witches', insisting that Jess deserved better; and Vinnie proved that day that whatever her domestic shortcomings, she was an excellent midwife.

Her own child was born a month later, this time with the local midwife in attendance, for Jessica had no experience of any confinements other than her own.

Vinnie was in labour for nearly twenty-four hours, and when Jess came wearily downstairs at midnight, to where Tom and Mace waited in the parlour, her face was so drawn with grief and fatigue that Mace leapt to his feet, crying out, "She's dead, isn't she? Vinnie's dead!"

"No. Only tired. But the baby . . ." Jessica shook her head, her face twisting with pain for her brother. "I'm so sorry, Macey. It was a boy. He was so weak . . . no one could have saved him."

Mace fought to control his emotions. In the past month he had crooned over little Annis even more than had the baby's father, and he had looked forward with joyful anticipation to the birth of his own child. More than all this, he knew what the baby's death would mean to Vinnie.

"Poor little mite, he wasn't even baptised," he said. Religion was not important to Mace, and yet somehow he could not bear to think of his own son buried surreptitiously in some forgotten corner of the churchyard.

Tom gripped his shoulder, saying gently, "Bear up, mate. Vinnie is all right, that's the main thing. There'll be other children."

"Can I see her, Jess?"

"She's sleeping. Macey, she doesn't know yet . . ."

He went upstairs anyway. The midwife was still clearing up. Mace paid no heed to the old woman, but he could not disturb his wife, seeing her so lost in exhausted sleep. He looked into the cot beside the bed. It was too big; the tiny corpse seemed so small and cold that he wanted to hold it and warm it, as he had with Smudge that icy morning two years ago.

He covered his son with Vinnie's moss-green shawl, and took the cot out to the landing, where Vinnie would not see it on waking. The midwife passed him and shuffled down the stairs, hunched in mounds of clothing, offering no word of sympathy or regret. Mace kept telling himself how lucky he was, to have Vinnie safe. He knew he would have to be strong for her in the weeks to come.

Trying desperately to concentrate on his many blessings, he thought of the flyer he would design some day, the one that would make them rich; the ultimate racer. He had seen its form in dreams; a sleek, streamlined hull, slicing through the waves like a sword. In the past, like a vision induced by opium, the lines had faded from his mind before he could define them on paper.

He went back into the bedchamber. He wanted to be there when Vinnie woke; no one else must tell her about their baby. The night stretched before him, long and full of sorrow.

Half ashamed, he took a pencil and a clean sheet of paper, and sitting on the floor with his back to the wall and a drawing board balanced on his raised knees, he began to sketch the lines of a yacht.

CHAPTER SEVEN

"Most impressive," said Gaspard Vaillant, adjusting his monocle for a closer look at the drawings scattered across the dining-room table. "Do you have a half-model yet?"

Mace was surprised by his interest. The Vaillants were paying a social call, which meant staying two or three days at Crosstrees, and he had assumed that courtesy alone had prompted the Frenchman to study the new drawings.

"Better than that," he said. "A scale model. Want to see her?"

"My dear fellow, I should be honoured."

The four Vaillant boys were as entranced as their father by the minutely crafted model yacht and, left to themselves, would cheerfully have dismantled it from sheer curiosity. Luke, who knew the time and loving skill that his uncle had put into its construction, challenged Raoul Vaillant to a fight, and all five boys were ejected from the room.

Gaspard spent another minute or two examining the yacht, turning it between his hands, holding it up to the light, stroking the lines of the hull. He glanced up to find himself the focus of every eye in the room – including those of twelve-month-old Annis. The blonde, inquisitive child stood swaying on the hearthrug, steadied by the hands of her elder sister.

"What scale is this?" the Frenchman asked Mace.

"One in thirty. Full size, she'd be around sixty feet overall. And less than a hundred and forty tons burthen."

"She has a very shallow draught. Will one be able to stand upright below decks?"

Mace grinned. "I won't. Tom will, just."

"The keel is abnormally long."

248

"Cuts down leeway in heavy weather."

"She is extremely . . . innovative."

Tom interrupted, pretending outrage, "Of course she is. You are looking at *the* Tandy flyer. A racer for the new decade. The ultimate product of my partner's genius."

Mace vigorously shook his head. "Perfection is only for dreams. Pursuing it is the best one can hope for. But . . ." he laughed. "Maybe this little lady comes close."

Gaspard arched his brows. "An utterly biased and unreliable judgement."

"Utterly," said Mace.

"You may build her for me."

Sophie Vaillant, whose attention had reverted to baby Annis, lifted her head in shocked incredulity. The assembled Elderfields and Tandys were staring at Gaspard as though he had materialised that instant out of the air.

Then Mace and Jessica simultaneously let out a whoop of joy. Jess hugged Tom first and Gaspard afterwards, while Mace waltzed a protesting Vinnie around the room and Honor tossed Annis above her head so that the baby squealed and gurgled with delight.

"Mad," Gaspard observed to his wife. "Quite mad, the lot of them."

Gaspard had not owned a yacht before, but he missed life at sea; missed also the freedom to take a risk now and then. He liked to keep up with the fashionable set; and as a timber merchant, he could commission the building of a yacht more cheaply than most people. He had seen Mace Tandy's ideas evolve over the years, while Tom's financial control of the company had enabled it to prosper. His chosen name for the yacht would be *Joie-de-Vivre*.

To Mace, she would always be what Tom had unwittingly christened her: *The Tandy Flyer*. That summer and autumn, as she took shape on the new, third slipway, her designer experienced a tremor of almost fearful happiness whenever he glimpsed her through a window or worked alongside the labourers on the scaffolding.

He knew that pride was inexcusable, that he should be objective and critical, seeking to improve the prototype; but he had sweated over the design, including interior fitments,

249

for a whole year, in addition to working on current projects and distributing political pamphlets. To see her now, created in the sun, the dream translated to a reality of hollow oak, was awesome indeed. Sometimes it terrified him. Only mathematics and instinct told him how fast she would be; and the design of a racing hull that would fly in all weather conditions was at best a juggling act between often contradictory principles.

The building of *Joie-de-Vivre* became something of a race in itself. Tom learned from Charles Pelham that the Earl of Wickham, disgusted by the consistently poor performance of his ageing cutter *Xanadu,* had commissioned an eighty foot yacht to be launched the following March. Tom and Mace were determined to follow Wickham's example by launching their flyer early in the season, allowing Gaspard as much time as the Earl to experiment with sails and rigging, and discover how the boat handled, before the start of the summer racing programme. The passage of time had convinced the partners that Wickham had either resigned himself to losing Jessica, or was powerless to harm them – and it was easy for Tom, the victor, to shrug his shoulders at the past. All the same, they would derive much satisfaction from seeing *Joie-de-Vivre* beat Wickham's new *Honeydew* next summer.

Mace's sense of fulfilment, both in his marriage and his career, heightened his awareness of the sufferings of the poor. It was said that dealers were withholding corn from the market, to create artificial shortages and keep prices high. Labourers were found huddled in ditches, dead from simple starvation. Children sickened and died for want of nourishment, their fathers taking home wages barely adequate to feed a single man. The Poor Relief, as well as sapping men's pride, offered too small a supplement. Mace had never noticed a scarcity of pretty faces about the countryside, but that autumn he was shocked by the pale cheeks and wasted limbs of cottagers' wives and daughters. He felt that he should be doing more to help them; they needed articulate spokesmen to put their case forcefully without recourse to violence.

"Nothing will change," Cobbett said, "until the labourers revolt."

Whether or not he intended the comment as an incitement to riot, his words were prophetic. With November came reports of gangs roaming the county, armed with all the deadly weapons of smithy and carpenter's shop, and prepared to terrorise farmers and landowners who would not meet their demands.

Jessica ceased her political activities, and would not join her brother in circulating Cobbett's revived news-sheet, the Twopenny Trash.

"Men are going too far," she said, on the night the Southampton saw-mill was burned by arsonists, with troops being brought in from Portsmouth to aid the companies of dragoons now stationed in the neighbourhood. "Speeches and petitions are one thing – but this! And machines are being smashed, hayricks set afire –"

"There's no harm in that, Jess," said Mace. "It's better than shedding blood – and it makes folk take notice."

"You don't condone these riots – do you? Macey, you can't!"

"I think the local papers are a mouthpiece for the landowners. Don't take everything you read as gospel."

But if the accounts of armed gangs were exaggerated, stories of damage to property were not. Threatening notes appeared under the doors of gentlemen farmers, in different handwriting but all signed by 'Captain Swing'. The hinged end of a flail was called a swingel; this was the implement being rendered obsolete by the hated threshing machines which deprived men of winter employment. Mace, along with most country people, accepted the 'Captain' as a mythical figure, a symbol of the labourers' unity under one banner. The landowners and the government thought otherwise; as did the press and many nervous townsfolk. The rumour spread that foreigners – Frenchmen, most likely – were infiltrating the South, stirring up the English labourers, setting class against class. It was claimed that Swing was a Frenchman who rode about the country in a fine carriage, firing ricks and sending the letters which warned farmers to smash their own machinery or take the consequences.

Mace habitually visited The Jolly Sailor on Sunday nights, to collect copies of the Twopenny Trash. The place was always lively, for the shipwrights and sawyers congregated there from their various billets around the village. Often, too, there were farmhands eager to discuss politics and empty bellies, or to accept a quart of ale from a friend.

The Sunday after the saw-mill was burned, Mace's entry to the taproom was greeted by a cheer from a group of men near the hearthfire. A shipwright called out, "Here, Tandy, take a peep at this!"

The workforce invariably addressed Tom as 'Mr Elderfield', whereas Mace had somehow failed to acquire the handle to his name. He was glad of it. Feeling himself equal to any man, neither better nor worse, he preferred to be treated as such.

He crossed the sanded floor, ducking to avoid the roof beams. A smocked labourer whom he did not know – had never seen before – was seated at a table, surrounded by fascinated onlookers. The table was covered with sheets of paper. Mace picked up one at random, arched his brows, and tossed it down among the rest.

"You can't spell 'starving condition', mate," he said.

The stranger – a pink cheeked fellow of about thirty, obviously no starveling himself – asked smoothly, "Care to write one, would you? Everyone's been taking a turn."

Mace was not convinced that 'Swing' letters did any good; although their efficacy rather depended on their content. Ordering farmers to destroy machines was a doomed last stand against progress; the important issues were high rents and low wages.

He shrugged, grinned and took the quill from the stranger. The ink in the bottle was red. Mace sniffed at it, then licked the end of the quill.

"Whose blood?" he asked curiously.

"Mine," said the stranger. "And willingly spilt in the cause of justice for all."

Had the man been less pompous, Mace could have liked him; but he asked anyway, "Where d'you hail from?"

"North of Botley. I'm travelling the length of the Hamble River, acquainting folk with the facts. The name's Kitcher. Pleased to see a gent like yourself coming down on the right side."

Mace nodded abstractedly, puzzling over what to write.

After a minute he penned the words with a flourish, reading aloud for the benefit of the audience.

> *Sir – Your name is down among the Blackhearts in the black book! Raise the wages of every man in your employ by four shillings a week, or consign your hayricks to the flames of Hell!*
>
> *Swing*

The men cheered. The shipwright who had first greeted Mace said in admiration, "Now that's what I call fancy educated writing. Here, you ought to write the petition."

There was general agreement, and Kitcher said, "Just what I was about to suggest. There's to be a march tomorrow, Mr Tandy. Should be a turn-out of a hundred labourers or more. We're taking a petition round, asking for signatures. Maybe you'd care to phrase it neat and proper for us – and join the march, if you've a mind to."

Mace was suspicious. "Will it be as peaceful as it sounds?"

"Lily-livered, are you?" sneered Kitcher.

"No, I'm bloody not – and if it comes to a fight, you'll find me as ready as any man – but the gaols are filling up with marchers who've started riots. While we fight with words and not bludgeons, there's a good chance of keeping public sympathy."

The men present were of the same opinion; especially as, for most, it was not their quarrel. But Mace decided after all to join the protest; and he willingly wrote the petition. It stated simply that each man must receive two shillings a day for his labour, every youth eighteen pence, and children over two years old to be given a loaf and sixpence a week. The aged and infirm should receive four shillings a week. Landowners were advised that they must reduce rents to enable farmers to meet the demands.

Mace was pleased with the document; farmers could presume a threat if they liked, but none was implicit. And at last he had the chance to do something positive; to stand by his beliefs. He gave no more thought to the absurd 'Swing' letter.

Reaching home before eight, he wanted to talk about his plans for the morning, but Vinnie and Jess would only worry, and the twins would raise hell when he refused to let them march with their uncle.

As for Tom, his callous attitude over the whole question had more than once astounded Mace. Jess seemed to think that Tom pitied the labourers, but he did not speak of them with compassion, and would not be drawn into political arguments on the subject – though Mace in recent weeks had nagged him constantly about it.

That evening, tense with excitement and a touch of nerves, Mace was disinclined to let the matter rest. He valued Tom's good opinion, and did not like to feel they were divided on such an important issue. His frustration grew, as Tom waved aside his arguments and sat smoking a cigar and trying to convince Luke of the need for some organised schooling.

"How can you stay so aloof from it all?" Mace asked savagely. He leapt to his feet and slammed his fist against the mantelpiece. "Don't you see the injustices, the suffering? Don't you care?"

Honor exclaimed, "Oh, Uncle Macey, don't let's talk politics *again!*"

"Of course he cares," said Jessica, laying her book aside. "Let it drop, little brother."

And Vinnie murmured, patting the vacated cushion beside her, "Sit down, Macey, and sing to us."

Tom's narrow gaze was fixed on his partner. "What I care about most," he grated, "are this family and this yard. Our men are paid a fair wage, and we've given to charities when we could afford it. I'll gladly offer food or shelter to anyone who comes here in dire need of either. But I don't like what happens to men when they hunt in packs – No, let me finish, damn it! The French mob hounded my mother's people into penniless exile. A gang of Hatchley louts killed my father and got away with it . . . and a trumped up judge and jury murdered my wife and called it a just execution." Tom's voice shook with the strength of his feelings, and Jessica slid her hand into his. He went on without seeming to notice, "If any thugs turn up here hoping to wring money out of us with threats, I won't stop to argue justice with them, nor to ask whether they're disciples of Cobbett or hired by Wickham."

"And you think I would?" But though Mace was angry,

his partner's words struck an odd and disturbing note. He added with a ferocity not solely aimed at Tom, "Hired by Wickham? Since when has his precious lordship been likely to set a gang of thugs on us?"

Tom breathed a long sigh, and ground his cigar stub on the fire-guard before flicking it into the grate. "Since our insurers cancelled the policy," he said. "I reckon I couldn't keep it from you indefinitely."

It drained a lot of Mace's anger. He said blankly, "What?" at the same time that Jess said, "No – they can't! How can they?"

"Very easily. The contract states their obligation to give seven days' notice of termination. They did that, two weeks ago."

"You could have told us," Jessica said. "You *should* have done. How dare they treat us this way – you've always paid the premiums on time."

"I can guess their reasons," said Mace, with a flicker of savagery. "Risks to person and property have been compounded of late, to a degree incompatible with continuation of the said contract. Or words to that effect. Farmers may be losing ricks and threshing machines, but in most cases it must be the insurance companies losing the money."

"Bullseye, partner." Tom's glance, fiercely blue, rested on every member of his family in turn. "None of this goes beyond these walls, is that clear? Luke? Honor?"

The twins nodded. Honor said, evidently speaking for them both, "Mama's right, you should have trusted us. We're all in this together. What are you going to do, Papa?"

"Try to change their minds. I've written to them. They've agreed to see me tomorrow, so I'll be in town all day. I don't hold out much hope."

"Bastards," said Mace; but he thought privately, with more than a twinge of conscience, that at least his partner would be out of the way when he joined the labourers tomorrow. If he had to fight Tom, which was not unlikely, he would sooner do so after the event.

The crowd that set forth from Hamble next day, gaining in numbers with every mile, was comprised mainly of farmhands, but there were some professional men among them. Most of the labourers carried bludgeons or sledge-hammers, with the intention of damaging machines rather than people, and then only upon extreme provocation. Mace walked with the leaders; for having a clear, strong voice he had volunteered to read the petition aloud at each stop. During that morning, the paper was signed by hundreds of folk from three villages, along with several farmers who were openly sympathetic to the demands of the men. Mace was proud to have his own name at the head of the list. His only slight disappointment was that the man Kitcher, after all his self-righteous words, had not appeared; but that was no real loss to the cause.

They did meet some opposition. A farmer in Botley refused either to sign the petition or to pay a forfeit of five pounds for his obstinacy. Standing squarely before a muttering and hungry crowd three hundred strong, he showed great resolve.

"When the squire lowers the rents, and the parson cuts the tithes," he said, "that'll be the time to think of upping wages."

Hensting, one of the labourers' spokesmen, said coldly, "Then I'll point out to 'ee, the nights are long. I can't tell what might happen."

"So 'tis threats now! You'll fetch your mob one dark night to murder my little ones in their beds –"

Mace cut in quickly, "You mistook my friend's meaning, sir. Your family is safe enough – but hayricks and threshing machines are expendable."

The farmer must have been well insured. He became reck-lessly abusive, and finally stalked into his cowshed. Hensting was all for taking action then and there, and the mob would have followed him.

Mace shouted above the growing clamour, "Have you run mad? How many of your faces are known around here? There are two hundred men filling Hampshire gaols, awaiting trial on charges of rick-burning and machine-smashing. Do you want to spend Christmas with them, and the next seven years in Van Diemen's Land?"

The men were not ready to make such a sacrifice. In spite of the many Special Constables sworn in, and the presence of foot-soldiers and dragoons in the area, sudden raids carried out at night were still a pretty safe bet, whereas a crime committed in daylight was indeed highly chancy. Disconsolate, but aware of the day's many small victories so far, the labourers shambled after Mace and Hensting.

They had not walked half a mile along the lane, when the sound of a troop of horsemen approaching at speed halted them in confusion. Hensting swore, and Mace glanced back at the crowd. The advance of a mounted but still unseen enemy had induced the beginnings of panic. Already some labourers were turning, backing away, preparing for flight.

The lane was wide, but the hedges were high and thick. It was likely that some men would be injured in the event of a stampede; but casualties would be far worse if they stayed to fight – and even attempting to wound an officer of the Crown was a capital or transportable offence.

Mace shouted, "Run! Run for your lives!"

Hensting turned on him in a rage. "You sodding coward–"

"Are you willing to stand with me, and face the troops?" The man stared.

"How else," said Mace, "do we give this crowd time to disperse? And drop that bloody hammer, unless you want to swing for the cause. I'm not fool enough to do battle on foot with armed and mounted men, even if you are."

Hensting flung his sledgehammer into the ditch.

The dragoons galloped into view, their blue coats dark against the gleam of unsheathed sabres. Mace stood his ground, along with Hensting and half a dozen others, blocking the road as behind them the mob fled back towards Botley.

The dragoons, seeing their opponents unarmed and not remotely dangerous, would not ride them down. They drew to a halt.

"Gentlemen," said Mace, holding out the petition. "This is no riot. We have here a document signed by more than three hundred and fifty –"

"Arrest them!" the Captain barked. "All the ringleaders. Let the rest go free – they'll be rounded up before the Assizes."

It was over quickly. The petition was snatched from Mace's hands, and when he made a grab for it a sabre glinted in front of his face. He looked up at the man holding the weapon.

"We are not guilty of riotous assembly," he said.

Another dragoon dismounted and tied his hands, roping all eight of the prisoners together in a line. Hensting put up a token struggle, but Mace's words had struck home; Van Diemen's Land had little appeal.

They were marched beside the horses towards the County Gaol at Winchester, some eleven miles away. As he tramped along the dismal November lane, Mace realised that being a first offender with no poaching or smuggling convictions, he might still get as much as three months' hard labour for unlawful assembly, if the judge was intent on making examples of the 'rioters'. If that happened, he would miss Vinnie unbearably – but at least he would be freed before the launching of *Joie-de-Vivre*.

His flyer . . . *The Tandy Flyer*. It would have been a fine name for her. To hell with modesty; he could hardly wait to see her in action against Wickham's *Honeydew*.

Mace knew that he was a lucky man. A short gaol sentence would be a very minor misfortune, by comparison with the labourers' sufferings these past few years.

His main concern was that Tom would be furious.

CHAPTER EIGHT

Only two of Elderfield & Tandy's workforce had dared to join the march, absenting themselves from the yard on a Monday morning; but a sawyer who had fled from the dragoons found courage to bring the news of Mace's arrest to Crosstrees. The family was horrified – for Mace had said nothing, even that morning, of his plans – but after the first shock, Jessica pointed out to Vinnie and the twins that after all Mace had not committed any dreadful crime, beyond signing a peaceful petition and passing a few cool words with a farmer.

When Tom came home, having failed to persuade the company's insurers to renew the policy, the news that greeted him sent him striding into the yard to interrogate the offending sawyer. He returned looking somewhat relieved, and gave Vinnie a comforting hug.

"Not to worry, little girl. Mace wasn't a ringleader, he only read the petition. But he did threaten to fire some ricks, and if he's convicted of that, you might not see much of him before spring."

By early December, peace had returned to the country-side; a silence born of fear. Warrants were still being issued for the arrest of scores of men who had escaped during various battles between dragoons and labourers; and nearly three hundred were now to be tried by a specially commissioned Court of Assize at Winchester, having appeared briefly before local magistrates. The story was similar in neighbouring counties. In many parishes, farmhands had been awarded the wage increases they so desperately needed; but this did not hearten those who faced possible transportation.

Winchester Gaol was so overcrowded that sanitary conditions were appalling. The eight men arrested outside Botley were lodged in one small cell, with two beds between them. However, there were no chains or leg-irons, and Mace did his utmost to keep morale high.

"We've done nothing worse than all the others," he said firmly. "Hellfire – if all three hundred of us are shipped out to Van Diemen's Land, we'll have enough men to raise a Navy and invade Old England. You've got a boatbuilder among you, don't forget!"

The men were not always able to laugh at their situation. They were allowed a visit from close relatives before the Assizes, and many of the labourers' wives were in despair, dreading the future.

Tom had to bribe the gaoler to let him take both Vinnie and Jess into the cell, and the stench as they entered rocked him on his heels. Mace scrambled up and rushed to Vinnie, clasping her in a fierce embrace. "I'm sorry, love – sorry to have deserted you for this hole," he said; and then, glancing wryly at Tom over her head. "Want a fight, mate?"

"I'll thrash you to kingdom bloody come, the minute you show your ugly face at Crosstrees."

They shook hands on it, the gesture acknowledging the words as nonsense. They were partners, still pulling together.

"Any luck with the insurance?" Mace asked.

Tom brought him up to date, surprised that Mace could think of the company at such a time; but they were both fairly optimistic about his chances of acquittal.

"The Assize starts on December 20th," Mace said. "D'you think I'll be home for Christmas?"

"Just don't get more than three months, or we'll have to postpone the launching party."

On the 18th of December, the coach carrying the three judges was escorted into Winchester by the Sheriff's javelin men and trumpeters, amid the pealing of cathedral bells. From the pageantry, one might have thought that the new King William IV had arrived in person.

When the court convened two days later, the Duke of Wellington was a fourth member of the judicial bench. Since the Whigs' recent return to office, the Iron Duke was no longer Prime Minister, and he had ample time to attend to his duties as Lord Lieutenant of Hampshire.

The Assizes were held in County Hall – the lofty Great Hall of Winchester, where hung the Round Table said to have seated King Arthur's knights. Due to the great number of prisoners, they would be tried in groups according to district. On the second day of the hearings, Mace was delivered to the Hall along with nineteen others, in a gaoler's cart.

The forecourt was packed with well-wishers and petitioners. Sympathy for the labourers had grown among the public as terror of the roving mobs had abated. The prisoners' escort of Special Constables noisily cleared a path to the door.

The court was being held at the opposite end of the Hall from the suspended Round Table, and proceedings took place behind a curved plaster partition. Tom, who was to be called as a character witness for Mace, had obtained seats for himself, Jess and Vinnie on the public benches, which on this occasion were reserved for relatives of the twenty accused. The twins, though mutinous, had been left at home.

Tom clasped the hands of Jess and Vinnie, as the prisoners filed in and took their places in the dock, hob-nailed boots clattering on the raised wooden platform. Mace, looking around with interest, caught his wife's eye and smiled encouragingly; but Tom sensed the girl's horror of that dim, ancient hall, with its columns of Purbeck marble soaring darkly towards the steeply pitched roof, and the single window at either side of the partitioned courtroom admitting too little light.

He himself experienced an almost superstitious chill a moment later; for seated among those to be called as witnesses – a veritable crowd, most apparently finding room on the public benches – was the Earl of Wickham. Tom could think of no reason for his being there.

The judges entered, awesome in scarlet and ermine. The proceedings began. The indictment was ponderously read – and the charge was not just 'riotous assembly', but also 'extorting money with threats'.

Mace could hardly be convicted of that, Tom thought, whispering as much to Vinnie and giving Jessica's hand a reassuring squeeze. The only farmer his brother-in-law had threatened had refused to pay.

All the prisoners pleaded Not Guilty. A Grand Jury of no less than nineteen men was sworn in; all titled gentlemen or MPs. Not a labourer among them.

The accused comprised the alleged ringleaders of two separate marches of protest. For the first hour, the court heard of the apparently warlike activities of the twelve men arrested a week before Mace. Then it was the turn of the labourers led by Mace and Hensting.

Mr Follett, the prosecuting counsel, chose as his first witness the courageous farmer, one Mr Jeffreys. Jeffreys took the oath with assurance, and answered each question in the same manner. Yes, the mob at Botley had mostly been armed, but not with firearms. No, they had not attacked him. The man with the petition had threatened to fire his ricks unless he paid up.

"Do you see that man present in this court?" asked Follett.

"I do." Jeffreys pointed straight at Mace. "No mistake, for he was the tallest of them all, and he wore that orange striped waistcoat, though it was cleaner then."

"Do you also see the first man who menaced you?"

Jeffreys indicated Hensting. "Him – with the black jerkin."

Follett moved to a small table of exhibits – papers, and a few hammers – and picked up three sewn sheets of paper.

"I should like you to study this petition, Mr Jeffreys, and inform the court whether it is the same as that carried by the tall prisoner on the day in question."

Jeffreys perused the document. "The words are the same, near as I recall. I couldn't swear to the handwriting, for I never saw it then. He only read it out loud. I wouldn't look at it."

Mr Missing, defending the labourers, had no questions for Jeffreys, asking him merely to confirm that Mace Tandy had not been armed.

Follett returned to the table, shuffling the papers, taking another. "I call Abel Kitcher to the witness box," he said.

The name meant nothing to Tom, but he saw Mace's head jerk; saw too his frowning profile, apprehensive and puzzled.

Kitcher took the stand proudly, glad to perform his duty.

"Mr Kitcher," said Follett, "you are resident on the estate known as Durley Park, and are employed as a bailiff by his lordship the Earl of Wickham, who occupies the Grange. Is that correct?"

"Yes, sir, it is."

Tom looked sharply at Mace; their eyes met, and Mace shook his head fractionally, miming the words, "I didn't know."

"On the evening of Sunday 29th November this year, you were present at the tavern known as The Jolly Sailor, in Bursledon?"

"That's so. His lordship wished me to find out from the shipwrights how work on the new flyer was progressing."

"Would you be so kind as to enlighten the court, Mr Kitcher? What is meant by the word 'flyer'? A fast yacht, perhaps?"

"Just that, sir. The yacht being built for Mr Vaillant, at the yard of Elderfield & Tandy."

"What was Lord Wickham's interest?"

"He's having a new cutter built at Cowes, to be launched next spring."

"We speak, then, of sporting rivalry between two gentlemen. Lord Wickham desired to know whether Mr Vaillant's yacht was progressing as well as his own."

"Yes, sir."

"And did anything unusual occur, while you were in conversation with the said shipwrights?"

"Mr Tandy came in – the tall prisoner – to fetch fifty copies of the Twopenny Trash. I was told he sells them round the neighbourhood."

Two of the judges murmured to each other, and the Duke of Wellington lowered his brows, the hooked nose jutting ominously.

"I see," said Follett. "Pray go on."

"Mr Tandy said there'd be a march the next morning, and did anyone want to join it. There were a good many labourers in the taproom."

"Tandy was organising this march?"

"He didn't say so – but I saw him write the petition, and sign his own name first."

"Was this the petition, Mr Kitcher?"

Wickham's bailiff gave it a cursory glance. "That was it."

"And this proposed march would be peaceful, I suppose."

"Mr Tandy thought it might be. But he did say, 'If it comes to a fight, you'll find me as ready as any man.'"

"Those were his exact words?"

"They were."

"What happened then? After Tandy had signed his own petition?"

"He wrote a lot of 'Swing' letters. He fetched out a little bottle of blood for the purpose."

Several members of the Grand Jury grimaced in contemptuous disgust. There were mutterings of surprise and interest from the public benches. Tom whispered, "Jesus Christ, you silly bastard." Mace looked like a man caught in some incredible nightmare.

Follett asked, "Do you mean that he wrote threatening letters in blood, demanding money from farmers, and signed himself 'Swing'?"

"He did."

"Is this letter one of those you saw penned by Tandy?"

Kitcher studied it closely. "Yes. No doubting all those loops and fancy squiggles."

"Quite." Follett addressed the judges' bench. "My lords, with your permission I shall circulate these two documents among the Gentlemen of the Jury. I believe that the most casual glance will confirm that they were written by the same hand."

The papers were duly circulated. Mace sent his family a look of helpless anger.

Follett went on: "How did the 'Swing' letter, which you have just positively identified, first come into your possession, Mr Kitcher?"

"It was shown to me some days after the march, by a tenant farmer on Lord Wickham's estate. The man begged me to apply to his lordship for a reduction in rent, as he had been obliged through fear to raise the wages of his men."

"The letter, then, had forced him to take reluctant action. Money had been extorted – however indirectly – by means of threats. Threats made by the prisoner Tandy, under the name of Captain Swing."

264

"That's the truth of it."

Mr Missing, the defence counsel, rose to his feet. "Objection, my lords! My learned friend wishes this court to infer that Mace Tandy and Captain Swing are one and the same. There have been scores of 'Swing' letters, and all penned by different hands."

Mr Justice Parke frowned. "Mr Follett merely stated the facts. Objection overruled."

Missing cross-examined Abel Kitcher, but could not shake his story. The prosecution called the supposedly intimidated farmer to testify; the man only confirmed Kitcher's fairy-tale.

Then it was the turn of the Earl of Wickham. His testimony was concisely delivered, and he cut a handsome and imposing figure. He exuded integrity.

"Kitcher has served as my bailiff for seven years. He is an upright, honest man. On the 29th of November I had indeed despatched him to Bursledon, to enquire into the rate of progress on Mr Vaillant's new yacht. If Kitcher states that he saw Tandy pen letters in blood, then personally I should not doubt it for a moment."

"You speak with certainty, my lord."

"I know Tandy to be a dangerous and volatile character, subject to outbursts of ungovernable violence."

Missing cried out, "Objection, my lords! With respect to his lordship the Earl, my learned friend is wilfully leading his witness astray. My client Mace Tandy is not charged with having committed any form of assault. This 'evidence' can have no bearing on the case whatsoever."

Mr Justice Parke scowled at him. "You will be given opportunity to cross-examine his lordship the Earl. Do not interrupt again without just cause."

Wickham inclined his head towards the judges' bench, and continued. "In the summer of '27 I attended a launching party at the yard of Elderfield & Tandy. My motives were entirely amiable, as Mrs Elderfield could easily verify." His eyes flickered towards the public benches, and he smiled at Jessica before focusing his attention once again on the prosecuting counsel and the Grand Jurors. "While in conversation with Mrs Elderfield, I was attacked by Tandy and brought to the ground. I was taken completely by surprise.

He punched me in the face before Mrs Elderfield was able to drag him off."

"This occurred without the slightest provocation from your lordship?"

"Entirely. There was a small postscript to the event, which might interest the court. After I had left the yard, a friend of mine – Sir Bevis Ponsonby, who will gladly confirm my testimony if desired to do so – overheard a snippet of conversation. Mrs Elderfield was telling her husband of the unrest among the labourers on my estate, when Tandy exclaimed, "It's about time!""

"So three years ago, the accused was already in favour of militant action?"

"Indubitably."

Missing began rather hesitantly to cross-examine the Earl, for Wickham had clearly impressed the Jury. His eagerness to condemn Mace's words and behaviour had not lost him any friends among the judges, either: the Earl was simply showing a high regard for his own person and property, and righteous anger at the young man who had threatened both.

Missing said, "Notwithstanding the account we have just heard, my lord, I . . . I submit that you had a long-standing grudge against Mace Tandy, before the alleged assault took place."

"On the contrary, I have been on amicable terms with Tandy and his sister – Mrs Elderfield – for many years."

The defence counsel opened his mouth and shut it again. He was obviously not about to accuse Wickham of having kept Mrs Elderfield as his mistress before her marriage; though the fact was an open secret among local people.

He cleared his throat, and said, "You freely admit that Tandy attacked you without provocation. I submit that, for this reason alone, you would perhaps feel justified in wishing to punish him."

"Had I wished to do that," Wickham said, his tone icily polite, "I would surely have pressed charges at the time."

Except, Tom thought, that fist-fights among gentlemen were not uncommon, and sympathies at that launching party had been evenly divided between Mace and Wickham.

Now, however, the Earl's logic seemed unanswerable.

Two more witnesses appeared for the prosecution;

labourers who had been at The Jolly Sailor when Mace wrote the 'Swing' letter. Both agreed with Kitcher in every detail. They must have been well bribed.

Tom realised, with dreadful foreboding, that the trial was no longer the Crown versus twenty labourers. It was the Earl of Wickham versus Elderfield & Tandy.

Beginning the case for the defence, Missing called two farmers who testified to the sober courtesy of the ringleaders, and the peacefulness of the mob in general.

Next came three shipwrights who had visited the tavern on the fateful evening. But these men were now seeing what happened to those who crossed the Earl of Wickham. They could not recall the details, they said. They had not paid Tandy and Kitcher much attention; though one of them ventured that things hadn't seemed quite as Kitcher reckoned.

"And," he added, twisting his hat between his hands, "I've never heard that his lordship had much affection for Mr Elderfield nor Mace Tandy, and most folk in this courtroom can very likely guess why. And that's all I know about it."

None of the shipwrights would look at Mace after they stepped down.

By the time Mace stood in the witness box, he was white-faced and plainly furious. He told the truth firmly and with conviction; but without peaching on his mates he could not suggest that others had written 'Swing' letters that night. When cross-examined by Follett for the prosecution, he admitted to having distributed various pamphlets since moving to Bursledon; but he denied with heat that the mob had intended violence to any person.

"The labourers are starving," he told the court passionately. "Anyone who sees their plight must sympathise with them. We didn't need to use threats, except on Farmer Jeffreys. People were glad to give a few shillings, if that was all they could afford, even though not all of them would sign the petition. You submit that we were a riotous assembly. No one read us the Riot Act. No one had reason to!"

"By your testimony," said Follett, "you label Mr Kitcher a liar. By extension, Lord Wickham must also have perjured himself in stating the motive for his bailiff's visit to Bursledon. Is that so?"

"His lordship," said Mace, glaring straight at the Earl, "would do all in his power to hurt Tom Elderfield. If getting me transported were to ruin the company, then maybe Wickham would consider he'd scored a point or two."

"Slanderous nonsense! You are seeking to blacken his lordship's character and thereby redeem your own. Do you deny that you penned this letter?" Waving the sheet of paper. "And signed yourself 'Swing'?"

"No! I've already admitted —"

"Thank you, Tandy. No further questions."

Due to the tight schedule — the judges had one week to decide two hundred and eighty-five cases — only one character witness was allowed for each prisoner. As Tom left his seat to speak for Mace, Jessica whispered, "Tell them! For God's sake, Tom, tell them everything!"

To do that would be foolhardy indeed. The Duke of Wellington, the three judges and the Grand Jury were all ranged on Wickham's side. To embark on a lengthy tale of plot and counter-plot would sound to them like an imaginative, scurrilous, last ditch attempt to save his brother-in-law from transportation and his boatyard from possible ruin.

Instead, he pointed out that he and the accused had been closely acquainted since Mace's birth, and for most of the ensuing twenty-seven years. He praised his partner's talent, integrity, and genuine desire to right the world's wrongs. He stated that Mace had stood unarmed against the dragoons, and that the prosecution had not disputed this.

"My lords," he said, " if my partner must be charged with a crime, it should be naivety, for having believed — along with all the men in the dock — that a few protest marches could accomplish a miracle —"

"That will do, Mr Elderfield!" interrupted Mr Justice Alderson. "Let me remind every person present that we are not here to inquire into grievances. We are here to decide the law."

The remark caused a ripple of anger in the public gallery. Tom could not credit that the labourers' motives should be totally discounted. He said quickly, afraid of being ordered to step down, "Mace Tandy did not inform this court of the whole truth. My wife was the Earl of Wickham's mistress for

268

the five years preceding our marriage. He has not yet forgiven me for taking her from him –"

"Hah!" Follett was incredulous. The noise from the public benches rose like a tide. "So now we are asked to believe in some form of elaborate vendetta!"

"Not elaborate. Very simple."

"And all these witnesses were bribed, I assume."

"Those who are not too frightened to speak out, yes, I imagine so."

"Order!" The Duke of Wellington roared. A hush fell. Someone coughed nervously. "You will be fortunate, Elderfield, if his lordship the Earl of Wickham chooses not to sue you for slander of the most repulsive and unforgivable nature. You were called in good faith as a character witness for Tandy. Take yourself back to your seat, sir, and spare this court any more of your sordid fantasies!"

Tom was as white with fury as his partner as he strode back to Jess and Vinnie.

Neither the prosecuting counsel nor the defence had anything new to say in conclusion; they merely reminded the Jury of the evidence placed before them – which, as Missing emphasized, did not include an account of old quarrels at a launching party three years previously. He drew the Jury's attention to the fact that Tandy and four other men on the same march had been unarmed throughout.

Mr Justice Parke summed up on behalf of the judges.

"Gentlemen of the Jury, it must be clear to you all that we are being faced this winter with a concerted effort by treacherous and misguided men to incite Southern labourers to revolution. The prisoners in the dock comprise the ringleaders – and in some cases the most savage members – of two separate mobs. Riotous multitudes, who roamed the county armed for rapine and plunder in defiance of the law. Whether or not every single man among them carried a weapon is of little moment. A General may command his troops to join battle and yet not fire a single shot. Would that render his command invalid? When considering your verdict, Gentlemen, I advise you to bear in mind the evidence against the prisoner Tandy; namely that letters penned by him did in fact terrify at least one honest farmer into raising wages. You may retire, Gentlemen."

Predictably enough, the Jury was not long absent; but there were some surprises in their verdict. Three of the twenty prisoners were acquitted – to the unconcealed annoyance of the judges – on the grounds of lack of evidence identifying them as members of either mob. Sixteen, including Hensting, were found guilty only of riotous assembly.

"We find the prisoner Mace Tandy," said the chosen foreman, "Guilty, as charged, of both riotous assembly and extorting money with menaces."

Vinnie gave a whimper of terror, and Tom clutched her hand. He glanced at Jessica, seeing that she too was bracing herself to hear the worst. Seven years, he thought; and too many transported criminals never came home.

It was customary to pass sentence at the close of the Assizes; but again at these hearings the sheer numbers made this impractical. Mr Justice Parke, after a brief conference with his colleagues, decided the fate of the prisoners at once. Ten of the convicted men received six months' hard labour; Hensting and five others would be transported for seven years. From the public benches came cries of outrage and grief; no one had guessed that the sentences would be so harsh for relatively minor offences. The judge called the court to order, before fixing his eyes on the one prisoner who had yet to hear his fate.

"Mace Tandy," he said, "the crime of extorting money with threats carries the same penalty as though actual force had been used. It is a capital offence, although more men are transported than hanged in this enlightened age. The court has heard today, from divers sources, of your conduct during the past five years. You have actively encouraged the spread of banned and seditious literature, and spoken openly in support of violent revolution. You have confessed yourself 'as ready as any man' for a fight, and certainly proved the savagery of your temper by your unprovoked attack upon Lord Wickham. You are prosperous, well known in the community, and therefore politically influential. You have been found guilty of extorting money, not under your own name, but using the alias of Captain Swing."

The judge paused. The courtroom was utterly silent. Mr

Justice Parke continued, leaning forward slightly, "There are some, I believe, who dismiss Swing as a mythical figure. Others argue that he is a foreign infiltrator. It is the opinion of this judicial bench that he is neither a myth nor one man, but a collection of disaffected, articulate and violently motivated men, all of whom we are bound by duty to flush out and destroy, if this land is ever to know again the tranquillity it once enjoyed."

Pausing for the second time, he snapped his fingers at the court chaplain, who shuffled forward and passed him a black square of cloth.

Mr Justice Parke placed the cloth over his wig.

"Hear, therefore, the sentence which the laws of man have awarded against you for your crimes – which is that you, Mace Tandy, be taken from hence to the place from whence you came, and from thence to the place of execution, there to be hanged by the neck until you are dead. And may God, in his infinite mercy, have compassion on your soul."

CHAPTER NINE

With a sense of unreality Mace listened to the judge's censorious voice droning on and on.

"I am bound to exclude from your mind any hope of earthly mercy, and must point your attention to that higher tribunal where the most wretched sinner may by repentance achieve salvation . . . Apply earnestly and immediately to the reverend gentleman who will be placed over you . . ."

Mace became aware of a girl's loud, uncontrolled sobbing. Looking over his shoulder, he saw Jess supporting his wife from the Hall. It wrenched at his heart; he could not bear that Vinnie should suffer.

The enormity of what had happened struck at him then. They were going to take him away from Vinnie. He would never see Crosstrees or the yard again. Never work singing alongside the men on the scaffolding. Never see his flyer launched.

He was led from the Great Hall with the other prisoners, and bundled roughly into the gaoler's cart outside. All around him on the forecourt were grief-stricken women, held back from their menfolk by the Special Constables. He did not catch sight of Vinnie until too late, when he was already in the cart. He stretched his bound hands down to her, and she clasped them tightly, running alongside until Jessica pulled her away, in fear that she would be trampled by the crowd.

At the gaol, he was placed alone in a condemned cell. The chaplain harassed him constantly, though Mace had neither interest nor belief in heavenly salvation. He did not want comfort in the Valley of the Shadow. He only wanted to live.

Tom came to the gaol three days after his conviction. Mace was shocked; his partner looked as though he had not slept since the trial.

"I've spoken to John Ekless," Tom said, pacing the length of the cell. "You're not to give up hope. Ekless has already saved two labourers from the gallows. If your sentence is commuted to transportation for life, we'll find a way to send Vinnie with you. And we've started a petition – I've been riding round the villages –"

"The judges think I'm Swing," said Mace.

"There's no such person, for Christ's sake! You've done nothing that deserves even transportation."

"I've been wondering if Wickham could somehow be made to confess."

"Confess to what? You wrote the petition, and that stupid bloody letter. You attacked him when *Spirit* was launched. You couldn't deny any of the words Wickham and Kitcher claimed you'd spoken. It was only the context that was twisted. How the hell is any of that going to save you?"

Mace sat on the edge of the hard bed, staring down at his clasped hands. After a moment he looked up at Tom, and said quietly, "I've got another three weeks. It's too long, just sitting and pacing and thinking. I'm not strong enough to die like this, mate."

Tom stood still, leaned against the wall. "We're partners," he said. "You're not going to hang. Damn it, I won't let it happen! I've written to the Duke, and Parke, and the Home Secretary –"

"Where's Vinnie?"

"Oh . . . she wanted to come. Jess is bringing her tomorrow. I was hoping – I thought we might have good news for you both by then."

Mace knew that his attitude must seem defeatist to Tom, but for as long as he continued to hope and yearn for a reprieve, he could not face the prospect of imminent death with any degree of resignation. In sheer self-defence, he dared not be too optimistic; though after those initial, despairing days he managed to put on a brave front for his wife and sister.

Vinnie was allowed to visit him four times, under the gaoler's watchful eye. After the first occasion she was resolute, composed, determined to make the best of their time together, even while she clung to the hope that Mace would be transported after all. He was proud of her, and thought of her every minute. Tom brought him some paper and charcoal – with the gaoler's dubious consent – and after that he would draw for hour upon hour: portraits of Vinnie, and then of everyone at Crosstrees; even a sketch of the flyer surrounded by scaffolding and wooden platforms, with men laughing as they worked. Only the colours were missing, but he could imagine those.

In the New Year, his elder brother came to the prison. Obadiah was staying at Crosstrees. Having recently moved lodgings, he had just received a letter written by Jess a month ago, and had travelled at once from Deptford. The brothers had not met in ten years, and although Mace was glad that Obadiah had cared enough to travel seventy miles, the meeting was awkward, neither of them knowing what to say, and Mace was relieved when he did not come again.

Mace forbade Tom and Jess to bring their children to the gaol, and they agreed it would be too upsetting for the twins, and the air of the place unhealthy for Annis. As well as drawing materials, Tom had brought him decent clothes from home, while a small bribe gave him the chance of a wash now and then; but the building as whole was still over-crowded with men awaiting transportation. The place was rank with the smell of ordure and the sweat of fear.

Of the seven Hampshire men sentenced to hang for their part in the 'uprising', four were eventually reprieved.

Mace was not one of them. Tom received a letter from Mr Justice Parke, reiterating his summing up at the trial, and stating that while he appreciated the nobility of Tom's motives in attempting to save his brother-in-law, Mace Tandy had been instructed not to hope for earthly mercy, and – petitions notwithstanding – the decision of the judicial bench must stand.

Mace was not surprised. He grew impatient with the nagging chaplain; but by the evening prior to his execution, he had come to terms in his own way with the necessity of losing everyone and everything he loved so much.

Or so he believed – until, just after lamplighting, the warder admitted five visitors to the cell. Honor ran ahead of

Vinnie, straight into his arms, and he bent his head over hers and held her tight.

"Why did you come?" he said brokenly. "Tom, you promised—"

"We wouldn't stay at home," Luke said. "Pa couldn't make us."

And Tom said softly, "I couldn't, mate. How could I?"

Honor looked up, her face wet. "I can't bear it, Uncle Macey."

Tom stepped forward, drew his daughter gently away. "Hush now," he said, "No more of that talk."

Mace hugged his sister before turning to Vinnie, who stood silent, shedding no tears.

"My loveliest girl," he said.

She came to him, and for long moments they clung to one another. At last a shudder went through Vinnie. "If our baby had lived," she said, "I would have had something of you still."

Mace bowed his head, then with tortured gaiety he looked at each of the people who were more important to him than life.

"Do you think," he said, "that I'll be content to rot along with my bones in some old churchyard? Oh, don't say you'll ever think of me like that. Vinnie, love . . ." He put his hands on either side of her head. "They can't kill the memories, can they? This is where I'll live – in your minds, all of you – and maybe your hearts for a while, if my luck holds. How's that for immortality, eh?"

Honor turned her face against Tom's chest and wept. Luke had an arm around his mother; he was nearly the same height as her now. He said, since his father could not speak, "The flyer's getting prettier every day. The men have been working at double speed. I think . . . I think sort of to make it up to you, for the things they didn't dare admit in court."

Mace did not know what he could say to comfort his family. Perhaps, after all, his own view of the truth would be enough.

"I'll tell you what to do," he said. "Ask Vaillant to take you out on the flyer, when there's a real forget-me-not sky and a stiff breeze blowing up the Solent, and the wave crests are white and curling. Seamen reckon, don't they, that birds that follow ships are the souls of drowned sailors. Maybe my soul will be the flyer. She's my share of eternity – her, and the new generation of yachts that you'll build, Tom, from her design."

Jessica shook her head. Vinnie said, speaking for them both, "It's not enough. She's not you."

He held her close, buried his face in her hair. Rosewater and lavender; the scent of her would be with him always – but always was only a night and a cold dawn. He shut his eyes against the treacherous tears. How could he let her go, knowing this was the last time he would ever feel her arms around him, or the warmth of her body against his?

The warder said from the doorway, not without compassion, "Hurry it up, Tandy, you're not allowed all night for farewells."

Blindly he held Vinnie from him, and embraced all his family in turn, even Luke who would not normally have suffered it. Seeing that Jess was near to breaking, he said, laughing through his tears, "Give Annis a great smacking kiss for me – and Smudge too, if you can bear to do it."

"Oh, Macey," she said.

He came last to Tom, and the partners gripped each other in a brief and fierce embrace. Then Mace stood back, and lightly punched Tom's shoulder.

"We were a grand bloody team, weren't we, mate?" he said.

"Knew we would be. Don't the best exceptions . . . make the world go round?"

The brightness and promise of that summer of '26 seemed very long ago. Mace raised a crooked grin.

"Only in a perfect world," he said.

Their eyes locked in a silent, intense communication. Mace nodded. "Anything planned?" he asked.

"I will have. Trust me. He's mine."

Mace had seen his friend look like that only once before; on the night Tom had decided to confront Wickham in East Cowes.

"Take care, Elderfield," he said. "Look after everyone."

"Bet on it, Tandy."

None of them said a literal goodbye. The gaoler, tolerant but mindful of his duty, ushered the visitors with firmness from the cell. Mace had only time to kiss Vinnie once more before she was gone.

The door was shut. The key rattled in the lock.

Stooping, he chose a portrait of Vinnie from the pile of sketches beside his bed. Then he lay down on the hard, thin mattress, and propped the sheet of paper upright against the wall a few inches from his head.

He gazed at her until the gaoler returned to extinguish the lamp, leaving him only darkness and memories to help him through the long night.

The winter morning dawned greyly. The chaplain came, to make a final, earnest effort to redeem Mace's soul. Mace had no time for such irrelevancies. Refusing the offered prayer book, he held the sketch of Vinnie while a warder bound his hands, and was permitted to take it with him from the cell.

It was almost eight o'clock. The other two condemned men were steered ahead of him to the back of the gaol, where the raised platform of the portable scaffold overlooked the prison yard and the shabby dwellings of Staple Gardens. It seemed that most of the convicted rioters had gathered to watch the executions from the yard. In the alleys and green areas beyond the wall, a hushed and shuffling crowd was still growing.

The first condemned man to mount the steps to the scaffold was hardly more than a boy. He was to die for aiming an unsuccessful blow at the head of an MP, who had captured one of his friends. By no means all of the marches had been peaceful. The youth was dressed in rags, and sobbed loudly with terror while the noose was tied around his neck. Only when the trapdoor swung open and his feet dropped into air, did his cries choke gradually to silence. The hangman as usual suspended his own weight from the body of the dying boy, to end his suffering as quickly as possible; but it was ten minutes before the corpse ceased to twitch.

Mace had resolved to be calm and show no fear, but the boy's lingering agony struck him cold to the heart. His mouth was parched; he trembled in every limb. A sideways glance showed him the face of Cooper, the other condemned

man, bent over the chaplain's prayer book in desperate concentration. An awed hush lay over the yard and beyond the
walls; there would be no cheers raised for these executions.

A breeze eddied about Mace; he thought it came from the
south. He smelled the odours of the city and the prison;
sweat and woodsmoke and baking bread. Through them
came a different scent; faint, half-imagined, drifting on the
sighing wind. Rosewater and lavender.

Then he knew – and though he had no faith in an afterlife
as the chaplain understood it, he whispered, "Vinnie," with
more love than reproach.

When his turn came, he climbed the steps with a determined tread, and did not flinch from the feel of the rope
around his neck.

By the time the trapdoor fell away beneath his feet, he was
no longer afraid.

Vinnie often woke early, before the household was astir;
but that night she had not slept. Jess had been with her until
an hour ago, and had left only when Vinnie insisted, with
composure, that she would prefer to be alone to rest for a
while.

They would not leave her undisturbed for long, she knew
that. Some member of the family would return well before
eight o'clock.

On the dressing chest, a clock ticked sombrely. Nearly
half past seven. The pink walls glowed with the dawn, for
Vinnie did not care for closed curtains. The bed felt cold on
the side where Mace should have lain.

She rose quietly and looked down from the window. The
warm light in the room had been deceptive, and the sky was
grey. The flowing river was edged with ice. Vinnie could see,
through the naked trees, the place on the bank where she and
Mace had taken their gypsy wedding vows.

"To go where thou goest," she murmured, "live wherever
thou livest . . ."

On the slipway the flyer stood proudly, near completion,
the beauty of her lines visible even through the network of
scaffolding.

"To share with thee all things . . ."

Vinnie put on her best blue skirt and embroidered bodice,

and tied the scarlet cravat – Mace's first gift to her – in her hair. She ran lightfooted down the stairs, and grimaced at the creaking of the front door as she opened it.

The boatyard was quite deserted. No one challenged her, nor called from the windows of Crosstrees as she approached the high, dark, looming hull of the new yacht. She stood for a minute gazing up at the poles and platforms that surrounded the flyer.

"All things, Macey," she whispered, "until the day of my death."

Vinnie had climbed the scaffolding before. It was not difficult for a young and supple girl. Gaining the horizontal pole above the lowest platform, she stood up straight, holding on with one hand.

A breath of icy wind made her shiver, as she untied the long cravat from her hair and knotted one end securely around the next pole above her, and the other end around her neck.

She turned her face towards the north, and Winchester. Then with neither hesitation nor fear she let her feet drop from the lower pole.

She had been dead some minutes when Jessica found her.

CHAPTER TEN

In the days following the double tragedy, it seemed that all life had gone out of the boatyard. The shipwrights worked harder than ever, but they spoke in low voices under a grey and sombre sky. There was no more laughter. None of them were told where Vinnie had died, for they were as superstitious as sailors, and would not have climbed the scaffolding again.

Tom and Jess drew strength from one another, doing their best to fill the gap left in their children's lives and to behave naturally with Annis, who was just learning to talk. The little girl had been spoiled by Mace in particular since the day she was born, and although he had been absent since the end of November she still missed his bright presence, and his voice singing her to sleep. Often when a door opened she would turn in sudden expectation, as if her gangling, tousle-headed uncle might stride into the room at any moment, to shout her name gleefully and toss her in his arms. It broke Jessica's heart.

Mace's body was conveyed home to Bursledon. He was buried in the churchyard, alongside the unmarked graves where Vinnie and their baby lay. A midnight trip to the churchyard and a bribe accepted by the sexton had allowed Vinnie to lie in consecrated ground. Tom knew this mattered to him more than it would have done to the young couple. For them, it would have been enough that they were together.

The Elderfields had assumed that Obadiah would return to London after Mace's funeral, but he remained at Cross-trees, having quitted his job in Deptford. He was a sullen guest, and showed scant affection for his sister or anyone else. Tom suspected that he stayed in the hope of being offered employment, perhaps even a partnership to keep the name of Elderfield & Tandy alive. Tom was not interested. He thought Obadiah a feckless drifter; and while yachts continued to be built to Mace's designs, Mace would be his partner still.

Three nights after the funeral, Tom lay awake into the small hours, as he had done every night since the execution. He stared up into the darkness, hands clasped behind his head. From the age of fifteen, he had had good reason to hate and despise those who stepped outside the law to commit murder and call it justice. Yet now, he would have struck down the Earl of Wickham in cold blood without a twinge of conscience.

If harm came to Wickham – even by accident – his friends would demand a full and careful inquiry. In the event of any hint of foul play, Tom would be the prime suspect. Either he would share Mace's fate, or his family would be in more danger than they were at present; for if the law could not gather sufficient evidence to punish him, there were men who would do so without that evidence. He had been given a taste of their methods in East Cowes.

Jessica stirred beside him, already half awake. "Can't you sleep, darling?" she said.

"How can Wickham – how can he believe that you'd ever go back to him now, ever love him, whatever threats he used?"

Jessica turned on to her side and touched her fingers to his lips. "I don't even know whether he still wants me back."

"Is it only vengeance, then? Nothing but that? He killed Mace for no other reason than to hurt me?"

"Don't you know," she whispered, "why Macey and those other men were hanged, and why all those hundreds of labourers from five counties are filling the convict ships? The mobs were a threat to property, not to lives. The rest was just propaganda by the press. Not one person was ever killed by a so-called rioter, were they?"

"No," he said, with bitterness. "The muskets and sabres were all on the other side."

"Because property is – well, it's sacrosanct to landowners like Wickham."

"That's always been true, Jess. Why else did keepers set traps and spring-guns in the old days, unless their pheasants were more important than men's lives?"

"Wickham loved me. I was stolen from him by a bold upstart, a blacksmith's son who dared to outwit and humiliate a peer of the realm and do so in front of witnesses. You poached his property . . . and his lordship was always death on poachers."

Tom grimaced at the ceiling. "I thought you said he was the poor man's friend."

"He used to say that he paid his men fair wages, and therefore they shouldn't kill his game. It was unsportsmanlike, he said."

"And spring-guns weren't?" Tom caught his breath suddenly, and raised himself to one elbow. "Guns and traps have been illegal for three years. Would Wickham be one of those to carry on using them regardless?"

"Yes," she said. "I think he would. The law can't be enforced, can it? When has a gamekeeper employed by a powerful landowner ever been arrested for murdering a poacher?"

Tom lay back, frowning. Jessica said, "What is it? What are you thinking?"

But his thoughts were hazy as yet. Instead of replying, he reached for his wife, needing her desperately; needing also to escape, just for an hour or two, from the plans for vengeance that might well result in failure and his own death.

Four years of marriage had not sated Jessica's appetite for his lovemaking, and by the time he took her she was aware of nothing beyond the breathless, joyful reality of their united bodies. Not until Tom sank down exhausted beside her did Jessica hear the sounds from the yard, and see a light leap across the ceiling from between the closed curtains.

"Tom!"

She leapt naked from the bed and rushed to drag back the curtains. Tom was at her side within seconds.

The tool-store and mould-loft were ablaze, with sparks blowing in a rising wind across piles of newly delivered oak timber and the upturned hulls of two skiffs under repair.

Blowing towards the flyer.

Tom and Jessica dressed frantically in the nearest clothes

to hand, and ran from the bedchamber fumbling with hooks and buttons, yelling to wake the household. The twins were easily roused. Annis was left in the care of the maidservant.

Jess and the twins, equipped with bowls and buckets, were at the front door when Tom came bounding after them. "Obadiah's gone. His bed has been slept in, and his knapsack is still there. What do you reckon, Jess?"

"You don't think – why should he? – and he doesn't know about the insurance."

"He does," said Honor. "I – I thought it was all right. Our own uncle –"

Tom gave her a look that made her flinch, and hustled her through the doorway with the others. "Run into Bursledon," he told her. "Yell at the top of your voice. Knock on every door. Not just where our men are billeted. Bring the whole bloody village. We'll need more buckets too. Now *run!*"

While Honor fled down the drive, the rest of the family sprinted to the river. At the end of the jetty they filled their buckets from deep water, racing then to douse the blazing tool store, the shed nearest to *Joie-de-Vivre*.

The fire was more widespread than at first appeared. The sheds and stores were not by any means tinder-dry, but each one of them had been set alight from the inside. Almost nothing within could be saved, even where the outer walls remained intact.

More than two hundred villagers eventually ran or shambled down the lane to the yard. Tom organised them to form chains from the jetty and slipways to the blazing buildings and smouldering piles of timber.

All four Elderfields formed one end of another chain, climbing the scaffolding to protect *Joie-de-Vivre* from the thousands of sparks and glowing pieces of thatch blown on to her deck and into the standing rigging. It was very clear in Tom's mind that if he lost everything else, the whole of four years' investment, he must not lose Mace's flyer.

The fact that he would have to declare himself bankrupt if *Joie-de-Vivre* burned did not occur to him that night.

It took an hour to bring the flames under control. At four o'clock in the morning, with the villagers and shipwrights trudging home in small, weary groups, Tom and Jessica stood at the gates to thank them individually and bid them a grateful goodnight. Around them, the ruins of the boatyard smoked in the darkness. The proud sign advertising the name of Elderfield & Tandy was charred at the edges, and hung crookedly on blackened posts.

Tom and Jessica returned to Crosstrees to find the twins sitting on the steps. In the dim light from the hallway the children's faces were flushed and charcoal-smeared, their clothes holed by flying sparks. Honor's long hair had been singed in places.

"We saved her," Honor said with a catch in her voice. "We saved the flyer for Uncle Macey."

The four of them went indoors, saying little, all of them knowing the extent of the disaster. Most of Tom's working capital for the coming year had been invested in the timber, ninety per cent of which would be unusable. Tom felt bone-tired and suddenly old. He had no idea whether saving *Joie-de-Vivre* would be enough to save the company.

Honor said, her eyes bleak, "It can't have been Uncle Obadiah. It just can't."

Tom hugged his daughter into his side. "Maybe it wasn't. Never mind, little girl. You weren't to know." But his tone was flat and not totally forgiving.

In the hall they stopped, in sheer disbelief. Obadiah was descending the stairs casually, morosely, knapsack on his back. To the Elderfields, his intention to leave the house before dawn was sufficient proof of guilt.

Tom let go of Honor and stood at the foot of the stairs. "Where the hell were you," he said, "when half the village was working to save my yard?"

Obadiah paused about six stairs from the bottom. An unpleasant smile twisted his heavy features. "Watching," he said.

Tom was on him almost before the word was out. Obadiah was more than ready for a fight; had sought one, surely, with his public exit from Crosstrees. He blocked Tom's first punch and tried to kick Tom's legs from under him. He received in answer a straight jab in the ribs, and with apparent rage he launched himself at his opponent. The two men rolled together down the stairs into the hall.

The battle did not last long. Obadiah found himself under

attack from two sturdy fourteen-year-olds who fought like wild animals, with fists, feet and teeth, while Jessica's nails tore viciously at him as she struggled to drag the men apart. Whatever damage Tom was doing to him was nothing by comparison.

Swearing obscenely, he rolled out of reach and staggered to his feet, backing against the wall. Honor would have flown at him again, had Jessica not grabbed her arm as Tom stood up from the floor. Tom knew how his daughter felt. It took a tremendous effort of self-control not to hurl himself at Obadiah.

He said, panting, "D'you fancy . . . telling us why . . . you felt the need to destroy my company . . .?"

Obadiah threw up his head and let out a great guffaw of mirthless laughter. "You," he said, "have destroyed more than that, Elderfield, in your time."

Tom snarled, "A pretty sight, eh, Jess? The cornered rat, striking out at everyone who stands too close. Don't push your luck, Tandy."

"Tandys stick together," said Obadiah harshly. "That's what folk reckoned, back in Hatchley. It wasn't ever quite like that, was it, Elderfield? You and Amos . . . mates from the start. Not Amos and me. But that wasn't enough for you – oh, no! You had to get him killed, and then take Jessie – take her from her own family. She came home pregnant. As for Mace . . . he always did think the sun shone out of your baby-blue eyes. I was the outsider. Never you."

"Your choice, then. Not mine."

Obadiah half laughed, then shook his head. "You bloody sicken me. His lordship was right about you, Elderfield. You're a sore that's been allowed to fester too long in this county. You needed . . . cauterising."

Tom was shaking with fury. "You told Wickham the insurance had been cancelled? You were paid – by Wickham – by the man who murdered your own brother –"

"No. He offered, all right, but I wouldn't stoop so low. I thought his idea a good one, that was all. I did it for the pleasure of watching your precious yard burn and seeing your face afterwards."

Tom held Luke's wrist as the boy started forward. "Get

out of our sight, Tandy," he hissed, "and if you value your miserable life, don't ever set foot on my property again."

Obadiah sneered at him. "Or you'll do what?"

Tom blinked. He heard himself saying, "Jess should have told you. I've got friends on the coast. A gang four hundred strong, led by an old seaman who once took something that was mine. If I needed the services of his men, even now, in compensation, and as a favour, he'd be honour bound to oblige me. Maybe you wouldn't mind fleeing from the vengeance of the Free Traders. After all, you've done it before and survived. Think about it, Tandy. Look over your shoulder now and then."

Obadiah's face was sallow and sweating. One might have thought he had been placed under a curse; as, in a way, he had.

Tom said through his teeth, "Now get out of my house."

Obadiah shouldered past him, looking neither to right nor left. As he walked fast down the drive, the Elderfields stood in the doorway to watch him go.

"You really meant it," Jessica murmured. "You'd go to Hicks, after what he did –"

"Because of what he did. I don't know." Tom narrowed his eyes at his brother-in-law's departing figure. "Maybe I should."

"Not to hurt Obadiah?" She shook his arm. "Tom, *don't*!"

"No," he said. "Not for that. Besides, the Free Trade doesn't wield that sort of power any more, although your brother is too far out of touch with South Coast people to realise it. These days, only the Earl of Wickham can engineer a 'just execution' and get away with it. Or think he has."

Whatever his family heard in his voice, Tom became aware that they were staring up at him with a kind of awe.

Luke said, "You've decided, haven't you, Papa? You know how to keep your promise to Uncle Macey."

"Yes," he said quietly. "I know, now."

CHAPTER ELEVEN

He was determined to keep his plans even from Jess. It was too soon to worry her; nothing was fixed or certain.

The first step, however, required her approval. He raised the subject next morning, when they were about to go downstairs for breakfast, and Jessica's reaction was much as he had anticipated.

"You want to send our children to *Guernsey?* To a woman who was your mistress for years? And you expect me to *like* it?"

"I'd rather you went too," he said, ignoring her look of outrage. "Though I know quite well that you won't be persuaded."

"Well, full marks for knowing your own wife, Tom Elderfield!"

He went to her, placed his hands on her shoulders. "Jessie . . ."

She folded her arms. "No. Annis is only a baby."

"She's nearly two years old, and Honor is used to looking after her. Jess, Mace is dead. The yard is a burnt-out ruin. If Wickham is only out for revenge, as you believe, he won't care what he does or who he hurts. For the next fortnight, I want our children well out of range."

Her eyes sought his, not in anger but with the stirrings of fear. "You're saying that in a fortnight it won't matter any more?"

"It won't, if I win."

"What you're going to do," she said, "it's dangerous, isn't it? I mean really dangerous . . . in the way that East Cowes was."

"This time I'll be holding all the aces."

"I want to help." She held his wrists and lowered his hands from her shoulders. "I love you, you proud stubborn bastard. Don't you dare shut me out!"

He kissed the end of her nose. "Then stay with me," he said, "and we'll keep the secret together. But the children should go to Madame de l'Erée."

He won the argument. Jessica would not risk her children's lives for the sake of petty jealousy over some long-dead love affair. Tom wrote to Hélène at once, and rode into Southampton with the letter, to ensure that it would catch the Guernsey mail-boat.

Jessica had been warned that he might be gone all day. When he had told her the plan she had been afraid for him, saying it would be worse than East Cowes, much worse, because this time the duel would be to the death. But he knew that she understood and shared his thirst for revenge. Mr Justice Parke had spoken of living in an 'enlightened age'. There was nothing enlightened or remotely civilised about Jessica's feelings towards the Earl of Wickham.

Besides, even doing nothing had become too perilous for sense.

Having delivered his letter aboard the appropriate sailing packet, he led his horse along the Quay to where a gig waited to row passengers out to the anchored Cowes ferryboat. Steamers still did not run during the winter. Jeremy Lomer stood in the bows of the gig, attempting earnestly to attract custom in the face of lively competition from the crew of a rival vessel.

His pleasure at seeing Tom was tempered by genuine regret over his partner's fate. Although Jem had visited Crosstrees occasionally, the house having been his child-hood home, he had always felt rather overwhelmed by Mace's personality; but he resented any blow that Fate dealt his one-time skipper.

Tom forestalled his sympathetic philosophising. "Can you spare me half an hour before you sail? I need to talk to you, Jem."

Jem willingly delegated his duties to the ship's boy, and jumped ashore. He walked at Tom's side beneath the ancient city walls that stretched right down to West Quay. They could be certain they were not overheard.

"What's become of old Hicks these days, Jem?"

"The Captain?" Jem was evidently surprised by the question. "He's still running things, I am told. *Winter Witch* has been sold to a yachtsman."

"Yes, I've seen her on the Solent. So Hicks keeps his finger on the pulse, does he? Tough old bugger. He must be all of seventy-five."

Jem slanted him an apprehensive glance. "You cannot be thinking, after so long –"

"Of vengeance? Not the kind you mean."

"The Earl of Wickham?"

Tom whistled softly. "That would be aiming high. What makes you think I've anything against such a good and loyal Englishman?"

"Rumours. Whispers. People surmising that more happened at County Hall that day than the trial of a handful of rioters. Hicks cannot help you, you know. The days of picking hired murderers from smuggling gangs are gone. And as for hoping to murder an Earl –"

"Hicks killed my wife, or at least sanctioned her 'execution'. He owes me. But murder is not what I'll be asking." Tom looked straight at Jem. "All I want are the men who crewed *Marshlight* while I was skipper. Their services, for a week or two. Nothing more. You're excused, being legitimately employed, but I'll need all the rest – including Eddie Verity."

Jem blinked. "I have not seen the Captain in years. Can you not approach him yourself?"

"I may be watched. I absolutely cannot afford to be seen visiting a man with Hicks' reputation until this business is sorted out. I trust you, Jem. You've a good brain in your head, and you'd put my case fair and square. Will you do it?"

Jem Lomer gave one of his rare, glowing smiles. "You had better fill me in on the details, skip," he said.

The men arrived by ones and twos, usually during the hours of darkness as Tom had instructed Jem. They ambled down the lane when the villagers were abed, or came ashore from small river craft that dwindled at once into the night. A furtive bunch, indeed, who found themselves greeted warmly by the family at Crosstrees. They were lodged in the spare rooms, and did not show their faces by day, when shipwrights and painters worked on the flyer, and general labourers began clearing the debris from the yard. There were none to question the strangers' presence; the maid had been dismissed with a month's pay, and departed to inform the people of Bursledon that it was a real shame that the master had lost all his money, but it came hard to folk done out of a job so sudden.

The last of the eleven seamen to arrive was Trekker Verity. Tom shook his hand – a gesture of truce, not goodwill – and Trekker nodded and said in an undertone, "Well . . . I owe 'ee some help, Aristo, if anyone does." All the same, they mainly kept out of one another's way.

Tom received a letter from Hélène, expressing her pleasure in being asked to do such a delightful favour for an old friend. She would adore to have the children with her, she said; for old times' sake. Tom was mildly embarrassed by such gushing sentiments from the calm and sophisticated Hélène, and wished he had not let Jessica open the letter. He wondered fleetingly whether Hélène had been more fond of him than he had been permitted to guess. Jessica arched her brows at the wording and pointedly made no comment.

Next day the twins and baby Annis set sail for St Peter Port, with Luke mutinous to the last, and Honor convinced that she would not see her father alive again. Mace's death had shaken the sense of security which the twins had begun to take for granted.

"Will you be angry with me for ever," Honor asked her father, "because of what I told Uncle Obadiah?"

"That's all forgiven and forgotten. We've got to think of the future, not the past. Don't cry, sweetheart, I'll make Crosstrees safe for us. Didn't I promise your Uncle Mace?"

But standing with Jess to wave at the children as their ship set sail, he knew too well that Honor could be right, and he may not live to see their return. Optimism had never come so hard to him before; but if the gamble cost him his life, so be it. Whichever of them were to die – himself or Wickham – the odds were that his family would be safe afterwards. Even if Wickham was the survivor, Jess would repel any advances pretty sharply, and he would surely not harm her for that alone, with no rival suitors on the horizon.

Tom's first job, on reaching home, was to set the boat-yard's smithy in order. Much of the interior had been gutted by the fire, but the place was adequate as a working forge, once the damaged tools had been replaced. Tom shut himself in for several hours each day, hammering and experimenting, drawing on the memories of his youth – and not only for the purpose of re-acquiring a blacksmith's skills.

He found the work shattering, and in the mornings could hardly move. It was a severe blow to a man's pride, as he told Jessica wryly, to realise that he had been tougher at fifteen than he was at thirty-two. But at the end of a week, he had created a couple of items that satisfied him. He kept the smithy doors locked, after that.

Meanwhile, a rather startling occurrence in Durley gave the villagers cause for gossip. A group of half a dozen smocked labourers called one evening at the alehouse. They spoke with New Forest accents, and declared themselves, with many a wink, to be a gang of ambitious 'night-workers' roaming Hampshire in search of 'suitable work'. They had heard there were rich pickings to be had on Lord Wickham's estate.

A group of men seated in the corner immediately wished to hear where the strangers had come by such information.

"For 'tis well known," said the villagers' spokesman, "that guns and traps are set all over the estate. And maybe there are men hereabouts who wouldn't welcome new-comers poaching his lordship's game. Maybe there are men who'd think that the right of Durley folk only."

The strangers left the alehouse with speed and little dignity, claiming they had not come looking for a fight, and would not make so bold as to trouble the villagers again. But the incident was considered odd and vaguely shocking, for gangs of itinerant poachers were fortunately not common.

Some few days later Mr Snelgrove, head gamekeeper at Durley Park, pondered the matter as he sat in his favourite chair, feet resting on the hearthstone before a log fire. The way he had heard the tale, the strangers would not show their faces at the alehouse again. The vexed question was, were they likely to start poaching on the estate despite their denials?

Thinking of the illegal but reassuring crop of spring-guns, Snelgrove grunted with callous humour. Let them try it, that was all. Let them try.

A sudden rapping on the front door of the cottage made him jump. He muttered a curse. The watchers on the night shift were not supposed to report for duty for another twenty minutes, and he had been hoping for a peaceful smoke and a cup of tea before then.

He rose grumbling, to admit the offending watchers.

The grumbles died in his throat. He retreated from the pistol aimed at his chest, and sat down heavily in the padded armchair. About a dozen men followed the man with the gun as he strolled casually into the room. Though he was evidently the leader, he was clad like the rest in the usual labourers' garb of smock and old-fashioned breeches, and a low-crowned billycock hat. He stood on the hearthrug looking totally at ease. Not too difficult, Snelgrove reflected sourly, for a man holding a loaded pistol.

The gamekeeper said in righteous anger, "What the hell do you mean by bursting into a man's own house in such a manner? If it's money you want, I haven't got any."

"Mr Snelgrove," said the leader, "you'll know me by name, if not by sight. I am Elderfield, of Elderfield & Tandy, boatbuilders for the Royal Yacht Club."

Snelgrove swallowed; he began to be really afraid. "I wasn't at the trial. I'm no friend of Kitcher's. I had nothing to do with any of it."

The blond man acknowledged this with a small, bitter smile. "I'd like you to understand, Mr Snelgrove, that the men with me tonight are not shipwrights, they are seamen. Six of them were at the alehouse some days ago, posing as poachers. You may not be aware that I was once very successful in the Free Trade. Old loyalties die hard. These are eleven men from a gang of four hundred – the number excludes a network of waggoners and middle-men stretching from the Forest to London. When someone betrays them, their vengeance is swift and sure. Wherever he tries to run, they'll find him. But I'm sure you're not going to betray us, Mr Snelgrove."

Snelgrove ran his tongue over dry lips. "Damn you, I'll not be threatened in my own house!"

The blond man arched his brows. "We'd like to ask a favour of you, Mr Snelgrove. It is up to you whether you agree to our terms, but your refusal would be taken very personally by every man in this room."

Snelgrove had never thought of himself as a coward; but Durley was several miles from the Solent. He had heard that the coastguards were making life impossible for the Free Traders. But he had also heard, like everyone else, of men shot down in front of their wives, of informers who disappeared during dark winter nights, and of thirty decomposed bodies once found dumped in a well.

He said, as steadily as he was able, "What sort of favour might this be?"

The man called Elderfield sat down, passed his gun to the smuggler next to him, and proceeded to explain.

Eddie Verity banged with both fists on the kitchen door at Durley Grange, and thought if that did not shake the wool out of a few heads, nothing bloody well would.

It was quite dark now; a clear, cold, moonlit night. Just what Aristo had been waiting for. It was over an hour since they had left Snelgrove's cottage.

The door was opened by the butler, who regarded his visitor with suspicion. Unknown faces were welcomed less since the Swing riots – and, at Durley Grange, since the trial of Mace Tandy.

Trekker cut across the butler's first words, saying with apparent desperation, "I have to speak to his lordship. 'Tis terrible important. I do beg 'ee, let I inside."

The butler was dubious, but the man on the doorstep was alone, small, and harmless-looking. There were sufficient servants to usher him firmly out again if he started any trouble.

Once in the kitchen, Trekker horrified Wickham's servants with as gruesome a tale of mayhem as they had heard for some time. Nothing like it had ever happened on his lordship's estate before, although the newspapers told of such incidents from time to time. The butler was convinced that, in the lamentable circumstances, Lord Wickham should be informed. Trekker, having proved that he was unarmed and therefore not one of the poaching gang, was escorted upstairs to the drawing-room.

The butler entered to announce him, and Trekker glimpsed the Earl standing at the window, abstractedly taking snuff as he peered into the dark. Lady Wickham, reclining on a sofa, was saying peevishly, "Must we have so little light? You know how it depresses me – and I am quite sure there is nothing of interest to be seen in the garden at this hour."

Wickham turned from the window. "Yes, what is it, Skelton?"

"Edwards, my lord. One of the watchers."

Wickham showed immediate interest. "I knew there was something afoot. Thank you, Skelton, you may go. Edwards, what is amiss? The hillside is alive with men."

"Sir – my lord – 'tis the poachers. A great gang, my lord. Ten at the least, we do think."

"Good God! I hope Snelgrove has his wits about him." Wickham frowned, and looked down his nose at Trekker. "Do you hail from the Forest?"

"I be living in Botley, my lord, since I was wed. Mr Snelgrove be dead, and three of the watchers."

Wickham's reaction was drowned by a shriek from his lady. He threw her an impatient glance, and made no attempt to reassure her. His attention fixed once more on Eddie Verity.

"What the devil are you saying, man? Is there a pitched battle being fought? How is it possible for four of my men to have lost their lives? What of the traps?"

"Most of the poachers be armed, and they do seem to know the placing of the traps as well as we. We've driven they up as far as High Coppice, but that be more like a wood, as you do know. We don't have the men to surround he. And there ain't traps nor spring-guns in there."

"Then there damned well should be! What the deuce was Snelgrove thinking of?" Wickham turned to his wife, who was fanning herself rapidly. "It seems that reinforcements are needed, my dear. And," he added to Trekker, "I shall take the greatest delight in shooting down personally any poacher who crosses my path."

Lord Wickham did not leave the Grange alone with Trekker. They were accompanied by three young footmen and the middle-aged butler Skelton. The Earl and two footmen carried loaded shotguns. Trekker, who had expected this, nevertheless experienced a qualm or two. Aristo must be stark raving mad.

Climbing the hill in the moonlight, Eddie Verity's doubts were overlaid by satisfaction at the scene being enacted just below High Coppice. Aristo Elderfield and the men of *Marshlight* had not been idle since he left them.

Tom had indeed been busy. He squatted now in the shadow of a holly bush at the edge of the wood, surveying his handiwork. Some distance away, a watcher lay apparently dead, his body partly concealed by his stooping comrades, one of whom was testing for signs of life. The crew of *Marshlight* had missed their vocation, Tom thought. They should have formed a travelling theatre company.

A dozen more men – assorted seamen and genuine watchers, though Wickham was not to know that – were taking their stations in a line along the perimeter of the wood, as if preparing to close in on the supposed gang of poachers.

Snelgrove was not present. He and several watchers and underkeepers, who had reported on time for duty, were passing an evening somewhat reluctantly in the game-keeper's cottage, under the eyes of two Keyhaven sailors. The penalty for informing on smugglers had been pointed out to them all; as it would be to Wickham's servants, if necessary. The watchers' silence could be guaranteed.

Wickham approached the group around the 'dead' man. This was one thing Tom could not risk – the Earl's close inspection of a corpse with normal breathing and no visible wounds. The time had come to act.

He carried no weapons. He might otherwise have been tempted to use one, if things turned out badly, thereby condemning himself to certain death.

He had seldom been so frightened.

He drew a deep breath, stood up and raced along the edge of the wood, before taking the first path into it.

There were shouts behind him, a shot fired hastily, without a hope of hitting its target. Tom's heart beat fast from more than the sudden exertion. It was up to the crew of *Marshlight,* now, to ensure that none of the servants followed him.

He glanced back. Three cheers for the seamen; only one man was on his track, though that man was obviously cursing his servants' cowardice.

The path curved, then forked after another few yards. Tom slowed his pace; it mattered that Wickham should see which direction he chose.

The Earl sprinted around the bend in the path. Tom was already running by the time he raised the gun to his shoulder and fired.

Hundreds of pellets spattered the undergrowth and smacked into the bark of a tree. Less than thirty found their mark.

Tom fell with an agonised oath and rolled at once to his knees. The back of his left thigh felt pierced by red-hot daggers. He looked at Wickham. The Earl was advancing without haste, sure of his quarry.

The brim of the billycock hat shadowed Tom's features from moonlight falling through the trees. Keeping his head low, he clambered awkwardly to his feet. Blood flowed warmly down his leg. He absolutely did not want to run another fifty yards.

Fifty yards might be all that was needed.

He broke into a lurching, hobbling run. He could hear the Earl walking behind hm, unhurried. Tom's painful progress was setting him an easy pace.

Wickham called out, with mocking courtesy, "You had better halt, if you value your life."

Tom recognised the tree ahead; the distinctive, twisted trunk. On his visit to the coppice an hour ago, he had chosen the place for that very reason. Further along the path was another place, chosen with equal care; but with luck he would not need that one.

He ducked behind the twisted tree, as anyone might if they feared a shot in the back, then emerged again on to the track.

Wickham shouted in grinding disbelief, "Elderfield!"

Tom turned, staggering on to his good leg, and looked

296

straight into Wickham's eyes. The Earl appeared astonished, even then, to have his suspicions confirmed. He
frowned, slanting wary glances at the undergrowth on either
side. Then he smiled at Tom.

"Throw down your firearms, Elderfield. Whatever you
carry beneath that convenient smock."

Tom shook his head, retreating before Wickham's steady
advance. "No firearms, " he said. "Nothing."

Wickham paused only to reload the gun. "Throw them
down, Elderfield," he said conversationally, "or I shall be
obliged to blow your head off."

"You'll do that anyway. What would I gain by obedience?"

Still smiling, Wickham raised the shotgun. Tom made a
bound for the sheltering undergrowth. His wounded leg
buckled. He fell heavily on the path and for vital seconds lay
in agony, unable to rise even though his life depended on it.

Jessie, he thought. *Jessie – Mace – I'm sorry*.

The Earl of Wickham did not fire. He continued to walk
towards Tom, with that small, gloating smile, and the
shotgun ready.

It came to Tom that the Earl wanted his enemy to sweat –
and wanted to be close enough to blow his head off literally.
Wickham drew level with the twisted tree.

The Earl tripped, and recovered his footing with a curse.
For Tom, it seemed an echo of the past, a dream from long
ago that still had power to make his skin crawl. The click, the
swivelling motion of that squat, grotesque machine hidden
in shadow beside the path. The flash, the deafening report.

The tall figure of the Earl of Wickham spun round, arched
backwards. The gun flew from his hand. The spring-gun,
grimly crafted in the forge at Crosstrees, squatted in silence.
Wickham's body thudded down on to the path. What
remained of his face stared up at the branching, naked trees.

He had been luckier than Mace. He could not have taken
more than a second to die.

CHAPTER TWELVE

In the striped marquee the champagne flowed freely. Guests were able to forget the greyness of the February day, as they celebrated the imminent launch of Monsieur Vaillant's new yacht, four weeks ahead of schedule.

Tom limped to the buffet table with the aid of a stick. It was nearly a fortnight since the encounter in High Coppice. His wounds had healed cleanly – thanks to Trekker's removal of the pellets, and Jessica's perseverance in applying cobwebs – but the muscles were taking longer to recover. A small price to pay.

He was refilling his glass with good French brandy, courtesy of absent comrades, when Lord Yarborough moved to join him.

"I owe you an apology, Mr Elderfield. I placed a small bet that you would not complete before Lord Wickham."

Tom smiled slightly. "I doubt it matters to his lordship now."

"Extraordinary business, Wickham's – er – sudden demise."

There had been an inquest, of course. The Coroner had heard – from an array of watchers and under-keepers – how Mr Snelgrove had been worried by the rumours of a gang of armed poachers in the area. He had been up in High Coppice on the evening in question, setting a pair of new spring-guns. He should have told the Earl at once, but maybe he didn't expect his lordship to take a late stroll. The watchers had not thought to inform the Earl; it was not their place to do so. But it was no wonder, really, that Snelgrove had disappeared after his employer was found dead.

To the Coroner the story had sounded plausible. But then

298

Lady Wickham, who had insisted on attending the inquest, had begun a confused tale of a man called Edwards, and four men brutally murdered. The Coroner, embarrassed, interrupted her gently, saying that begging her ladyship's pardon, not a single poacher had been seen that night, nor had any watchers died. Nor, in point of fact, did a watcher named Edwards exist. Had not every one of the servants, including Skelton the butler, stated that no visitors had called at the Grange? Surely her ladyship did not suspect a conspiracy involving the entire staff? What would they have to gain? Her ladyship, he suggested kindly, had been deeply affected by her tragic bereavement, and disturbed by reports of a gang having visited the local tavern.

Lady Wickham had been led away by friends, bemused and sobbing, trusting Skelton's integrity so completely that she almost believed the Coroner.

She could not know that one Mr Elderfield of Bursledon had spent most of his remaining capital on bribes. With the exception of Snelgrove, who would have required too huge an amount of money to persuade him to leave Hampshire, even if he had not been insulted by the offer, threats had been used only as a last resort. The staff – watchers, underkeepers and household servants alike – had been detained by *Marshlight's* crew that same night, not by Tom in person. The crew members, without naming names, had explained their intention of righting wrongs done to a certain young man – an outspoken friend of the poor – at a certain trial. There was no doubt about the young man's identity. Rumours were rife at Durley Park concerning the amount Abel Kitcher and others had been paid to ensure Mace Tandy's conviction. On the whole, Wickham's staff had pocketed the generous bribes with alacrity. Only Skelton had been offended; but he had said that Lady Wickham would be better off now, and he for one was glad to see justice done.

The country people's innate sense of fair play had done more to help Tom's case than any number of threats.

Lord Yarborough was saying with casual good humour, "Your lady wife tells me that you were injured by falling downstairs. Strangely clumsy, sir. I always thought you as neat-footed as a cat."

"My baby daughter tends to abandon her toys in treacherous places."

Yarborough's eyebrows rose. "I gathered from Mrs Elderfield that your accident occurred at – yes, at approximately the same time that Wickham met his death, while your little girl was with friends in Guernsey."

Tom blinked. "Concussion," he said, "must have affected my memory."

"Oh, quite. Quite. Did you not mention once, sir, that you had been apprenticed as a blacksmith?"

"I'm sorry, my lord, I don't follow your line of –"

"Reasoning? Don't try, my dear sir." Yarborough beamed. "I am plucking thoughts at random from the air. A deplorable habit, and most disconcerting to everyone but myself, I dare say." He raised his glass in a subtle toast, his eyes shrewd and piercing. "I always liked young Tandy. I'm glad to have lost my bet. I should have guessed that you would finish ahead of Lord Wickham."

"Yes, my lord." In gratitude and understanding, Tom touched his glass to the Commodore's. "You should."

When the rain stopped, there was an exodus from the marquee to the slipway. The scaffolding had gone, now. Mace's flyer, painted, fully rigged and all but ready for sea, was a beautiful and imposing sight. It was hoped that the Vaillants would sail her home to Lymington.

Most of the shipwrights and sawyers were enjoying their own celebrations at The Jolly Sailor, but a few stood to free the last ropes securing the flyer. Sophie Vaillant nursed a bottle of champagne, while her husband addressed the shivering crowd.

"My lords, ladies and gentlemen." Gaspard, in spite of his dandified appearance, spoke gravely and without affectation. "A launching party should not be a solemn occasion. I shall not dwell on the circumstances which have surrounded the building of this vessel. They are known to you all. Mr Elderfield assures me that he now has every confidence in the future of his yard. It is my hope and belief that the performance of my flyer during the coming season will prove that confidence well-founded. I know that I speak for you all in wishing him well."

There were murmurs of assent, and some scattered applause.

Gaspard glanced at Tom and Jessica. "However," he said, more quietly, "a few words of explanation are necessary, for the benefit of those among you who have expressed surprise today at the name painted on the bows. When I first saw the scale model of this yacht, Tom Elderfield remarked that the prototype would be *the* Tandy flyer. He has since told me that Mace Tandy looked upon my yacht as the realisation of a long-held dream."

Gaspard paused again, his gaze sweeping the aristocratic company. "You all knew Mace Tandy, to some degree. Whatever your political views, I know that you must regret, as I do, the waste of so much talent, imagination and zest for life. Tandy put all of those qualities into the design and building of this yacht. *Joie-de-Vivre* would have been in many ways an appropriate name; but it is not the name by which her designer thought of her." He turned to Sophie. "My dear, if you would be so kind . . ."

Sophie cleared her throat, and said proudly, "I name this yacht *The Tandy Flyer*. God bless her, and the men who built her for us. Both of them."

The bottle smashed. The lines were let go. *The Tandy Flyer,* crewed only by half a dozen shipwrights, slid from her raised and inclined keel blocks, and smacked into the quiet river.

A great cheer went up; not just from the members of the Royal Yacht Club, but from the men thronging the riverbank outside The Jolly Sailor. Tom and Jessica hugged each other, too overcome with emotion to speak.

Gaspard and his four sons spent much of the afternoon preparing their yacht for the short voyage home. Before she set sail, Luke and Honor edged politely through the crowd in the marquee to reach their father.

Luke, this time, was the twins' spokesman. "Papa, M'sieur Vaillant has said – if we'd like to help take *The Flyer* down to Lymington –"

"Mama thinks it's a good idea," said Honor. "We asked her."

Tom knew how much it would mean to both of them, to crew for Gaspard on the maiden voyage.

"Go and pack yourselves a seabag, then," he said. "And don't keep M'sieur Vaillant waiting."

The light was fading when the yacht finally weighed anchor. Tom and Jessica stood with their guests on the bank, as the cheering died to a murmurous hush. The sails were set; the children waved from the deck.

Jessica leaned her head back against Tom's shoulder. "If only," she said, her voice breaking, "if only Mace and Vinnie . . ."

"If there's any justice in this world or the next," he said, "they'll be out there with Gaspard tonight."

The yacht dwindled, sailing close-hauled on the wind. A last red glimmer of sunset shafted between the clouds, gleaming on the new paint and touching her sails to a momentary radiance.

Even when the colours had gone, the white sails were a line of unextinguished light amid the winter dusk.

MALCOLM MACDONALD

HIS FATHER'S SON

On a winter's morning in 1915, a baby boy is quietly brought down to a Cotswold gamekeeper's cottage.

Fitzie is the love child of Miriam Lessore, the wayward daughter of the manor house. The father is rumoured to be the Prince of Wales — although one man knows differently.

Brought up as their own by Patrick and Martha Davy, the gamekeeper and his wife, the scandalous truth will never be known.

Until Patrick returns from the war, his obedience to the old order gone, and ambitious now to become wealthy and independent. Until Martha joins Miriam in a business venture. Then, as the traditional divisions between squire and servant change, the pressures for the truth to be revealed become ever more unbearable . . .

'Will bring pleasure and entertainment to Macdonald's many readers' *Western Mail*

MORE FICTION TITLES AVAILABLE FROM HODDER AND STOUGHTON PAPERBACKS

MALCOLM MACDONALD

☐ 51593 7	His Father's Son	£2.99
☐ 20010 3	World From Rough Stones	£3.50
☐ 49749 1	The Sky With Diamonds	£4.50
☐ 38454 9	In Love and War	£2.95

RAYMOND HARDIE

☐ 51118 4	Fleet	£3.99

BARBARA WHITNELL

☐ 50924 4	Freedom Street	£4.50

JANE AIKEN HODGE

☐ 51588 0	First Night	£2.99

NOEL BARBER

☐ 28262 2	Tanamera	£3.99
☐ 48843 3	The Weeping and the Laughter	£3.99
☐ 37772 0	A Woman of Cairo	£4.50

All these books are available at your local bookshop or newsagent, or can be ordered direct from the publisher. Just tick the titles you want and fill in the form below.

Prices and availability subject to change without notice.

Hodder & Stoughton Paperbacks, P.O. Box 11, Falmouth, Cornwall.

Please send cheque or postal order, and allow the following for postage and packing:

U.K. – 80p for one book, and 20p for each additional book ordered up to a £2.00 maximum.

B.F.P.O. – 80p for the first book and 20p for each additional book.

OVERSEAS INCLUDING EIRE – £1.50 for the first book, plus £1.00 for the second book, and 30p for each additional book ordered.

Name ....

Address ....

....